DREAMS OF FEAR

Hilary Bonner

This first world edition published 2019
in Great Britain and 2020 in the USA by
SEVERN HOUSE PUBLISHERS LTD of
Eardley House, 4 Uxbridge Street, London W8 7SY.
Trade paperback edition first published
in Great Britain and the USA 2020 by
SEVERN HOUSE PUBLISHERS LTD.

British Library Cataloguing in Publication Data
A CIP catalogue record for this title is available from the British Library.

ISBN-13: 978-0-7278-8907-2 (cased)
ISBN-13: 978-1-78029-653-1 (trade paper)
ISBN-13: 978-1-4483-0368-7 (e-book)

Typeset by Palimpsest Book Production Ltd.,
Falkirk, Stirlingshire, Scotland.

For
Alan St Clair

ACKNOWLEDGEMENTS

Grateful thanks for their inestimable assistances are due to:

Former Detective Constables John Wright and Chris Webb, Devon and Cornwall Police; former Detective Sergeant Frank Waghorn, Avon and Somerset Police; Michael Johns, doyen of Instow and the North Devon Yacht Club; Pete and Sandra Morris, long-time friends from my home town of Bideford.

PROLOGUE

The child appeared suddenly right in front of the car as Gerry Barham turned into Estuary Vista Close.

A little girl, starkly illuminated in the beam of their headlights, was running towards Gerry and Anne's vehicle, as if totally unaware of the danger she was in.

Her long blonde hair was flying around her face, her feet were bare, and her mouth was wide open as if she might be screaming, but inside the car Gerry and Anne could hear nothing but the rumble of the engine and the shrieking noise of burning rubber on tarmac as Gerry slammed on the brakes and the wheels locked into a skid.

Anne cried out in shock. The child kept on running. Gerry swung the steering wheel to the right. The car continued to skid. It seemed for ever before it slowed at all. But the child was no longer before them, having disappeared from their narrow field of vision as suddenly as she had appeared in it. There was then a dreadful moment when Gerry thought they and his treasured Mercedes were going to smash into the Morgan-Smith's newly erected natural stone wall. Involuntarily he closed his eyes.

Ultimately the vehicle jerked to a halt just in time, slamming Gerry and Anne against their seat belts. Gerry wondered if his safety airbag would open. That had happened once before when he'd made an emergency stop. Not this time thankfully.

He turned to his left, staring through the passenger window at the stretch of road where the child had been. Gerry didn't know the exact time, but he thought it must be well after midnight. Possibly nearer to one. The rain, which had started just as they left Bideford, was falling steadily now. There was no moon visible. No stars. The Close, half a mile or so up the hill to the rear of the North Devon seaside village of Instow, had no street lighting, and was the type of residential road where, by and large, most of the residents retired early to their beds. Except directly ahead, where his headlights were illuminating the Morgan-Smith's wall, Gerry could see nothing but blackness.

'What the heck was that?' he muttered, reaching into his pocket for his mobile phone.

'Little Joanna Ferguson, I'm almost sure, in her pyjamas,' responded his wife. 'Oh my God, Gerry, we didn't hit her, did we?'

'I don't think so,' said Gerry. 'But I can't be certain.'

He switched on his phone's torch. A shaft of light bounced around the interior of the car, primarily illuminating his wife's pale face.

'I'm going to go and look,' said Gerry. 'I don't dare move the car in case she's behind us.'

'I'm coming with you,' said Anne, reaching for her own phone.

The Barhams had been to dinner with friends in nearby Bideford. They were rarely out that late, but it had been a little party celebrating a ruby wedding anniversary, a particularly jolly affair, and considerable quantities of good food and wine had been consumed. Upon which, Gerry sincerely hoped, for his own sake as well as hers, that the child had not been hit. He was usually very careful about drinking when he was driving. Indeed, throughout his life he had been the sort of man who made sure he would never be caught falling foul of the law, and he was pretty sure that he was within the limit. But he knew he'd drunk at least a glass more than he would normally.

'Shit,' he muttered to himself under his breath. Anne didn't like to hear him swear. But on this occasion she did not seem to notice.

Once they were both out of the car he could see that his wife had switched on her torch and was shining it from side to side. He started to do the same, hunching his inadequately clad upper body against the driving rain.

'I can't see her, can you?' he called.

'Not yet,' Anne called back. 'What on earth is she doing out at this time of night? I'm sure it's little Jo— oh, thank God, there she is . . .'

She stopped speaking. Gerry could see that she was shining the light from the torch onto her own face.

'It's me, Jo, it's Anne,' she said. 'Don't be scared.'

Gerry hurried towards his wife.

Joanna Ferguson, whom he knew to be just six years old, was

half concealed by the wheelie bin she seemed to be trying to hide behind. Anne had reached for the little girl's hand and was trying to coax her out onto the pavement, speaking to her in that soothing comforting way she had with children. Finally Joanna stepped forward. Both Anne and Gerry knew her and the rest of the Ferguson family reasonably well, albeit as neighbours rather than friends. They had even occasionally babysat Jo and her twin brother since they'd retired to Instow seven years earlier and moved into the house next door to the Fergusons.

Joanna looked to be in quite a state, her appearance worsened by the effects of the heavy rain. Now that she wasn't running, her blonde hair lay flattened to her head, lank and dark. She was sobbing uncontrollably. Her pyjamas were sodden.

'What is it, darling?' asked Anne gently. 'Whatever's wrong?'

The little girl looked as if she was trying to speak, but didn't seem able to get any words out. Her breath came in short sharp gasps. She was shaking from head to toe. Gerry wasn't sure whether that was just because of the cold and the rain or something else. Something more. He was beginning to think it was something more.

He slipped off his jacket and, although the shoulders were already thoroughly damp, passed it to Anne. She stepped forward and took the jacket, then wrapped it and her arms around little Jo.

'What's happened, darling?' she asked again.

Again the child seemed unable to reply.

'Look Joanna dear, we must get you into the warm,' Anne continued. 'Shall I take you home? Are Mummy and Daddy there? They wouldn't leave you on your own, I know that.'

The little girl stopped sobbing quite abruptly and looked up at Anne through wide eyes.

'M-m-mummy is . . . is there, I want my mummy and d-daddy,' she stumbled. 'I c-can't get to my m-m . . .'

The child's voice tailed off, as she started to sob again.

'You want Mummy and Daddy,' echoed Anne. 'Yes, of course you do.'

Anne lifted the little girl up, keeping Gerry's jacket wrapped around her, and pressing the child tightly against her upper body.

'That's better, isn't it?' she soothed. 'Your feet must be cold and sore, I should think. You've not even got your slippers on, have you?'

The child did not reply, but her sobbing abated very slightly.

'I think Mummy must be asleep,' Anne continued. 'Or she would never have let you wander off out into the street, would she? How did you get out of the house, anyway, you little monkey?'

Anne's voice was light. But, then, of course it was, thought Gerry. Clearly Anne's principle intention was to reassure the little girl and get her to safety.

Gerry still had a lurking sense of unease, and felt sure Anne did too. He told himself that Jo's mother, Jane, must have failed to lock the front door properly, or something like that.

Jane's husband, Felix, had told him how badly she was sleeping. He knew she had all sorts of problems in that regard. Maybe she'd been desperate for sleep and had taken a sleeping pill. More than likely that's what she had done.

'Is little Jo, OK?' Gerry asked Anne quietly.

'I think so, just frightened,' replied his wife.

A light suddenly appeared in the Morgan-Smith's bedroom window, presumably as curtains had been pulled open.

Gerry realized he had left his headlights full on, and they were still directed at the house. He had been in such a hurry and so shocked by the appearance of the child in front of him in the road, that he'd not even switched the engine off.

'Look, Gerry, I'm sure everything's fine,' said Anne. still keeping her voice light. 'Why don't you move the car before we wake the entire road. Go home. I'll call you if I need you. I'm sure I won't—'

Gerry felt doubtful. Very doubtful. He did not share Anne's confidence.

'No, you go home, I'll take Joanna back,' he interrupted.

'Don't be silly, Gerry, you have to move that blessed car.'

Not for the first time during their long marriage, Gerry wished his wife could drive. His feeling that all might not be well at the Fergusons was growing stronger by the minute. He was about to protest further when he saw another light go on in the Morgan-Smiths' house. The one on the landing, he thought. Damn. They were probably on their way downstairs to investigate. Gerry wasn't overly fond of the Morgan-Smiths, and in any case didn't really feel like answering a lot of tom fool questions in what was, for him, the middle of the night. Anne was right, he really must move the car. He would so much have preferred to be the one returning little Jo.

'All right,' he agreed reluctantly. 'I'll park up at home and unlock whilst you take Jo back. But call if you're uneasy about anything. Promise?'

'Promise,' replied Anne.

Gerry turned and started to walk quickly to the abandoned vehicle.

As he approached he saw the figure of a man, or a woman, standing by the Morgan-Smiths' gate, weakly silhouetted against the lights from the house. Or he thought he did. There was something or someone there, surely.

He cursed under his breath. Had one of the Morgan-Smiths' come outside already? He feared he was about to have to face the cross-examination he so wanted to avoid.

Which Morgan-Smith was it? He marginally preferred the prospect of having to deal with Frank over Daphne. Though there wasn't much in it. He narrowed his eyes, peering ahead.

The figure had not moved, surely. But it did not seem to be there anymore. And if it had been Frank or Daphne they would sure as heck have made their presence felt. Gerry was relieved. Or half relieved. He had been so convinced someone was standing there. And if it hadn't been one of the Morgan-Smiths, who on earth was it?

He felt most uneasy. He told himself firmly that he must just be the victim of a trick of the light. He was seeing things that simply weren't there. He made a mental note to get his eyes checked, and see if he could be prescribed some glasses which might help with night vision. After all, he had found driving at night difficult for some time now. Yes, he was getting old and he was seeing things. It was as simple as that.

However, he wasn't able to entirely convince himself.

Still holding Joanna Ferguson tightly in her arms, Anne Barham turned away from her husband and headed for the Ferguson home, number eleven. Joanna started to cry more loudly again. The little girl seemed to be in total shock. But then, she was only six, Anne told herself. Just being alone in the dark would be shock enough at that age to spark a near hysterical crying fit.

Joanna was a fair weight too. Anne, hurrying as fast as she could through the rain, would have quite liked to put her down and make her walk, but she wasn't sure if the tot was capable of that right then. Certainly, the easiest thing to do was to grit her teeth and carry the six-year-old. But she had to do it more or less with one hand as she needed the other to aim the phone torch before her.

She made it to the Fergusons' house and into their drive. The big iron gates stood open. That momentarily surprised her because they were electronically operated security gates, and they were usually closed and locked. Then she realized they would have had to be open, for whatever reason, for Joanna to have been able to wander out in to the street. The garden lights didn't come on automatically like they normally did. The front door was slightly ajar. It was all more than a little disconcerting. As Anne approached, little Jo's weight became too much for her. She lowered the child carefully to the ground and took her hand.

A pale light shone into the porch. From the landing, she thought.

'Right, let's go and wake Mummy up, shall we,' she murmured to Joanna, pushing the door with one foot.

It swung easily fully open. A shadow, not immediately recognisable, from an object that seemed to be moving slightly in the subsequent draught, passed over Anne's head, once and then again.

Anne looked upwards.

Jane Ferguson was suspended from the bannisters, her body swinging gently where it hung in the stairwell, suspended by a rope fastened tightly around her neck.

Her tongue protruded through her open mouth. Her eyes were also wide open and protruding unnaturally in their sockets.

She was clearly dead. She had been hanged.

For several seconds Anne couldn't quite take in the terrible scene before her. She stood quite still staring ahead, as if she were rooted to the spot.

'There's Mummy,' said Joanna. 'Are you going to wake her up now, Anne?'

The child's voice jerked Anne into action. She bent down and picked up the little girl again.

'Come on,' she said. 'I'm going to take you over to our house. Then I'll come back to . . . to . . . look after Mummy.'

Jo didn't argue.

Anne, valiantly fighting the trembling fit which was threatening to engulf her entire body, turned away from the grotesque scene before them and was about to carry Joanna out of the house when a thought suddenly occurred to her. Joanna had a twin brother.

'Jo, wh-where's Stevie?' she asked.

'I-I don't know,' stumbled the little girl.

'Did he leave the house with you?' Anne persisted. 'Is he outside somewhere?'

'I-I don't think so. He was asleep . . .'

Anne glanced back, almost involuntarily, over her shoulder.

So, Stevie might still be asleep in his bedroom, with his mother hanging dead from the bannister directly outside. She needed to check the bedroom. But she couldn't do so with little Joanna in her arms. Neither could she inflict any closer proximity with her clearly dead mother on the little girl. Nor on herself, come to that, she thought.

She'd just decided that she would continue with her intention of taking Jo home and get Gerry to seek out Stevie, when she heard a sound from the landing. She looked up. Stevie, wearing a dark blue sleepsuit decorated with silver star-bursts, was standing on the top stair. His spiky blonde hair was tousled, he had the thumb of one hand in his mouth, and in the other hand carried his toy teddy bear. He looked like something out of Christopher Robin.

But this was no Christopher Robin story, thought Anne, wondering exactly how she was going to cope with both children in these shocking circumstances.

Stevie was staring at his mother, hanging there in front of him. But it was almost as if he did not see her. He kept looking, yet didn't react. Anne knew she had to get him away from the house too. And as quickly as possible. She coaxed the little boy down the stairs and handed him her phone.

'Right Stevie, you and Joanna are going to come next door to ours with Gerry and me for a little while, and I want you to shine the torch right in front of us as we go. Can you do that?'

'Of course, I can,' said Stevie.

'Let's go, then,' said Anne.

She took his hand as they walked awkwardly down the short drive and onto the street, Stevie's steps uncertain and Joanna a near dead weight in Anne's arms. The little girl had buried her face in Anne's shoulder and was continuing to sob. The little boy still seemed more bewildered than anything else, and was clearly trying to be brave.

Anne could see the lights of her own house were now on, including the outside lights, and that Gerry was making his way towards her, shining the torch from his phone in front of him. She narrowed her eyes and peered into the gloom. At least she hoped it was Gerry. Then she told herself off for letting her imagination run away with her. Of course it was Gerry, and he was just in time. Anne feared her knees were going to buckle. It was not just the weight of stocky little Jo which was making it difficult for her to remain standing. She felt as if all her strength had left her.

Gerry noticed at once that she was struggling, and took the child from her. She leaned against her husband, desperately glad of his physical as well as his emotional support.

'What on earth has happened?' asked Gerry.

'Just help me get these children away from here,' said Anne, in a voice so curiously high pitched she barely recognized it as her own.

'Anne. What is it?'

'Let's get these children away from here,' Anne repeated. 'Then I will tell you.'

ONE

Just under three weeks earlier the lives of Felix and Jane Ferguson had finally and irrevocably changed for ever. They had both been forced to accept the unacceptable, and to embrace a terrible stark reality which they had previously continued to deny the very existence of.

For Felix, the day, which they both came to refer to as Black Monday, had begun like any other. He ran a café, the long established Cleverdon's, in Bideford, the historic little market town a couple of miles up-river from Instow. He had been given it, and control of one of the family property businesses, by his father.

People who knew Felix were inclined to remark on his extreme good fortune. Everything Felix had seemed to have fallen into his lap with very little effort required, including his marriage, his children, and his beautiful home.

He certainly had no great love of hard work, whenever possible escaping to sail his boat, the twenty-one-foot drop keel shrimper he kept at the North Devon Yacht Club, ten-minute's walk down the hill from his home.

He made an appearance most days at Cleverdon's, but employed a chef to cook the assorted cakes, scones and pasties for which the establishment was well known. On leaving school, Felix had undertaken a catering course at college. He'd learned to cook professionally and also studied for a diploma in business studies, and had managed to successively achieve the minimum acceptable grades with the minimum possible work. *PRINCIPAL*

On the insistence of his father, after leaving college Felix had become the principle chef at Cleverdon's. This had involved rising at five a.m. six days a week. Felix had not been at all keen, and only reluctantly agreed when his father promised that his taking the job would be an experiment for both of them, and that they would re-examine the situation after a year.

Perhaps unsurprisingly Felix proved unable to make those early starts on a regular basis. And although he was actually a talented cook, he was also an absent-minded one who bored easily. Felix's attention, both physical and mental, was all too often diverted onto matters he found more interesting and consuming. The Fastnet yacht race on the TV in the office, or a major golf tournament, a quick pint in The Heavitree Arms, a coffee front of house with a passing chum. The result was that he burnt the cakes. And the pasties. Literally. And failed to achieve risen scones with any consistency at all.

His father's experiment lasted a scant six months.

However Sam Ferguson made it clear that he still wanted his only son to assume his rightful place in the family business. The otherwise unfortunate experiment at least allowed Sam to become aware of his son's strengths as well as his weaknesses. Felix brought in the customers to Cleverdon's, enticed by his smiling demeanour and gentle humour. He had a certain natural charm, and every so often even proved himself able to negotiate better business deals than Sam was able to.

And so Sam Ferguson had embarked on a new course of action, that of playing to his son's strengths. Instead of falling out with Felix and demoting him, he promoted him, making him managing director of Cleverdon's and a director of the family property business.

Felix promptly brought in his mother, always besotted with him, to manage the café, and a distant cousin – one trait he had inherited was that of keeping everything possible in the family – to manage the nitty gritty of the property business. Meanwhile Felix himself concentrated on what he called 'the frilly bits' – in the main the wooing of customers of the café and of the various business associates involved in the property business, over long lunches, and days out sailing, or playing golf at the Royal North Devon Golf Club on the burrows at Westward Ho!.

The arrangement, seeming somewhat bizarrely to suit all involved, had continued with perhaps surprising success through Felix's bachelorhood, withstanding his preference for boats and golf and fast cars over any form of work, and into and beyond his marriage to Jane. The café did better than ever before, and when Felix realized that his mother was begin-ning to struggle with the workload, he found another distant cousin to manage that too.

Nowadays Felix, using the need to look after, indeed to watch over, Jane, as his excuse should he ever need one, rarely arrived at any of his workplaces before eleven. Sometimes midday. And sometimes not at all. Particularly on a good sailing day.

Jane did not know that Felix used her as his excuse in that way. And Felix knew that she wouldn't like it. He was genuinely a kind and caring man who wanted nothing more than to be able to help his wife through the difficulties which they were both finding harder and harder to deal with, but one of his less endearing traits was that he did like to be seen to be doing good, and indeed to be admired for it.

This particular fateful day, the day that became Black Monday, began, as usual, with Jane preparing a family breakfast. Then she cleared the breakfast things away and washed up whilst Felix completed the morning school run, also as usual. After Felix returned, she continued to clean and tidy the house whilst he sat with his papers and his coffee.

One good thing about Jane was that she had never required him to do anything much in the house. He did occasionally put the rubbish out. Men did, didn't they? And every so often he would cook a special meal, if only to show off his professional skills. Albeit not nearly as often as when they were first married.

All of this suited Felix's indolent nature down to the ground.

However, although Felix was not by nature a worrier, he was becoming more and more concerned by Jane's 'little problem'. She was all right during the day, he told himself for the umpteenth time. Indeed, perfectly all right. She didn't really need his supervision.

The sun was shining, and a moderate easterly breeze was blowing. The tides were right too. Felix thought he might treat himself to an entire day off and take the *Stevie-Jo*, named, of course, after his children, out for a blow around the estuary. They'd put her on her river mooring ready for the season just a couple of days previously, and this really was an exceptionally good day for mid-April. To be comfortable, and Felix wasn't big on discomfort, he needed one crew. He glanced towards his wife and considered asking her if she would like to go sailing with him on this glorious morning.

But no, that would never do. He would be able to pick up

somebody at a loose end at the yacht club, for sure. After all, he didn't entirely trust Jane on a boat, did he? Indeed, who would? She was no natural sailor.

He informed Jane of his intentions, which, as usual, she accepted without any adverse comment, and a little later began the stroll down the hill to Instow sea front and the North Devon Yacht Club at the Bideford end of Marine Parade. Leaving his car behind meant he could drink as much as he liked. And by the time he faced the uphill walk home he was usually feeling no pain.

Felix was aware that he might be beginning to drink too much. Jane had tentatively mentioned it once or twice, but had never laboured the point. After all, she was in no position to criticize him. And Felix had swiftly responded that if he wasn't worried sick about her, he probably wouldn't drink at all. Although he didn't really believe that was true. He'd always enjoyed bar-room bonhomie.

On that day it was well after four before he left the yacht club. He'd found a sailing companion without difficulty, as he had predicted that he would. An old school chum, working on his own vessel not yet ready for its river mooring, had been delighted to be offered a diversion from a day of tedious tasks. He not only crewed for Felix, but then spent a convivial afternoon in the bar with him.

Felix was an amiable drunk, whose nature led him largely towards agreeable melancholy when under the influence of alcohol. As he stepped out of the clubhouse into the fresh sea air, he began to reflect on his first meeting with Jane. It had been love at first sight, it really had, even though, at the time, Felix would have said he did not believe in such a thing.

There'd been a vacancy for a waitress at Cleverdon's. Jane, who'd recently moved into the area following the death of her mother and was living in a bedsit over at East the Water, applied for the job. As soon as she walked into the café for her interview, Felix was captivated by her natural prettiness, her warm shy smile, the beautiful glossy brown hair which fell to her shoulders, and the look in her bright eyes which held just a hint of unknown sadness. His heart had melted. And he'd known, with devastating clarity, that this was the woman he would marry.

Was he glad that he married her? Yes, of course he was, he

told himself. Apart from anything else, she had given him two beautiful children. Was he happy with his life? Well, until recently the answer to that would have been a resounding yes. Nowadays he wasn't quite so sure. There were certainly problems in his marriage. Problems he'd never imagined could have happened. Not to him, anyway. Not to him and Jane.

Felix didn't like problems, and he had no real capacity for dealing with problems.

He caught his toe on a piece of uneven pavement along the seafront, stumbled slightly, and hung on to a lamp post for support.

Was he still in love with Jane, he asked himself? Obscurely he found himself thinking about the fateful news coverage of Prince Charles and Princess Diana when they became engaged to be married, and Charles had been asked if he were in love with Diana. That had been before Felix was born, of course, but the footage was still shown repeatedly on TV and, like so many, in view of subsequent events, Felix always found himself chilled by it.

Charles had memorably replied, 'Whatever in love means'.

Felix suspected that if he even had to ask himself that question, then he wasn't still in love with Jane. But he had been once, by God he had. He certainly wouldn't have needed to ask 'whatever in love means' when Jane had consented to be his wife. And how many couples were still in love with each other after seven years of marriage?

Loving your husband or wife, now that was a different matter. Did he still love Jane? Felix squinted into the bright sun. He told himself he was being ridiculous. He really shouldn't go there. He was half pissed and fully pickled. Did that make sense? He didn't know. Did he still love his Jane? Of course, he bloody well did.

He loosened his grip on the lamp post and hoisted himself up to his full six foot one inches, making a monumental effort to stand straight and generally pull himself together.

Then, walking with any sign of inebriation now so very slight that only the most intent observer would notice anything amiss, he stopped off at Johns, the village shop.

The shop often stocked flowers from local suppliers. Felix hoped there might still be some late daffodils on offer, Jane's favourite. There were. A large bucket stood outside containing four or five bunches.

Felix bought the lot, and proceeded along the Parade, still concentrating hard on his walking, whilst clutching an armful of budding yellow daffs.

By the time he reached Estuary Vista Close, Jane had collected the twins from school, as she routinely did, and was in the process of preparing their tea. Fish finger sandwiches. Their favourite.

Felix pecked Jane on the cheek and presented her with his daffodil offering. She responded with smiling thanks. If she noticed that he had once again been drinking heavily – and he was pretty sure that she would have done, Jane knew him far too well not to – then she passed no comment.

Felix assumed she was getting used to it. He supposed that was what all married couples did sooner or later. They just got used to each other. And put up with each other, of course.

Some things, however, he thought to himself, were more difficult to get used to than others.

He bent to attend to his children, who had, upon his arrival in the kitchen, jumped from their chairs at the table and wound themselves around his legs, noisily demanding his attention.

After only a few minutes of playfulness, fatherly teasing, and listening to their tales of the school room and playground, Felix, who was beginning to feel extremely weary, was grateful when Jane announced that the twins' beloved fish finger sandwiches were ready, and they should return to the table. Smartish.

He then took the opportunity to retreat to the bedroom. There he did what he often seemed to do nowadays: slept off his afternoon excesses before joining Jane for dinner.

TWO

Jane Ferguson was definitely no longer happy with her life. But she didn't blame Felix. By and large he was a good husband. And she believed that he loved her. As she did him. In spite of everything. He was kind, and he was an excellent provider; albeit not entirely through his own efforts. He was also the best of fathers.

She didn't mind his streak of lazy indolence. She had been aware of it from the very beginning of their relationship, and had always regarded it as being the flip side of the coin to the charmingly easy-going man she'd fallen in love with.

She wished he did not drink quite so much. This was a relatively new thing. And she could understand his desire to seek an escape from reality, but she didn't like it that Felix's increasingly frequent afternoon drinking encroached upon his time with his children. All too often he would retreat to bed to sleep it off just at their tea time, when he would otherwise be joining in and making this ordinary evening event so much more fun than she ever seemed able to. Felix was good at that.

But no. Jane didn't blame Felix for anything. She blamed whatever it was that was going on inside her own head. The wretched curse gnawing away at her very being, making it increasingly more difficult for her to cope with even the most basic challenges of her day-to-day life. She had almost totally lost confidence in herself. She only went out when she had to, preferring to remain in her own familiar territory. Even then, her days were filled with nervous uncertainty.

Jane was beginning to dread bedtime more and more. And she suspected that Felix was too.

Nonetheless she continued to proceed with the routine of a normal family evening as if there were nothing wrong. Or she tried to, anyway. After all, what else could she do?

Felix emerged at around six thirty p.m., just as Jane was preparing to put the twins to bed. He seemed very nearly sober. He'd always been a quick recoverer.

'I'll do it,' he said.

Jane happily demurred. Felix nearly always took charge of bedtime duties. Even his drinking rarely got in the way of that.

She went back to the kitchen to make dinner for them both, leaving the door open so that she could hear the cheery sounds from upstairs. First the splashes and shrieks emulating from the bathroom, and then, later, the low hum of Felix's voice as he read the twins a bedtime story. This was a nighty ritual at which Felix was also rather good.

The whole thing usually took around an hour.

By the time she heard her husband's footsteps on the stairs, Jane had set the little table in the conservatory, with its panoramic views across Bideford Bay, where they almost always ate when alone, and made a green salad which she placed in the centre of it. Two decent-sized sirloin steaks from their local butcher were marinating in oil and seasoning ready to be sizzled in the griddle pan waiting on the hob. A tray of chips in the oven were about to brown. There was fruit and ice cream for afters.

Jane had never been what she called a proper cook. And she was certainly no match for Felix, on the rare occasions nowadays when he made the effort. But she was reasonably adept at putting good healthy meals together, and, by popular demand, sometimes not so healthy ones for the children. Felix always said that he loved her cooking. Mind you, he would say that, wouldn't he, if it meant he didn't have to do it. Jane smiled indulgently. However, she knew she cooked a mean steak, and that this simple meal was a favourite of Felix's.

She lit the gas burner beneath the griddle pan and turned to face Felix as he entered the kitchen. He was smiling. He had a lovely smile, Jane thought, which rarely failed to lift her spirits, even if only a little.

'You'd never guess what little Stevie just said to me . . .' he began. 'I told him I loved him and he said, "I love me too, Daddy."'

'Oh, that's funny, Felix,' Jane said.

'I know,' Felix replied, smiling that smile again. 'Maybe we've bred a stand-up comic.'

'Maybe we have,' responded Jane. 'Although it might be just a little early to start booking theatres.'

Felix remained in the kitchen with her until the steaks were cooked and plated, then picked them up and carried them into the conservatory.

He began to tuck into his meal at once, somewhat unusually not returning to the kitchen to select a bottle of wine from the rack. Jane was glad about that, although she would have made no comment had he done so. But she knew that if he consumed any more alcohol after a heavy earlier session he would become quite drunk again almost immediately.

An old friend of her late mother's, who'd had an alcoholic husband, called it the chemical tip. Not that Felix was an alcoholic, she reminded herself. And even if he were, that would surely be her fault too.

But, just for the moment, she really was not going to let her thoughts drift down that particular road.

This was turning into the kind of evening when she almost began to believe that they could be a normal family again, living a normal family life.

Felix was behaving quite like the old Felix. She made a conscious effort to try to behave like the old Jane, instead of the angst-ridden neurotic she knew she had become.

After dinner they watched a movie, sitting together on the sofa, not quite the way they used to, when Felix would wrap a long arm around her and she would settle contentedly into his nook. But it felt to her that they were close that evening. Both physically and mentally.

Indeed, so much so that Jane wondered if Felix might make a move towards the love-making which had once been at the very core of their marriage, and was now such a rare event.

Or even if she might dare make a move on him? Something she would once never have hesitated to do. But nowadays she feared rejection too much. She believed, or certainly she hoped, that Felix did not reject her because he no longer wanted her. No. He rejected her, or at least showed no active desire to make love to her, because of his fear of what would come after. The sleep which would surely follow. The sleep which brought her no rest at all. And all too often destroyed his.

But perhaps tonight would be different. She had been ten days, a whole ten days, without a problem. She had, of course, barely allowed herself to sleep. Nonetheless, could this be the start of a new beginning?

The movie ended. Felix turned to her, reached for her hand. Her hopes rose. Her heart soared.

Unfortunately, Jane's hopes were about to be dashed. In every possible way. This was the night that was to change everything. This was Black Monday.

'That was fun,' remarked Felix with a smile. 'I'll go on up then. Let's hope for a peaceful one, eh?'

Jane smiled back, careful not to show her disappointment. She knew exactly what he meant, of course, but neither of them liked to talk about it.

'Yes,' she murmured obliquely. 'I'll be right behind you.'

She watched him make his way from the room, trying to move softly, as they both did after the children's bedtime.

Jane had for some time been all too aware of the cracks in their perfect life. And continued to believe the blame lay almost entirely with her.

She couldn't even remember when it all began. However hard she tried. Not exactly anyway. And she had no idea of the cause. Although sometimes she didn't think Felix believed that.

There appeared to be little she could do about it. The nights were worse, of course, far worse, but the fear was always with her, twenty-four-seven. All day long it wrapped itself around her like a blanket of ice-cold fog. And it had been so much worse lately, since the cause of it all had so very nearly revealed itself to her.

At night the fear tightened its grip until she felt as if she were being suffocated, until she believed that she could no longer draw breath. Indeed, in her blackest moments, she thought that was what would ultimately happen. That she would just stop breathing. At least it would all be over then.

Bedtime had become an ordeal. Felix remained kind and supportive. Most of the time. But she could see the strain within him, eating him up. She was asking too much of him. And she knew it.

She rose from the sofa and walked from the sitting room into the kitchen, then back again, several times, keeping her footsteps light, taking long deep breaths. Exhaling slowly. Inhaling again. She had been told that she should ensure that she controlled her breathing before attempting to sleep. That she needed to develop a rhythm, a discipline, in order to contain the more extreme ramifications of her mind.

She gave Felix fifteen minutes or so before following him upstairs. She didn't want to cause him the embarrassment of feeling he had to pretend to be asleep when she entered their bedroom, as she knew only too well that he had on a number of occasions.

She moved as quietly as Felix had done, slipping almost imperceptibly into the room. The bedroom door always stood ajar and the light from the landing was left on after dark, in case the children, or indeed anyone else, stirred in the night. Felix's face was gently illuminated.

She could see that he was already sound asleep in the big double bed. And he definitely was not pretending.

His chest rose and fell in perfect rhythm. He was lying on his back. Felix, although his hair was a light sandy blonde and his complexion fair, had a heavy beard. His chin already bore a faint shadow which would need immediate attention in the morning. Felix would shave as soon as he rose. He did not subscribe to the modern style of designer stubble. He was more the clean-cut type, square jawed, classically handsome, like the hero of an old-fashioned boys' comic.

Jane smiled. She loved Felix, and told herself she should not doubt that he still loved her. In spite of everything.

Watching him sleep gave her pleasure. How she envied him though. He was so at peace. He slept with his mouth very slightly open, lying so still that when they had first come together she had sometimes put her cheek almost to his lips to gently check that he was breathing.

It also gave her pleasure to think of those early days together, when they had so deliriously explored each other's bodies and minds.

Almost at once they'd started to plan a life together. They were lucky, Felix had told her. They would have plenty of time to play, plenty of time for holidays and nights out, particularly in the early years. And they would at the same time acquire a beautiful family home. And then the family to go in it would arrive. Just like that. Effortlessly.

And so it had come to pass. Pretty much how Felix had promised from the very beginning. Their twins, Stephen and Joanna, were now tucked up in the bedroom just on the other side of the landing.

Jane walked softly across the room into the en-suite bathroom where she changed into her night things in order not to disturb Felix. This had become a more or less nightly routine, and one she did not like at all.

When she returned to the bedroom she paused by the window, looking out across the River Torridge to the lights of Appledore. The curtains were open, as they both preferred.

Jane told herself how lucky she was. She tried to convince herself that if she counted her blessings, the demons might cease to plague her. After all, she had Felix, two fabulous children, and a perfect home.

If she believed it, wished with all her heart for it to come to pass, maybe, just maybe, she would be left alone. Jane had also been told that if she could think calm happy thoughts before she slept it would help. And indeed, it had. Up to a point.

The night was so still. The tide was high, and the moon reflected a rippling silver on the dark water. It was so peaceful, and Jane longed for peace.

She had everything else, after all, and she reminded herself of how she and Felix were the envy of most of their friends and neighbours. Therein lay the rub. They didn't know, of course. Only Felix knew. Really knew. And he preferred not to dwell on it.

Her husband stirred very slightly. He curled himself a little more into the foetal position, quickly settling again.

Jane continued to watch him. She couldn't actually remember the last time they had made love. The physical side of their relationship had once been so good, from the very start. Until bedtime began to turn into a horror story. She wondered if Felix was missing it as much as she did. And not for the first time, she wondered if he was seeking release elsewhere. He had given her no reason to believe that, but he was still a young man. One thing was certain, if Felix had found an occasional sexual alternative to his angst-ridden wife, and she didn't see how he could fit much more than that into their lifestyle, then, again, Jane blamed only herself.

She pulled her dressing gown close, wrapping her arms tightly around her body. She wasn't cold, just forlorn. Her attempts to focus on the happy positive aspects of her life had not worked well.

She made a last effort. She let the dressing gown fall loose again and set off for the children's room, carefully pushing their door open just a little more, in order not to wake them.

The twins, in their matching wooden beds – Stevie's painted pale blue, Joanna's pale yellow – were sleeping as deeply and as peacefully as their father. Their room was also painted in shades and shapes of blue and yellow. In the days when she had still felt able to bother about interior decoration, Jane had considered pink and blue to be a tad too obvious for boy and girl twins. And, in any case, blue and yellow, whilst such nice colours for little ones, were also rather stylish. The colours of Monet.

Each child lay very still. Stevie had his thumb in his mouth, and was half lying on his toy bear. Joanna, a bunny hugger through and through, was clutching her white rabbit close. Actually Loppy, Jo's favourite cuddly toy since she was a baby, wasn't really white any more, but rather more a murky grey.

Jane made a mental note to pop Loppy in the washing machine in the morning, whilst Joanna was at school.

Feeling slightly better again, she returned to the master bedroom, removed her dressing gown, and slipped beneath the bedclothes alongside her husband, moving as little as possible in order not to wake him.

She pulled a pillow from the pile at the head of the bed and wrapped her arms and legs around it. Sometimes she thought that helped her.

She'd barely slept at all for three nights. And not a great deal for more than a week before that. She'd got into the habit of deliberately keeping herself awake half the time. In spite of the resultant all-consuming exhaustion, it was often preferable to the alternative. That night she knew she would not be able to do so again. Her body craved sleep. So did her mind. The warmth of the bed cocooned her. Her husband's gentle breathing soothed her, enticing her to forget her fears. Ultimately, she had no choice but to let go, telling herself everything was going to be all right, and she could be well again, as she gave in to the waves of sleep washing over her.

The next thing Jane was aware of was the sound of screaming. Desperate loud screaming. A child's screaming. And her own screams too. As one. Close yet distant.

At first, she couldn't see anything. She didn't know where she was. She had no idea what was happening. She had no concept even of whether she was awake or asleep. Had she gone blind? No. Her eyes were closed. She opened them. And immediately wished she hadn't. She was still screaming, unable to stop. The screaming child was her daughter, Joanna, whom she was holding tightly in her arms. Too tightly. She slackened her grip at once, desperate to find a way of comforting her daughter.

'There, there,' she mouthed.

It was too late. Joanna did not respond to her mother's voice. Not at all. She continued to scream, and she looked terrified. Was Jane responsible for that? Jane supposed she must be.

She was still trying to work out how she could calm and sooth her daughter, whilst she was herself still in the grip of a panic attack, when Joanna was snatched from her arms.

Felix was tousle-haired and bleary-eyed, clearly fighting his way back from a deep sleep. He also looked absolutely furious. Angrier than Jane had ever seen him. Yet he held Joanna tenderly, and his natural gentleness had a swift effect on the little girl, whose screams abated as she snuggled into her father's chest. The look he focused on Jane was anything but gentle.

'Go back to our bedroom,' he instructed her. His voice was level but icy cold.

Jane wanted to try to explain. To apologize. But at the same time to reassure. To tell him she would never ever harm their children. Not under any circumstances. But the words wouldn't come out. And she wasn't even sure that they were true. Not anymore. She just stood there, looking at Felix, trying to control her breathing, fighting to calm herself down.

'Go back to our bedroom,' Felix repeated, his voice low but all the more foreboding for that.

She knew she should obey Felix, try to explain later, wait until they were both over the shock of the moment. But she couldn't move.

'She's all right, i-isn't she?' she queried hesitantly. 'I mean, I haven't hurt Jo, h-have I?'

'I don't know,' muttered Felix through gritted teeth. 'You were squeezing her. And shaking the life out of her.'

'I didn't shake her,' protested Jane. 'I didn't do that. I'm sure I didn't.'

'Yes, well that's the problem, isn't it, Jane?' Felix continued, spitting out the words. 'You're not sure. You can't be sure of anything. You don't know what the hell you're doing.'

'But I wouldn't harm them, never, I-I couldn't . . .'

Jane was unable to finish the sentence. Felix, her Felix, was looking at her as if he hated her. She didn't blame him.

'Just go,' he said, his voice low and all the more menacing for that. 'Go back to our room before I do something I regret.'

Finally, she obeyed him, pausing at the door of the children's room just long enough to watch him lay Joanna on her little yellow bed.

It was probably ten minutes or so before Felix returned to their bedroom. Jane was again by the window, staring out at the lights twinkling across the estuary, trying to overcome the fears that raged within her, threatening everything that she treasured in life, trying to make sense of the senseless. This had been the worst, the worst ever. Jane turned to look at him when the door opened. His face was ashen. There was a resigned grimness about him. He was trembling.

'I'm so sorry . . .' she began.

There was so much that she wanted to tell him, had to tell him.

But he didn't give her time. His face darkened with anger. He strode purposefully across the room, and, before she could speak again, raised his right hand, the palm flat, and struck her once across the cheek. The edge of his wedding ring caught her, cutting into her flesh. Her cheek stung. She could feel wetness on her skin. She knew she was bleeding.

It was the first time Felix had ever hit her. The shock of it was far greater than any pain.

'This is it,' he told her. 'I will make sure you never touch our children again.'

With chilling calmness, he turned away from her, walked over to the door, locked it and removed the key, then returned to bed.

Jane wanted to tell him everything that was going through her head. But she was afraid to do so. And in case she hadn't made sense of it herself yet. It couldn't be how it seemed, could it? Did she dare confide her deepest fears to her husband? She wasn't sure.

'Felix, we need to talk,' she began.

'Jane, we've talked and talked,' he replied. 'Nothing helps. This time you've gone too far.'

'Bu . . . but, I couldn't help it, I didn't know what I was doing,' said Jane.

'I know, and that's the most frightening thing about it, isn't it?'

'All I have to do is control what happens to me. I think last night I was halfway to understanding . . .'

'Yes Jane, but unfortunately, we can't expect our children to understand, can we?'

'Oh Felix, can't we just talk . . .'

'Look, in the morning we'll get the twins up together. Then we'll see . . .'

Felix's voice tailed off. Jane wondered exactly what they would see. She didn't ask the question though. Indeed, she didn't reply at all. He was tired, and he was angry.

Felix closed his eyes and clearly had no intention of opening them again. She didn't want to join him in bed until he was asleep. But she knew he was not sleeping, just as earlier she had been so sure that he was.

She would have gone to the spare room, for the very first time ever, but he had locked the door.

Eventually she climbed into bed beside him, and lay rigid, her legs and arms straight. Would he hit her again? Later that night, or in the morning? He had never hit her before. It was not in his nature. But she had frightened him half out of his wits. She had frightened her children, particularly poor Joanna. She had frightened herself. Not for the first time, but more than ever before.

The events of the night were laid out before her like a tableau. Mixed up with other things. Other people. Other children. Parts of dreams, or were they dreams? Parts of happenings that were nothing to do with her and her life, and her husband, and her children. Or were they?

Her injured cheek was sore. She reached up with one hand. The little cut inflicted by Fergus' ring was still tacky with her blood. She reached under the pillow for a tissue and held it to her face.

Being careful only to move her head so that she didn't disturb him, Jane peered through the half-light at her husband. The moon remained bright outside, shining as strongly as a moon ever can, through the bedroom window. Just as before, before she had again done her best to destroy everything, she could see clearly enough the shape of Felix's body and the way his chest moved rhythmically up and down as he breathed.

He had fallen asleep again. How on earth could he sleep, she wondered? Felix always seemed able to sleep, whether or not he had been drinking, whatever was happening in their lives. But there had never been a night like this one before. She would not sleep again that night, she knew that for sure. Sleep was her enemy. She had earlier allowed it to overcome her, and look what had happened. It was a wicked trick of nature that this enemy of hers was one no human being could live without.

She had to talk to Felix.

The alarm sounded at six thirty a.m.

Felix stirred then went back to sleep. She shook him gently awake again. He opened his eyes looking towards her. She watched as he began to remember.

'You have the key to the door,' she prompted him. 'You said we should get the twins up together.'

Felix was not by nature an early riser. However, he reached under his pillow for the key to the bedroom door, then sat up at once and swung his legs over the edge of the bed.

He led the way to the children's room without speaking to her. With the resilience of childhood, both Joanna and Stevie seemed to have slept through the rest of the night, and they appeared to have woken without any clear recollection of what had happened.

'C'mon you two,' said Jane, in her cheeriest voice, hoping beyond hope that was how things would remain. 'Daddy's going to get you dressed whilst I make breakfast.'

She glanced at Felix enquiringly.

'I sure am,' he agreed, his voice even more overtly cheery. 'Now, where are those school uniforms? I know. We put them in the shed, didn't we, in case the elves and the goblins and the fairies who live at the bottom of the garden needed them in the night?'

'Don't be silly, Daddy, elves and fairies and goblins don't go to school,' said Stevie, sounding very grown up. 'Everybody knows that.'

Felix smiled his 'Daddy' smile. It stretched from ear to ear and lit up his eyes, so they shone with love. Usually it warmed Jane's heart and made her feel, even on her darkest days, that all could not be entirely bad with the world. But not this morning.

She left the room and made her way to the kitchen where she prepared breakfast on auto pilot.

About half an hour later the twins came running down the stairs and into the kitchen, fully dressed in their school uniforms. Jane had boiled an egg for Felix. But it didn't look as if he was coming to eat it. However, the twins sat down at the kitchen table and tucked in to their usual fruit and cereals. At first sight everything seemed normal with them. Although Joanna seemed a little quieter than usual.

'Are you all right, baby?' asked Jane.

'I d-don't know,' stumbled Joanna. 'I think perhaps I had a bad dream in the night. Did I have a very bad dream, Mummy?'

'Oh, darling,' said Jane. She felt her heart lurch inside her chest.

'Oh, darling, perhaps you did.'

She hurried around the table to her daughter's side and wrapped her arms around her, hugging her close.

At just that moment, Felix, also dressed and ready for the school run, arrived in the kitchen.

'OK kids, if you've finished your breakfasts off you go and get your shoes on,' he instructed at once. 'I'll be right with you.'

His voice was strained. For the first time since the horrors of the night, he looked directly at Jane. His eyes were full of pain. Or might it have been loathing? She realized that for Felix, seeing her clutching Joanna like that must have been all too reminiscent of the scene he had walked into in the early hours.

'I-uh, I was just comforting her—' Jane began.

'Bit late for that,' interrupted Felix abruptly, in the same strained tone of voice.

He glanced behind him, checking, she assumed, to see that the twins had left the room and were safely out of earshot in the hall, where their shoes and outdoor clothes were kept.

'We can't carry on like this, Jane,' he said.

'I know, I'm so sorry, I just don't know what more to do—'

He interrupted her again.

'I tell you what we're going to do in the short term,' he said.

'We're going to move the twins' beds into the master bedroom. There's enough space, just about. I will sleep there with them every night. And the door will be locked. You will sleep in the spare room until we have found a solution to this mess. That way at least I will know our children are safe. Do you agree to this?'

Jane felt a fleeting sharp stab of self-pity. She was being punished for something that was not her fault. The twins might be kept safe, but would she be? On the other hand, she had to admit that last night she had caused her darling Jo considerable distress, mentally if not physically. The little girl had made that clear only a few minutes previously. And who knows what might have happened if Felix hadn't come running into the twins' bedroom when he did? Certainly not Jane, that was for sure. She knew very little except that she had no choice but to go along with whatever Felix wished.

'Of course, I agree,' she replied. 'But I would never hurt our children. You must know that.'

'We've been through that,' snapped Felix. 'You are no longer in a position to even say such a thing.'

She supposed he was right. She certainly could not tell him he was wrong. Maybe, locked in the terrifying grip of the nightmare world inside her own head, she was capable of harming those she loved most in the world. Joanna and Stevie, and even Felix.

'I don't really know anything anymore,' Felix continued, as he turned and headed out of the kitchen to join the twins.

In the doorway he looked back over his shoulder.

'I'm sorry about your face, though,' he said. 'I won't let that happen again, I promise you.'

'It's all right,' Jane began lamely. 'I don't blame you. I blame myself for everything. Can we talk some more, when you get back? Please.'

'You've told me all I need to know,' said Felix.

His expression softened a little.

'Look, Jane, you must see that none of it is real, don't you? You must see that.'

She made no reply.

Then he was gone. She could hear him out in the hallway,

joshing and jesting with Joanna and Stevie as the three of them bustled through the front door.

This was the family she loved. This was her life, the only life she had ever wanted. She couldn't bear to think that she might lose it. That, unless she could change, move on from the unthinkable, she would lose it.

Jane sat down at the kitchen table, lowered her head into her hands, and wept.

THREE

A nd so began the chain of events which led, two weeks and five days later, to little Joanna Ferguson finding her mother hanged in the hallway of the family home.

A stunned Gerry Barham dialled 999 as soon as his wife told him what she had found at number eleven.

PCs Phil Lake and Morag Docherty of Devon and Cornwall Police were the first officers on the scene. Phil was a new boy, recently qualified from Hendon. Not only had he not encountered a dead body since joining the police force, he had never actually seen a dead body in the whole of his life.

But he didn't want anyone to know that. Least of all Morag Docherty, who was not only one of the most experienced officers at his nick, but was also cool. Real cool.

Phil tried to look as if this were just another day at the office. Nonetheless he could feel his stomach heaving. He so hoped he could control it. He had heard about police officers throwing up all over crime scenes. That was not how he wanted to start his career.

In the background he could hear Docherty speaking. She'd stepped forward until she was just a couple of feet or so away from the hanging body, the position of which was such that the dead woman's face was on the same level as their own.

Phil gulped.

'They told us suicide, suspected suicide to be precise, which is what anyone would think at first, but you know I'm not entirely

sure about this one,' Docherty remarked thoughtfully. 'This
woman may well have previously been the victim of a violent
assault by a third party, regardless of whatever happened tonight.
Look at that old bruising on the side of her face. And there's a
freshly healed scar there, too.'

Phil made himself study the corpse, still hoping that he
wouldn't disgrace himself and foul the scene.

'Yes, so there is,' he said, trying to sound matter of fact.

'Ummm, and do you see the way her right arm is hanging?'
Docherty enquired.

To Phil's relief she continued before he was forced to come
up with some sort of answer.

'It's either broken or dislocated at the shoulder, if you ask me.'

Phil struggled to concentrate and to find something intelligent
to say.

'But couldn't that have happened even if she did throw herself
off the landing?' he queried. 'I mean she probably swung on the
rope when it tightened. Couldn't her arm have been broken just
by smashing against the wall or the bannisters?'

'Ummm,' murmured Docherty again. 'You may well be right.
But combined with the old bruising and the scar on her cheek
. . . I dunno. Then there's the matter of the children being alone
in the house with their mother, certainly after her death if not
before. Would she really hang herself from the bannisters of her
own home, with her children there? Also, she has a husband,
apparently, but no sign of him. One way and another, quite enough
to get my antennae waggling.'

Phil wished he had antennae and wondered if he would ever
develop any, and what it would feel like when they waggled.

Docherty was still talking.

'Certainly not cut and dried, is it? I don't think so, anyway. I
reckon we've at least got a suspicious death on our hands. 'Course,
we won't know for sure until CSI and pathology have done their
stuff.'

She turned to face Phil.

'Do you want to call it in, or shall I?' she asked.

'Oh, you do it,' replied Phil.

With only the hint of a smile Docherty proceeded to do so.
Phil fleetingly wished he had volunteered himself for the task,

rather than deferring to the more experienced PC, as she had clearly expected him to.

It remained a good decision however. Docherty was professionally lucid as she reported what they had found at number eleven Estuary Vista Close, and relayed her suspicions that all might not be what it had at first seemed.

When she ended the call, she turned to Phil.

'They're going to contact CID and get back to us,' she said.

Phil nodded. His eyes were riveted on the dead woman now, with a kind of morbid fascination.

He and Docherty had been dealing with a domestic in nearby Fremington when control diverted them to Instow, following Gerry Barham's 999 call.

So they already knew that Jane Ferguson's body had been discovered by her six-year-old daughter, Joanna. And that the little girl's brother, Stevie, had also seen the body hanging dead from a rope; shocking and upsetting for any adult, devastating beyond belief, surely, for children. And children horribly aware that the dead woman was their mother.

Phil found the very thought profoundly upsetting. He had a much younger half-sister whom he adored, seven-year-old Lillian, from his father's second marriage, and he could only imagine the terrible effect any such discovery would have on her.

From what he and Docherty had been told it seemed that both children must somehow have slept through the actual act of suicide, assuming for a moment that is what it was. But they couldn't be sure. Could they? He wondered what had disturbed the little girl. Had there been some sort of commotion which awakened her? He had no idea how long Jane Ferguson had been dead. Maybe the child heard something at the moment her mother fell from the upper landing. Maybe Jane Ferguson cried out, regretting too late what she had done. Maybe, even, the six-year-old had seen her mother jump. That thought sent a shiver down PC Lake's spine.

He made himself continue to consider the scene of the crime. The landing light had been on when he and Docherty arrived. The Barhams may have switched it on. But it was quite likely that the light had been on throughout. Lots of families left at least some sort of night light on when they had young children.

Had Joanna Ferguson seen a shadow move outside her bedroom door? Perhaps some trick of the light had led her to see the silhouette of her dead or dying mother.

Phil Lake had no way of knowing.

He shuddered and turned away. It was probable that neither he nor anyone else would ever know the effect this terrible sight had had on the little girl. He did know the effect it had had on him. Docherty was still studying the body, in her usual cool way, standing close but being careful to touch nothing. And Phil was trying desperately not to show how totally uncool he felt.

'I don't think there's anything to stop us going upstairs and having a shifty round, do you, Constable Lake?' Docherty enquired with false formality.

'I can't think of anything at all, PC Docherty,' replied Phil, in exactly the same tone.

The two officers were halfway up the stairs when Docherty's radio bleeped. It was the return call from HQ.

'Right then,' he heard her say. 'Of course, I understand. OK, yes. We'll just tape everything up and stand guard until they arrive then. Over.'

The disappointment was clear in Docherty's voice. She switched off her radio with an irritated flick of one finger.

'We must do nothing except protect the crime scene, if that's what it is, and wait,' she muttered. 'The new head of CID is sending in some crack team from outside division, and God knows how long they'll take to arrive. Seems this is considered too hot a potato for a couple of lowly plods like you and me, Phil. Apparently HQ have just realized who we have hanging here before us. The daughter-in-law of the mayor of Bideford, no less.'

Phil looked blank.

'You don't really get local politics yet, do you?' Docherty continued.

Phil shook his head.

'You soon will in this neck of the woods,' said Docherty, in a resigned sort of way.

FOUR

Detective Inspector David Vogel was in bed and asleep at his home on the outskirts of Bristol when he got the call from Detective Superintendent Reg Hemmings, his immediate superior in the Major Crime Investigations Team of Avon and Somerset Police.

'You and Saslow have been co-opted over to the Devon and Cornwall,' said Hemmings without prevarication. 'Woman found hanged in her home. At first sight looks like a suicide, but they're now considering treating it as a suspicious death, and one they'd rather have someone from outside handling. Plus, they're chronically short of personnel at the moment, even more than the rest of us apparently.'

'W-what? When? Where?'

The monosyllables were all Vogel could manage. He had propped himself up on one elbow to answer his mobile, and not even put a light on yet. But the electric clock on the bedside table – an old-fashioned radio alarm clock, Vogel was that sort of man – had illuminated hands. It was just after three a.m. He groaned silently.

Hemmings started to speak again.

'I've just told you what,' he said. 'Right now. And you have to go to a little seaside resort called Instow.'

'Instow?' Vogel repeated. He was very nearly in shock. Where the hell was Instow anyway?

Hemmings was ahead of him.

'The North Devon coast,' he said.

Vogel's West Country geography was still pretty shaky, but he had a fair idea he could get to London more quickly from Bristol than to almost anywhere on the North Devon coast.

'How far away is that?' he asked.

'About two hours' drive if you're lucky,' Hemmings replied. 'So just get on with it, will you.'

'What?' queried Vogel again. 'But I've got a lot on, boss.

There's that historic abuse case for a start. We're beginning to untangle a right can of worms there—'

'Look Vogel, do you really think I like this any more than you do?' interrupted Hemmings. 'This was chief constable to chief constable. None of us have any choice.'

'It's another police force,' Vogel continued. 'What is it exactly that makes their need greater than ours, anyway?'

'Vogel, do you always have to argue?' responded Hemmings. 'The D and C covers the largest geographical police area in England, extending over 180 miles from the county borders with Dorset and Somerset, right down to the tip of Cornwall and beyond. Would you believe its territory even includes the Isles of Scilly?'

'I believe everything you tell me, boss,' said Vogel, who was beginning to clear his head but wasn't entirely sure that he wanted to.

'I should bloody well think so,' countered Hemmings. 'Right well, the D and C's Major Crimes Team is stretched to breaking point at the moment, an ongoing double murder enquiry in Penzance and that missing child in Dorset that's all over the press. So we're helping out, Vogel, whether you like it or not.'

'All right,' muttered Vogel resignedly. 'Do I not even get a proper briefing?'

'I'll email you all that I have. Full name and address of the deceased obviously. And the preliminary report from the two uniforms who were first on the scene. They were the ones who alerted the brass to the fact that this might not be the domestic tragedy it first seemed.'

'All right,' said Vogel again. 'I'll call Saslow then. Get her to come and pick me up on the way—'

'Leave Saslow to me,' interrupted Hemmings. 'I'll alert her and make sure she gets her skates on. All the D and C people have instructions not to touch anything until you get there, so you can see the scene for yourself, Vogel.'

'I can hardly wait,' said Vogel.

'I do hope you're not being sarcastic, detective inspector?' Hemmings enquired.

'What me, sir?' asked Vogel.

'Just behave, Vogel,' he said. 'This is a tricky one. If the woman has been murdered, the number one suspect would seem to be her husband who may well have gone missing.'

'Well that's not unusual,' replied Vogel. 'Some sort of domestic then? So why on earth have we got to get involved? Why don't the Devon and Cornwall brass just put it in the hands of local CID?'

'That's where we come to the tricky bit. The husband's father is a pillar of the local establishment, big businessman thereabouts, and the mayor of Bideford, the nearest town.'

'Ah,' said Vogel, trying to sound as if he understood everything now. He swung his legs over the edge of the bed and sat upright. His head still felt as if it was stuffed with cotton wool.

'Yes, it's been decided they have to have an investigative team from outside the area, further away the better,' said Hemmings. 'They don't want the local boys and girls anywhere near it. Justice has to be seen to be done and all that. So I've agreed that you and Saslow will be seconded to the Devon and Cornwall.'

'Right,' replied Vogel, still struggling to take everything in. 'Instow, you said . . .'

'Yes, pretty little place, wonderful estuary views, good beach too. Mrs Hemmings and I spent a weekend there once, soon after we were married.'

'Did you, sir,' murmured Vogel, who really couldn't care less about the detective superintendent's weekend break, nor the scenic attractions of the location of the incident which had caused him to be so rudely awakened and dragged from his marital bed.

'How long are we going to be there for?' he asked lamely.

'For God's sake, Vogel, how the hell am I supposed to know how long the investigation will take,' responded Hemmings forcibly. 'You'll be there for the duration.'

'Does that mean staying over down there?' Vogel queried, trying not to sound as unenthusiastic as he felt.

'Of course it damned well does,' said Hemmings. 'I just told you, Instow's a good two hours' drive from Bristol, and can be longer. The North Devon link road is a right bastard. I want you working, not stuck in traffic.'

'Whatever you say, boss,' muttered Vogel, who so wished he could go back to sleep and somehow or other erase this phone call from his life. Vogel didn't like going away from home. He was a family man. He liked to spend whatever spare time he had, which was never enough, with his wife, his daughter, and his dog. He really did not want to be stationed away from home for an indefinite period. And he knew that Hemmings was well aware of that.

'I should think so,' replied Hemmings. 'You've been asked for specially, by the way, by the new head of MCT at the Devon and Cornwall.'

Vogel was surprised. He wasn't aware that he knew anyone in the D and C, let alone a copper senior enough to be in charge of the major crimes unit.

'Really, boss?' he queried, his interest awakening just a little.

'Yep. Newly appointed. Old chum of yours, only been in the job a few days. Transferred from the Met. Detective Superintendent Nobby Clarke.'

Vogel was suddenly wide awake. Being stuck away from home in North Devon might not appeal to him, but the opportunity of working again with his old boss from the Met's Major Incidents Team excited him at once. It always did.

'I'd never have thought Nobby would leave the Met,' said Vogel, more or less thinking aloud.

'Yes, well, I think there might be a bit of a story there,' replied Hemmings. 'All in good time, eh?'

Vogel smiled. He wondered what Nobby had done this time. She was famous, or notorious as her superiors might say, for doing things her way and brooking no interference. As Hemmings had inferred, he'd find out soon enough.

'Yes, sir,' he said.

He would still have preferred to stay at his home base, but things were definitely looking up.

'Right, Saslow will pick you up within half an hour,' Hemmings instructed. 'And I'll have all the info that's been compiled so far pinged over so you can study it on the way. Oh, and Vogel, one more thing. You get Acting DCI rank for the duration, and Saslow acting DS, with the appropriate salary and pension increases. OK?'

Vogel managed an ungracious thank you. It was, however, very OK. Vogel had a daughter with special needs. There was always something else that could, or should, be done to help

Rosamund lead a better and as normal a life as possible, often at considerable expense. The extra money would be a real bonus. He knew that in their present circumstances, as far as his wife Mary was concerned, it would go quite a way towards making up for his absence from home. And for him too.

Perhaps things weren't turning out so badly after all.

Meanwhile, there had been a development at the scene of the crime.

PC Docherty received another call from a senior officer. She listened for a few minutes, responding only briefly with a succession of murmured 'yes sirs' and 'no sirs'.

When she'd finished she turned to face PC Lake.

'That was Inspector Braddock at Bideford,' she said. 'Seems like he's also had his beauty sleep interrupted for this one. They've roused Mr and Mrs Ferguson senior, and broken the news. Felix Ferguson isn't with his parents. And they're in shock, of course, but they did say, regarding the whereabouts of their son, that we should try the North Devon Yacht Club. He's just been made commodore, apparently, and there's been an inaugural dinner.'

Phil glanced at his watch. It was 3.05 a.m.

'And they think he might still be there at this hour?' he queried. 'That's some night out, even if it is a special occasion.'

'Indeed,' agreed Docherty. 'Anyway, they're on their way here to pick up their grandchildren. Adamant they should be with family. The Bideford team are driving them. Markham doesn't want them blundering about unsupervised, or so he says. Treating 'em with kid gloves, if you ask me. He said HQ are diverting a team from Barnstaple to take over our sentry duty. As soon as they come they want us to check out the yacht club, see if Felix is there.'

She paused.

'Could be a death call, so they want a woman there, of course . . .'

Phil Lake was mildly surprised. He remained steeped in the principals of political correctness. Equality and diversity had formed a substantial part of his training at police college, and he was only just beginning to learn that the everyday reality of policing did not always abide by the codes of practice which had been instilled in him.

'Did they say that?' he asked.

Docherty shot him a withering look.

'They didn't need to,' she replied.

For a moment she looked as if she might have a lot more to say, but the attention of both officers was drawn to a sudden rumpus at the end of the driveway. They had earlier closed the iron gates as a basic security measure, but had no means of locking them even if they had wished to. Somebody now seemed to be more or less falling through them. All the exterior lights were now on, having been switched to permanent by the two officers. Docherty and Lake could not only hear but also see the approaching figure. It was a man, and it was pretty clear he was very drunk.

'I think our missing father and husband may just have arrived home,' said PC Docherty calmly. 'That's saved us a job, then.'

With the exaggerated deliberation of the inebriated, the man, wearing a dinner jacket but no tie, made his way determinedly up the short driveway towards the two officers. It was still raining heavily. He looked as if he was wet through, but barely even aware of it.

Docherty stepped forwards.

'I'm sorry, sir, you can't go in there,' she said.

'Whaddya mean, I can't go in?' countered the man belligerently. 'I bloody live here. What's going on anyway? Why are you here? What's happened?'

The man sounded as if he was starting to panic. Even in his drunken haze, thought Lake, he must be beginning to realize that something serious had occurred to necessitate a police presence in the early hours.

'Could you tell me who you are, please, sir?' asked PC Docherty politely.

'Who I bloody am?' came the reply. 'Who the bloody hell do you think I am, for God's sake?'

'I need you to tell me your name, sir,' said PC Docherty, enunciating with the exaggerated patience usually reserved by sober adults for the excessively young, the excessively elderly, or, as in this case, the excessively drunk.

'My name? I'm Felix Ferguson. Thish is my bloody house.

My wife and children are in there. Now will you get out of my bloody way.'

He stepped forwards. So did Lake, who was a big lad and a rugby player. He might still have a lot to learn about the niceties of policing, but he was not at all phased by the prospect of a little rough and tumble.

'Sir, you need to calm down,' he said in his most authoritative fashion.

The man focused on Phil Lake with some difficulty.

'Don't you tell me what to do,' he began. But he did take a step backwards.

'Right,' said Docherty, in an equally authoritative manner. 'Could you please tell me where you have been until this hour of the morning, Mr Ferguson?'

'What'sh it got to do with you?' asked Felix, still belligerent. Then he looked around him, as if trying to make sense out of what was going on.

'Why are you stopping me going into my own home?' he asked loudly. 'I fucking live here. What are you all doing here?'

With the last sentence, Ferguson's voice rose even higher in pitch.

Lake looked at Docherty, hoping she would take over. Which she did, with only the hint of a weary sigh.

'Look, Mr Ferguson,' she said quietly. 'I'm afraid we have some very bad news for you. Um, perhaps you would come with me and we could sit in the patrol car over there . . .'

Ferguson lurched forwards again. He now seemed not only drunk but was also near hysterical.

'What'sh happening, what'sh going on?' he screamed. 'Is it the children? Oh my God, hash something happened to my children?'

The words came out in a torrent, and were not entirely comprehensible.

'Your children are safe . . .' Docherty began.

'It's my wife then? It's Jane. Tell me, tell me what'sh happened?'

'I'm trying to, Mr Ferguson,' responded Docherty quietly. 'But you really do need to calm down and listen.'

Her calm and restrained manner seemed to infuriate Ferguson even more. Suddenly he let out an animal roar of anger and threw himself at the woman PC, arms flailing as if he were about to attack her. Lake was ready for him. The young officer simply wrapped his big arms right around Felix again, and pulled him away. The man stopped struggling at once.

'Jusht tell me, tell me what's happened,' asked Ferguson again. This time a tad more quietly and with a note of near pleading in his voice. He leant back against Lake, his body suddenly limp. Lake wondered if this was because he was no longer confident of his ability to stand unassisted, or out of fear of what was to follow.

'I'm trying to, sir,' said Docherty patiently.

She so hated these moments. In spite of her bravado, and air of having seen it all before, Docherty believed that breaking the news of the death of a loved one was the most difficult thing a police officer ever had to do. Particularly when the circumstances might still be suspicious. Or, equally hard for many to accept, when suicide was the most likely cause of death. None of this was helped, of course, by the imminent recipient of the bad news being drunk as a skunk.

She decided the best thing to do was to get on with it, as quickly as she could.

'Mr Ferguson, there is no easy way to break this news to you,' she said. 'I am afraid your wife is dead.'

Ferguson's legs buckled. Without Lake's support he would almost certainly have fallen.

'Dead?' he queried in a bemused sort of way. 'How can she be dead? I was with her jusht a few hours ago.'

'I am afraid there is no doubt, sir. She will need to be formally identified, of course. But the body of a woman has been found in your home. And we have no reason to assume it might be anyone other than your wife.'

'Oh my God. How?'

Ferguson still looked bewildered, and was clearly desperately fighting the fog of his inebriation in order to understand.

Docherty braced herself.

'I'm afraid your wife's body was found hanging from the bannisters.'

For a moment it seemed Felix Ferguson hadn't fully grasped what the PC was saying.

'Hanging? How? What do you mean?' he asked.

Docherty braced herself further.

'Hanged, by the neck, sir, I'm afraid,' she said.

Ferguson again stared at her, for what seemed like a very long time. Then stark light seemed to dawn.

'Oh my God,' he said eventually, and for the second time.

Far more calmly this time, he struggled to pull himself away from Lake's grasp. Lake glanced towards Docherty. She nodded almost imperceptibly. All she could do at this stage was accept Ferguson to be a genuinely grieving husband. Drunk he may be, but he would also be in terrible shock and should not be forced to deal with the news he had just been given whilst being held in an armlock by a rugby playing policeman.

Lake let go. He kept a warning hand on one of Ferguson's arms, but the man no longer looked so much of a drunken nuisance, nor as if he might be a danger to anyone.

He did, however, still seem to be struggling to take in what had happened. And that was a common enough reaction, in Docherty's experience.

'Who-who found her?' Felix asked, stumbling over his words, but no longer just because he'd been drinking, Docherty reckoned.

'I am afraid it was your daughter,' Docherty replied. 'Little Joanna found her mother.'

Again, Ferguson just stared at the police officer for several seconds.

'Oh my God,' he said eventually and for the third time.

Then he leaned forward, and was mightily sick. A rush of vomit hit the concrete driveway directly in front of the porch, splashing over the feet and legs of both officers.

The crime scene, or certainly the approach to it, had been sullied, just as PC Lake had feared, albeit that he wasn't responsible. Or not directly, anyway.

After that, Ferguson's recovery from his drunkenness was surprisingly swift. He gave the impression of being very nearly sober almost immediately after emptying the contents of his stomach. Which did not surprise either officer. Lake was not unused to the varied effects of heavy drinking, and its aftermath, experienced on nights out with his rugby mates. Docherty had noted more than once before in her police career how extreme shock can trigger sobriety, even without the assistance of a good old-fashioned vomit. But Ferguson was clearly still quite unable to deal with the situation in a realistic manner.

'I want to see my wife,' Ferguson demanded. 'And I want my children. I want them now. They should be with me.'

Docherty explained that Felix would not be permitted to see his wife's body until the pathologist had completed her examination.

For just a fleeting moment Ferguson looked as if he might throw up again.

'And I am afraid you will not be allowed back into your home until the crime scene investigators have finished their work, which won't be for at least twenty-four hours, probably more,' Docherty continued.

'Really, well where do you suggest I go then?' asked Ferguson, now speaking with considerably more lucidity. 'And will you please tell me where my children are? You have no right to keep them from me.'

'We are not keeping your children from you, Mr Ferguson,' continued Docherty patiently. 'They are with your neighbours, the Barhams, the people who called us here when they realized what had happened . . .'

'But why are they involved? How did they know?'

'I'm not sure of the details, Mr Ferguson. But when they realized what had happened to your wife they took Joanna and Stevie into their home, and dialled 999.'

Ferguson still looked puzzled.

'Just let me go to them,' he said. 'That's all I ask.'

'Of course, I will take you over to the Barhams' house myself,' said Docherty, who had no intention of letting this man out of her sight for a moment until she was told to.

'And you should know that when we could not locate your whereabouts we had to alert your parents, and they are on their way here now, with the intention, I understand, of taking your children back to their home,' Docherty continued. 'Perhaps you may like to go with them.'

'Oh yes, constable,' responded Ferguson. 'I'd like nothing more.'

Docherty studied him carefully. She thought he was being sarcastic, but she wasn't sure. It was hard to be sure of anything concerning this case, she reckoned. One thing was certain, it wasn't going to be straightforward. She already reckoned that little concerning the death of Mrs Jane Ferguson would turn out to be how it at first seemed.

FIVE

Vogel and Saslow arrived in Instow less than two and a half hours after Detective Superintendent Hemmings' middle of the night call to the acting DCI. It was still only five thirty a.m. But this was May at the bottom end of England. Narrow stripes of yellow, white, and pale grey, were already streaking through the darkness heralding the imminent arrival of daybreak. They had driven through rain, which had now stopped, and it looked as if a pretty decent morning was about to break.

A CSI van was parked outside number eleven Estuary Vista Close, alongside two police patrol cars and an unmarked vehicle. A grey VW Golf. Vogel had a feeling that Karen Crow, the Home Office Regional Pathologist, drove a VW Golf. He wasn't very good at colours – which his wife Mary always said was immediately apparent from the way he dressed, unless she managed to have a hand in it.

He knew one thing for certain. If Karen had been waiting all this time for him and Saslow to arrive before being allowed to start her preliminary investigation, she wouldn't be in the best of moods.

Vogel could see that there were lights on in the house and also just one other in the close, the house next door to number eleven, on the east side. He guessed that was the home of the Barhams, the couple whom, he already knew, from the preliminary report forwarded by Hemmings, had reported the discovery of Jane

Ferguson's body. All the other properties were still in darkness. They clearly slept well in Estuary Vista Close, thought Vogel. But, of course, these were large and solid detached houses, set well back from the road in their own substantial gardens.

Saslow parked deftly between the Golf and one of the patrol cars. A uniform standing on sentry duty by the gate stepped forward.

Vogel climbed out of the car and introduced himself.

'Yes, sir, we've been expecting you,' said the young constable, greeting him politely. 'I'm PC Phil Lake.'

'Ah, you were first on the scene, weren't you, along with a woman PC?'

'Morag Docherty, sir,' said Phil Lake. 'She's nipped back to Fremington to check on the domestic we were dealing with before we were diverted here. The neighbours have been complaining it's still kicking off. She shouldn't be long though.'

'I see. Any sign of the husband at all?'

'Oh yes, sir. I thought you knew. He came staggering back here in the early hours, and he was well pissed I can tell you . . .'

PC Lake stopped abruptly. In the ever-brightening early morning light Vogel could see the young constable's face colouring beneath his uniform cap.

'S-sorry, sir,' Lake stumbled. 'I mean, the deceased's husband appeared to be inebriated, sir.'

Vogel couldn't help smiling.

'Well-pissed will do nicely, thank you, constable,' he said. 'But I haven't been told anything yet about his return. You'd better fill me in.'

Phil Lake did so, in what Vogel considered to be a highly satisfactory manner. The young officer seemed to have a clear mind, and was one of those who paid considerable attention to detail. Vogel liked that in a copper.

'So where is Mr Felix Ferguson right now, then?'

'He's with his parents in Bideford, as far as I know, sir,' he said.

'And the children?'

'He took them with him.'

'Terrific,' muttered Vogel.

'I'm sorry, sir, we had no reason to detain him,' said PC Lake.

'At first everybody thought this was just a suicide, and then, well, then, of course . . .'

PC Lake's voice tailed off.

'And then what, constable?'

'Uh nothing, sir,' replied Lake.

'And then, Felix Ferguson is the son of the mayor of Bideford, the commodore of the North Devon Yacht Club, and a prominent local businessman. Is that what you were going to say, constable?'

Constable Lake straightened his back, stood very nearly to attention, and treated Vogel to a display of quite impressive inscrutability.

'Certainly not, sir,' he said.

Vogel did not press him further. Privately he considered that this young man might go rather a long way.

'Right then, let's go look at what we've got in there,' he said, with just the faintest of smiles.

Karen Crow appeared, apparently from nowhere, just as Vogel and Saslow were getting kitted up in the protective coveralls and over-shoes handed to them by a waiting crime scene investigator.

'At bloody last,' she muttered to no one in particular.

'And good morning to you, Dr Crow,' said Vogel affably.

Karen Crow grunted and inhaled deeply from the cigarette she was carrying between the extended first and second fingers of her right hand. So, she'd been lurking somewhere in the street having a smoke, thought Vogel with a certain amount of distaste. He hated smoking. He'd watched his maternal grandfather die from emphysema, and, in any case, Vogel was a fastidious man who could not understand why anyone would willingly poison their own lungs, let alone what was left of the world's atmosphere, with smoke and ash.

Then Karen Crow exhaled. The DCI breathed in at just the wrong moment. He started to cough as soon as the smoke hit the back of his throat.

She turned away – totally unapologetic, if indeed she had even noticed – and along with Phil Lake, led the way up the short driveway to the house, with Vogel and Saslow following as quickly as they could.

'As we are approaching a crime scene, don't you think you should put that thing out?' Vogel enquired.

Karen Crow shot him a withering look. But she reached inside her protective suit, took from a pocket a little folding ashtray, clearly carried for just such occasions, opened it, stubbed out her cigarette, closed it again, and returned it to the pocket.

By then the four of them had almost reached the front door. Lake held out a cautionary hand.

'Watch where you put your feet,' he warned. 'I'm afraid Mr Ferguson had a bit of an accident.'

Vogel looked down with distaste at the pile of vomit on the ground just outside the porch. He was beginning to take a dislike to Felix Ferguson.

Lake, who was wearing gloves but not a coverall, opened the door and stood back for his senior officers and the pathologist to enter. Then he retreated down the driveway to his sentry duty by the gate.

CSI had already set up their lights and were at work. One investigator was on his hands and knees, shuffling backwards down the staircase checking out each tread.

As Vogel had been assured, nobody had touched the body, which was swinging very gently from side to side, a phenomenon brought about, Vogel assumed, by the slight breeze caused by the opening of the front door.

The high intensity floodlights, which had been erected, illuminated the scene with stark brilliance, their beams crossing each other, so that numerous shadows of the hanging body were cast around the hallway.

It was an eerie sight. Vogel stood for a moment taking it all in. Unlike Phil Lake he had seen more death, and almost always violent death, than, in his opinion, any one man ever should. He'd never got used to it, and he knew that he never would. He looked up at the woman's distorted face. His stomach heaved involuntarily, as it always did, and as Phil Lake's had done earlier. But the young officer would never know that.

She hung there, suspended, like a puppet waiting to be jerked into life by its puppeteers. However, this poor broken soul would never know life again. The striped men's pyjamas she was wearing gave her the look of a somewhat obscene Andy Pandy.

Vogel took a step closer, in order to more intensely examine the body, making himself set aside those feelings he had never quite been able to overcome, and concentrate hard on the scene before him.

David Vogel was a most meticulous man. He had a natural eye for detail, and a rather decent brain which had yet to be numbed into submission by the routine drudgery so often required of the modern police officer, whether or not he might be a fine detective.

This was a fairly large house, probably 1930s built, with high ceilings and a tall ornate staircase. He guessed the drop from the landing to the hallway below to be about fifteen feet. The spacious hallway was probably about ten feet square, and the staircase curved around it. There was little doubt that it was a location rather well suited to a successful suicide.

'What do you think, Saslow?' enquired Vogel.

The young detective was standing to one side also carefully scrutinising the body. If she were at all alarmed or distressed by the sight before her, she gave absolutely no sign of it.

Not for the first time Vogel considered that Dawn Saslow was probably made of sterner stuff than him. Indeed, during her relatively brief police career she had successfully dealt with, or at least given every impression of having done so, one almost cataclysmic personal experience far more extreme than anything Vogel had ever faced.

'Hard to tell, boss,' replied Saslow. 'You can see pretty much from looking at this woman that the cause of death was almost certainly strangulation, can't you? But it does also look as if someone might have been knocking her about.'

'Indeed,' agreed Vogel. 'Which naturally makes us turn our attentions to the husband, of course. Whether or not Mrs Jane Ferguson ultimately did take her own life.'

'What, an esteemed local businessman, the son of the mayor of Bideford, and the commodore of the local yacht club, boss?' responded Saslow sardonically, echoing Vogel's own words to PC Lake. 'Surely not.'

Vogel smiled wearily.

'Do not fret, Saslow,' he said. 'At least we can escape back to Bristol when the job is done. No wonder Nobby Clarke wanted to farm this one out.'

He made himself concentrate on the task in hand, taking in

the old bruising and the freshly healed cut on the woman's face, and the way her arm dangled in such a way that it had surely been wrenched from its socket.

Vogel could see at once why the two uniforms had called in as a suspicious death what must have, at first sight, looked like a suicide. Smart work, all the same, which had led to him and Saslow being summoned in the early hours of a Sunday morning all the way from Bristol to the scene of what might otherwise have been dismissed as a domestic tragedy. That and all this local political nonsense. Vogel groaned silently. He hated that sort of thing.

Stealing himself, he continued to study the grotesque tableau before him.

'So, on balance, Saslow, do you think this still might be a straightforward suicide, our Jane here just got her arm entangled in the bannisters somehow, and there could prove to be an innocent explanation for the old injury to her face?' he asked. 'Or do you think, as the D and C bigwigs clearly suspect, that we might be faced with something more sinister here?'

'Well, suicide could remain a possibility, boss, but—' Dawn Saslow began thoughtfully.

She got no further before being interrupted by Karen Crow.

'One thing's certain, Vogel, if you give the go-ahead for that body to be brought down so that I can examine it properly, we might well all gain a far better idea of what really happened here,' proclaimed the district Home Office pathologist forcefully. 'We waited long enough for you to get here, for God's sake. It really would be nice if we could all now get on with what we have to do.'

Vogel treated her to one of his most benign smiles. He knew that Dr Crow, whose extensive territory also stretched across much of the Avon and Somerset's beat, was based in Exeter, which even he realized was one heck of a lot closer to the North Devon coast than Bristol. About an hour and a quarter's drive away he guessed. And the doctor would have been notified almost as soon as the incident was called in, whereas he and Saslow were alerted only after a conflab between two chief constables. So she had possibly been hanging around for as much as three hours waiting for him and Saslow to arrive. He had earlier speculated that she wouldn't take kindly to that sort of wait. And he had just been proven absolutely right.

David Vogel did not give the appearance of being in any way a forceful or assertive man. He was tall, thin, and heavily bespectacled. He walked with just the slightest hint of a stoop, and tended to wear honourably ancient corduroy jackets and comfortable slip-on suede shoes even when the weather and terrain rendered them highly inappropriate. He rarely appeared to be in a rush either to speak or to act. And it was invariably apparent from every iota of his body language that he was unlikely to speak, or certainly not to venture an opinion, without giving the subject of his vernacular considerable thought and consideration. Indeed, Vogel resembled rather more an academic, a school teacher, or perhaps a clergyman, in his bearing, than he did a police detective. Nonetheless, twenty years or so of being a fairly exceptional detective, or certainly an exceptionally clever one, had resulted in appearances being significantly deceptive.

Vogel could be rather impressively forceful, both physically and mentally, if required, and was actually by nature an assertive man, albeit a quiet one.

In this instance a demonstration of assertion was not required. There were few people Vogel would allow to speak to him in the way Karen Crow just had. But she was definitely one of the exceptions. In the first place she was a pathologist, and pathologists and senior police officers were programmed to indulge in a certain degree of banter, if only as a diversion from the horrors with which they were usually confronted when working together. And in the second place, Karen Crow had earned the right. She was one of the most experienced Home Office pathologists in the country, with a reputation for brilliance. When she had first plied her trade almost thirty-five years previously, hers had been a ground-breaking appointment. And for many years she was the only woman in the UK to acquire and to hold down such a job.

'My dear doctor,' he began, in the slightly old-world manner he sometimes adopted. 'Please feel free to go ahead. Who am I to stand in your way?'

He inclined his head in what might have been a gesture of gracious acquiescence were it not for the persistent twitch of a smile around his lips and the twinkle in his dark brown eyes, which was only partially disguised by his thick-lensed spectacles.

Karen pursed her lips and frowned at Vogel. She knew him pretty well. She said nothing more. Vogel indicated to the waiting CSI team that they could start to bring down the body. And he watched with some admiration as the CSIs worked together to release the body of Jane Ferguson whilst causing as little disruption as possible to it or to the crime scene. The two tallest male CSIs lifted the body from the ground floor, whilst another two forensic investigators untied the rope used to hang the woman from around the upper bannister. Ultimately the CSI team lowered Mrs Ferguson's body carefully to the ground and lay it on the floor in the middle of the hall directly below where it had been found hanging. The dead woman was positioned on her back, legs straight, with the noose which had caused her death still tight around her neck.

Karen Crow stepped forward at once to begin her preliminary examination.

All the banter left her as she checked Jane Ferguson's body for any further signs of external injury which may have contributed to, or have born some significance to, her death. The doctor paid particular note, of course, to the left arm, which had seemed to Vogel and Saslow, and before them to Docherty and Lake, to have been dangling unnaturally from the shoulder. She also checked out the signs of old injuries on the dead woman's face. She did not attempt to remove Jane Ferguson's clothing. That would come later on the mortuary slab. But she did lift Jane's pyjama jacket so that she could examine her abdomen. As far as Vogel could see this revealed nothing out of the ordinary. Then Karen Crow pushed the sleeves and legs of Jane Ferguson's pyjamas upwards, so that her lower arms and legs could be seen.

This revealed several small narrow horizontal scars on both arms, around the area of her wrists.

Only then, and with some difficulty, did she loosen the noose which had strangled Jane Ferguson to death and begin to check out the bruising around her neck, the position of her tongue in her throat and so on.

Eventually the doctor looked up at Vogel.

'I can confirm that the left arm is dislocated at the shoulder, and there is considerable old bruising to one side of the victim's face, consistent with her having been hit by a clenched fist, although not necessarily so; plus a partially heeled cut, which again, if she was punched, is consistent with having been caused by a ring worn on one of her assailant's fingers,' the pathologist began. 'The victim's left hand shows signs of new bruising which could have been caused by her fall from the bannisters, but was more probably sustained a little earlier. It's hard to say. As for the scars on her wrists, they're quite old. And, well, we've both seen plenty of this before, Vogel. Lacerations caused by a small sharp knife, or possibly a razor blade. Classic signs of self-harming. Although not necessarily so. It is, however, highly unlikely that any of this would have directly contributed to her death.'

'So, what do you consider to have been the cause of death, Karen?' Vogel enquired. 'Is it as one would first assume, or might there indeed be more to this?'

'Not to the cause of death as such,' replied Karen Crow. 'I am quite confident that the victim died due to strangulation, presumably caused by being hanged; although that is off the record, of course, until we get her back to the lab and conduct a full post-mortem examination, and it's impossible for me to rule out internal injuries or any other contributory factors not immediately apparent.'

Karen Crow paused again, as if concentrating her thought process. Vogel waited expectantly.

'OK,' he said eventually when it became apparent that the pathologist wasn't going to speak again without some sort of further encouragement. 'But as a result of your preliminary examination alone you are prepared to venture your off the record verdict that this is death by strangulation, as indicated by Mrs Ferguson having been found hanged from the neck. But do you think it is suicide, or not? Or to put it another way, is there enough doubt in your mind for this death to continue to be treated as suspicious, at least for the time being?'

'Yes, Vogel, I have plenty of doubt in my mind about the way Mrs Ferguson died,' Karen Crow replied. 'Certainly, and in common with the first responders to the scene, I have yet to be fully convinced that this is the straightforward suicide it might have initially appeared to be. So yes, my opinion is that Mrs Ferguson's death should definitely be treated as suspicious until or unless we have good reason to be convinced otherwise.'

'Thank you, I have no doubt at all that you are quite right, Karen,' said Vogel.

He turned to Saslow.

'Well, Nobby told me she's setting up an incident room at Bideford nick, and has already appointed a deputy SIO to run it, so hopefully we can leave that side of things to them for the time being and get stuck in to the nitty gritty,' he said. 'Whilst we are here we may as well interview the neighbours who found the little girl out in the road. But there's little doubt who is the person of most interest to us at the moment, is there? One Felix Ferguson. Jane's husband.'

SIX

As they stepped outside and into Estuary Vista Close Vogel glanced towards the house he now knew to be the Barham home. The lights were still on even though the day was brightening rapidly. He glanced at his watch. It was six twenty a.m. He doubted the Barhams had been to bed at all that night. They certainly wouldn't have slept. He knew he wouldn't have done if he'd inadvertently encountered what they'd been confronted with in the early hours of the morning.

The Barhams' house was like all the others in Estuary Vista Close. Each was detached and of differing design, but what they had in common was their near immaculate presentation, perfect paintwork and beautifully tended gardens.

Saslow rang the doorbell. The response was almost immediate. Gerry Barham, a trim narrow-shouldered man with thinning grey hair, probably in his early to mid sixties, shorter than average, answered the door. He was fully dressed, weary looking, and in need of a shave. Vogel had been right. Gerry had definitely not seen his bed.

'Come in, come in,' the man invited, ushering Vogel and Saslow into a sitting room offering the panoramic sea and river views which were clearly standard in this street. It was, after all, called Estuary Vista Close.

'I'll just give Anne a shout,' he continued, gesturing for Vogel and Saslow to sit, which they did. 'It was she who first . . . uh, first saw Jane. Had a terrible shock, poor dear. I insisted she go upstairs to try to get some rest, but I doubt she's sleeping . . .'

Gerry was interrupted by the appearance of his wife in the doorway. She was wearing night clothes and a dressing gown, but did not have the appearance of someone who had been woken from sleep.

'I heard the doorbell,' she began, her eyes taking in Vogel and Saslow.

The two officers stood up again as Gerry introduced them to his wife.

'Oh hello,' she said just a tad vaguely, followed by, what was surely an automatic response, 'can I get you something? Tea or coffee?'

Vogel glanced at Saslow. Saslow glanced at Vogel.

It had been a long drive through the night from Bristol, and neither of them had had anything like enough sleep.

'Coffee would be lovely,' said Vogel, answering for them both.

'I won't be a moment,' said Anne Barham.

She had a very modern, short-cropped haircut and, although slim, a slightly plump face which was largely unlined and, in spite of her obvious distress, somewhat defied the age Vogel guessed her to be.

Her husband offered to make the coffee. Anne Barham turned him down quite firmly. Vogel thought she might need a further minute or two to try to clear her head. The woman had a look in her eyes which Vogel had seen many times before. It was shock. Total shock.

Once Mrs Barham returned with the coffee, Vogel began his questioning.

'I wonder if you could tell me exactly how you came to discover Mrs Jane Ferguson's body?' he asked.

The Barhams did so, in commendable detail, Vogel thought, beginning with how they had been unexpectedly confronted by six-year-old Joanna Ferguson running along Estuary Vista

Close towards them when they were returning from their night out.

'It was lucky we didn't hit her, I can tell you,' said Gerry, who clearly meant every word of that.

'The little mite was screaming her head off, gave us such a shock,' contributed Anne Barham. 'God knows how she got their front door open, she's only little. But she must have done. Or I suppose she must have done. Unless it had been left open. The security gates were open when we got over there . . .'

Mrs Barham's voice tailed off.

'Go on,' prompted Vogel.

'Well, I jumped out of the car and went to find her. She was in a dreadful state, wet through and sobbing. She could barely speak. Just about all she said was "Mummy, Mummy" really. And she was calling for her daddy, too.'

Mrs Barham paused again.

'So, what did you do next?' prompted Saslow gently.

'I told Joanna I would take her home to Mummy, and I just picked her up in my arms. She tried to tell me about her mother, I think, but she couldn't get the words out. I didn't understand. When we got to the house the front door was ajar, and there were lights on. I just walked straight in, with Joanna in my arms. Jane was hanging there right in front of us. Dead that's for sure. Strangled. What little Joanna had been trying to say made sense then. Terrible sense. But until I saw it before my very eyes . . . well, I mean, it hadn't occurred to me.

'Her face . . . Oh my God. It was the most awful thing I have seen in the whole of my life. I know I cried out. I couldn't help myself. Then Joanna started wailing again, bless her. I'd taken her back into the house. To see her mother like that again. Poor little thing. I just wanted to be anywhere else but where I was. And get Joanna out of there. But I was rooted to the spot at first. It was as if my feet were nailed down. I couldn't move. Then little Stevie suddenly appeared on the top landing, looking down at that awful sight. I knew I really must get them both away, and I simply had to pull myself together. We were just at the bottom of the drive when Gerry arrived. He'd been parking the car, you see. I mean, we thought Jane was asleep or something—'

'But, obviously, it was all very odd,' Gerry interrupted. 'And

as I was parking up I started to really worry, so I hightailed it
next door as quick as I could.'

'Yes, and thank God,' said Anne. 'I'd never been more glad
to see him, that's for sure.'

Mrs Barham turned towards her husband, before continuing.

'We got the children back here as quick as we could, didn't
we? It was still raining. We were all wet, particularly Joanna and
I. I found the night things we keep here for our grandson, he's
only five, but he's a big boy, and the twins could just get into
them. I put theirs in the dryer. Then we just tried to comfort
them, until their father and their grandparents got here. It was
terrible, really terrible.'

'I'm sure it was, Mrs Barham,' Vogel commiserated. 'I don't
want to upset you further, but I do need to ask you one or two
more questions. How well do you know the Fergusons?'

'Well, we moved here just under seven years ago now, before
the twins were born,' said Anne. 'So that's how long we've known
them. We've even babysat occasionally. Not for quite a while though.
And we've never been friends exactly, but always friendly. I'd
say we know them reasonably well, or I would have said so anyway.
They always seemed like very nice people. I can't imagine why
Jane would have done what she did. Although, well . . .'

She stopped abruptly, as if unsure whether or not she should
continue.

'Although, when you met her out shopping last week, you did
say she wasn't looking well, didn't you?' encouraged Gerry. 'You
thought something might be wrong.'

Anne nodded.

'Well yes, that's quite true,' she continued. 'I bumped into her
shopping in Barnstaple. She had bags under her eyes, and her hair
needed doing. She was wearing an old track suit. Not at all like
the Jane we knew. She was a good-looking young woman, you see,
and we were used to always seeing her immaculately turned out.
I was a bit shocked, actually. I asked her if she was all right. She
said she was, but she just hadn't been sleeping well. I understood
that, of course. It's terrible, you know, when you can't sleep. I
suffered like that after our Angela was born, didn't I, Gerry?'

Her husband agreed that she did.

'Yes. She was a good baby, slept all night most nights. But

that was more than I could. I used to lie awake worrying if she didn't stir at all, and I'd worry myself even more if she did wake up and start to cry.'

'Was there anything else about Jane Ferguson which concerned you that day?' Vogel asked, in a bid to get Anne Barham back on track.

'Well, yes, there was something. I told myself it was nothing, but . . . Jane had a fresh bruise on one cheek, and a small cut. It looked quite nasty. I asked her about it and she said she'd had a fight with her car door. Then she laughed.'

'Was that the last time you saw Mrs Ferguson?' asked Vogel.

'Yes, to speak to, that is. We've waved at each other a couple of times since, like you do, when I was tying back our daffs the other day and she was getting into her car. That sort of thing.'

'And what about Mr Ferguson?'

'Only yesterday, just to pass the time of day with. I haven't seen him to talk to for weeks. Actually, maybe months.'

'And did you notice anything amiss?'

'No, everything seemed normal.'

'I saw Felix at the yacht club last Sunday lunchtime,' interjected Gerry.

'I see. He's the commodore, is he not?'

Gerry agreed that he was.

'And so he is presumably a pretty frequent visitor.'

'Well yes.' Gerry agreed again. 'But I'm not. I mean I like the place, and I had these romantic ideas when we moved down here. Bought a boat. Just a little motor cruiser with an outboard, you understand. But I don't seem to get round to taking it out much. Nice bar overlooking the bay, though.'

'Did you speak to Mr Ferguson at all, last Sunday?'

'Ummm, yes.'

Gerry Barham seemed hesitant.

'Can you recall your conversation?'

'Oh, you know. Just the usual stuff. The weather. It was a terrible day. I sometimes wonder if the weather changes faster anywhere in the world than it does on the North Devon coast. Already looks like it's going to be a beauty today, after all that rain in the night.'

'Did you discuss anything else?'

'Bit of sport. He likes his rugby, does Felix, same as me. And golf. Only . . .'

Gerry seemed reluctant to continue.

'Only what, Mr Ferguson?' prompted Vogel.

'Well, shall we just say Felix wasn't at his most coherent.'

Vogel knew he was blinking rapidly behind his thick-rimmed spectacles. It was pretty obvious what Gerry Ferguson was getting at, but he was too experienced a police officer to put words into the mouth of a potential witness.

'What exactly do you mean by that, Mr Barham?' the acting DCI asked levelly.

'OK. He was pretty drunk.'

As he had apparently been when he returned to his home in the early hours of that morning to find a police presence there, and his wife hanging dead in the hallway; if he hadn't known about that already, thought Vogel.

'Do you by any chance know if this is a regular occurrence?' Vogel asked in a neutral tone of voice. 'Is Felix Ferguson a particularly heavy drinker?'

'I don't really know the answer to that,' responded Gerry. 'But he certainly likes a drink—'

'Yes, and perhaps a bit more than he used to, we've been thinking, haven't we, Gerry?' interjected Anne Barham. 'We've seen him walking home a bit unsteady on his feet a few times lately.'

'We have, yes,' agreed Gerry. 'But not that often. He is a successful businessman. And he wouldn't be commodore of the yacht club if he weren't a capable young man.'

'So just a social drinker who overdoes it a bit occasionally, is that what you are saying?' enquired Saslow.

'I would think so, yes,' responded Gerry. 'Always seems to be a very nice chap. Felix. And a devoted family man. We've never had any doubt about that, have we, Anne? Well, not really.'

Gerry sounded only very slightly doubtful.

'Well, no,' agreed Anne. 'Not until very recently anyway, when we've just had that feeling that things may not be quite right.'

'You mentioned that before,' said Saslow. 'Can you tell us any more about why you both had that feeling.'

'Well, the drinking, I suppose, Jane looking so bad and her face bruised, and once or twice we've heard a bit of a commotion, shouting, that sort of thing,' continued Anne. 'One night I woke up to go to the bathroom and I felt a bit hot and uncomfortable, so I opened the bathroom window, which faces towards the Fergusons, and I just stood there for a couple of minutes breathing in the fresh air. Then I thought I heard screaming, coming from their house. But it was over almost as soon as it began. And, in any case, I couldn't be entirely sure where it came from. I didn't think any more about it, at the time, to tell the truth. But now, well . . .'

'So what conclusion did you draw?'

Gerry came in swiftly.

'We didn't really, I mean, every married couple has rows. Like Anne says, we didn't think there was anything serious going on. But . . .'

Gerry's voice tailed off.

'But now, well, you can't help wondering if there were some real cracks in that marriage, I suppose,' said Anne. 'We've been talking about it most of the night. Or what was left of it after we found Joanna. I mean, whatever actually happened, something must have been very wrong, mustn't it?'

Vogel inclined his head very slightly.

'But until last night, or rather today, you weren't aware of any obvious problems in their marriage?'

'Well, like I said, we're not really friends,' responded Anne. 'Although we have been neighbours for a long time, and no, I'm sure they had their ups and downs like all of us, but I would say we both always thought of them as being happily married, didn't we, Gerry?'

'Certainly,' said Gerry.

Anne turned to face Vogel.

'Mr Vogel, I'm beginning to wonder where you are going with all these questions? I mean, even if the Fergusons had a terrible marriage and that's why Jane took her own life, suicide isn't a police matter, is it?'

'No, Mrs Barham,' agreed Vogel. 'Not in itself, that is. But we do need to examine the circumstances.'

'I still don't understand,' said Anne. 'I mean, what's this all about? There can't be any doubt that Jane killed herself, can there? I saw her. She was hanged. From her own bannisters. And nobody else was in the house except her two poor little children. Are you saying you have some reason to believe her death was not suicide? Is that it?'

'I'm afraid, Mrs Barham, I am not at liberty to discuss that with you at this time,' Vogel recited formally.

Gerry Barham suddenly butted in.

'Oh my God,' he said. 'You think Jane was murdered, don't you? And Felix is a suspect.'

Vogel found himself blinking rapidly behind those thick-rimmed spectacles again.

'I suppose I can tell you, sir, that at the moment we are treating Mrs Ferguson's death as suspicious,' he said. 'Until a post-mortem examination is completed I cannot give you any more information concerning this. Meanwhile I am grateful for your assistance. But you should know that we may need to see you again.'

With that he and Saslow took their leave.

Once outside the house, Saslow turned to her senior officer.

'He's about right, boss, isn't he,' Saslow remarked. 'If Jane was murdered, and Karen Crow seems to think that's pretty likely, then who else would or could have done it apart from her husband?'

'But could Felix Ferguson have done it?' countered the DCI. 'If he was at the yacht club all night playing at being commodore and getting rat-arsed with his mates, then, he may have had motive, something we don't know about yet, but he sure as heck didn't have opportunity.'

'I don't know what to make of it, boss,' said Saslow. 'Perhaps Karen Crow is wrong. Perhaps Jane Ferguson did take her own life, and we're all wasting our time.'

'Perhaps,' responded Vogel. 'And, like I told the Barhams, we need to know the results of the PM before we can be sure of anything. But in the three years I've been working in the west of England I've never known Karen Crow's first impression be proven wrong. Not least because she never shares her opinion unless she's pretty damn sure of herself.'

'Doesn't like to stick her neck out, you mean, boss,' said Saslow.

Vogel glanced at the young detective, wondering, in the context of the night's events, if she meant to make a bad joke in even worse taste, or if she had no realisation of what she had said.

Saslow's face was giving nothing much away and he wasn't sure. So he decided to carry on as if he had noticed nothing.

'Something like that, Saslow,' he remarked casually. 'Anyway, we'll hopefully get confirmation one way or another at the post-mortem later today.'

He glanced at his watch. It was just gone seven.

'We're booked in to a pub across the estuary in Appledore, The Seagate. 'Fraid we've missed out on the best part of a night's sleep. But we might as well bowl over there, get ourselves checked in, have a shower and maybe some breakfast. By then the world will be awake and we can crack on.'

Saslow smiled weakly. It suited her ill to lose a night's sleep.

'A visit to the family Ferguson first, I reckon, after we've freshened up,' Vogel continued.

Saslow managed a little nod. Her smile had faded. It was all right for the DCI, she thought, not for the first time, he hadn't had to drive for hours as well as doing the job. If her room was ready, she would probably give breakfast a miss and see if she could squeeze in a nap. Even if it were for only an hour or so.

SEVEN

It took less then fifteen minutes for Saslow and Vogel to drive to Appledore, crossing the river over the Torridge Bridge, an impressively tall sweeping concrete structure which by-passes Bideford and is still known locally as the new bridge even though it was built in 1987.

The views, to the left upstream towards Bideford and to the right towards the estuary and out to sea, were spectacular. So much so that even Vogel noticed and was mildly impressed.

The Seagate, an attractively renovated period property, holds an enviably central position right on the front of the one-time fishing village and ship-building centre. There was one room available for immediate occupancy when the two police officers arrived. Vogel offered it to a grateful Saslow, who retreated straightaway to grab some rest, albeit briefly. Vogel wasn't good at catnapping, and instead preferred to tuck into a plate of scrambled egg washed down with copious quantities of coffee.

After he had eaten, he walked outside and crossed the street to the waterside. The sun was shining now. Instow, the village where they had so recently visited what he now believed to be almost certainly the location of a vicious murder, was immediately across the estuary, looking just like a picture postcard brought to life. It was hard to believe that anything bad or evil could happen in such a place, thought Vogel, who was still rather more used to the underbelly of metropolitan London where you accepted violent crime on a daily basis.

He found a bench, texted Saslow to tell her where he was, and sat there enjoying a few minutes' peace before immersing himself in the hurly-burly of the investigation again.

A little later the acting DS joined him. Vogel checked his watch. It was just before eight thirty a.m., the time they had agreed they would set off on the next stage of their enquiries, that visit to the Fergusons. Saslow was almost always punctual.

The home of the mayor of Bideford – called All Seasons, and in its glorious but exposed position it would certainly experience a full-frontal assault from all four, thought Vogel – was a large sixties- or seventies-built house in Bay View Road, in the borough of Northam. As the name suggested the plot commanded a stunning view of Bideford Bay.

The sun was still beating down over the water, white horses danced in a dark sea. Vogel, although a city boy through and through, was beginning to discover that he was not entirely immune to the beauty of nature, but, as usual, his mind was totally preoccupied with the case in hand.

Saslow parked in the driveway. As they stepped out it became apparent that quite a breeze had blown up in the ten minutes or so the drive from Appledore had taken them. Vogel was surprised. Unlike Gerry Barham, he had yet to learn first-hand how quickly the weather changes on the North Devon coast. He and Saslow found themselves hurrying to the protection of the porch around the front door, bending forward into the wind which was beginning to blast powerfully off the Atlantic.

The woman who answered the door almost before Vogel had rung the bell was of average height, five foot five or so, Vogel guessed, but held herself so well she appeared much taller. Her grey-blonde hair had clearly been quite strenuously coiffured into submission and framed a strong well-boned face with carefully arranged waves and curls which did not look as if they ever dared move much. It was, Vogel supposed, a rather old-fashioned look. Not unlike the hairstyle of our own dear queen, as Vogel's mother may have remarked.

She was wearing a twin set. Vogel didn't think he'd seen one of those in a long time.

A pair of Cavalier King Charles spaniels, yapping excitedly, were at her feet.

'Mrs Amelia Ferguson?' he enquired.

The woman nodded curtly.

'Police,' said Vogel, and proceeded to introduce himself and Saslow.

She looked him up and down without enthusiasm.

'You'd better come in then,' she said, stepping back into the hallway.

Her manner was disconcertingly abrupt, which Vogel assumed was her intention. She was not only immaculately coiffured, but fully made-up and perfectly dressed, even though it was not yet nine a.m. and her daughter-in-law had met a violent death during the night. If this had disturbed her in any way beyond having suffered a broken night's sleep, Amelia Ferguson showed no sign of it. And, in what most people would regard as the worst of circumstances, Mrs Ferguson displayed no visible distress. This was clearly a formidable woman. A force to be reckoned with, thought Vogel.

She had the look of someone who had never shed a tear in her life. But in Vogel's experience that was sometimes only a façade. He wasn't sure about this one, though.

Amelia Ferguson led the way into a vast sitting room with floor-to-ceiling picture windows offering sweeping views over the bay. The room was perfectly presented, just like its owner.

Two large cream brocade sofas, standing on a spotless cream

carpet, flanked the windows. Vogel was mildly surprised that he hadn't been asked to remove his shoes before entering.

Through a wide arch Vogel could see a second smaller room containing a large solid-looking dining table. Two small children, a boy and a girl, sat at the table. They had pencils or crayons in their hands and seemed to be drawing in books, or perhaps colouring-in.

The twins, Vogel guessed correctly. Joanna and Stevie Ferguson. Joanna in particular looked pale, perhaps unnaturally pale, but there was little else about either child to give any indication of the terrible night they had just experienced.

Joanna's long blonde hair appeared to be freshly washed, and had been neatly tied into bunches with two pink ribbons. Her brother's hair was also quite long, but had been parted to one side and combed flat to his head. The attentions of Grannie were evident, Vogel thought.

Both children were neatly dressed, Joanna in a grey woolly skirt and a pink jersey with a teddy bear motive, and Stevie in little blue jeans, with the crease ironed in, and a blue and yellow plaid shirt. Vogel assumed they must have been transported from Instow in their nightwear, but presumably they kept clothes at their grandparents' house, and doubtless Amelia Ferguson was the sort who would require children to wash and dress as soon as they were out of bed. On this just like any other day.

This family had been through some kind of nightmare already. But, superficially at least, there was little to show for it at the home of the Fergusons senior. Vogel had no doubt that was largely down to Amelia.

The two children looked up from their books as Vogel and Saslow entered the sitting room.

'Hello,' said Vogel, treating them to what he hoped was his most reassuring smile.

Amelia Ferguson clearly had little time for life's niceties, even where her own grandchildren were concerned.

'Right, you two, Grannie has to talk to our visitors, why don't you both go upstairs and play in your room for a bit,' she commanded.

Vogel thought that was quite an unfeeling way to talk to a couple of little kids who had been through such an awful experience. Only a few hours previously they had witnessed their mother hanging dead in their home.

Joanna and Stevie merely stood up and proceeded to do as they had been told.

Vogel took the opportunity to introduce himself.

As the twins walked past him he crouched down.

'I'm David,' he said. 'You must be Stevie and Joanna.'

The little boy nodded, and very formally held out his hand to be shaken. Vogel obliged. He found such grown-up courtesy rather disturbing in one so young.

The little girl just stared.

'I may see you later,' said Vogel. 'Will that be all right?'

The little boy nodded again. His sister more or less ignored Vogel, turning instead to her grandmother.

'Aren't we going home to Mummy now?' she asked suddenly.

'No dear, not today,' replied Mrs Ferguson, her voice full of forced cheeriness. 'You're going to have a day with Grannie. Isn't that nice?'

Neither child looked entirely convinced of that.

'I want to see my mummy,' said Joanna, looking disconcertingly close to tears.

'We'll talk about that later, dear,' said Amelia quite brusquely. 'Just run along now, there's a good girl.'

Mrs Ferguson senior really did appear to be the most insensitive of people, considered Vogel. He watched as the children left the room without further protest. There was something so very sad about them. And he wasn't at all sure that this rather austere woman would be much help to them. There was also already a question mark over the father. In any case surely under these tragic circumstances he should be with his son and daughter.

'Where is your son, Mrs Ferguson?' he asked curtly, as soon as the door had shut behind them. 'I shall need to talk to him too.'

'He's in bed, he's had a dreadful shock, you know, he needs to sleep, to recover,' replied Amelia Ferguson, immediately displaying rather more sympathy for her son than she had so far for her grandchildren.

Vogel was surprised.

All he said was: 'I see.'

'Yes well, Mr Vogel, shall we get on with it then?' she continued.

Only it wasn't so much a question as an instruction. Amelia gestured for Vogel and Saslow to sit on one of the big sofas. There was no offer of coffee or tea. Vogel didn't want either. He had just enjoyed a large breakfast. But he suspected the thought of providing two visiting police officers with a beverage wouldn't even occur to this woman.

'Could I start by saying how sorry we are for your loss, Mrs Ferguson,' he began, forcing himself to use the quietly sympathetic tone which was the norm for him when dealing with the recently bereaved. Even when suspicion might have already fallen upon them, or he simply found himself instantly disliking them.

Amelia, who had remained standing, towering over Vogel and Saslow in a domineering sort of way, grunted.

'Yes, yes,' she said. 'Now what do you want to ask me exactly?'

Vogel thought he'd better at least attempt to take charge of this interview.

'Won't you please also sit down, Mrs Ferguson,' he said.

In spite of his mild-mannered approach, Vogel would never let anyone he was interviewing assume a dominant position – not even to the extent of sitting in a significantly taller chair.

With just the merest flicker of further annoyance in her eyes, Mrs Ferguson sat.

'Right,' said Vogel. 'First of all, you should know that the reason we have come to see you so quickly is that your daughter-in-law's death is being treated as suspicious.'

Vogel's tone was now quite sharp. He would try not to show it, but Amelia Ferguson's manner had already annoyed him considerably. Not least because of the way she had been with her grandchildren under such awful circumstances.

He was gratified to see the woman's excessively confident and somewhat overbearing manner evaporate like steam on a hot day.

Her jaw dropped. It really did. She sat forward in her chair, clasping her hands tightly in her lap, as if making a determined effort to maintain her strict self-control.

'Whatever do you mean?' she asked. 'Jane took her own life, the s—'

Amelia Ferguson stopped abruptly. Had there been a bookie handy Vogel would have taken a decent bet that she had been about to say 'silly girl'. Or something worse. He really had taken an instant dislike to this woman. Something he rarely did. And something he knew he must disregard while completing this investigation. He met Mrs Ferguson's eye with his, keeping his expression as neutral as possible, and remained silent.

'But, Jane hanged herself,' the woman continued. 'Little Joanna found her. The police, I mean, the two officers who came first to the house, they told my Felix that. Didn't they? It was suicide. That's not a suspicious death, is it?'

Amelia Ferguson no longer sounded quite so much in control. Not even of herself. Vogel knew he was being small, as his wife would say, but he found that rather gratifying.

'Indeed, suicide is not a suspicious death,' he said. 'But the pathologist who attended the scene has reason to believe that there is a strong possibility that your daughter-in-law did not take her own life.'

'Reason to believe?' repeated Amelia Ferguson. 'What possible reason could there be? Jane hanged herself from the bannisters when the only other people in the house were her own little children. And if that's not the height of selfishness I don't know what is . . .'

The woman stopped abruptly again. This time a light flush spread across her features. Vogel suspected that she realized she may have gone too far.

'I'm sorry, Mrs Ferguson, I am not at liberty to go into any details. However, I would like to ask you why you are so sure your daughter-in-law killed herself?'

'Well, it didn't occur to me that it could be anything else. Not from what Felix told me, and the two constables who broke the news to us said much the same. She'd been found hanged by little Joanna, that's what they told us. The whole thing was just totally shocking. I could barely believe my ears. Neither Sam nor I could quite take it in at first. I mean, Jane, was, well, never what you might call well-adjusted. But it didn't occur to me, not to any of us, that she would take her own life. I mean, have you seen her beautiful home? Felix has always been such a good provider. Like his father. Well, to tell the truth, the whole family have been involved. Jane wanted for nothing. Never had to work once she was married. Not that we'd have let her carry on working as a waitress, obviously. That wouldn't have done at all . . .'

Amelia stopped in mid-sentence. Vogel wondered if his face might have given away too much of what he was thinking. He was vaguely amused by the way Amelia Ferguson seemed to have so little idea how her words would sound to almost anyone listening. He considered what she had told him. Jane had been a waitress before her marriage, had she? That would certainly not have pleased her future mother-in-law who was clearly a proper old-fashioned snob. He certainly wanted to hear more from her, though. She was revealing so much more than she realized.

'Do go on, Mrs Ferguson,' he encouraged.

'Right, yes,' the woman continued readily enough. 'And then there are those beautiful children. I don't see how there can be any doubt that Jane committed suicide, surely. But as for why, I have no idea, detective chief inspector.'

'Could you tell me when you last saw your daughter-in-law, Mrs Ferguson?' Vogel asked levelly.

'Oh yes. Yes, of course. It would have been, uh, about two months ago. Felix's birthday. His thirty-fifth. We gave a little party for him here.'

Vogel considered for a moment.

'Two months seems quite a long time ago for you to have last seen your son's wife,' the detective remarked casually. 'Particularly considering she and your son only live fifteen minutes or so away from you.'

'Yes, well. You may as well know, detective chief inspector, because you'll find out soon enough if you're going poking around in matters that don't concern you, my daughter-in-law and I did not get on.'

Poking around in matters that don't concern you? Had she actually said that? The woman really was infuriating. And she had already made her low opinion of her son's wife pretty darned clear. Vogel found himself blinking rapidly behind his spectacles. It always happened when he was aroused, either emotionally affected, or, as in this case, battling to keep his anger in check.

'Mrs Ferguson, we may well be mounting a full-scale murder investigation, of which I expect to be in charge,' he responded with a certain quiet menace. 'There is therefore nothing that does not concern me or any of my investigating officers. Nothing at all.'

Amelia Ferguson flushed again. She opened her mouth as if to speak and then shut it. Vogel suspected she had thought that he was a pushover. People often made that mistake. Vogel's natural demeanour was to be mild-mannered and courteous. He was a thoughtful man, whose hobbies were compiling crosswords and playing backgammon at the highest level. He never looked well dressed. His dark brown hair was long to the collar and somewhat dishevelled. He sometimes seemed a tad on the vague side, and gave every appearance of being a bit of a dreamer not entirely at ease in the modern world. But appearances can be deceptive. Vogel was a very modern policeman, technically highly skilled, an incisive detective with a brain like a bacon slicer. And he expected, indeed demanded, to be treated with respect.

It seemed possible that Amelia Ferguson was beginning to realize at least part of this. She remained silent until he spoke again.

'Right,' Vogel continued firmly. 'Perhaps you would tell me when you last saw your son before his wife's death.'

'Oh, that would be yesterday, when he picked the twins up. He usually brings the children here on Friday evenings, then they stay with us overnight. More often in the school holidays. I see Felix most days, Mr Vogel. When he's working, he almost always pops in at lunchtime or early evening before he goes home.'

'But not accompanied by his wife?'

'No, Mr Vogel. I'm afraid things had got to the stage where Jane and I only met up at family occasions when that could not be reasonably avoided. Like birthdays. Christmas. Events at the children's school. Important social occasions connected with the businesses, not that she was keen on that sort of thing. Rarely otherwise. Not for two or three years now.'

'And might I enquire if there was any particular reason for this situation to develop?' asked Vogel.

'Nothing in particular, not really. Things just went from bad to worse between us, over the years. I mean, Felix should never have married her. He could have had anybody, taken his pick of the girls around here, handsome young man like him, family business and all of that. But no. He chose her. That . . . that . . . silly . . .'

She stopped yet again.

'Silly girl?' prompted Vogel.

'Well, she was. She really was.'

Mrs Ferguson blurted the words out. Vogel was starting to get interested. For all her controlling ways Amelia Ferguson clearly had problems governing her tongue. Certainly as far as her daughter-in-law was concerned. Which, for an investigating policeman was extremely good news.

He didn't say anything. Neither did Saslow. She'd learned fast that one.

Mrs Ferguson soon began to speak again, as Vogel had known she would.

'Look, Mr Vogel, Jane was never happy. She was one of those who found life difficult. She was never content. The children would often get to be too much for her. She would call Felix and say she couldn't cope on her own. That's why I had them so much in the school holidays. I always thought she had . . .'

Mrs Ferguson paused, took a deep breath, and then continued.

'To tell the truth, and there can't be much doubt about it now, I always thought she had mental health issues. We, Sam and I, begged Felix to get her to seek help. He told us she did agree to see someone. A while back. I never knew the details. She needed medication if you ask me. Lately, well . . . Felix seemed so unhappy. I've suspected he and Jane were having problems. Not surprising. A man like Felix needs a proper wife. Someone who will look after his children and his home, and be there to socialize with him. She never wanted to get involved with that side of his life. Not a bit interested in going to the yacht club with him, for example, even though he is commodore.'

'You said that your son never should have married Jane,' Saslow remarked. 'Why? Did she always show signs of these mental health issues you believed her to be suffering from?'

'Well, I don't know about that. Not at first, anyway. And she was a pretty girl. You can't take that away from her. But she never fitted in. She just wasn't one of us, if you know what I mean.'

Vogel feared he very much knew what the woman meant. She really was one of the worst snobs he had ever met.

'So what was Jane's background, then?' Saslow continued. 'Was she a local girl?'

'She most certainly was not local,' said Mrs Ferguson, as if that in itself had been enough to cast doubt upon her daughter-in-law's character. 'And we know hardly anything of Jane's background. Next to nothing about her family history. She admitted early on she didn't even know who her father was. Can you believe that? Next to nothing about her medical history, either. I don't think Felix ever knew much, either, although he wouldn't admit it, of course. Besotted with her, he was. To begin with anyway. But Jane's past was always a mystery as far as Sam and I were concerned. If you asked her anything she would clam up at once, or change the subject. I've always thought she was ashamed of her background. And I don't like that sort of thing. It's all in the breeding, you see, isn't it? People. Dogs. Horses. If you know their breeding, you know what you're getting, don't you?'

Neither Vogel nor Saslow passed any comment. Amelia Ferguson glanced down at her two Cavalier King Charles', now lying at her feet, both of which were staring at her adoringly. Vogel had a vague memory of a scandal a few years previously concerning the in-breeding of these pretty little dogs. As a result the majority of them ended up with a severely painful condition causing malformation of the skull, plus heart, and other health problems. He suspected many of those responsible would be the same type of person as Mrs Amelia Ferguson.

'Everything is down to breeding,' she repeated, stroking the little dogs' heads proprietorially.

Vogel had an almost overwhelming urge to pick up the woman and shake her. Instead he concentrated on extracting from her as much information as possible.

'Was your son aware of how strongly you had come to feel about his wife?' Vogel asked.

'Well, yes. I suppose so. There was no secret about it.'

'And how did he react to that?'

'He accepted it. He must have known himself that he'd made the wrong choice. But we didn't talk about it.'

'Yet you had no qualms about making your opinion known, Mrs Ferguson?'

'No. I didn't. What would you expect? She most certainly wasn't what I'd wanted for my boy. But, look, if you want to know more you're going to have to ask Felix. I don't see how I can help you any further.'

'I certainly intend to be asking Felix a number of questions,' said Vogel.

'I just said, he's upstairs asleep. It's been a terrible ordeal for him, so I told him just to stay in bed and get all the rest he can. He's been extremely distressed by everything, you know.'

Yes, and very drunk, from all accounts, Vogel thought. He was unimpressed. He considered how he would behave if, heaven forbid, anything happened to his beloved Mary. He would be in bits, but he would still be there for his daughter. Indeed, he would not leave Rosamund's side.

'His children are going through quite an ordeal, too, Mrs Ferguson,' said Vogel. 'I'm a bit surprised he isn't up and looking after them, to tell the truth.'

He glanced at his watch.

'It is nearly nine thirty,' he said.

'My son has been up half the night, detective chief inspector,' responded Mrs Ferguson defensively.

'And so have his children,' countered Vogel quickly.

There was more he would like to say. He stopped himself. Baiting Amelia Ferguson was not going to get him anywhere. Tempting though it was. He changed tack. Made his voice gentler.

'Look Mrs Ferguson, I do understand, everyone is upset and everyone has a different way of dealing with shock and grief. However, we will need to wake Felix and get him down here, I'm afraid. But I do have one last question for you. You say that you believe Jane committed suicide. Is there anything you know of that has happened, anything that has changed, possibly in the last weeks or even days, that might have induced your daughter-in-law to take her own life? Anything that might have pushed her over the edge?'

Vogel's conciliatory approach seemed to work. Mrs Ferguson looked as if she were genuinely considering how best to correctly answer his question.

'Well, there were the dreams, of course,' she said.

Vogel felt a little frisson of excitement.

'The dreams?' he queried.

'Yes. But she's had them for years. From soon after they were married. Felix told us. Bad dreams. Nightmares. She'd be inconsolable, Felix said. But whether or not they'd been getting any worse, or anything like that, I don't really know . . .'

Her voice tailed off.

'Did Jane talk to you about the dreams?' asked Vogel.

'You've got to be joking,' muttered Mrs Ferguson. 'No. I thought I'd made it clear. Jane never talked to me about anything. Barely spoke to me at all, actually. Which suited us both. We felt exactly the same way about each other. There was never much doubt about that. Felix told me, of course. He was worried about Jane, poor dear. Terribly worried. The dreams were pretty persistent, you see. Sometimes he'd say she was going through a bad patch, and another time he'd be pleased because she hadn't had one in a while. He always hoped they would just stop. Ever the optimist, my Felix.'

'I see,' said Vogel. 'OK Mrs Ferguson, thank you for your help. I think the time has come for you to go upstairs, wake up your son, if he really has managed to sleep, and fetch him down here to me.'

Amelia Ferguson appeared to hesitate. She looked as if she might be about to argue. She really was a piece of work, thought Vogel.

'At once, Mrs Ferguson,' he commanded. 'Oh, and by the way, where is your husband? We will need to speak to him too.'

'He's at the council. Went off very early.'

'What, just hours after his daughter-in-law was found hanged? And today is a Sunday, unless I'm much mistaken.'

'Sam doesn't take any notice of weekends, he's a very busy man, and he is the mayor, you know,' responded Mrs Ferguson defensively. 'This is all most difficult for him. He said he'd come home as soon as he could.'

What a family this is, thought Vogel.

'Right, Mrs Ferguson, while you are upstairs I want you to phone your husband and tell him to get back here straight away,' he ordered.

Again, Amelia Ferguson looked as if she might be able to argue. Ultimately, she seemed to think better of it, and left the room.

EIGHT

Within just a few minutes Felix Ferguson joined Vogel and Saslow in the sitting room. He was wearing a black velveteen dressing gown and apparently little else. Certainly a considerable expanse of bare chest was exposed where the gown gaped open to the waist in a wide V, and his lower legs, protruding from beneath the knee-length garment, were also bare.

Vogel and Saslow stood up as he entered the sitting room. Felix walked straight up to them both, albeit with a somewhat uncertain gait, and offered his hand in greeting.

He definitely had the dishevelled look of someone who had just been woken from a deep sleep. He seemed not to be functioning properly, although there may have been more than one reason for that. His wavy blonde hair was tousled. He was unshaven.

Nonetheless Felix Ferguson was very nearly an extremely handsome man, albeit let down by a weak fleshy mouth and one eye which failed to precisely line up with the other.

This made it difficult to ascertain exactly where he was looking, which Vogel found mildly unnerving.

The DCI was intrigued. If he had just lost his wife, particularly in such dreadful circumstances, he couldn't imagine that he would ever be able to sleep properly again, let alone immediately afterwards.

On the other hand, of course, Felix Ferguson may have taken sleeping pills or some kind of sedative. Vogel studied the other man carefully.

Those unnerving eyes were bleary and red rimmed. Maybe he had shed a tear or two. If so it was possible that he at least had a little more heart than his mother had displayed so far.

'Uh, I'm sorry I didn't come down before,' said Felix, clearly trying to stifle a yawn and not entirely succeeding. 'I didn't know you were here.'

'That's quite all right, Mr Ferguson,' said Vogel, once he'd
formally introduced himself and Saslow. 'I am sure you needed
to rest.'

Vogel's tone was neutral, but a certain underlying criticism,
or at least curiosity, had been intended. In spite of his dopey
appearance, Felix Ferguson seemed to pick up on this.

'Uh, yes, well, my mother thought so, anyway,' he said. 'Made
me take a sleeping pill.'

He shook his head as if trying to clear it. At that moment his
mother returned.

'I've called Sam, Mr Vogel—' she began.

Felix interrupted her, sounding angry.

'For God's sake, Mum, what the heck was that pill you gave
me?' he enquired loudly. 'I went out like a light, and I still can't
wake myself up properly.'

'Oh, nothing out of the ordinary. Just a zolpidem. But, of
course, you had been drinking, dear . . .'

'For God's sake,' said Felix again.

He glanced at his watch.

'I can't believe the time.' He paused. 'Where are the children?'
There was suddenly a note of panic in his voice. 'Mum, where
are the twins?'

'They're upstairs, playing in their room.'

'I don't believe it, Mum. You've left them up there? On their
own? Today?'

Felix began to move towards the door, presumably intending
to go to his children.

Vogel interceded at once.

'Mr Ferguson, I really need to talk to you right now,' he said.
'Perhaps your mother could go up to your children.'

Felix stopped in his tracks.

'All right. Yes, of course. Mum, go up to them, will you? And
don't leave them again. Just call me. How could you leave them
alone? Think what they must be going through.'

'I didn't think, dear,' said Mrs Ferguson senior apologetically.
'I'm so sorry. Of course. I'll go at once. I'll look after them.
Don't you worry.'

She half ran from the room, almost embarrassingly eager to
please. Vogel had seen this before, both in men and in women.

A person who was strong and dominating with everyone in their life except just one person. Usually someone they hero-worshipped. It seemed clear that her much-adored son was Amelia Ferguson's weak spot. Indeed, she had already indicated that in the way she'd talked to Vogel about him.

Felix sat down again and addressed the detective chief inspector.

'You'll have to excuse me, I can't get my head around anything right now,' he said. 'And that bloody pill of Mother's hasn't helped. Still, I suppose she meant well.'

'I'm sure she did,' responded Vogel, who supposed much the same thing about Amelia Ferguson in this instance, at least in regard to her son's welfare, if nothing else.

'So, I understand you have some questions for me?' Felix continued. 'I'm not sure that I'll be able to help you much. I wasn't even there when Jane . . . Jane . . .'

Felix Ferguson stumbled to a halt. He seemed quite unable to get the words out. And, like his mother, he was obviously under the initial impression that nobody believed his wife's death to be anything other than suicide.

'I realize that, sir, and I know this must be a very difficult time for you,' said Vogel. 'I would also like to say how sorry we both are for your loss—'

Felix interrupted, almost as if he hadn't heard, or certainly not taken in what Vogel was saying.

'It's the twins, you see, they're only six, seeing their mother like that. They told me it was little Jo who found Jane first. It's just too much. I don't know what to say to them. I really can't bear it . . .'

And then Felix began to cry, tears started to roll down his cheeks, his shoulders heaved. Soon his whole body was wracked with sobs.

Vogel looked at Saslow. Saslow looked at Vogel. At least it seemed apparent that Felix had a heart, which remained question-able in his mother's case. Either that or he deserved an Oscar, thought Vogel. But Felix's grief appeared genuine enough, and Vogel would never criticize anyone for showing their emotions when they'd lost a loved one, particularly in circumstances like these. However, in his time he had seen many parents battling to cope with tragedy, even the death of a child, while somehow or other managing, on the surface at least, to hold themselves together for the sake of any siblings of that child.

He couldn't help questioning what use the weak-mouthed Felix Ferguson was likely to be to his traumatized children in this state. Maybe his mother had not been entirely wrong to keep him out of the way for a bit.

The two police officers waited in mildly embarrassed silence until Felix's sobbing finally abated.

He took a handful of paper tissues from his dressing-gown pocket and blew his nose loudly.

'I'm sorry,' he said. 'I suppose I'm in shock. I don't seem able to control myself. I keep breaking down.'

He glanced at Vogel, or at least Vogel thought he was glancing at him, in a manner that suggested he was hoping for sympathy and reassurance. Like a little boy. The little boy he once was, who, Vogel thought, still formed a big part of his character. The DCI was not interested. He just wanted to get on with the job in hand.

'Firstly, I would like to ask you to go through with me your movements yesterday evening and through the night, if you will, Mr Ferguson,' he instructed, almost as if the man's sobbing fit had not even taken place. 'When you last saw your wife alive, where you were when she died, and so on.'

'I see,' said Felix.

He sat down on a chair facing Vogel, making no attempt to volunteer any information.

'Right, so let's begin with you telling me when you last saw your wife then, shall we, Mr Ferguson?' Vogel continued, his voice a little more forceful.

'Uh, yes, of course. It was when I left to go to the yacht club. About seven yesterday evening. We put the twins to bed together. We always try to do that. I read them one chapter of a story, and then Jane read one . . .'

Felix Ferguson looked as if he might burst into tears again. Vogel was not impressed.

'Please continue, Mr Ferguson,' he prompted sternly.

'Sorry. Yes. Then I walked down to the village. To the yacht club. I knew I'd have a few drinks. It was a special night, you see. The inaugural dinner marking my appointment as commodore. Or maybe you know about that already?'

Vogel nodded impatiently.

'And how was your wife?'

'How was she? She was fine. Absolutely fine. That's what's so crazy about this . . .'

'So, there was nothing about her to give you any cause for concern?'

'No. If there had been I wouldn't have left her, would I?'

'Well, you said yourself, Mr Ferguson, it was an important night at the club. Your formal inauguration as commodore.'

'I wouldn't have left my wife if I'd been worried about her in any way,' Ferguson persisted, with more than a hint of stubbornness.

Vogel wondered if this was a usual characteristic, or just something brought about by the tragic circumstances.

'Might I ask, as this was such an important night, why your wife didn't accompany you to the yacht club?' he enquired.

'She decided to stay home with the twins. We might have asked Mum and Dad to keep them another night, they'd actually been here the night before, Mum probably said. But they were going out.'

'I see. Was there nobody else?'

'Well, not really. The Barhams have babysat for us before. But not lately. To be honest, Jane tolerated the twins going to my mum and dad, but she had come not to like leaving them with anyone, really. And to be honest, she wasn't mad about yacht club events.'

'Your mother told us that relations were strained between her and Jane,' commented Vogel. 'Your father too. She was quite frank about it . . .'

'So what's that got to do with anything?' interjected Felix tetchily.

'I am not at all sure yet,' responded Vogel quickly. 'Perhaps you would like to tell me?'

'My wife has died. Whether or not she got on with my parents is really not relevant.'

'We are still looking into what is relevant, and what is not, in the events leading up to your wife's death, Mr Ferguson, and that is why I need your help,' recited Vogel with an exaggerated patience he did not feel. 'You are clearly under the impression that your wife took her own life, and that might be so, but we are also investigating other possibilities—'

'What do you mean, other possibilities?' interrupted Ferguson.

'As I have just explained to your mother, Mr Ferguson, there seems to be evidence indicating that foul play may have been involved in your wife's death.'

'For God's sake, are you saying you think Jane may have been murdered?'

'I would not go as far as that at this stage, but we are already treating her death as suspicious.'

Felix Ferguson seemed to visibly pale before Vogel's eyes.

'Suspicious,' he repeated. 'What was suspicious about it? She hanged herself, didn't she?'

'Mr Ferguson, you clearly accepted straightaway, when you heard of your wife's death, that she had killed herself,' Vogel continued. 'That indicates to me that you must, at the very least, have been concerned about her in some way. Isn't that the case? Would you mind telling me if there was something wrong with your wife in the weeks and months leading up to her death?'

'Wrong with her? There was nothing wrong with Jane. She was fine. I wasn't concerned about her at all. I accepted that she'd committed suicide because of the manner of her death. The officers last night, they told me she'd hanged herself. I'm sure they did.'

'I doubt they would have put it quite like that, sir.'

'Well, they certainly told me Joanna found her mother hanging . . . I mean, what else would you expect me to think?'

'I don't know, sir. That's why I need you to answer my questions. You just told me that when you went out last night you had no concerns about your wife. Yet a few hours later she was dead, and now you say it was obvious that she took her own life. Regardless of the circumstances, you must see that doesn't quite add up, don't you?'

'Doesn't it? I don't see why not. And I'm damned if I'm going to answer any more of your questions, not now. Absolutely not now.'

Felix jumped to his feet. He glowered at Vogel. His expression and his voice were both angry.

'Look. This is a family tragedy. And you are intruding on our grief. I need to be with my children. I am going to my children.'

He turned his back on Vogel and began to walk to the door leading to the hallway.

'Mr Ferguson, I need you to sit down and continue to answer my questions,' Vogel called after him. 'I am sorry to be insistent at this time, but this is officially an investigation into a suspicious death and we shall be enquiring into the circumstances accordingly. You should know that if you will not cooperate here and now, I shall have you taken to the nearest police station.'

Vogel was at his most authoritative. He did not excessively raise his voice. He did not need to.

Ferguson turned to look again at the policeman. Vogel's gaze was level.

'Please sit down, Mr Ferguson,' he said again.

'But . . . but, my children. Of course, I'll cooperate. I just should be with my children. Can't this wait?'

'No, Mr Ferguson, it cannot.'

There was a definite warning note in Vogel's voice now.

Felix Ferguson sat.

'Joanna found her mother hanging, there was no one else in the house,' he said, his voice quiet again. 'Why on earth would you suspect anything other than suicide?'

'I'm not able to go into that, at the moment, sir,' said Vogel.

'For God's sake,' said Ferguson.

Then he fell silent as if struggling to come to terms with a whole new scenario.

'You think someone killed my Jane. You clearly do. And you must have good reason for that. I want to know why you think it. That's all.'

'I'm not able to discuss it, sir. Not yet, I'm afraid.'

'But I'm her husband. I have a right to know . . .'

Vogel remained silent. He could almost see the light switching on behind Felix Ferguson's eyes.

'For God's sake,' he said again. 'You think I did it, don't you? You think I killed my Jane?'

'I don't think anything of the sort, sir,' responded Vogel mildly. 'We are treating your wife's death as suspicious, yes, but it may well prove that we ultimately conclude that she did take her own life. Meanwhile, of course, as the husband of the deceased, you are a person of interest. And this may well be only the first in a series of interviews with you to be conducted during the course of our enquiries. But no assumptions of any sort will be made until we have assimilated and evaluated all possible evidence.'

'A person of interest? What's that supposed to mean?'

'I'm sure you understand what that means, sir. As I explained, you are the husband of the deceased. In addition, you are most probably the last person to have seen your wife alive, excluding, possibly, your children. And, also, I have reason to believe you are not being entirely honest with me about Jane. I will ask you again, was there nothing at all in her behaviour to cause you concern last night?'

'Of course, I am being honest,' Ferguson responded quickly. 'There was nothing that caused me concern last night. Jane seemed perfectly normal when I left the house. Really, she did.'

'I see, sir,' said Vogel. 'And what do you mean by normal, exactly?'

'Well, normal's normal, isn't it. She got the twins' tea. I left as soon as we'd put them to bed. She seemed fine. Really.'

'Are you quite sure of that?'

'Yes, yes . . .'

Ferguson paused abruptly.

'You've been talking to Mother, haven't you?' he blurted out. 'What's she said? What's she said about Jane?'

Vogel had absolutely no intention of sharing anything Amelia Ferguson had said about her daughter-in-law.

'Mr Ferguson, for the umpteenth time, if there was anything about your wife which was giving you or any of your family cause for concern I need to hear it. Now. From you.'

Felix sighed, in a resigned sort of way.

'Well,' he said. 'There were the dreams, of course.'

'The dreams, sir?' Vogel queried, again experiencing that small frisson of excitement he always did when he felt that he might be about to learn something highly significant to a major investigation.

He gave no indication that he already knew at least something of Jane Ferguson's history of bad dreams. Even if Felix did already suspect his mother of some sort of indiscretion. He wanted to hear this man's version uninfluenced by anything he may already have learned.

'Well, yes. Jane had been having bad dreams. Full blown nightmares, really. Sometimes they were worse than others. She would have periods of them not being too bad, nor all that frequent. But, well, she'd been going through a bad patch these last few weeks. She would wake screaming and hysterical. It had got so bad that she was afraid to go to sleep half the time. And, uh, that's another reason she was quite happy to stay home with the twins last night. She'd barely been sleeping, you see. She was tired, terribly tired.'

'But that didn't give you cause for concern?'

'Well no, not in the way you mean. You asked what I meant by normal. Well, I suppose it had become normal. A part of our life. Jane would have these dreams. Either not be able to sleep, or not allow herself to sleep. Then, as a consequence of that, she was always tired. Dead tired.'

He paused, as if suddenly realising the nature of the words he had used.

'I didn't mean to say that,' he murmured.

'Of course not, sir,' said Vogel.

'She was still a good wife, though, I need to tell you that,' Ferguson continued. 'In spite of everything. And a wonderful mother.'

Vogel studied the other man carefully. He reckoned Felix Ferguson's last remark was just a tad trite.

'I'm sure she was, sir,' the detective remarked mildly, at the same time changing tack a little. 'And her death must be an enormous loss to you.'

'Yes, it is. Just terrible. I can't quite believe she's gone. That we will never see her again . . .'

Ferguson looked and sounded vaguely surprised by the DCI's

sympathetic tone. As well he might, thought Vogel, in view of the somewhat aggressive nature of his previous questioning.

'I'm sure, sir,' he continued as gently as possible. 'The nightmares must have disrupted both your lives though, didn't they?'

'Well yes. But we didn't think about it that way; I didn't anyway. I just wanted Jane to get better. She was an incredible woman you know, just incredible . . .'

'I'm sure, sir,' said Vogel again. 'May I ask, were you doing anything about these dreams? Was your wife having any treatment at all?'

'Yes, of course. We had to try to do something. I guess you kind of deny these things at first. We did for years. But eventually, well, Jane first went to her GP about it around two years ago. She'd had bad dreams occasionally ever since we were married, and before, I think. But they got progressively worse after the twins were born. Even then we managed to cope most of the time. It was very stressful, obviously. The GP tried to help, mainly by putting Jane on various courses of medication. But things just continued to get worse. Ultimately, he referred Jane for psychiatric help. He tried to arrange for her to see a consultant who specialized in sleep disorders. There was a three-month waiting list, would you believe?'

'So, had she actually seen a psychiatrist at all?'

'Oh yes. We decided to arrange something privately.'

'I see. Could you tell me the name of this psychiatrist, and how often your wife saw him or her?'

'Yes. Dr Miriam Thorpe. She's in Exeter. Jane saw her every week.'

'Did the therapy seem to be doing any good?'

'I'm not so sure now. It would seem not, wouldn't it? But I thought it was. We both thought it was. The nightmares had become not quite so bad and seemed to be getting less frequent. Until, like I said, a few weeks ago when she went into a really bad patch.'

'Was this bad patch still going on?'

'Actually, I don't think Jane had had a nightmare for more than a week before . . . before she . . .'

Ferguson seemed unable to complete his sentence.

'So she was feeling better, again, was she?' Vogel encouraged him.

Felix shook his head.

'It wasn't like that really. Not right after a bad patch anyway. The tiredness alone was terrible for her. But we were used to it, Mr Vogel. And I swear to you, on my children's life, that there was nothing about Jane when I last saw her that made me think for one second that . . . that . . . something like this would happen.'

'Did you or your wife have any idea what caused these nightmares?' asked Vogel.

'No. Neither of us did. We hoped Dr Thorpe might be able to shed some light on that. But she was as puzzled as the rest of us, apparently.'

'Could Jane ever remember her nightmares when she woke up?'

'No, Mr Vogel. She always said she had no idea what they were about.'

'And yet they frightened her to the extent that she would scream out loud and become quite hysterical?' interjected Saslow.

'I'm afraid so. The worst ones anyway. She said it was as if there was something there in front of her, but she couldn't quite grasp it. She said she felt as if her brain was being torn apart, that one half of her wanted to confront her dreams and the other half was holding her back.'

'Presumably these dreams were violent in some way?' Saslow continued. 'Did she know where they took place?'

'I don't know about violent. But it was terrible to see the state she got in. As for where they took place, we never really talked about that. I don't think she knew, though, or she would have mentioned it.'

'Did she know if they were dreams about people, or events, disturbing and frightening happenings, maybe a disaster, like a plane crash, or something natural, like an avalanche or a tsunami, or perhaps something smaller and more personal?' asked Vogel.

'She had absolutely no idea, Mr Vogel. That was the worst of it. She didn't know what these terrible dreams were about and she didn't know why she had them, nor when they were going to strike. It used to drive her mad . . .'

Felix stopped abruptly. Once again, thought Vogel, he had inadvertently chosen words which were chillingly appropriate.

Felix Ferguson was clearly under great strain, and had not really had time to fully absorb the grim reality of what had occurred. Sometimes that was of advantage to a police interviewer. In this case, Vogel thought it was probably a mixed blessing, and that he'd leave Felix Ferguson to cogitate a little before interviewing him further.

He had one last line of questioning.

'Your wife had old scars on her lower arms which our pathologist says are consistent with self-harming,' Vogel remarked. 'Do you know what happened?'

'Not exactly. It was well before I knew Jane. She used to just say that she was in a bad place at the time.'

'Jane also had old bruising on one side of her face, and a partially healed cut on her cheek, unrelated to the manner in which she died,' the DCI continued. 'Can you tell us how that was caused?' HEALED

'She fell in the garden,' Felix answered quickly. 'She was playing with the twins, stepped on a toy car with wheels and went flying.'

Vogel was not entirely convinced. Nonetheless he was about to tell Felix that he was free to go, when he heard the front door slam and into the sitting room walked a man who was quite clearly Felix's father. Samuel Ferguson, the mayor of Bideford, was an older version of his son. Still handsome and with a full head of wavy hair, albeit totally white. The two men were strikingly alike. The only difference was that there was no hint of any sort of weakness in Sam Ferguson's features. The eyes were clear and level. The mouth was set straight and strong.

As his son had done earlier, Sam walked right up to Vogel offering an outstretched hand. Vogel took it.

'You must be DCI Vogel, from what my wife has told me, the man in charge,' he said with a small but confident smile. 'Sam Ferguson. Sorry I wasn't here when you arrived. I just had to put one or two things in place, explain to the staff, people at the council, that sort of thing. Such a dreadful business. So very sad.'

'Indeed, sir,' said Vogel, as he introduced Saslow.

'They're all at work on a Sunday, are they?' the detective continued, with only the slightest inflection in his voice.

'Uh, some of them came in, and I did a bit of a phone-round,' Sam Ferguson replied vaguely.

'Now, how can I help you?' he asked in a much more brusque fashion, as he lowered himself into what Vogel suspected was his usual armchair.

This was a man used to taking control, thought the DCI. He would, of course, learn, sooner rather than later that, in a police investigation of this nature, only the senior investigating officer was in charge of anything.

'Well, I have already interviewed your wife and your son, sir, but I do need to ask you some questions, in particular where you were last night when you daughter-in-law died?' Vogel enquired mildly.

'I see. Yes. Amelia told me on the phone you were treating Jane's death as suspicious. I don't suppose you can tell me why?'

'No sir, I'm afraid I can't. Just that we have reason to believe that suicide might not be the only possibility. Now, will you please answer the question.'

'Yes, of course. I was here with my wife, all evening. We went to bed about midnight. And we were woken when the police came around about three a.m., I think it was, to break the news. Didn't my wife tell you that?'

'Yes, she did, sir. But I needed to hear it from you. And your son told me he believed you were going out last night.'

'Oh yes, we were. To dinner with friends. An anniversary party actually. But Amelia had a tummy bug or something. So we stayed home.'

Vogel turned to Felix.

'I meant to say, sir, if you would like to go to your children now you are quite free to do so,' he told him.

Felix thanked the DCI and left the room. Which was what Vogel wanted. He thought he already knew the answers to the further questions he was about to ask Sam Ferguson, because he had more or less covered the same ground with Felix and his mother. But he wanted to see if Sam Ferguson told the same story.

By and large the man did so. Down to when he had last seen

his daughter-in-law. He claimed to know little about Jane's dreams, saying he always took that sort of thing with a pinch of salt. Whatever that meant, thought Vogel.

The DCI found Sam Ferguson an intriguing character. The epitome of a tough businessman probably, but with an easy manner and a natural charm. Even under these circumstances.

Once he had exhausted every current line of questioning, Vogel stood up to say goodbye.

As he shook hands again with the mayor he held on for just a second or two longer than normal, thus giving the other man every opportunity to try, or at least indicate, a Freemasons' handshake. Ferguson's handshake remained normal, without any indication of the tell-tale thumb pressure on knuckle which Masons use to recognize each other. Vogel didn't like Freemasonry. He'd seen too much of it in the police force at the most senior level, where officers had been known to favour their fellow Masons and sometimes protect them when they should not have been protected. Vogel had half expected Ferguson to be a Mason, and he considered it in the older man's favour that it now seemed likely that he wasn't. He could just be being cagey, of course. But Vogel didn't think so. The man was too content in his own skin. He was unlikely ever to hide what he was. Too pleased with himself, even on a day like this.

'May I just say, sir, you don't seem unduly upset by your daughter-in-law's death,' Vogel remarked. 'Would that be a fair comment?'

'Mr Vogel, I am used to holding things together in this family. My son is a broken man this morning, and I have two very vulnerable little grandchildren who have been through a quite terrible experience. I cannot afford to indulge my emotions.'

'Is that all there is to it, sir?' asked Vogel politely.

The other man sighed.

'Look, I suspect my wife wouldn't have been able to keep quiet about this, there has never been any love lost between either of us and Jane. We didn't think she was right for Felix when he married her, and nothing that has happened since has led us to change our minds. She was the mother of his children, two beautiful children, so we tolerated her. But we never grew to like her, nor her us. I am, actually, deeply upset by what has happened,

and the affect it will have on all of us; Amelia, Felix, the two
little ones, and yes, myself, and indeed the position I hold in the
community. I will confess to being concerned about that too. But
I am not upset by the loss of my daughter-in-law. And I will
certainly not miss her in any way.'

Vogel was thoughtful as he and Saslow left All Seasons.

'Well, that was blunt, Saslow, wasn't it?' he said.

'He obviously prides himself on being a plain-speaking sort
of man, boss,' commented Saslow ambiguously.

'Maybe. A tough one, that's for sure. Of course, it is still
possible that we won't ultimately have anything to investigate.
And the fact that both her in-laws clearly hated Jane Ferguson's
guts will prove to be none of our business.'

'You don't believe that, though, do you, boss?'

'I'm not entirely sure yet, Saslow,' responded Vogel. 'Maybe
Felix's words will prove to be prophetic. Maybe Jane was driven
mad by the nightmares that plagued her. Mad enough to take her
own life. And maybe the post-mortem examination won't reveal
anything to disprove that.'

'But what about the stuff that has already led us to suspect
third party involvement?' asked Saslow. 'The door that had surely
not been locked, the immediately visible injuries to Jane
Ferguson's body, some old and some new, and the unlikelihood
of any mother allowing even the chance of her little children
finding her dead hanged body.'

'There could still prove to be logical explanations for all of
that,' said Vogel. 'This could be a simple straightforward case
into which you and me, Saslow, Nobby Clarke, and all, have
been reading far too much.

'Perhaps Jane Ferguson ultimately became unable to cope any
longer with the madness raging inside her. Perhaps she really did
become crazy enough to hang herself regardless of any considerations about her children or anything else. Perhaps her death is
just another domestic tragedy. Suicide while the balance of her
mind was disturbed.'

'I think you're playing devil's advocate, boss,' commented Saslow.

'Perhaps,' said Vogel.

'And I don't reckon you really think for one minute that Jane
Ferguson took her own life.'

Vogel grunted in a non-committal sort of way.

'Let's just hope the PM examination gives us a definitive answer to that question,' he said.

'What d'you make of Felix Ferguson, Saslow?' asked Vogel, as they settled into Saslow's car.

It occurred to him that the arrival of Felix's father had diverted both their attentions from their earlier interview with his son, still their most significant 'person of interest'.

'I don't know quite what to make of him,' responded Saslow. 'On the one hand he seems plausible enough . . .'

Saslow let the sentence trail off. Vogel finished it for her.

'And on the other, you get the feeling he's hiding something, not being entirely honest. Which he denied, of course. But then, he would, wouldn't he? Something more about those dreams, maybe.'

'Exactly—'

Saslow didn't get to finish that sentence either. She was interrupted by the strident ring of Vogel's mobile.

He glanced at the screen and half smiled. Saslow was pretty sure she had a fair idea who was calling.

'Morning, boss,' said Vogel.

He could have been speaking to Detective Superintendent Hemmings. He wasn't though. Saslow was quite sure of that. She knew the difference.

'All right, all right,' muttered Vogel half apologetically into the phone. 'Nobby. Morning, Nobby.'

Saslow congratulated herself on her astuteness, and how well she knew her senior officer. He reacted to any contact with Detective Superintendent Nobby Clarke in unique fashion. She listened as Vogel continued to speak.

'Well, no, I don't know quite what to make of it yet, Nobby,' Vogel began. 'Jane Ferguson was clearly a disturbed young woman, and yet there was more than enough potential evidence at the scene to at the very least call suicide into question. And I've got the feeling there's a lot more going on that we don't know about . . . What? Now? We're on our way to the post-mortem. Oh. Lunch! OK. Sorry. I suppose we could make it to Exeter. Yes. All right. See you there.'

The DCI was frowning as he ended the call.

Saslow glanced at him enquiringly.

'She wants to talk about it over lunch,' Vogel remarked, his voice incredulous.

Saslow barely suppressed a chuckle. Her senior officer was not the sort of police officer who would build a lunch break into the first day of a murder enquiry. Or, come to that, probably any day of a murder enquiry.

'So we're going to Exeter?' she queried, somewhat surprised he'd agreed to that. Even if it was Nobby Clarke who'd made the suggestion.

'Yes, that's where the Devon and Cornwall's MCT is based, of course,' Vogel replied. 'Some restaurant Nobby likes, near the cathedral, apparently. We need a word with Jane Ferguson's trick cyclist anyway, and she's based in Exeter. So it kind of fits in.'

Vogel didn't sound totally convinced.

'But first, it's Barnstaple, and the post-mortem,' Vogel continued.

Saslow pulled the car out of the Fergusons' driveway and turned left along Bay View Road in the direction of Northam and the Torridge Bridge.

The entire Torridge and Taw estuary lay to the left of the bridge. The sun was still shining and reflecting on the water. The wind might have got up, but perhaps because of it, the sky was spectacular, lines of yellow and white were splashed across a pale blue backdrop.

Saslow was one of those who had an inborn love of the sea. She thought this part of North Devon was one of the most beautiful places she had ever been to.

She glanced at Vogel. He was sitting quite still, hands clasped in his lap, his eyes cast downward. As was often the case, he did not seem aware of anything much going on around him except the case he was working on.

NINE

Karen Crow had fast tracked the post-mortem for eleven a.m. at the North Devon District Hospital. She was just about to start work when Vogel and Saslow arrived at the mortuary.

The body, lain on its back with arms and legs outstretched, was no longer clothed, its nakedness adding to the vulnerability of this small slight woman. That was something else Vogel always found difficult to deal with.

Jane Ferguson had certainly sustained a number of bruises and other injuries of varying degrees of severity, and of varying longevity. There were old bruises on one of her upper legs, and also on one thigh, as well as the scars on her lower arms and wrists which the pathologist had earlier suggested could be signs of self-harming. There was also, of course, the faded bruising and the half-healed cut to Jane's face which had been apparent when her body was first discovered. Most of these could not have been sustained as she fell from the landing of her home, because they couldn't be post-mortem. And then there was the injured arm, dislocated at the shoulder according to Karen Crow's initial examination at the scene.

Vogel leaned closer to examine the body.

The dead woman's head lay very slightly at an angle. Vogel already knew that her neck had been broken, as he would suspect in the case of someone who had hanged to death. He stared for a moment or two at her distorted features, the swollen discoloured flesh where the rope had tightened around her neck, the protruding tongue. Then he looked away. He had already seen Jane Ferguson's body once, at first hanging from a rope and then lying on the floor of her home. This was far from the first death by strangulation that he had encountered in his police career, and would almost certainly not be the last. He still found it one of the most disturbing causes of death, and probably always would, whether self-administered or by a third party. Vogel fought to keep his facial expression neutral. He just had to accept that if he continued in police work until the end of his days he still would not get used to it. Nor to what he regarded as the equally horrific mechanics of a forensic post-mortem examination, come to that.

He glanced at Karen Crow. He could see that she was preparing the instruments she would use to saw open the dead woman's torso and remove the top of her head. He steeled himself. He suspected Karen could already answer most of the questions he needed to ask, but she was notoriously tetchy concerning what she considered to be interruptions whilst she was at work.

Eventually she turned to Vogel.

'I can see no initial signs of any internal injuries that may have contributed to death,' she said. 'There seems little doubt that my initial prognosis was correct and that the victim died of strangulation. The protrusion of the tongue, the bulging eyes, the skin discolouration, all point to that, in addition to the obvious circumstantial evidence of a rope which was tightened around her neck by her own weight when she fell from the bannisters on the landing of her home. Which she quite clearly did. And this is consistent with the fracture of the axis vertebra which she sustained.'

Karen Crow paused again.

'Hangman's fracture,' said Vogel.

Karen nodded.

'What, boss?' queried Saslow, who had never encountered a death by this kind of strangulation before.

'The name given to the fracture commonly sustained by those sentenced to death in a court of law in the days of judicial execution by hanging,' explained Vogel. 'Isn't that right, Karen?'

'Yes, it is,' said the pathologist. 'Although more recent studies have shown that the axis, which is the second spinal vertebra and the one that carries the pivot upon which the head rests, was not actually fractured in judicial hangings as often as used to be supposed. If it is fractured, particularly in circumstances like this, then it certainly serves to confirm that death was by hanging. But . . .'

'But . . . Karen?' interjected Vogel eagerly.

'But,' Dr Crow went on, 'there may also be indications of manual strangulation. The deceased's hyoid bone, that's the

U-shaped bone which supports the tongue, is also fractured. Now, according to what is generally regarded as probably the most authoritative study, in the States in 1990 something, thirty-four per cent of victims of manual strangulation suffer a fractured hyoid bone, but only eight per cent of victims of hanging. So, we have something of a conundrum here.'

'I see,' mused Vogel. 'But couldn't both these kinds of fracture occur in a suicidal hanging? Is that not possible?'

'I suppose it must be,' responded the pathologist. 'Although I personally have never encountered it. There is another explana-tion, of course, which at the very least would be equally likely.'

'That an unknown assailant manually strangled Mrs Ferguson and then staged a hanging so that her death would look like suicide, and she would sustain injuries consistent with suicidal hanging?' queried Vogel quickly.

'You're keeping up, Vogel. Well done. And yes, that has to be a possibility.'

'But can we prove it?' asked Vogel, who was too intrigued by what was being suggested to indulge in any banter.

'Well, I do think there is enough forensic evidence to strongly indicate that Mrs Ferguson has been murdered. And there's something else, Vogel. If you look closely . . .'

She glanced up at the DCI in invitation. Trying not to wince, Vogel obediently leaned forward in order to give himself a better view.

'If you look closely you can see certain indentations in the flesh around the victim's neck and throat which may not be directly related to the effects of the rope when she fell,' Karen Crow continued.

'So, are you saying that you think these indentations might be caused by fingers pressing into the flesh?' asked Saslow.

The pathologist nodded absently.

'You're keeping up too, Saslow,' she remarked. 'Yes. I do think these marks could have been made by fingers. And the victim suffered a quite severe blow to the head, probably around the time of her death. Difficult to be sure which. Do you see? There's a small but distinct dent in the cranium. Now, assuming for a moment that this is suicide, that injury could obviously have been caused by the deceased knocking her head against the bannisters, or perhaps a wall, when she fell. But it does also arouse suspicions that it was caused by a third party, perhaps using some sort of blunt instrument, and that it actually contributed to her death.'

'Well, in that case, and this time assuming Jane Ferguson was murdered, if the killer knocked her unconscious why did he need to manually strangle her?' asked Vogel. 'I can understand the difficulty in staging a hanging with a fit conscious young woman to deal with. But not too difficult if she's unconscious, surely.'

'Maybe not,' replied Dr Crow. 'But I am unsure if this particular blow to the head would have been sufficient to render the victim unconscious, or not for a long enough period of time, anyway. The assailant would almost certainly have known, or at least suspected, that there were children sleeping in the house too. He would have wanted to be able to move with maximum speed and minimum noise—'

'OK,' interrupted Vogel, who could not quite control his eagerness to grasp every possible option. 'But neither can you rule out the possibility of the blow to the head having been sustained when the victim fell from the upper landing with a rope around her neck – either of her own volition or at the hand of her killer, can you?'

'No, I can't,' agreed Karen Crow.

'What about the old bruising?' continued Vogel.

'Well, it's quite extensive. You know what I am going to say, don't you?'

'I think you are going to say that the pattern of the bruising is in keeping with domestic violence, as we have all suspected from the beginning. Not least because the bruising is primarily in areas which would probably normally be covered by clothing and therefore not seen.'

'I am indeed.'

'And so, the finger points even more at the husband. As usual.'

'That's your territory, Vogel.'

'Yes. And my enquiries so far have revealed that whatever personal suspicions I may have, the husband, our principle person of interest, appears to have a cast-iron alibi. In addition, your evidence is not conclusive, is it?'

'Well, no.'

PRINCIPAL

'Therefore, whilst there may well be reasons to suspect otherwise, Mrs Ferguson could still have taken her own life, as was initially suspected. Is that not so?'

'I'm afraid it is,' agreed the pathologist. 'Yes.'

'Yes,' echoed Vogel. 'Nonetheless, I think we have enough here for me to get the brass to agree to stepping up this operation to a murder investigation. Nobby Clarke is halfway there anyway. But I'm going to have to do a lot more digging before I take any action against Felix Ferguson, that's for sure.'

Vogel turned to Saslow.

'Come on, Dawn. Let's leave Karen to get on with her work and head for Exeter.'

He glanced at his watch. It was just noon. He had agreed to meet Nobby Clarke at one p.m., and he had no idea whether they would get to the restaurant on time. If not Nobby would have to wait. Knowing her, she wouldn't mind as long as she had a drink in her hand.

'First, lunch with the boss, then we'll see what Dr Miriam Thorpe has to say for herself,' he told Saslow as they headed for the hospital car park.

Nobby Clarke was already sitting at a window table at the restaurant, overlooking the city's lovely old Cathedral Yard, when Saslow and Vogel arrived. As usual Vogel barely noticed his surroundings.

'So,' Nobby said by way of greeting, 'I've just more or less got booted out of the Met because I took a moral stand on a contentious issue, or I thought that's what I was doing, anyway, and within days of arriving here I'm stuck with the son of a local bigwig as number one suspect in the murder of his wife . . .'

'I've just been telling Mr Ferguson junior that he isn't the number one suspect,' muttered Vogel, as he sat down.

'Of course, you have, Vogel, and we both know what a load of bollocks that is.'

'Whatever you say, boss, I mean Nobby. And it's not a murder enquiry yet, is it? Not officially anyway. But I think it should be.'

'Ummm. From one pile of horseshit to another. Apparently, Mr Ferguson senior, the mayor of Bideford, is a bloody tin god around here. More than likely I'm about to wreck yet another career move. Particularly with you on board, Vogel.'

'You asked for me, Nobby.'

'Yeah, I did, didn't I? I must be barking mad. What any intelligent copper in my position would try to do is brush this shit into a very dark corner, not heap it into a bloody great pile and sift through it.'

'Very lyrical,' said Vogel. 'When did you start worrying about career moves, anyway?'

'About the time I began to wonder what I'd do when they ran out,' growled Nobby.

'Ah.'

Vogel thought for a moment.

'So you didn't exactly choose to move to this very beautiful part of the world then?'

'Like you hadn't bloody guessed that, Vogel,' muttered Clarke.

'The thought did cross my mind.'

'I bet it did. The alternative seemed to be a demotion and back to uniform. I only hung on to my rank by the skin of my teeth as it was. The top brass at the Met were so desperate to get shot of me that when the MCT job down here became vacant they pushed like hell for me to be drafted in. God knows what lies got told. But, I didn't bring you here to talk about my career prospects, or lack of them.'

There was a glass of white wine on the table in front of Nobby Clarke. She raised it and took a deep drink.

Vogel watched in silence.

'It's my first,' offered the detective superintendent.

'I didn't say anything,' responded Vogel.

'You didn't have to,' growled Nobby. 'You sanctimonious born-again, vegan, ginger-ale drinker.'

'I'm not vegan, just vegetarian,' muttered Vogel, turning towards Dawn Saslow.

'What would you like to drink, Saslow?' he asked quietly.

'Think I'll stick to coffee, thanks,' said Saslow. 'I haven't had my caffeine quota yet today.'

'It's on the way,' said Clarke, without enthusiasm. 'And a ginger ale. In case you need a fix, Vogel.'

Saslow failed to react visibly in any way to the banter between her two superior officers. She'd heard it all before. If the exchange had been between anyone except Vogel and Clarke, it would have surprised and even embarrassed her. Neither, Vogel was quite sure, would she be fazed by Clarke's frank revelations concerning her career in front of a junior officer she didn't know that well. Nobby was that sort of person. She always treated everyone on her team as her equal. Albeit superficially. There was never any doubt about who was in charge.

'You all right, Dawn?' Clarke enquired conversationally. 'Still keeping the old bugger in check.'

'I don't know about that, boss,' Saslow murmured.

'No. Far too much to expect.'

Clarke picked up two menus and handed them to Saslow and Vogel.

'Let's order first,' she said. 'I'm having a veal escalope Milanese. With spaghetti.'

Vogel winced. Clarke laughed.

'Got you!' she said. 'Even I don't eat veal. It's a chicken escalope. All right, Vogel?'

'I am not your conscience,' said Vogel, aware that he probably sounded even more sanctimonious than he had intended.

Saslow said she would have the same. A waiter brought the coffee and ginger ale. Clarke ordered chicken escalope for them both. Vogel chose mushroom risotto.

Clarke leaned back in her seat, her hands behind her head.

'So, we have forensic evidence indicating that Jane Ferguson was murdered,' she began.

'Yes, but not irrefutable,' said Vogel.

'And yet you want me to officially launch a murder investigation?'

'It's as near as dammit if you ask me, Nobby,' said Vogel. 'However, we have to put a full-scale murder investigation in place in order to widen the scope of our enquiries. We need more evidence, and then there's the little matter of our number one suspect appearing to have a pretty good alibi.'

The obligatory Vogel-Clarke banter was over, apparently. For the moment anyway.

'Yes, our grieving husband, doubtless expressing his undying love for the deceased to anyone who will listen,' Clarke mused. 'Are we absolutely sure of his alibi?'

'Well, he was at this big night at the yacht club, and as the new commodore he was guest of honour,' responded Vogel. 'Gave a speech. Hoovered up the booze. It looks cast iron. At first sight anyway. Although we'll go along there later and double check it out.'

'Nobody else in the frame?'

'Not really. Not yet anyway. Felix Ferguson's mother clearly loathed her daughter-in-law and makes no bones about it. Thinks she wasn't good enough for her precious son. Same with Ferguson senior. Neither made any secret of their feelings when we interviewed them earlier. But it's hard to believe either of them would go as far as to whack our Jane on the head, strangle her, then hang her over the bannisters. Indeed, hard to believe Mrs Ferguson would have had the physical strength. Not on her own, anyway. Same for Sam really, even though he looks like a reasonably fit man for his age. They're both well into their sixties.'

'What about if they did it together? Do they have alibis?'

'Only each other. But, like I say, disliking your son's wife and doing her in are two different things. We'd have a load more corpses on our hands if they weren't! I don't see it, Nobby, really I don't.'

'Neither do I, to tell the truth. So, we don't have a lot to go on, yet, do we? As things stand, Vogel, what sort of chance do you see of us getting to the bottom of this thing, finding out beyond reasonable doubt who did what and why?'

Vogel glanced curiously at his senior officer.

'That's an odd sort of question to ask,' he said. 'I mean, it's very early days. We've teams doing door-to-door in Instow, Estuary Vista Close and thereabouts. See if anyone suspicious was seen hanging about, and so on. We'll do all the routine grinding police work, like we always do, and see where it takes us. I won't give up, boss. I never do. You know that.'

'Of course, I know that. It's why you're here.'

Vogel noticed that she hadn't picked up on his calling her 'boss'. She always picked up on that. Unless she had something more important on her mind, of course.

'What is it?' he said. 'You know something, don't you? Something I haven't been told.'

Clarke's second glass of wine arrived, along with the food they'd all ordered. She allowed herself to be momentarily distracted, and took a sip from the new glass before replying to Vogel, who was waiting more than a tad impatiently.

'Actually, Vogel, I don't *know* anything,' she said, with emphasis firmly on 'know'.

'It's just that the old super in Barnstaple, who's been in charge for ever, turned quite green when I told him we were looking at a suspicious death which might possibly turn into a murder enquiry. Kept asking me if I was absolutely sure and so on.'

She paused.

'Well yes,' said Vogel. 'But you would expect that, wouldn't you? I mean, you said from the beginning, the mayor of Bideford is like a little tin god in this part of North Devon. And your old super has been here since the year dot. Barnstaple's his home town. I'd guess?'

Vogel raised his eyebrows quizzically. Clarke nodded briefly.

'Bideford actually.'

'Ah, even worse, then,' Vogel continued. 'He wouldn't want to rock the boat of any local political bigwig, would he? And particularly not the mayor of his old home town. He probably also has retirement closing in on the horizon, and really doesn't want his own boat rocked either?'

Another query. Another nod from Clarke.

'Then what's bothering you, Nobby?' asked Vogel. 'Everything's panning out how we'd have expected so far, isn't it? That's how it seems to me, anyhow.'

'Yes, but you're a city creature, and as a copper you're Met through and through. Always will be. You know what they say. They can take the boy out of the Met, but you can't take the Met out of the boy.'

'I don't quite see where this is going,' responded Vogel.

'Oh, come on, yes you do,' replied Clarke. 'You have that awful Met thing in you, of assuming that anyone out in the sticks is at the very least inferior to, and quite probably considerably less intelligent than, you, and indeed most people in the metropolis.'

'I dunno about that, Nobby,' replied Vogel mildly. 'I've been down west for a couple of years now. I may have thought that way to begin with, but I don't reckon I do any more.'

'Really,' said Clarke, sounding totally unconvinced. 'Sure of that, are you, Vogel?'

He opened his mouth to tell the detective superintendent she was a damned sight more likely to be guilty of Met superiority than he was. Then a certain aspect of his last big case for Avon and Somerset Police flitted across his mind. He had very nearly missed vital indications of criminal activity because of a lurking inclination to regard people with broad West Country accents as being not quite as bright as those without. Even though he would never admit it.

'Well, maybe not entirely sure,' he said. The nearest to an honest answer he was prepared to give.

'Indeed. Have you looked around you at all whilst you've been here, Vogel?'

Vogel glanced at Saslow. He had been aware of her taking in the sea views, and generally enjoying the scenic quality of the place they had been sent to. Aspects of life that meant very little to Vogel. Was that what Clarke was getting at? If so, she was, in his opinion, moving from mild eccentricity into weirdo territory.

'It's a very beautiful part of the world, Nobby,' he remarked tentatively.

Nobby Clarke clicked her teeth impatiently.

'Anything else you noticed?'

'Uh, well, we only got here a few hours ago and I've been concentrating on the case—'

'This is about the case,' Clarke interrupted. 'This chunk of North Devon by the sea has something of a boom town about it. Recession and even Brexit haven't really touched it. Not to the degree that they have most of the rest of the country, anyway. The holiday trade is booming. It's quite a sophisticated trade nowadays too.

'Look at that lovely little boozer, where you're staying. Everything about it is high end, from the furnishings to the food. And consider the location. You've got the river right in front of you, and Instow across the water, the pretty little white village which we believe is now the scene of a major and not yet explicable crime. It doesn't fit, Vogel. That's for sure. But when does crime fit? Nonetheless, another thing that's for sure, is that the people who live on the North Devon coast aren't seaside Worzel Gummidges. Neither are they inbred idiots desperate to protect an insular way of life. There is nothing insular about North Devon anymore.'

'I still don't get exactly where you're going with this, boss,' said Vogel again.

'Don't you?' the detective superintendent replied. 'Thing is, Vogel, you're actually not here because the local mayor's family are at the heart of a murder enquiry, and I want someone in charge who will dig his way to the truth regardless of any pressure from those on high.'

'I'm not?'

'No, Vogel, you're not. Neither you nor Saslow. You're here because I don't believe one jot of this hick town nonsense. The Barnstaple super might be old fashioned but he's a thoroughly decent police officer, and I think every instinct in his body would lead him to conduct a thorough investigation into any serious crime on his patch. By the book to the nth degree, maybe. But he'd do it. And the fact that a local mayor is involved would probably make him more determined to conduct a proper investigation rather than less. Yet he would still like nothing more than to find a way to shut this enquiry down and dismiss Jane Ferguson's death as a tragic suicide.

'That's why I wanted to meet you today, Vogel. To make my thoughts on this clear. And that's why I wanted you leading the investigation. Because I believe there is something far bigger going on than the possibility of some small-town scandal, which those who pass for the great and the good round here want brushed under the carpet in order to protect reputations and civic status.

'In fact, I think all that is a load of old bollocks, Vogel. You are here to find out what really lies behind this desire for a cover-up. Because there's no doubt something is going on. There remains considerable pressure from on high, and I don't think for one moment that it is confined to within Devon and Cornwall Police, for the case of Jane Ferguson to be buried as quickly as possible.'

Nobby Clarke paused.

'If you'll excuse the pun,' she said.

Vogel allowed his lips to twitch.

'Saslow and our number one suspect have already beaten you to it in that area, Nobby,' he murmured.

The detective super ignored him. She looked and sounded like a woman on a mission. Vogel had seen her in that mode before. It almost always led to trouble. For all concerned. She never learned, of course, and neither, he supposed, did he.

'I'm not sure exactly who is applying this pressure, in fact I've no bloody idea,' Clarke continued. 'But it comes from the very top. I'm quite sure of that. Trust me.'

Vogel took a sip of his ginger ale.

'You really are determined to run out of career moves, aren't you, boss?' he commented.

'Do you mind?' queried the detective super. 'If I go down again, I could well take you with me.'

'Naw, I'm Met. You said so yourself. I'm slippery. I'll blame it all on you.'

'Vogel, you are all kinds of things. Slippery is not one of them. And neither have you ever been any better than me at keeping out of trouble.'

Vogel knew he couldn't argue with that. He smiled and changed the subject.

'One thing though, I don't get, boss,' he said. 'If the D and C brass want a cover-up so badly, why did they take this case away from the local boys and girls, authorize you to bring in Saslow and me. Chief constable to chief constable too.'

'It's all changed, Vogel, from when this death was called in not much more than twelve hours ago, and it really was just about local politics,' she said. 'The brass are now regretting your appointment big time, I suspect. They are under some sort of mega pressure from on high, seriously on high, and I don't know why, what, or bloody whom. I will bloody well find out, though.'

For a while the three officers concentrated on their food. Saslow was clearly hungry, she had missed breakfast, and she demolished her chicken escalope at appropriate speed. As usual Nobby Clarke was more interested in the wine and only picked at her escalope.

Vogel only picked at his risotto. He'd eaten a hearty breakfast and hadn't wanted lunch in the first place.

When they rose to leave the restaurant, Clarke placed a hand on Vogel's arm.

'Sod it, you've officially got your murder enquiry,' she said. 'I'll tell the CC. He'll be thrilled.'

With a new spring in his step, Vogel headed for the door. He couldn't wait to get on with it.

That was one of the things he liked best about working with Detective Superintendent Nobby Clarke. She didn't ask the chief constable, even the CC of a force she was new to, at which she had arrived under something of a cloud. Even under the increasingly bewildering circumstances which seemed to be developing.

She told him.

TEN

D r Miriam Thorpe's consulting rooms were in a narrow street of tall Georgian houses situated, rather conveniently for Vogel and Saslow, just a few minutes' walk from Exeter's Cathedral Yard.

The doctor was an unusually tall woman, probably in her late thirties. Her wavy dark hair was attractively untidy, and she was casually dressed in jeans and a loose-fitting sweater. Vogel assumed this kind of style was probably the norm nowadays for someone in her profession – on the basis that in the twenty-first century it was the sort of look required to encourage patients to relax and talk about themselves without feeling intimidated.

Dr Thorpe ushered Vogel and Saslow into a spacious high-ceilinged room, bade them sit on a sofa facing the window, and lowered herself into the armchair alongside. No formal seating arrangement for this one, and certainly no question of her sitting behind a desk while her visitors were forced into low seating accommodation, thought Vogel. Even when in this case the visitors were not patients but police officers, Dr Thorpe was careful to ensure that no party enjoyed a physical advantage over another.

She looked suitably shocked when Vogel explained that he was investigating the death of Jane Ferguson.

'I h-had no idea,' she said, somewhat obviously, stumbling very slightly over her words. 'Jane is dead? My God. Wh-what happened?'

Vogel considered for a moment if the woman might be dissembling. But, in view of what had originally been regarded as the probability of Jane Ferguson's death being suicide, no announcement had yet been made to the press. And whilst there was already doubtless plenty of local gossip, and probably at least some mention on social media, there was no reason why Dr Thorpe should be aware of it.

'Mrs Ferguson's body was found hanged from the bannisters of her home in the early hours of this morning,' the detective explained bluntly. 'By her six-year-old daughter.'

Miriam Thorpe gasped.

'That's terrible,' she said. 'Absolutely terrible. Poor Jane. And the poor child.'

'Indeed,' said Vogel. 'We are here to ask you, doctor, if you are aware from your consultations with Mrs Ferguson of anything which might have led her to take her own life. And further to that, if you had ever regarded her as a person at risk.'

Miriam Thorpe looked doubtful.

'Well, yes and no, detective chief inspector,' she said. 'Most people who seek out the counsel of a mental health professional are vulnerable. So yes, almost all of them are at some level of risk. But as for fearing that Jane might take her own life: no, I don't think I ever thought that was likely. Although when dealing with someone who has reason to seek psychiatric help, one knows better than to rule anything out, my consultations with Jane never led me to actively consider that possibility. However, I really can't go into detail, Mr Vogel. I'm sure I don't have to remind you that everything that takes place between a patient and someone in my position is highly confidential. That's the only way we can maintain the necessary trust. Mine is after all one of the most sensitive areas of medicine . . .'

'I am sure it is, doctor,' replied Vogel. 'But perhaps I need to remind you that your patient is no longer with us, and that I am investigating the manner of her death.'

'The manner of her death, detective chief inspector? You said she'd been found hanged, that she had taken her own life, didn't you?'

'I asked you if you knew of anything that may have led to Mrs Ferguson taking her own life, doctor. Now look, I totally understand your reluctance to breach a professional confidence, but there are extremely troubling aspects of Mrs Ferguson's death which we are investigating, and I suspect it would be of considerable assistance to us if we had access to your notes concerning the deceased's mental health. I feel sure you would be as anxious to get to the truth of the matter as we are, for everyone's sake, not least her husband and her children.'

Miriam Thorpe still looked doubtful.

'I take your point, inspector,' she said eventually. 'But I would like to check with Jane's next of kin first, with her husband.'

'I'm afraid I have to ask you not to do that, doctor,' countered Vogel quickly.

Miriam Thorpe stood up abruptly and turned away from the two officers for a few seconds. Then she swung around to face them again.

'So, you think Jane's death may be suspicious and you suspect her husband may be involved, is that the nub of it, Mr Vogel?' she asked eventually.

'We are investigating Mrs Ferguson's death, doctor, and Mr Ferguson is helping with our enquiries. That is all I can possibly tell you in that regard at the moment. You must understand that in our line of work, also, there are areas of considerable sensitivity.'

'Of course. And shall we just say that my contacting Mr Ferguson in advance of any assistance I might feel able to give you could be counter-productive. Is that so, Mr Vogel? Please don't prevaricate, will you?'

Vogel smiled, very slightly. He was beginning to think that Miriam Thorpe was someone he could work with after all.

'That is absolutely so, doctor,' he said. 'And, if it helps at all, I can tell you that we are about to launch a full-scale murder investigation. This will be announced through the media very shortly, either, I would expect, by the head of the Devon and Cornwall Police Major Crimes Team, or the chief constable.'

Miriam Thorpe nodded. She stood looking at Vogel in silence for a few seconds, then walked to her desk and sat down.

'All right, Mr Vogel,' she said, as she fired up her computer. 'A woman who was under my care has died a violent death, you and your superiors believe she has been murdered, and I accept that any information I have might be of considerable significance in your investigation. Under these circumstances, I will give you all the help I can. You should know that Jane Ferguson's case is, or should I say was, a very challenging one. She came to me because she was suffering from terrifying dreams. Nightmares, in fact. Were you aware of these dreams?'

'Yes, but not in any detail,' said Vogel. 'We have interviewed Jane's husband and other members of the Ferguson family concerning this, but they claim to know nothing of either the content or cause of her dreams.'

Dr Thorpe nodded.

'They may well be telling the truth, Mr Vogel,' she said. 'Certainly, Jane always claimed that the nightmares were a mystery to her.

'We began a series of standard therapy sessions which revealed very little. At first sight Jane Ferguson seemed like a perfectly normal young woman. She claimed to be happily married. She appeared to have only happy memories of her childhood. There were causes of concern, things that had happened in her life which could possibly have caused her to have bad dreams. Her mother was a single parent, and she never knew her father. To all intents and purposes, she had no father. Her mother, Alice, had, Jane said, been quite honest about that. Alice told Jane that she had been going through a promiscuous stage when her daughter was conceived, that she'd been a child of the sixties, everybody was sleeping around, and she'd been no exception. Alice also said that she did a lot of partying as a young woman, she drank heavily, and she experimented with drugs. She claimed she did not know which of a number of candidates was Jane's father, and she didn't care. Jane was an accident, but a welcome one. Alice's message to Jane was that she never for one second considered any alternative to having her child and bringing her up on her own in the best way that she could.

'Now, you might think that in itself could have caused Jane to be disturbed. But she was quite adamant that she was untroubled by the question of her paternity. She said her mother's love had been quite enough for her. That her mother always gave her a sense of security and supported her in everything that she did. And, although as you can imagine, I questioned her intensely on this issue, she never gave me the slightest cause to disbelieve her. Now, Alice died nine years ago, of an aneurism. Obviously, that was deeply upsetting for Jane. She said herself that her mother was everything to her. And it is quite possible that it was Alice's death which sparked off Jane's nightmares. But I was never able to get anything from Jane which proved that either way. She couldn't even really remember when they started. Or so she said. Although she did say they got worse after her own children were born. Regarding her father, or rather her lack of a father, Jane seemed extremely well adjusted to that. Her reactions were so reasoned that I concluded that it was certainly unlikely that anything concerning her paternity was at the root of her problems.'

Dr Thorpe glanced at the screen.

'Ah yes, and then there was the matter of her relationship with her husband's family, particularly her mother-in-law. This was clearly very strained, not least because of Mrs Ferguson senior's attitude to Jane's family background. Apparently, Felix, who clearly knew his mother rather well, had suggested to Jane that they gloss over the issue of her father, and indeed let his parents think that Jane's father had died when she was a baby. Jane was adamant that she was not going to enter married life on a lie. This caused terrible problems with the mother-in-law who apparently has strong ideas about what she calls "breeding".'

Dr Thorpe paused.

'Yes,' said Vogel, with a little smile. 'I have encountered that. Mrs Amelia Ferguson is certainly a woman of strong opinions.'

'So I understand. Well, Jane admitted that there had been times during her marriage when she'd wished that she hadn't been quite so principled on the issue of her paternity. But you know, although she disliked the unpleasantness, she didn't seem to me ever to be unduly upset by it. This was a young woman who considered herself to be happily married, who made it quite clear that she loved her husband deeply, and was absolutely sure that he loved her.

'She was perfectly well physically. She had two beautiful children whom she clearly adored. Her only unhappiness, it seemed, was these dreams. However, she talked about them frankly, and without embarrassment. And she certainly did not link them in any way to the two issues which seemed to be the only flaws in an otherwise charmed life: her lack of acknowledgeable paternity and her strained relationship with her in-laws. She did say if she'd been a brain surgeon or a famous television personality when she'd met her husband, instead of a waitress, it may have helped, but she wasn't entirely sure. She had a nice sense of humour, and seemed able to see the funny side of most of the negative things in her life. But not those terrible dreams.'

Dr Thorpe paused again, studying intently the computer screen before her.

'Yes, here's something I was looking for. She said concerning her lack of a father: "You don't miss what you never had." Of course, often in these sorts of circumstances the relationship between the single parent and their child is particularly close, and there is little doubt that was so with Jane and her mother. When Alice died suddenly and unexpectedly, Jane was devastated. But she also seemed to have come to terms with it well enough. By the time I came in contact with her, anyway. She said that when she met Felix, just a few months after her mother died, he brought such joy and support into her life that . . .'

There was another brief pause, then Dr Thorpe read directly from the screen again: '"It was almost as if my mother had sent him to love and look after me in her place."'

Vogel was thoughtful.

'And yet, in spite of her professed happy life, or by and large happy, she suffered from nightmares so severe that both she and her husband thought it necessary to seek professional help,' he remarked. 'Isn't that the case?'

'It most certainly is, Mr Vogel. She discussed freely the effect the nightmares were having not only on her, but also on her husband and her children—'

'Her children knew about these nightmares then?' Vogel interrupted.

'Well, to some degree, yes. Apparently, her screaming was sometimes so bad that the children were woken up. I pushed her repeatedly on the content of her dreams, but she was adamant that she had no memory of them when she awoke. She described the fear she experienced pretty graphically, though.'

Again Dr Thorpe read from the screen before her.

'"I feel as if I cannot breathe, as if my breath is being taken away from me. I am in shock, I think. I am never sure whether something terrible is actually happening to me in my dreams, or I am witnessing something terrible. I have never experienced such terror when I've been awake, not in the whole of my life, thank God. Felix has always been very good at calming me down. But lately I know I have been quite out of control. I hyperventilate. A couple of times I have lashed out at him. It's just so awful for both of us."'

'That really is extreme, isn't it?' interjected Saslow.

'Yes, indeed,' said the doctor. 'And on a regular basis, pretty unbearable. Ultimately I concluded that there was no way I could help Jane without knowing the cause of her dreams. That's why I suggested regression therapy.'

'Right. When you take a patient back under hypnosis to their childhood, or some time in their past?'

'Yes, DCI Vogel. As there seemed to be nothing in Jane's present life, or in her conscious memory, that might have been causing her dreams, this seemed to be the logical next step.'

'And she was agreeable to it?'

'Absolutely. She told me she was desperate to get to the bottom of her problem, and would do anything to do so.'

'At that stage did you not think suicide was something she might consider? After all, you said yourself she was desperate.'

'Well, it was clear that something was triggering a severe psychological reaction within Jane, so under those circumstances any medical professional would be irresponsible to dismiss suicidal tendencies entirely, but this was a young woman who was desperate to solve her only real problem in life. There appeared to be no desperation in her concerning the life that she led. She was more than happy with her lot. She just wanted to live free of the nightmares, and she gave every impression that she considered herself to be someone who had everything to live for. I never felt for a moment that she wanted to die. But, I guess I did have to admit, after what happened next, that I came to

realize that Jane Ferguson might be considerably more compli-
cated than she appeared to be . . .'

'We have reason to believe she may have been self-harming.
There were old scars of small cuts on her wrists and lower arms.
Did you have any knowledge of this?'

'No, no, not at all. I'm a psychiatrist, I do not usually examine
people physically. Come to think of it, I don't recall ever seeing
her wearing anything that didn't have long sleeves. Or I would
have thought I would have noticed. But she certainly never
mentioned anything like that, and there was nothing in her
behaviour that might have made me suspect it.'

'We also discovered bruising on her body which has led us to
explore the possibility of ongoing physical abuse—'

'Really?' interrupted the doctor. 'By her husband, do you mean?'

'Well, I couldn't possibly confirm that. But her husband would
be a suspect, obviously. Did you have any reason to consider
anything of that nature?'

'No, not at all. Certainly not at her husband's hands. She
repeatedly praised his kindness and his patience.'

'So, what was it that happened next? Did you have the
regression therapy sessions?'

'Well, we had one. It was not conclusive in any way. But it
was definitely disturbing. Jane proved to be easily susceptible to
hypnosis, and, at first, I was confident we were going to have a
successful session. I follow fairly standard procedure in such
cases, trying to take the subject back to his or her earliest memories. Jane began to talk freely about her childhood. She appeared
to have been happy both at home and at school. She needed little
encouragement to tell stories of days out with her mother, the
little dog they acquired, her schoolfriends, her teachers, her first
bicycle, one of those with the two little balancing wheels at the
back. All very normal stuff. And she showed no sign of distress
as she regressed back into her childhood. But I did realize that
everything she spoke about was after school-going age, five, or
maybe six. She couldn't be drawn on anything earlier, any stories
about herself as a baby or a toddler, learning to walk and talk,
that sort of thing. Now, it's pretty usual for people not to have
first-hand memories of that time of their life, but they nearly
always have quite extensive second-hand memories.'

Dr Thorpe paused.

'You understand what I mean, Mr Vogel? I expect you know how much you weighed when you were born, what your first words were, how you behaved as a baby, that sort of thing. But it's not because you actually remember it. It's because your parents told you. Isn't that so?'

Vogel nodded his agreement. He did not mention that his early childhood had also not been entirely straightforward.

'Well, with Jane Ferguson, it seemed almost as if she had been born aged five or six,' Dr Thorpe continued. 'That was the most curious thing about the session. I kept pushing the point. And I think I may have pushed too hard. Suddenly she started to scream, uncontrollably, just the way she described doing when she experienced one of her nightmares.

'I brought her around straight away, of course. She was white as a sheet and trembling like a leaf. Then she just leaned over and was sick on the floor by the side of the couch.'

Dr Thorpe waved a hand in the general direction of her consulting couch.

'I have actually never witnessed such an extreme reaction to regressive therapy, although I have read about it,' the doctor went on. 'I gave her water to drink, and called the practice nurse in. I was very anxious about her condition, obviously.

'But she made quite a quick recovery. Superficially at any rate. After just a couple of minutes she swung her legs over the side of the couch and sat up. "How silly of me," she said. I shan't forget that, in a hurry. Particularly now that her life has ended so . . . so violently. "How silly of me."

'Anyway, I reassured her that it wasn't silly at all. That she'd clearly had an extreme reaction to something she remembered whilst under hypnosis. She didn't respond at all to that. I asked her if she could remember what it was, if she could remember what had been in her mind when she'd started to scream.

'She said that she couldn't remember a damned thing. Again, her exact words. "I don't remember a damned thing."'

'Is that usual?' asked Vogel. 'Or would you expect a patient to remember the experiences they relived whilst under hypnosis, or certainly the more extreme or significant elements?'

'It varies, Mr Vogel. Regressive therapy is not an exact

science. I had no reason at all to doubt that Jane was telling me the truth.

'Anyway, I was clearly going to get no further with her that day, and it may well have been dangerous to try. I was anxious about her leaving alone, so I suggested we call her husband and get him to come and pick her up. She was adamant that she didn't want to do that. She said she had already caused him enough anxiety, and she was going to be just fine.

'I did insist that she sat down and rested for a while before driving home. She agreed to that, and the nurse took her into the waiting room and made her a cup of tea. I saw her again, briefly, before she left. About forty-five minutes later, when I had finished with my next patient. She seemed to have recovered well. She apologized profusely for having been sick on my floor, and said she really had no idea what had come over her. She even tried to make a bit of a joke of it. She said, "Well, you won't forget me now, my mum used to say I'd do anything to be the centre of attention." Then she made an appointment for the following week, and left.'

'When you saw her again, did you attempt another session of regression therapy?'

'I never did see her again, DCI Vogel. She failed to keep her next appointment and never made another one. We wrote to no avail, and tried calling her, of course. But she didn't pick up.'

'How long ago was that, doctor?'

Miriam Thorpe glanced at her screen again.

'Just under five weeks.'

'I see. May I ask, if you were so anxious, why didn't you do something about it, doctor? Contact her husband, perhaps?'

'I wanted to. But we are bound by such strict rules of confidentiality nowadays. We are not allowed to contact any third party concerning a patient, not even a husband or wife. I wish I had done so now, of course.'

Vogel was thoughtful as he and Saslow walked to the car.

'I think we'd better look into Jane Ferguson's background ourselves, don't you, Saslow?' asked Vogel. 'Starting with giving our Felix another grilling. I'm beginning to believe more and more that the key to all this lies in Jane's past.'

'Yes, boss,' replied the young officer. 'But everything Dr Thorpe told us would be more relevant if Jane had killed herself. And we now know ninety-nine point nine per cent that she was murdered.'

'There was a deliberate attempt to make her murder look like suicide, which could easily have been accepted, particularly in view of her medical history. And, after finding that hangman's fracture at the top end of Jane Ferguson's spine, a lot of pathologists not as meticulous as Karen Crow mightn't have looked much further.'

'Really, boss?' queried Saslow. 'With that old bruising indicative of domestic abuse surely any pathologist's suspicions would be aroused? To me what's surprising is that the murderer wouldn't realize that.'

'Good point, Saslow. But all the old injuries, apart from the bruising and the healed wound on her face, were on parts of Jane's body which would normally be covered by her clothing. Perhaps the murderer didn't know about it.'

'Her husband would have known about it though, surely, boss? He certainly would if he'd inflicted it. And Felix Ferguson is our principle suspect in all of this, and will remain so until we have evidence to indicate otherwise. In spite of what you told him this morning.'

'Absolutely right, Saslow,' said Vogel. 'But even spouses and partners remain innocent until proven guilty. And there's only one thing I'm getting more and more sure of, Saslow, concerning this case. I think almost nothing about it is quite how it seems. We are going to be opening up a real can of worms. Nobby is obviously quite sure of that. All we can do is take it step by step.'

'We're going to need to talk to those children some time, boss, aren't we?' said Saslow. 'Probably formally. Maybe one of them, particularly Joanna, saw something more than we know already.'

'Yes, I'm afraid so,' agreed Vogel. 'And the nearest children's suite is at Exeter, I expect. I'm going to hold off for a day or two, though, Dawn. See if we can clear this up without dragging them off there and causing them any more distress than necessary. Next step, let's go back to Bay View Road and seek out Felix Ferguson again. We can start by finding out exactly what he does and doesn't know about his wife's background and early life.

'Oh, and we can tell him that we are now officially upgrading the investigation into Jane's death to a murder enquiry. That should take him out of his comfort zone.'

ELEVEN

As Vogel and Saslow had expected, Felix was still at his parents' house.

Again, Mrs Ferguson senior answered the door to All Seasons and ushered Saslow and Vogel into the big living room, albeit not with very good grace.

Felix was lying on the floor, playing with his children. He seemed unaware that anyone had entered the house and was laughing as the two officers entered. His children seemed in surprisingly high spirits. A good game was obviously going on.

'You're cheating, Daddy, you're cheating,' cried little Stevie Ferguson, as his sister attempted to climb on her father's back.

'No, I'm not, you are,' countered Felix, still laughing.

Then he looked up and saw Vogel and Saslow.

He stopped laughing immediately. The light faded from his eyes.

'What do you want now?' he asked, his voice gruff.

'I'm afraid we have some more questions for you, sir,' said Vogel mildly.

'Look, you've already given me the third degree once today,' responded Felix tetchily. 'Surely you don't have to do it again. Not now. You can see I'm spending time with my children, and I'm sure you realize how important that is right now. I want to get everything back to normal for them, as soon as possible.'

Vogel thought there was little chance of life getting back to normal for little Joanna and Stevie Ferguson for a very long while.

'It shouldn't take too much of your time, sir,' Vogel continued in the same mild tone.

Ferguson glared at him. His mother stepped forward.

'I'll take the children into the kitchen,' she said. 'Come

on, you two, let's see if we can find any of those special biscuits you like.'

Stevie jumped to his feet at once and ran eagerly to his gran. Joanna, by then fully astride her father's back, did not move.

'I want to stay with you, Daddy,' she said, a tad sulkily.

'You can come back in just a minute,' said her father. 'Now off you go with Granny and Stevie.'

With reluctance the little girl climbed off her father and began to do as she had been told. Very slowly.

'Hey, and don't forget to bring me one of those special biscuits when you come back,' Felix called after her, as she finally reached the kitchen door.

Then, his displeasure still apparent, he hauled himself up from the floor and sat down in the nearest armchair. He did not ask Vogel and Saslow to sit. They did so anyway.

'I've come to tell you that we are now treating your wife's death as murder,' said Vogel formally. 'And we are in the process of launching a full-scale murder enquiry.'

'Murder?' queried Felix, his expression one of total shock. 'You said this morning you were treating the matter as a suspicious death. I thought that was probably just a formality. Now you suddenly tell me you've decided Jane was murdered. I don't believe that. Not for a moment. I believe Jane took her own life. She must have done.'

'The post-mortem examination on your wife has taken place,' continued Vogel, almost as if Felix hadn't spoken. 'The results have led us to conclude beyond all reasonable doubt that there was a third party involved in your wife's death, and that she was killed by a person or persons unknown.'

'What results? What are you talking about?'

'I am afraid we cannot go into details yet, sir, but we thought you should be the first to know. And there are matters arising which we need to discuss with you urgently. We have just come from interviewing your wife's therapist, Dr Thorpe, and she has revealed to us certain information which I would like to ask you about—'

Felix Ferguson butted in straight away.

'I didn't give my permission for you to poke around in my wife's medical records,' he said. 'I hope the bloody woman didn't give you any personal information. I thought that sort of thing was confidential.'

Ferguson sounded significantly different to the way he had been earlier. Previously his grief and distress had been quite transparent. He had shown every sign of being desperately upset. That was understandable and normal. Now he seemed merely angry and aggrieved. Vogel wondered if the man was nervous. The DCI had had plenty of experience of sudden and violent death, and its effect on all concerned. People dealt with it how they could, and in ways that sometimes seemed unlikely and even disconcerting. He told himself that could well be all it was with Felix Ferguson. He was struggling to come to terms with his grief in his own way. Nonetheless Vogel found himself studying the man more closely than ever.

'I have just told you, we are conducting a murder investigation now, Mr Ferguson,' he said in the same level tone. 'That over-rides matters of medical confidentiality, as I am sure you must realize.'

'Look, this whole thing is nonsense,' Felix countered, still sounding angry. 'Jane committed suicide. I have no idea why, but what else could it be? Who on earth would want to kill Jane? Everyone loved Jane.'

Apart from your mother, that's for sure, thought Vogel. He said nothing. He kept his gaze expressionless and focused coolly on Fergus.

Suddenly the man jumped to his feet and took a step towards Vogel.

'Oh my God,' he cried. 'You really do think I killed my Jane, don't you? That's bullshit. Total bullshit. I loved her, for God's sake. I adored her. She was the mother of my children. And anyway, I wasn't even there.'

'Indeed, sir,' responded Vogel, standing his ground and continuing to keep his voice level. 'And, in fact, whilst as the husband of the deceased, you are what we call a person of interest, as I pointed out to you this morning, I have no evidence that you killed your wife, and would not at this stage suggest any such thing.'

'I should think not,' said Ferguson, his voice still raised. 'And of course you haven't got any evidence. Because there damned well isn't any. Because I didn't damned well do it.'

'It would be helpful if you would calm down, sir. All I want at this stage is for you to help us with our enquiries. Presumably you would like us to find your wife's killer?'

Ferguson stepped away from Vogel and sat down again as abruptly as he had stood up.

'I suppose so,' he muttered.

'Thank you, Mr Ferguson,' said Vogel evenly. 'Now, we are trying to put together a picture of your wife. There was no sign of a burglary or forced entry at your house. This indicates that her killer knew her. Was she expecting a visitor last night perhaps?'

'No, nothing like that.'

'And you were not aware of anyone in her life who might have wished to harm her?'

'No, of course I wasn't. There wasn't anyone.'

'Somebody harmed Jane, Mr Ferguson, somebody killed her. Was there anyone from her past, possibly someone you didn't know, who had recently come back into her life?'

Felix looked puzzled.

'I don't think so,' he said. 'No. Definitely not. Jane would have told me. Anyway . . .'

Felix looked as if he was about to say more, but stopped himself.

'Anyway what?' persisted Vogel.

'Uh, nothing, only that she didn't keep secrets from me,' said Felix.

Vogel wasn't at all sure about that. He did not push the point. Instead he asked Felix how and when he had met Jane.

The young man answered fully, telling him the story of how Jane moved to Bideford after the death of her mother and then applied for a job as a waitress at Cleverdon's.

'It was love at first sight, Mr Vogel, for me anyway,' he said, smiling very slightly at the memory. 'That was eight years ago, and we were married the year after.'

'I understand Jane's mother had died not long before you met?' queried Vogel.

Felix nodded.

'Yes. The year before. That was when Jane moved to Bideford. She and her mother had been very close. Jane was only twenty-one, and she took her mum's death very hard. They'd lived together in a little flat in Essex, Chelmsford. Jane had been at college, studying to be a primary school teacher, but she just chucked it all in, sold the flat and took off. Always said she was desperate to make a fresh start. She wanted to live by the sea, and she and her mother had been down this way on holiday a couple of times. I was secretly not altogether sorry about all of that, otherwise I would never have met Jane, but I didn't tell her that, of course.'

Felix managed another small smile.

'Was it after the death of her mother that Jane self-harmed?' asked Vogel.

Felix stopped smiling.

'Yes. I think so. That was when she was in the "dark place" I told you about this morning.'

'Obviously you never met her mother, but did you meet any other relatives or friends from her previous life?'

'There weren't any relatives. Jane's mother was an only child, and she never knew her father. Never even knew who he was. I expect my mother has already told you that?'

Vogel nodded.

'Yes. She rarely misses an opportunity to mention Jane's lack of breeding.'

This time Felix's smile was more of a grimace.

'There was a couple from Chelmsford, neighbours, and two old college friends, that I knew vaguely, and they all came to our wedding,' Felix continued. 'But I don't think Jane kept in touch with them.'

'Do you know where Jane was born?' asked Vogel.

'Yes. She was born in Chelmsford, and lived there all her life until she came down here.'

'Have you ever seen her birth certificate?' asked Vogel as casually as he could.

Felix looked at him quizzically.

'You're beginning to sound like my mother,' he said. 'Yes, of course I've seen Jane's birth certificate, when we got married for a start. And it's still in the safe at home. What are you getting at, Mr Vogel?'

'Just routine,' murmured Vogel. 'We do need to look into your wife's early life, though, not least to try and find out the cause of those extreme nightmares she suffered.'

'I told you, she and I went over it again and again. There was nothing. In any case, what could there possibly be that might be relevant to her death?'

'That's what I keep asking myself, Mr Ferguson,' said the DCI. 'Meanwhile, do you know when your wife last attended a therapy session with Dr Thorpe in Exeter?'

'Uh, what?'

Ferguson seemed momentarily nonplussed by Vogel's abrupt switch in his line of questioning.

'Oh, yes, of course,' he said eventually. 'She was going weekly. Tuesdays. Every Tuesday. I would take the twins to Mum's in the morning in the holidays, or to school in term time, and she would drive to Exeter. Been doing it for about a year. So last Tuesday, I suppose.'

'You never went with her?'

'The first couple of times I did. Just to suss it out really. But after that she said she was quite happy going on her own. I do have two businesses to run, you know.'

Vogel noted the tetchiness in the other man's voice again, but did not comment on it.

'Mr Ferguson, your wife hadn't been to see Dr Thorpe for over a month before she died,' he said instead. 'Were you not aware of that?'

Felix looked genuinely surprised.

'I had no idea,' he said. 'She went somewhere every Tuesday. Sometimes I would go back to the house. She was never there . . .'

'I see. Well, I can assure you she didn't visit Dr Thorpe. Were you aware that Dr Thorpe had embarked, or tried to embark on, a series of regression therapy sessions with your wife in order to try to find the cause of her nightmares?'

'Yes. Jane told me so. She told me she'd had regression sessions, in fact. Was that not so?'

'She had one session with Dr Thorpe. It ended with your wife becoming extremely distressed. Did she tell you about that?'

'No. She didn't mention anything like that.'

'According to Dr Thorpe, Jane became hysterical and had to be brought around from hypnosis prematurely. She then vomited on the floor of Dr Thorpe's consulting room. And that is a matter of medical record.'

'I had no idea,' said Felix.

'Dr Thorpe suspected that she may have relived something which caused her so much distress,' Vogel continued. 'Do you really have no idea at all what that could have been? Something extreme enough to cause Jane to vomit?'

'No, I don't. She said that she remembered nothing under hypnosis about her childhood that she wasn't already aware of, and that I didn't know about. Everything you are saying is news to me, detective chief inspector.'

Felix looked thoughtful.

'Of course, it might explain why she became suicidal,' he remarked suddenly. 'Or have you completely ruled out that possibility, Mr Vogel?'

Vogel blinked rapidly behind his spectacles. Felix had sounded disingenuous enough, but Vogel was not oblivious to the barb which undoubtedly lay behind his remark.

'I haven't ruled anything out, Mr Ferguson, not totally, anyway. But I have already explained that unless further evidence is revealed indicating the contrary, we are treating your wife's death as murder.'

Ferguson lowered his head into his hands, wrapping long fingers around his forehead. Vogel watched. After a few seconds the man looked up.

When he spoke his voice was surprisingly calm.

'And I'm your number one suspect, however much you deny it, isn't that right?' he queried.

'That is not right, Mr Ferguson,' responded Vogel levelly. 'You are a person of interest, obviously. I have already told you that—'

'And what other "persons of interest" do you have?' interrupted Ferguson, his voice still calm.

'Mr Ferguson, our investigation has only just begun. But I can promise you that it will continue until we have found out exactly what happened to your wife, and apprehended her killer. Whoever that might be.'

TWELVE

After Vogel and Saslow left the Bay View Road house, Felix asked his mother if she would look after the twins whilst he took the dogs for a walk.

He told her he needed to clear his head.

And that, thought Felix, as he set off along Abbotsham Cliffs, the dramatic coastal heathland which stretches for miles to the west of Westward Ho!, could be the single most true thing he had said since his wife's death.

He so needed to clear his head.

Through all the years of their marriage, until very recently, Felix had managed to cope with his wife's nightmares. He and Jane had both coped. Or he'd thought so, anyway. The nightmares had been the sole blot on a bright horizon. And only in the last months had the dreams which, in spite of what he had told Vogel, had grown more and more frequent and extreme, gradually become his nightmare too.

He realized he'd probably been naïve in thinking that Jane's death would bring them both release. The horror of it all seemed even bigger now. And the fear too. How could he have even hoped for anything else, he wondered.

He had been kidding himself to ever allow the possibility that everything would turn out all right. In any case, he'd never really believed it, had he? After all, his excessive drinking bore testament to that.

Felix didn't think he was a bad man. He knew, however, that he was lazy, and that he was a coward.

Two thriving businesses with trusted staff had been offered him on a plate. Felix had never had any ambition for anything else. Why would he? He'd led a privileged childhood, and sailed through a minor public school where little or no pressure was put on him to succeed academically, certainly not beyond a pretty lowly average.

Felix knew that he did have his talents. His easy manner and generally relaxed demeanour meant that, both in business and in his personal life, he was often able to deal successfully with tricky people and situations where a more focused and driven man would probably fail.

Felix's father had always recognized this. In addition, the self-made Sam Ferguson was a control freak. And this suited equally well both father and son. There was none of the friction between them, common amongst successful fathers and their sons. Felix had never been competition to his father nor had any desire to be. He had remained content to run his side of the business according to his father's wishes, and to reap the considerable rewards for so doing. And his father was content to let him do so, leaving him alone in the areas in which he was able, whilst stepping in when a firmer hand was needed at the helm. Felix never minded. Why would he? That was how he had been brought up. A privileged unstressful childhood had drifted into a privileged unstressful adulthood.

He was also protected. If stress threatened, in almost any form, his mother clacked and his father acted. Again, both father and son exhibited complementary characteristics. Both accepting, and indeed actively enjoying, their roles as protected and protector.

But marriage proved different. Sam Ferguson could not reasonably be his son's protector within that institution. In any case, one of Felix's stronger and better characteristics was loyalty. When he'd married Jane he'd fully intended to be loyal to her for the rest of his life. In every way. Which for him went way beyond mere sexual fidelity.

And for the first time in his life, when the cracks began to show in this union, which he had been so sure would be perfect, Felix had not run to his parents to share his misery and seek their assistance. Although he knew they had guessed all was not well. He had not turned to his father and stood aside whilst Sam made everything all right again. Like he usually did.

Upon reflection, it may have been better if he had confided more in his parents.

As it was, he was not at all sure what they did and did not know. He suspected that his mother was, as usual, sticking rigidly to her own vision of her son's life – which varied from day to day in many aspects but never much swayed from adoration and a total conviction of his lack of blame in anything. In other words, Mrs Ferguson senior's head remained firmly buried in the sand. If she had suspected anything beyond the ordinary in her son and daughter-in-law's affairs, she would probably have pretended not to notice.

Felix's father, on the other hand, was a different prospect. Sam Ferguson didn't miss much. Although Felix had no idea at all what conclusions his father may have drawn from what could only ever have been a disjointed and incomplete view of his son's married life.

If Felix had shared with his father what was really going on things may have turned out differently. Sam Ferguson might, like his wife, love his only son unconditionally. But he was a realist. And he had the steadiest of heads on his shoulders.

If Felix had gone to his father, told him the truth, the whole truth, he supposed it was possible that Sam Ferguson may have found a better way out of the whole damned mess. Although Felix didn't know what the hell that could have been. And neither did he know how he, the man who previously had always told his father everything, could have shared the details of the last few weeks of Jane's life with anyone.

But one thing was for certain now. It was too late. Irrevocable decisions had been made. Jane was dead. The beautiful wife Felix had fallen head over heels in love with was no more.

Felix bent down and picked up a stick which he threw for the dogs. Pedro and Petra took off after it in yelping writhing delight, every pace, every leap, every sound, a chorus of total happiness.

The sea breeze of earlier in the day was growing stronger and there were dark clouds gathering. The first drops of rain were beginning to fall. Felix didn't care. He stood still for a moment looking out to sea. This part of Westward Ho!, the start of Abbotsham Cliffs, where the tors reached up to the south and the ocean stretched to the north, was quite possibly his favourite place in all the world. It was beautiful whatever the weather.

Lundy Island, jewel of the Atlantic, standing dark and proud on the horizon, had yet to disappear within a gathering mist.

Pedro galloped back to Felix and was at his feet, excited,

joyful, insistent on another throw of his stick. Felix bent forward, and took the stick from the dog's mouth.

When he stood up, ready to oblige, there were tears pouring down his cheeks.

THIRTEEN

B ack in Instow, Gerry Barham had also decided to go for a sea walk. But not along the front of his home village, that was far too public.

He had a meeting arranged with someone he was not sure he wanted to meet at all. But he felt that he had little choice.

He drove to Westward Ho!, heading for Sandymere at the furthest end of Northam Burrows, where he parked by the seawater pond, known as the inland sea, which, at low tide, is actually little more than a large puddle.

Even though this was a Sunday in May, there were few other cars there, probably belonging to stalwart dog walkers. The changeable weather had seen to that, as Gerry and the man he was meeting had expected. By the time Gerry arrived the wind had turned into something of a gale and the rain was tipping down.

Nonetheless Gerry pulled on the heavy duty waterproof he had learned, since moving to North Devon, to always carry in the back of his car, and clambered over the pebble ridge. The tide was a long way out. He strode towards the distant sea until he felt his feet begin to sink in the sand. Then he stopped and stood for a moment just staring over the water.

The wind bit into his face, driving droplets of rain down his neck inside the waterproof. He hoped he wouldn't have to wait for long.

After a bit he checked his watch, turned around, and peered back towards the pebble ridge and the sand dunes. A tall burly man wearing a dark hooded coat and wellington boots, body bent almost horizontally into the driving wind, was moving across the sand towards him.

He walked straight up to Gerry Barham, all the while looking around as if to make sure nobody else was nearby.

'Hello, Sam,' said Gerry.

Sam Ferguson, the mayor of Bideford, father-in-law of the recently deceased Jane Ferguson, unenthusiastically grunted something which might or might not have been a greeting.

'Hope nobody knows we're meeting today, Gerry,' he muttered.

'Nobody knows we're meeting, Sam, and certainly not that we're doing so way out here with our feet sinking in the sand,' replied Gerry. 'We could have talked in the early hours when you came to collect the twins. You didn't even come into the house. Why do you always have to be so bloody cloak and dagger anyway?'

'For God's sake, Gerry, it's not cloak and dagger enough, not nearly enough,' replied Sam. 'I wasn't going to try to talk to you with the Close crawling with coppers. In any case, Felix was already with you, ready to bring the children out to Amelia and me. Look, let's cut to the chase, my daughter-in-law met a violent death in the night. I want to know what you know about it?'

'I-I don't know anything,' said Gerry haltingly. 'Except that Anne and I discovered Jane's body, or Anne did – well, after your poor little Joanna, of course.'

'Ummm, we'll see about that,' said Sam. 'I just got a text from Amelia saying the police have now launched a murder investigation. Did you know that?'

'I . . . uh . . . I didn't know for certain,' stumbled Gerry.

'They've been around to interview Felix for the second time,' Sam continued. 'My son seems to be the number one suspect, and I doubt I'm far behind him on the list.'

Gerry looked anxious.

'But you didn't do it, Sam, did you?' he said. 'I mean, I know more than anybody how you felt about Jane. Whatever you say. And you were supposed to be at that anniversary dinner at the Waltons last night. You didn't turn up.'

'Have you taken leave of your senses, Gerry? I'm not a bloody murderer. I've just been looking out for my family, that's all.'

'So where were you last night then?'

Gerry had decided that attack might be the best form of defence, but he spoke with a confidence he did not feel.

'Why weren't you at the Waltons?' he continued.

'You know why we weren't there. Melia was a bit under the weather. Some sort of tummy bug. We phoned.'

'Yeah. So I understand. And I for one didn't believe a word of it. Your wife's as strong as an ox. Shouldn't think she's gone down with a tummy bug in the whole of her life.'

'All right, all right. Joan Walton has put Amelia's nose out of joint. Woman probably not even aware of it. God knows it's easily enough done. Got herself elected chairman of the Inner Wheel over Amelia's head. Or that's how Melia sees it. I thought she was prepared to let it go, move on. But no. Not her. At the last moment yesterday she refused to go. So I made our excuses . . . Gerry, what is this? Why are you giving me the third degree? You're the one who's been snooping on my son and his wife. You're the one who knows what was really going on in that house.'

'I don't know anything more than I've told you. We made an agreement and I stuck to it. Any information I have, you have.'

'I don't have any information, Gerry. You've given me nothing. And neither have you told me what any of this is about, and what you've really been up to.'

'Just a little retirement job, Sam. I've explained all I can . . .'

'It's something far more sinister than that, I suspect, Gerry.'

'Really. Didn't stop you getting me on board to do your dirty work though, did it? To do some snooping on your behalf.'

'That woman was ruining my son's life, she was a danger to her children, my grandchildren. What did you expect me to do? I just took the opportunity to find out what was happening. So that I could maybe sort the whole damned mess out.'

'And is that what you've done, Sam. Sorted out the mess by killing Jane. Is it?'

'No. I promise you. It isn't.'

'Your son, then?'

'Felix? You know him. I love my boy. But, quite frankly, apart from any other considerations, he wouldn't have the gumption. He wouldn't be able to do it, he couldn't kill anybody, let alone his wife. You must see that.'

'Then who, Sam, who?'

'That's why I wanted to see you. I thought if anybody knew, it would be you.'

'I know no more than you do. Unlike you, I was at the Waltons last night, as I was supposed to be . . .'

'So I hear. And I've checked that. Otherwise, well otherwise, I'd be quite prepared to believe you killed our Jane.'

'Our Jane, is it now? That's not how you thought of her when she was alive, is it? Look Sam, the first I knew anything was wrong was when little Joanna ran plumb in front of our car.'

'I don't trust you, Gerry,' said Sam, spitting the words out. 'I don't trust you as far as I can see you.'

'Well then, that's at least something we have in common, Sam. Because I sure as hell don't trust you either!'

'Look, whether or not we trust each other, we need to work together here,' said Sam. 'I need to get the heat off Felix, and put my family back on track. You don't want anything to upset your cosy little life. So, let's make sure we both get what we want, shall we? The police clearly don't have a clue what's going on here. But you do, don't you, Gerry?'

'I don't know what you're talking about, Sam.'

'Really. You know what I caught you doing that night at number eleven. The only surprise is that the police haven't yet discovered what you were up to. They will, though, surely. It must only be a matter of time. And if you don't come clean with me I will make sure they find out. And I will destroy you. I promise you that. All I have to do is drop a word in the right ear and the whole of the Devon and Cornwall police force will come down on you like a ton of bricks.'

'Don't be so ridiculous. Come down on me like a ton of bricks for what?'

'Are you being deliberately stupid? You were doing something not only highly questionable but totally illegal . . .'

'And you went along with it, you became a-a conspirator.'

'Really? You just try proving that, Gerry boy. I shall deny all knowledge. And there's more, obviously. The little question of historic sex abuse.'

'For goodness sake, Sam. What are you talking about?'

'Oh, those unfortunate little incidents in your past life that might pop up at any moment.'

'We both know you're making that up.'

'And what if I am? In the present climate even the merest

suggestion of historic sexual abuse has to be fully investigated. And it will be. Believe me. Even more so than the allegations might otherwise merit, probably, because I shall be behind the scenes pulling the strings like some extremely able puppet master.'

'You evil bastard.'

Gerry had been on tenterhooks ever since the discovery of Jane Ferguson's body. Sam Ferguson's words sent a shiver of pure fear through his entire body. But not entirely for the reasons Sam might expect. Gerry made one last attempt to mediate with him.

'Look Sam, you don't know what you're getting into here, really you don't—' he began.

'Maybe not,' Sam interrupted. 'But if you don't start talking, I will destroy the life you've built for yourself down here in no time at all. The parish council, the yacht club, the golf club, it will all be over for you. And as for your marriage . . . I think you can say goodbye to that once the press and social media come alive with stories of all your nasty little sexual shenanigans, don't you? It won't matter whether they're true or not, will it?'

'I'm telling you, Sam, you are meddling with matters you don't understand.'

'So make me understand then. That's all I'm asking. Tell me everything you know. Everything you have learned about Jane's past, and about the people you are working for.'

Gerry sighed. He reckoned he had no choice. In any case, he could do with confiding in someone. He feared he was out of his depth. Perhaps Sam might prove to be an ally. Someone to lean on.

'All right,' he said. 'I will tell you all I know. I just hope we don't both come to regret it.'

FOURTEEN

After leaving the Ferguson's home for the second time that day, Vogel and Saslow decided that a visit to the North Devon Yacht Club should be their next move.

'Motive and opportunity, that's what you look for in a murderer, is it not, Saslow?' Vogel murmured as they turned into Instow's Marine Parade. 'We have yet to find a motive as far as Felix is concerned, and at first sight it seems he didn't even have the opportunity, either. So at least let's check that out, shall we?'

They arrived at the yacht club shortly before six p.m.

The NDYC occupies a couple of acres of seafront land on the site of Instow's former railway station, bounded on one side by the tidal River Torridge, and on the other by what had once been the railway line between Barnstaple and Bideford and is now a coastal path, part of the famous Tarka Trail.

Its premises even include the original signal box, still standing proud on the site of the old level crossing. The changing rooms are housed in the wooden clad building which had once been the station waiting room.

The club, founded in 1905 as the Taw and Torridge Sailing Club, moved into its intriguing current home after the infamous Beeching cuts in the early sixties destroyed local railway networks throughout Britain, digging up railway lines nationwide.

Vogel had Googled most of this on the short drive from Northam. Whilst not always impressed by the beauty of nature in the way that most people are, Vogel was fascinated by unusual architecture and the history of buildings. However, whilst he had at least acquired a halfway decent raincoat since moving to the West of England, Vogel the city boy remained inadequately clad to dally outside in the proper North Devon gale which was now blowing in from the estuary. He hoped he might have opportunity to take a longer look around another time, but meanwhile he and Saslow hurried inside.

The club steward, Ronnie, was just opening up the bar, at the rear of the function room where the commodore's dinner had been held the previous evening.

He seemed friendly and helpful enough, at first.

'I am sure you know about the tragic death of Mrs Jane Ferguson,' Vogel began.

Ronnie, a sharp-featured neat little man of a certain age with silver hair so precisely arranged that it looked as if it might have been parted by a geometric instrument rather than a comb, agreed that he did.

'Terrible business,' he said. 'You wonder what could possibly drive a young woman like that to do what she did. I mean, she had those lovely children and everything.'

'Do I gather from what you have just said that you are assuming that Mrs Ferguson committed suicide?'

Ronnie looked surprised.

'Well, yes, of course,' he said. 'She was found hanged, wasn't she? By her poor little daughter, I heard.'

'That much is true,' said Vogel. 'But you should know that we have reason to believe that Mrs Ferguson did not take her own life. We believe she was murdered.'

'Oh my God,' said Ronnie.

'So we are making enquiries concerning the whereabouts last night of everyone connected with Mrs Ferguson,' said Vogel. 'Starting with her husband.'

'Oh my God,' said Ronnie again. 'Well, Mr Ferguson was here. But I expect you already know that. It was the annual do for the new commodore.'

'Do you know whether or not Mr Ferguson was here all night, throughout the proceedings?'

'Yes, of course he was,' Ronnie confirmed swiftly. 'There were drinks first, then the dinner, then speeches, then awards for people who'd won the most sailing races during the last twelve months, and so on. Mr Ferguson had to make a speech, and a very good one he made too.'

'Did he indeed?' remarked Vogel.

It wasn't really a query, but Ronnie responded as if it were, all the same.

'Oh yes. He's a very good speaker, Mr Ferguson. One of the best we've ever had as commodore actually. Only I didn't say that, if you know what I mean. Don't want to upset anybody.'

Ronnie tapped the side of his nose.

Vogel didn't think he'd actually ever seen anyone do that before.

'Oh yes, I know what you mean,' he agreed, in the matiest manner he could muster. 'Are you sure he was up to his best form last night?'

'He most certainly was.'

'Only we have reason to believe that Mr Ferguson may have been somewhat under the influence of alcohol.'

'By the time he left the club, perhaps,' said Ronnie. 'But he's always very professional, is Mr Ferguson. When he's speaking he'll barely have a drink at all until afterwards. Gin and tonic man usually. But every so often he tips me the wink and I know just to serve him tonic. Later on, like, he'll let his hair down, so to speak. Last night, a few of them settled into the back room for a few drinks after the main proceedings ended. I stayed behind to serve them. I didn't mind. He's always been very good to me, Mr Ferguson.'

'I see,' said Vogel. 'And until what time did Mr Ferguson and his drinking companions stay in the back room?'

'Well, I'm not entirely sure. I served them a final round, so they were stocked up, so to speak, and then I left just before two, I think. They said they'd lock up and everything.'

'Is it usual for you to leave members to lock up?'

'It's not usual, no. But the dinner for the new commodore is a special night. And there's not a problem about it. This is a member's club. You trust people, don't you?'

'How many people were drinking with Mr Ferguson, and who were they?'

'Let's see, four, no, five. There was Jack Crossley, last year's commodore. And two couples. Married couples. The Conway-Browns and the Smythes. They'd been sitting on the same table. Mr Ferguson and Mr Crossley were together on the top table, of course.'

'And you are quite sure Mr Ferguson didn't leave the club at all, during the course of the evening, at any time before you closed the bar?'

'How could he have done?' asked Ronnie. It was a rhetorical question. He clearly did not expect a reply and carried on speaking without giving Vogel time to make one. 'It was Mr Ferguson's night. The commodore is expected to be the host, like.'

'You couldn't be sure he didn't slip out, though, could you? I mean, you had a bar to run on a very busy occasion.'

'Well, no. I suppose I couldn't be absolutely sure. But I don't see how he would have had the chance. Somebody would have noticed . . .'

The bar steward stopped in his tracks.

'Why are you asking me this, sir?' he enquired. 'What are you suggesting?'

'I'm not suggesting anything, Ronnie,' said Vogel. 'I am just asking you to help us with our enquiries, that's all.'

Ronnie stood up, stretching to his full five foot six inches or so, and puffing out his chest. It was a clear display of righteous indignation.

'Well, I'm not answering any more of your questions. I'm not saying any more at all, not without someone with me, someone from the committee. I don't like where you're going with this, sir. I don't like it at all. Mrs Ferguson took her own life. That's what I was told this morning. And until you lot can prove anything different, that's what I'm going to believe. It's a tragedy, a terrible tragedy. I realize you never know what goes on behind closed doors, but the commodore and his wife were close, real close. There was no doubt about that, you can ask anyone. She must have been ill to do what she did. She must have been. That's the only explanation.'

Ronnie stopped talking abruptly. Perhaps remembering that he hadn't been going to say any more. Vogel had difficulty stopping himself smiling. He liked this sort of witness. They couldn't stop talking even if they wanted to.

He passed no comment – refraining from pointing out again that there was certainly another explanation, and that he was, in fact, conducting a murder enquiry – because he thought that would be counter-productive. Instead the DCI began to ask another question which he felt quite sure Ronnie would answer quickly enough. In spite of his pledge to remain silent from now on.

'Those people who were drinking with Felix Ferguson last night, the previous commodore, the Smythes, and . . . and . . . who were the other couple?'

'The Conway-Browns,' supplied Ronnie readily enough.

'Yes, the Conway-Browns. Are any of them likely to come in this evening?'

'I shouldn't think so,' said Ronnie. 'Not after the night they had last night. Mr Smythe popped in at lunchtime, hair of the dog, he said. Only a couple of other members turned up at all, and just for a quick one. Nobody stayed. We only opened for an hour.'

'Well, we're going to need to speak to that little late drinking group,' said Vogel. 'I'd like their contact details please.'

'You'll need to speak to Janice in the office in the morning,' said Ronnie a tad sullenly. 'I don't have that sort of personal information. And she'll have to get permission from the committee too . . .'

'Ronnie, I'm going to tell you again. We don't think Mrs Ferguson took her own life. We are conducting an investigation into a murder, and I really must insist that you cooperate fully. Now, you mentioned last year's commodore. Jack Crossley? I want his contact details.'

'He lives over Fremington way,' Ronnie answered in a resigned sort of way. 'I don't have his full address.'

'But no doubt you have his phone number?'

'Well yes, I do, but . . .'

'No buts, Ronnie. Give me that number.'

Even more sullenly Ronnie picked up his phone from the bar and began to read out Crossley's number.

As he did so the door to the club room opened. A tall rangy man, possibly into his early forties, but with a full head of dark blonde hair which flopped boyishly over his forehead, walked in and approached the bar.

Ronnie glanced towards him.

'Evening, Ronnie,' said the man. 'Hair of the dog for me. I could have done with it a lot earlier too, but I couldn't spare the time.'

He looked around the bar, which apart from Saslow and Vogel remained empty.

'Thought there might be a few other sufferers here,' he remarked.

Ronnie offered briefly that there had been a few in at lunchtime, as he'd told Vogel, but he certainly didn't expect many that evening.

The tall man, who had almost startlingly blue eyes, studied Saslow and Vogel for a brief moment, then stepped towards them, hand outstretched.

'Don't believe I've had the pleasure,' he said. 'Jimmy Granger, pleased to meet you.'

'Mr Granger is one of our newer members,' volunteered Ronnie.

'Yes,' said Granger. 'Moved into a flat in Marine Court just over a month ago. Relocating after a divorce. Goodbye family home, hallo bachelor pad. You know the sort of thing, I'm sure.'

Vogel did not. And he had no intention of ever finding out. But he chose not to remark on that.

Instead he took Jimmy Granger's outstretched hand in his, and introduced himself and Saslow.

'Police, eh,' said Granger. 'All right, officer. I give in. It's a fair cop. I was drunk as a skunk last night.'

He laughed loudly at his own joke. If indeed it was a joke. To make matters worse his voice, with a hint of Midland twang about it, was a little too loud, and his whole personae a tad too hearty.

Vogel managed a weak smile.

'Do I take it you were at the commodore's dinner, sir?' he queried.

'Yes, I was. As far as I remember.'

Granger again laughed loudly.

'But you would remember seeing Mr Ferguson here, I presume?'

'Felix? Of course. He's the new commodore, for goodness sake. Gave a speech. Played host. What are you asking about Felix for? Nothing's happened to him, I hope.'

'Uh, are you unaware, then, sir, of a certain tragic incident in the village which occurred in the early hours of this morning?'

'Tragic event? What tragic event? I have no idea what you are talking about. Got off to a late start. Hangover and all of that. And I've been chained to my desk ever since, catching up on work. Graphic designer me. Self-employed. One good thing about it, I can do it anywhere. That's why I thought to myself, Jimmy my boy, you're on your own again, why not go to live at the seaside, buy yourself a boat . . .'

Granger paused.

'Sorry. I'm rambling, aren't I? Has something happened I should know about?'

'Mr Ferguson's wife was found dead in the early hours, sir,' said Vogel.

'Oh my God. I'm so sorry. How? I mean, she was a young woman, wasn't she? Why's it a police matter?'

Vogel explained as briefly as possible.

'A murder enquiry?' Jimmy Granger queried. 'Jesus. When I moved into Instow they told me nothing ever happened here. And you're asking about Felix? Surely you don't suspect him, do you?'

'I can't comment on that, sir,' said Vogel. 'I am just enquiring about Mr Ferguson's whereabouts last night, and anyone else who may have been nearby at the time of the incident. Can I ask you if you were here for the entire evening, sir?'

'Yes. Yes, I was. From just after seven.'

'And when did you leave, sir?'

'Oh, about twelve thirty. Maybe one a.m.'

'So you weren't one of the group I understand were drinking with Felix Ferguson in the back room.'

'You're joking? I'm just a new boy. Be a while before I graduate to a lock-in with the commodore.'

'I see, sir, well, thank you very much.'

Granger ordered a pint of lager and a whisky chaser and took his drinks to a table by the window.

Vogel watched him idly, wondering if he always drank like that. But maybe it really was just a hair of the dog after an unusually heavy night's drinking, as Granger had said. The man was fit looking and lightly tanned. He didn't have the appearance of a habitual boozer.

After he finished serving Granger, Ronnie moved back along the bar to re-join Vogel and Saslow. In spite of his earlier comments, he couldn't quite leave them alone, thought Vogel.

He suspected that Ronnie was the sort of man who always wanted to appear to know more than others did, particularly about something as juicy as the sudden violent death of a young woman, even whilst so volubly expressing shock and concern.

'Lovely woman, Mrs Ferguson, and those two lovely children,' he remarked for the second time, clearly trying to draw Vogel and Saslow into conversation again, regardless of his professed intention not to provide them with any more information. 'A tragedy, that's what it is . . .'

'Yes indeed, Ronnie,' interjected Vogel mildly. 'The sudden death of a young woman is always a tragedy. Particularly when she has been murdered—'

'I just can't believe it,' interrupted Ronnie. 'Who would want to murder Mrs Ferguson?'

'That is what I am trying to find out,' remarked Vogel patiently. 'Clearly you knew and liked Mrs Ferguson. Did you see her often in the club then?'

Ronnie seemed to have yet again forgotten that he was answering no further questions.

'Not often, no. There are the two young children, aren't there? But in the summer, particularly at weekends, the members often bring their children with them. His little ones are too young for proper sailing, of course, but Mr Ferguson takes them on the river sometimes, motoring upstream to Bideford at high tide, that sort of thing. And they seem to enjoy being here. As did Mrs Ferguson, I'm sure. Though we haven't seen her here in a while.'

'Can you remember when you last saw her in the club?'

'Not really. Not this year. I'm pretty certain.'

'I see. And she wasn't here last night, was she? Wouldn't you have expected the commodore's wife to be with him on such an important occasion?'

Ronnie looked blank for a moment. Then his face clouded over, and he scowled at Vogel. It seemed he'd remembered his earlier pledge.

'I'm saying nothing more,' he said. 'I told you that, and I mean it.'

Vogel smiled at him, which he hoped Ronnie found as annoying as he meant it to be. He didn't think the man was hiding anything deliberately, although it was possible that he knew something significant without realising it. But Ronnie was the sort of irritation the DCI could do without.

'C'mon, Saslow,' he said heading for the door.

'Do you ever long for the days when a copper could just give an irritating little bugger like that a slap, sir?' Saslow asked conversationally as she followed him out of the club.

'Not worth the effort, Dawn,' said Vogel, smiling more genuinely. 'And we've got better things to do. Like heading back to our gaff and getting some sleep before we both fall over. Early night and an early start tomorrow, when I think we should spend a few hours at the Bideford incident room, make sure we're abreast of everything. Meanwhile, I'll call Nobby and keep her up to speed. I want you to phone that former commodore fella, pick his brains about last night first, then tell him exactly what we want from the NDYC. Starting with a list of all the members who were at the dinner last night, and their contact details. Then we'll get a team onto checking 'em out.'

'Quite a job, boss.'

'Yep. The glamour of policing, Dawn. But all we need is one person, just one person, who saw Felix Ferguson slip away from the dinner – after all his home is only just up the hill – or even someone with a reasonable suggestion of how he might have been able to do that, and we have our opportunity.'

'But still no motive, boss.'

'Early doors, Saslow. Give it time. Give it time.'

FIFTEEN

In Estuary Vista Close the forensic examination of number eleven had continued throughout the day. Crime scene investigators arrived and left, moving in and out of the house, sometimes carrying boxes.

Anne Barham, sitting by the window of her spare bedroom, which, like the main bathroom, faced the Ferguson's home, had a bird's-eye view of the driveway. She wondered idly what the boxes might contain. She read crime novels occasionally, and more frequently watched the big detective series on TV. She assumed there might be mobile phones and tablets, laptops, or even a desktop computer in them. She knew the Fergusons had an iMac desktop in their home office off the kitchen. There would be paperwork too. Maybe clothes, and shoes. What else? Anne wasn't sure, but at least she was occupying her mind on what was proving to be a very difficult day.

She took a sip of her cappuccino, freshly prepared from her new all-singing, all-dancing coffee machine, a present for her birthday a month earlier from her daughter and son-in-law. Anne loved cappuccino. Possibly more than any sort of alcohol. Although Gerry certainly didn't understand that. Nor anyone else much that she knew. The group of retired people who seemed to comprise the bulk of hers and Gerry's social circle in North Devon were like expats in some ways, she thought. Desperately seeking alcohol in a bid to fill the hours left empty by retirement from jobs which no longer seemed unattractive at all, and the absence of children who had long flown the nest and were now consumed, and quite rightly so, by their own careers and families.

Anne realized that her mind was wandering. The cappuccino was wonderful. Rich and creamy. Angela and Ralph always gave her and Gerry extravagant presents. They lived in London. Ralph was an architect and Angela was a barrister, who had returned to work just a couple of months after the birth of their five-year-old son. Anne knew that their presents were intended to compensate a little for the fact that she and Gerry hardly ever seemed to see them nowadays. But Anne was inordinately fond of all three of them. And usually she didn't mind too much. Today she so wished they lived closer, and were less busy.

She emptied the coffee cup. Ever since the arrival of the doubtless expensive machine, it had given Anne such pleasure to be able to make and enjoy a truly excellent cappuccino in her own home. Not today.

She was still getting over the events of the early hours. Actually, she wasn't getting over it at all. And she didn't think she ever would.

Anne had seen death before. Her mother lying stiff and grey in the bedroom of the old family home in Harrow. Her father at the undertaker's chapel. And once, a stranger, a motorcyclist, dead and broken in the road, when she had found herself the first on the scene of a fatal traffic accident.

But she had never, ever seen anything akin to what she had so recently witnessed in the house next door.

Jane Ferguson hanging, unnaturally crooked, her face distorted and discoloured, in the hallway of her own home. Then there were the little children, finding Joanna in the road, caught in the glare of the headlights of their car, and little Stevie wandering onto the landing. Both of them disorientated. Distraught. And Anne trying so hard, yet, she felt, so ineffectually, to comfort them.

She shivered. The bedroom was cool, although that may not

have been the cause. Outside the wind was getting up, and rain was now falling steadily. The glorious weather of earlier in the day had evaporated. That was North Devon for you. The CSI people, in their pale blue protective suits, were hurrying as they went about their business, hoods up, and heads down. It was probably a trick of the angle from which she was watching them, but their legs looked too small for their bodies, and seemed to be moving unnaturally fast, as if they were part of a speeded-up film sequence. Anne thought they looked like a swarm of blue plasticised ants.

She had only recently dressed properly, having spent most of the day in her dressing gown, wandering aimlessly around the house. And, most unusually, it had been a real effort to do so. But it was an effort she had ultimately made on the grounds that she would feel better. She had showered and washed her hair, applied her make-up with care, dressed nicely in her favourite silk shirt and a faux leather waistcoat over a rather good pair of Eileen Fisher trousers.

However, she didn't feel better. She thought she would probably never feel better. And her fragile state of mind had not been helped by Gerry's behaviour, which had actually been distinctly odd.

He had seemed fine at first. The usual supportive kind Gerry, so concerned about her after she had been confronted by Jane's body. He had taken charge the way he usually did, phoning the police, making hot drinks for the children, whilst she calmed herself down, assuring her that he would see to everything, dealing with the arrival of the emergency services, and later Felix. Then encouraging her to go to bed, to at least try to sleep.

But almost immediately after those two detectives had left, DCI Vogel and DS Saslow, at around seven a.m., he'd retreated to his study and remained there for most of the rest of the morning.

Anne, continuing to feel truly wretched, had two or three times popped in with a cup of coffee and asked him if he wouldn't come and sit with her for a bit. Each time he'd been bent intently over his laptop, and when he'd looked up at her he'd shut the lid.

'I promise I'll be with you in a minute,' he'd said reassuringly. But he hadn't kept that promise at all. And when she'd asked what he was doing, he had merely muttered something only half comprehensible about wanting to take his mind off everything.

She'd hovered outside the study door every so often, something she would never normally think of doing, and once heard the murmur of his voice on the phone, but he'd been speaking so quietly that she'd been unable to decipher a word that he was saying.

He finally emerged for a late lunch, but only after she had stormed into his study and told him she was going to scream and burst into tears if he didn't come out. Then, as soon as he'd finished eating, just two or three of the sandwiches she'd prepared, he'd risen from the kitchen table and told her he was going out for a walk.

She'd broken down then, and begun to cry.

He had put his arm around her, kissed her lightly, apologized profusely and said that he just needed some fresh air, and he wouldn't be long.

She'd reached into the pocket of her dressing gown for a paper tissue, blown her nose, told herself she was over-reacting, and tried to pull herself together. As she had been brought up to do.

'Well, all right then, fresh air does sound like a good idea, I suppose, so why don't I come with you?' she'd enquired, trying to sound cheery.

'Look, my love, I really need a little time alone to clear my head. You don't mind, do you? I'll be back before you know it. And you're not even dressed yet.'

She hadn't been dressed, of course. And she supposed she hadn't minded. Not really. Not too much, anyway. But it was all so unlike Gerry. He was not the sort of man who needed to go for a walk to clear his head. Gerry's head was always clear. Or so Anne had always thought, and she had been married to him for thirty-seven years. It was one of the things that she'd always loved about him. Whatever happened in life, there was Gerry, level-headed, calm, brain engaged, sorting it all out.

Some women looked for excitement, for partners who were exciting. And God knows, Gerry had never been that. But he suited Anne down to the ground. She loved her dependable man. And she'd never really had a thing to worry about since she'd married him. Gerry had invariably seen to everything.

He had even managed to assist her in producing a daughter who never gave either of them anything to worry about. A clever girl, also pretty, who launched herself with apparent ease into a near brilliant career and married a charming handsome man who was equally clever and absolutely right for her. Anne had little doubt that their son would turn out in the same mould. That was Gerry for you. He managed things right. Even his only offspring.

However, that morning, that morning of all mornings, Gerry had definitely not been like Gerry.

Anne was puzzled as well as upset. So much so, that after he left for his alleged walk – taking the car, she noticed – she gave in to her curiosity. She went to his study and jacked up the laptop, still on the desk, which had monopolized so much of his attention that day. She'd never done anything like that before. It would just not have occurred to her. Not before this awful and peculiar day. She found that the laptop was password protected. Well, there was nothing unusual or suspicious about that. She also had a laptop, though she did not often use it, and that was password protected too. The only difference was, she suddenly realized, that whilst Gerry knew her password, she had absolutely no idea what his was.

Anne had closed the laptop and walked away, asking herself what on earth she thought she was doing. This was her husband of thirty-seven years, kind, dependable Gerry, who had never given her reason to doubt him for a moment.

Or had he? Gerry was a night owl, she was an early bird. She often went to bed before him, and was aware that he might spend hours sometimes on his laptop before joining her. He played backgammon. He was a keen amateur historian and enjoyed creating his own research projects, looking into famous characters from the past, and indeed his own family. He also liked to browse YouTube, Twitter and Facebook, sites which held no interest at all for Anne.

Or is that what he did? As she sat with her coffee gazing unseeingly now at the blue ants next door, it occurred to her that she really had absolutely no idea what Gerry was doing when he spent all those hours at his computer.

He could be downloading unspeakable porn. He could be

conducting some sort of weird internet affair. He could be a criminal mastermind, or an alien in human guise contacting his distant planet.

She let her imagination run riot, because it reassured her that Gerry downloading porn or having a cyber affair was no more likely than him being a criminal or an alien. And the latter two thoughts made her want to laugh. Which also made her feel just a little better.

She told herself there would be a logical explanation for his behaviour that day, because there always was with Gerry. Wasn't there?

Then she checked her watch. Gerry had left for his little walk to clear his head just after two thirty p.m., promising that he would be back in no time. That was another promise he had totally failed to keep.

He had now been gone for more than three hours, and she had not heard from him at all. He could have gone to the yacht club for a drink, but he had the car. If he'd intended to do that he would have left the car at home.

She was becoming quite anxious. Again, it was so unlike Gerry not to keep in touch. Particularly on a day like this.

She told herself he could have gone shopping to take his mind off everything. He could have driven to Bideford, or slightly further away to Barnstaple. He could just have gone for a very long walk, along any one of the so many lovely beaches near their home, then onto the network of paths which stretched along the North Devon coast. But for over three hours? Gerry was not that sort of walker. And the weather had broken. In any case she would have expected him to call.

She had called him, of course. But he hadn't picked up. Each time his phone rang briefly, then switched to voicemail.

She didn't know what to do. She half wanted to call the police. She had the business card that nice DCI Vogel had given her. But he was investigating Jane Ferguson's death. A death regarded as suspicious. And she didn't think DCI Vogel, or any other police officer come to that, would be very interested in the case of a grown man who had been away from his home for three hours. They would think Anne was being ridiculous. A silly old woman. And when she put it into words she could fully understand that. It was what she would think about anyone else.

But this was Gerry. Her Gerry. And it just wasn't right.

Sighing, she reached for her phone to call him one more time. Finally, he answered.

SIXTEEN

S am Ferguson was in a total state of shock as he tramped back across the sand and over the pebble ridge onto Northam Burrows.

Sam was a man accustomed to knowing what to do. He would invariably assess a situation quickly, decide upon a course of action, and execute it without hesitation. He was good at making decisions. That was what Sam Ferguson did.

Not this time though. What Gerry Barham had told Sam had shaken him to the very core. He still did not know what it really meant.

He did know that he was afraid. He believed now that his surviving family were under threat. He was sure of it. And whilst what he had told DCI Vogel was absolutely correct, that he felt no grief for the passing of his daughter-in-law, he found himself wishing with all his heart that she were still alive. He glanced at his watch on a kind of autopilot. At almost exactly the same time as Anne Ferguson had looked at hers, and Vogel and Saslow had arrived at the NDYC.

It was a few minutes before six p.m. The two constables who had broken the news of Jane's death had arrived at his home just before three a.m., around fifteen hours previously.

In the whole of his life Sam Ferguson had not experienced a more devastating fifteen hours. He couldn't believe what had happened. Not any of it. But particularly not what he had just been told by Gerry Barham.

He was devastated. He did not know whom to turn to or what to do. And Sam was not used to feeling that way.

He unlocked his car, climbed in, and allowed his upper body

to slump over the steering wheel for a few seconds, then he sat up and tried to make himself think, to concentrate, to come up with some sort of course of action. Any sort.

He supposed he could just do nothing at all, something he had always found most difficult. In any case he feared that events would overtake themselves. And Felix was so vulnerable. He'd always been like that, charming, not without talent, not without a brain, but weak and rudderless.

Sam had never minded. It had always suited him to have a son whose path he could mould, a young man he could guide and steer who, unlike most sons in Sam's experience, seemed to welcome that level of interference from his father.

But for a fleeting moment, and for probably the first time ever, he wished Felix were a different sort of man, a young man he could confide in, who might, for once, even be able to support his father in the way Sam had always supported him.

But that was not how things were. And Sam didn't want Felix, or his grandchildren, ever to have to face the consequences of what he had just been told. Yet he feared that day would come, and sooner rather than later.

He sat there alone in his car for more than half an hour wracking his brains to come up with a workable plan, something that might yet save the day, without any success.

He needed to get home too. He'd told Amelia he'd had to go back to the council offices to deal with some vital issues.

She had echoed Vogel's thoughts of that morning. Sam didn't know what Vogel had thought, of course, although he might have guessed.

'What possible council business could there be to take you away from your family yet again on this day of all days?' Amelia had asked. 'It's a Sunday, too.'

Sam had apologized but insisted that there were pressing matters he needed to attend to before the offices opened for normal business the following day.

'I'd always intended to go in this afternoon,' he told Amelia. 'I didn't know Jane was going to get herself topped, did I?'

As soon as he spoke he'd regretted his choice of words. Amelia, not a woman known for her sensitivity, looked at him quite aghast.

'I'm going to forget you said that, Sam,' she said.

He knew he had been unconvincing in explaining his intentions, and his wife, who was certainly no fool, had clearly not believed a word he said. Indeed, even as he sat in the Burrows car park, momentarily too shocked to move, she was probably calling his direct line at the council offices to see if he was really there.

And if he didn't pull himself together and get back fast, he was likely to be greeted by an explosion of fury, swiftly followed by an angry cross-examination which he didn't feel up to.

With a huge effort of will he made himself start the engine and head home, all the while his mind was in turmoil. He had to do something, and he had to do something quickly. There was no one to turn to. There never was. It was down to him. As always.

SEVENTEEN

Gerry Barham watched Sam Ferguson stride across the beach, his tall burly figure shrinking into the distance as he reached the pebble ridge, climbed it with surprising speed and agility for a man in his sixties, and disappeared over the top.

Gerry made no move to follow Sam. He wanted the other man well gone before he made his own way back to the car park. He already wished he hadn't told Sam all that he had. But Sam hadn't left him much choice.

Gerry picked up a piece of driftwood and threw it into the sea. Was it really only yesterday that his life in retirement, or very nearly retirement, had seemed so pleasant and carefree – his one extramural activity adding just the smallest pinch of spice to an existence which might otherwise have been almost humdrum.

Even as he threw the piece of wood he noticed that his hand was trembling. Just like Sam he wondered what he should do next. There were people he needed to speak to. One in particular. He had been waiting for her to call all day. That's why he'd left the house right after lunch. To chase her up. He'd needed to get seriously to work on the phone, and he couldn't do that at home with Anne. So far, he had only managed to speak to minions. And they'd been no help at all, that was for sure. Now he really ought to get back to Anne. He knew she was puzzled by his behaviour. He had tried to behave as normally as possible, in spite of all those hours at his laptop and the whispered phone calls. But he knew he hadn't made a very good job of it. He just hoped Anne would put it down to the shock of discovering Jane Ferguson's body. Even though she was the one who had actually made the discovery.

His mobile, switched to silent to prevent unwanted interruptions, was tucked into the top pocket of his leather jacket. Suddenly, for the umpteenth time that afternoon, he felt it vibrate against his heart. Or what was left of his heart, he thought wryly. He quickly removed the phone and checked the screen, willing for the call he both dreaded and longed for. It was Anne again. Still no word from the other woman who was so important to him. The other woman who might yet wreck everything. Not a mistress, or someone with whom he'd had a casual affair, or even a one-night stand. No. A woman whom he suddenly regarded as far more of a potential danger to his way of life than any manifestation of personal indiscretion might be.

He continued to study the screen for a few seconds. He knew he could no longer avoid speaking to his wife, or she was going to be quite frantic. He accepted the call.

'Hello, darling,' he said.

It was how he always answered a call from Anne. Ordinary words, and he tried desperately to make his voice sound ordinary.

'Gerry, where on earth are you? Are you all right?'

Anne sounded both anxious and bewildered. As well she might, thought Gerry.

'I'm on the beach beyond Northam Burrows, over by the estuary,' he answered truthfully.

The sea breeze was whistling in his ears. He rather hoped Anne would have difficulty in hearing him. It seemed that she did.

'What did you say, Gerry?' she asked. 'Where are you?'

'On the beach,' he repeated more loudly. 'There's a fair wind blowing. And it's raining. I told you I was going for a walk, didn't I?'

'What? Gerry, this is impossible. I can't hear you properly. You've been gone for hours. I've been worried sick.'

'I'm sorry, I . . . uh . . . I suppose I didn't realize the time . . .'

'Look, never mind, just come home will you?'

'Yes. Yes. I'm on my way.'

Gerry began to walk towards the pebble ridge, as if to prove to himself, if not to Anne, that he was again telling the truth.

'What?' said Anne, clearly still unable to hear him properly and sounding frustrated.

'I'm on my way,' Gerry shouted. 'I shan't be long.'

He ended the call relieved that the poor reception had enabled him to avoid having to give Anne any sort of explanation. That would come of course, but hopefully he would by then have had time to think of a suitable one. And he may even have received the call he was waiting for from the other woman. Perhaps some reassuring news. Although he wasn't holding his breath.

To his surprise, and somewhat to his discomfort, Sam Ferguson's Range Rover was still in the car park, parked not far away from his Mercedes. He couldn't see if Sam was still inside it, and he wasn't going to approach any closer to check. It made no difference anyway. He suspected Sam was trying to think through all that had happened and what he should do, just as he was.

As he climbed into his own vehicle he shut the door as quietly as possible, before driving slowly along the track across the Burrows, and out over the cattle grid onto the Northam road.

He crossed the Torridge Bridge and had just reached Instow when his phone rang again. It was her. On his hands-free. Her voice was all too familiar even though he had only actually spoken to her a handful of times over the three years or so that she had been his contact. Her name was Martha. And he was as sure as he could be that wasn't her real name. After all, Gerry had an ear for voices, and he was pretty sure this was the third Martha he had spoken to in total since he had entered into the agreement which had seemed such a good idea at the time. An agreement that had facilitated his retirement in a style and a manner he had not expected, allowing him and Anne to indulge in various luxuries, like their top-of-the-range Merc, and occasional exotic holidays.

He did not know Martha's last name.

'I've been wanting to speak to you, Gerry,' she said. 'I thought you might have some information for me.'

'Really?' responded Gerry, turning the word into a question. He wasn't entirely a pushover. 'I thought you might have some information for *me*. I've been waiting for you to call all day,' he continued.

'You are our man on the spot,' said Martha, ignoring any criticism which may have been inferred by his last remark. 'I hope you haven't forgotten that.'

She paused. Gerry thought she was waiting for him to speak again. He said nothing.

'I understand our potential problem is no longer a problem,' she continued eventually.

'Is that some sort of riddle?' asked Gerry, who found that he was suddenly more angry than anything else. He glanced at his hands on the steering wheel. His fingers were still trembling. And he couldn't control it.

'I think you know what I mean,' said Martha in the same level tone.

'If you mean that a young woman has died in violent circumstances, then yes, that is the case,' Gerry continued, fighting to keep his voice level and give no hint of just how afraid he was beginning to feel. 'As her death is being treated as murder and the police have launched a major investigation, then it could be that one "problem" has been replaced by another "problem".'

'Gerry, I would remind you we are speaking on an open phone line. Please be careful what you say.'

'Bit late for being careful, isn't it?' snapped Gerry.

'Look, you have been dealing with this situation for a long time now, you must have realized there were certain inherent dangers—'

'I never in my wildest imaginings thought it would end like this,' interrupted Gerry.

'Gerry, you made an agreement with us for which you have been and continue to be extremely well rewarded. There's no such thing as a free lunch, you know.'

'Jesus,' growled Gerry.

'Look, you have to keep calm. We need to debrief you. Obviously.'

'I am calm,' Gerry lied. 'I can't get up to London. Anne would never stand for it. And the police would be all over me like a rash. I'm sure they're suspicious already . . .'

'Maybe, or you could just be panicking. But I do agree it would be unwise for you to act in any way out of character right now, and you certainly aren't in the habit of hopping on a train to London at short notice. So, we will get someone to you.'

'Who?'

'Someone who can give you all the assistance you need. Someone who will do your thinking for you for a bit, and ensure that you and your wife are kept safe. How does that sound?'

It sounded good, of course. Only he wasn't sure he believed a word of it. He'd just had his sixty-fifth birthday. He was in reasonable health, able to enjoy life, his occasional games of golf, his even more occasional estuary forays on his boat, and so on. On that particular day he felt about 105.

'I'm too old for all this, Martha,' he said.

'You weren't too old for it when it wasn't causing you any trouble,' Martha reminded him.

'Murder is a step too far,' said Gerry, only vaguely aware that he had said something rather ridiculous. 'One huge step too far. To be perfectly honest, Martha, I didn't know today whether to call you or just to go to the police and tell them everything I know.'

'Well, I'm very glad you decided to call me, Gerry,' responded Martha. 'That was definitely your best option. Now, you will get another call. Tonight. It will be from someone who will make an arrangement to meet you, and allow you to go back to your retirement. Full time.'

'That's what I want, Martha. I can't do this anymore.'

'You won't have to.' There was a pause. 'Uh, Gerry, have you told anybody else about your part in all of this? Your wife. Anyone?'

Gerry remained silent for a few seconds, trying to think on his feet. What should he tell her? It would have to be the truth, or more or less. Lying to Martha would be far too dangerous. People like her had ways of finding things out. He had little choice but to trust her. And he so wanted all this to go away, just as she was promising.

'Only somebody who half knew already,' he said eventually.

'What do you mean by that? Who?'

'I told you at the time what happened. I was confronted by Sam Ferguson, Jane's father-in-law, when . . . when I was . . . Look, I told you. He hated his daughter-in-law. He was happy, more than happy, to overlook everything in exchange for information. Don't you remember?'

'Of course, I remember. So why did you feel the need to share anything more with him?'

'He was threatening to go to the police. He said he knew people in high places and if I didn't tell him what was going on he would destroy my life and my marriage. My "cosy little retirement", he called it. I'm now beginning to think I should have let him go to the police.'

'Well, you were clearly put in a difficult position. Have you any idea what he is going to do now? Is he still planning to destroy your "cosy little life"?'

'How the hell do I know? He just stomped off huffing and puffing. But he is an important man around these parts.'

'I'm sure he is, Gerry. Just try to stop worrying, and wait to be contacted later. Once you have been properly debriefed everything will seem clearer, I promise you.'

'I just never thought things would turn out like this, that's all.'

'Quite,' said Martha, ending the call.

EIGHTEEN

Amelia Ferguson wasn't so much furious as, like Anne Barham, bewildered at her husband's behaviour. To outsiders it might have seemed that she was the dominant partner in their marriage, and that her husband, whilst successful and rather important out in the world, deferred to her in everything concerning home and family. Not a lot of people knew it, but the truth was rather different. When it came to the bigger issues in their lives, Amelia looked to her husband in everything. Sam was her rock.

He finally arrived home just after six thirty p.m., looking damp and dishevelled. His wife greeted him in the hallway, closing the door to the sitting room firmly behind her.

'For God's sake, what have you been doing?' she demanded.

'I told you,' replied Sam curtly. 'I needed to go to my office at the council, I had business to sort out before tomorrow.'

'I called your direct line, several times, you didn't answer. You weren't there, were you? I mean, look at you. You're wet through.'

'It's raining and blowing a gale, haven't you noticed? Of course I was there. Since when did you feel the need to check up on me, anyway?'

'Since you disappeared on the day your son's wife died, that's when.'

'I'm sorry. It was unavoidable.'

Amelia noticed that he didn't sound very sorry. In fact, he barely sounded like Sam. But she was still too angry to pay that much attention.

'Well, now that you're finally back perhaps you could give the remains of your family five minutes,' she snapped. 'Felix is in a real state. When he returned from walking the dogs he sat himself down with a bottle of whisky, and he seems to have drunk the lot. He's slumped on the sofa in the sitting room, barely conscious. Will you see if you can get him upstairs to his bedroom to sleep it off?'

For a moment Sam looked as if he were about to protest. Ultimately, he muttered a reluctant assent.

'Now, Sam,' continued Amelia. 'I want him out of the way of the children, although I get the feeling they've seen it all before.'

'Where are the children?' asked Sam.

'They're in the kitchen, I've got them playing with cake mix, and a right mess they're making too . . .'

'Go back to them,' instructed Sam. 'I'll sort Felix out. Just make sure those children are safe.'

Amelia was thoroughly puzzled.

'What on earth are you talking about, Sam?' she asked. 'Safe? Of course, they're safe.'

'Yes, of course,' echoed Sam. 'I meant, well you know, you've left them alone in the kitchen. There are knives and things around . . .'

'Sam, you know perfectly well we redesigned our kitchen when the twins reached toddler age so that they couldn't reach anything that might harm them.'

'So, I do,' said Sam, smiling a rather forced sort of smile. 'I don't seem able to think straight today, that's all.'

'Yes, well, that I can understand.'

Amelia paused at the kitchen door and looked back over her shoulder.

'Look, I think we should have something to eat. You deal with Felix, it'll soon be the little ones' bedtime, and then I'll get us some supper.'

'I'm not hungry,' said Sam at once.

'Neither am I. But we must eat, we are going to need all our strength.'

'You're not wrong there,' Sam muttered.

When Amelia woke at six a.m. the following morning she found her husband had already left the house. It was a Monday morning, the start of the working week. Sam always started early and worked long hours. So this was not unusual. Or it would not have been at any other time.

But this was still only the day after the death of their daughter-in-law, and the day after learning the equally shocking news that the police were treating her death as murder. Although Amelia supposed she had to accept that Sam's behaviour was nothing if not consistent.

She tried his mobile at once. Her call went straight to voice-mail. His direct line at the council offices also went straight to voicemail. This, too, would not have been unusual on any other day. Sam was a very busy man and a very independent man with his own agenda to follow. When he was out and about running his various businesses, he rarely answered his mobile; neither did Amelia expect him to. Usually she would text him if there was something she wished to tell or ask him.

Neither of them had the time or inclination for idle chat on their mobiles. They weren't those sort of people.

But she couldn't quite believe he'd again walked out on her like that, at such a stressful time, leaving her to deal with their son, who was still sleeping off his excesses of the previous afternoon, their grandchildren, and quite possibly, further police enquiries.

Amelia did something she would not normally dream of doing. She set out to find Sam, wherever he was.

She knew that the council offices opened at nine a.m., and almost on the dot she called the switchboard, asking to speak to her husband, only to be told that he was not in his office. She then began a ring around of the family businesses, the café, Cleverdon's, the estate agency, the department store in Bideford High Street, and the office at the Westward Ho! holiday complex. Nobody had seen Sam.

Angry, and becoming increasingly more anxious, she blitzed Sam's phone with calls and texts. She even emailed, and messaged him on WhatsApp.

Finally, just before twelve noon he called back.

'What on earth's wrong?' he asked. 'You must have called a dozen times, and texted. Didn't you realize I was obviously busy? You don't usually behave like this.'

'No,' said Amelia. 'But this isn't a usual day, is it?'

'No, of course not,' said Sam, in a more reasonable tone of voice. 'I do realize that, darling. I don't understand why you have been chasing me, that's all.'

'Where have you been, Sam?' asked Amelia.

'I've been working, just like always. I've been busy. Life has to go on, you know. Somebody has to get a grip if this family is going to survive.'

'Sam, I've phoned the council, I've phoned the café, the estate agency, Westward Ho!, I have phoned every one of our businesses trying to find you. Nobody has seen you all morning. I asked at each place that they call me if you turned up there. Nobody called back. What's going on, Sam?'

'Nothing's going on, Amelia. Don't be ridiculous.'

'Well, will you tell me honestly, then, what have you been doing?'

She heard him sigh down the phone.

'Look, I had things to do, could we just leave it at that. I'm not always quite as strong as everybody thinks I am.'

'Really?' queried his wife. 'Well, you're not alone in that, Sam. So, where did you go?'

'I went for a drive.'

'For the best part of six hours?'

'No. I stopped. Parked up. I'm sorry, darling. I was just trying to get my head around everything. I'm having difficulty coping.'

Amelia felt most uneasy. This really wasn't her Sam. Did he really say he was having difficulty coping? This was a man who always coped. Coping was what Sam Ferguson was best at.

'Just come home, Sam,' she said, her voice displaying more emotion than she would normally reveal to anyone. 'Your family needs you. I need you. Together we will cope. Just come home.'

NINETEEN

In Instow Anne Barham woke at seven a.m., almost exactly an hour after Amelia Ferguson. At first she felt better than she had at any stage since discovering her neighbour's body. She had slept well. She felt rested, as if she might be beginning to recover. Just a little.

She reached out with one languid hand for Gerry. He was no longer in bed beside her. She was mildly surprised, because he rarely rose before her now that he was retired, but it was another glorious morning. The sun was shining through the windows. Yesterday's storm had passed over during the night. She propped herself on one elbow and listened to see if she could hear him moving around the house. There was no sound except the tick of the bedroom clock and the occasional drip of the tap in the en-suite bathroom, which they really must get fixed. Gerry, like her, was a keen gardener, but he was no handyman. He had probably made tea and gone out into the garden for a potter. More than likely he would soon bring her up a cup.

Once Gerry had finally arrived home the previous day he had been profusely apologetic and promised Anne his full attention for the rest of the evening. A promise he had delivered absolutely. He'd prepared supper, scrambled egg and smoked salmon, one of her favourites. Then they had sat together on the sofa watching an old movie. They hadn't talked about Jane Ferguson and her terrible death. They hadn't needed to. Gerry and Anne were good at companionable silence, and in Anne's opinion they almost always knew what each other was thinking, anyway. Although she hadn't been entirely sure of that yesterday afternoon.

By bedtime she had not only forgiven her husband for worrying her so, but made herself at least begin to forget all about it. She was just as determined to forget the terrible scene she had been confronted with at number eleven. And Gerry, who by then really had seemed like her Gerry again, had come up to bed only ten minutes or so after her, although she did think she had heard him on the phone again. And for her to be able to do that from upstairs, when he was in his study, meant that his voice must have been raised considerably. Which in itself was unusual for Gerry.

She hadn't asked him about it though. She hadn't wanted to risk upsetting him again. She just wanted things to get back to normal. And, after all, she trusted him, didn't she?

Anne still felt deliciously sleepy. She thought she would give herself another ten minutes or so. In fact, she drifted off into a deep sleep again and did not wake for well over an hour.

When she did wake, she sat up in bed at once. This time completely without her feeling of renewed wellbeing. The clock on the wall told her that it was eight thirty-five a.m. There was no cup of tea on her bedside table. And when Gerry was up first he always brought her a cuppa. She was also surprised he hadn't woken her. He knew it made her feel rotten if she lay in for too long.

She got out of bed, pulled her dressing gown over her shoulders, and trotted downstairs, calling out Gerry's name as she did so. There was no reply.

Could he perhaps still be in the garden? The conservatory off the hall afforded a pretty good view of most of their little plot. She could see no sign of him, nor of the gardening paraphernalia, from wheelbarrow to spade and fork, which he was inclined to leave all over the place when he was at work.

She opened the garden door and called out. Still no reply. Where could he be? Feeling distinctly anxious again she headed for the kitchen. There was a note on the kitchen table.

'Just popped out for a walk, darling. You were sleeping so

peacefully I didn't want to wake you. I'll do a bit of shopping and pick us up something nice for dinner tonight. Gx.'

Anne reached for her mobile phone at once and tried to call her husband. The call went straight to voicemail.

For God's sake, not again, she thought, as she left a brief, somewhat curt, message asking him to call her back.

Half an hour or so passed during which she tried his number twice more, each time getting no response.

She made tea for herself and took it into the conservatory, all the while keeping her phone close by. Her anxiety was growing. Where was he and what was he doing?

She went upstairs, showered, and dressed. There was still no word from Gerry.

She tried telling herself she was worrying unnecessarily. He could be somewhere without a mobile signal, particularly if he were walking along the cliffs. He could have run out of battery. He'd done that before. The worst-case scenario, surely, was a repeat of the previous day, when he had just wanted to be alone and get away from everything and everybody. Including his wife. She hadn't liked it yesterday. She didn't like it today. But was it really so difficult to understand? Perhaps she just had to accept that Gerry had been much more deeply affected by what had happened than he'd let on. Possibly more affected than her. She told herself she should not bother him anymore, that she should leave him to get over it all in his own way. Meanwhile she should concentrate on keeping herself occupied, mentally and physically. And that, she determined, was exactly what she would do.

She hadn't even made the bed. She did so, tidied the bedroom, and cleaned and tidied the bathroom. Then she went downstairs into the kitchen where she emptied the dishwasher and scrubbed and polished the white stone worktop until it shone like opaque glass.

Finally she heard the little bleep from her phone which indicated that she'd been sent a text. The time was eleven forty-seven a.m. The text was from Gerry:

> Just to let you know, it's such a lovely morning, I thought
> I'd take the boat out for a bit. Take my mind off everything.
> Gx

Anne was both surprised and alarmed. Gerry had bought his small second-hand, two-berth motor cruiser soon after they'd moved to the North Devon coast from their previous home in the London suburbs, not far from where their daughter and son-in-law still lived. He'd said that he wanted to feel as if he were really part of the seaside community of Instow. And he liked the idea of joining the yacht club.

But it had proved to be pretty much the fad Anne had suspected it might be. Gerry barely used the boat. Virtually never, in fact, except when Ralph and Angela visited. Ralph had learned to sail as a boy, and although rather scathing about Gerry's motorized 'gin cottage' as he called it, enjoyed trips around the estuary when the weather and the tides were right.

So why would Gerry want to take the boat out today? Why on earth today?

Anne glanced anxiously out of the window at the sky. The sun was still shining intermittently, and it had indeed been a glorious morning. But there were definite signs that this was not going to last and that once again some pretty grim weather was blowing in from the Atlantic.

She checked the weather forecast on her phone, the hourly regional BBC one. To her horror she saw that heavy rain and high winds were forecast for early afternoon, and there was a coastal storm warning off Bideford Bay.

Gerry's little boat, with its planing hull and big but single outboard motor, was only really seaworthy in perfect conditions. Certainly, with a sailor as inexperienced as Gerry at the helm. As far as Anne knew he hadn't taken it out at all that year, although she was aware that he'd arranged for it to be moved from winter storage to its river mooring, and she wasn't sure if he had ever before taken the boat out on his own. She wondered when the outboard had last been serviced. Maybe it wouldn't start. That, she thought, would be the best result. What on earth was Gerry thinking of? This was a kind of madness.

She picked up her phone again and once more tried to call him. Once more she got only voicemail.

She left a message: 'Gerry, have you not seen the weather coming in? The forecast is terrible. Please don't take the boat out. Just come home, will you? I know you are still upset. We both are. I think we need to talk properly about what's happened. Just come home.'

A few minutes later she received a second text:

> Sorry. Already aboard. Signal bad. Don't worry. I shan't be
> long Gx.

Anne didn't like it, she didn't like it at all. But she told herself the best thing she could do was to keep as calm as possible and continue to busy herself about the house. Gerry hated being fussed over. Particularly by his wife. All the while she kept her eye on the weather, both through the windows, and on the BBC weather app. By two o'clock the gentle sea breeze of earlier was approaching gale force. Rain was falling heavily, and the sky was leaden. The BBC was now predicting a force nine gale with coastal winds in excess of fifty miles per hour. And there had been no further contact from Gerry.

Anne could not wait any longer. First she phoned the yacht club. The barman answered. No, Gerry wasn't in the bar, and he hadn't seen him all morning. He had no idea whether or not Gerry had taken his boat out. He would see if he could get somebody to find out and call her back.

Anne paced the floors waiting to hear. She was quite sure now that something terrible had happened to Gerry. What other explanation could there be? Just as she was going to call the club again, her phone rang.

'Hello, Mrs Barham,' said a voice she did not recognize. 'I'm Sid Merton, mate of Gerry's at the yacht club. I'm the chef at The Boathouse, on the front. When I arrived at work about seven thirty this morning, I saw him heading out towards the estuary. I didn't think much of it. I thought he was just taking an early turn while the weather was good. But we've checked, and the boat isn't back. No sign of Gerry either. I don't want to worry you, Mrs Barham, but we've already phoned the coastguard and the RNLI. He shouldn't be on the water in that vessel of his in this weather.'

Anne could hardly believe what she was hearing.

'Are you sure you saw Gerry?' she asked lamely.

'Oh yes, Mrs Barham, I'm really sorry to be giving you such

disturbing news, but it was Gerry all right. I know the boat. And we waved to each other. Look, try not to worry. He may have put in somewhere, and be riding out the storm. We'll be in touch as soon as we hear anything.'

She ended the call and took another look out of the window. The wind was howling now.

Could Gerry really be at sea in his little boat in this weather? It made no sense. And if Sid Merton was correct in what he said he'd seen – and Anne had little doubt that he was, he said they'd waved to each other, for goodness sake – Gerry had been aboard his boat for at least seven hours. He must have left the house far earlier than she'd thought, probably before six, and had surely already decided that he was taking his boat out.

As for putting in somewhere to ride out the storm, well, Anne knew even less about boats and sailing than her husband did, but she had learned a little about the coast where they lived. There wasn't anywhere to put in once a vessel had left the estuary of the Torridge and the Tor. Not within range of Gerry's boat, that was for sure. Which led Anne onto yet another frightening train of thought. The boat would surely have run out of fuel by now. In fact, probably some time ago.

Anne started to weep. What was happening? she wondered. Until the night before last she and her husband had been living happily in quiet retirement in a beautiful part of the world. Then came the shock of finding the body of a neighbour who had died in the most awful way. And already their lives seemed to have been turned upside down.

Now Gerry was missing. There seemed little doubt about that. He could be in trouble. He could have drowned. Gerry could be dead.

Anne was distraught. She didn't know what to do or who to turn to.

TWENTY

Earlier that day Saslow and Vogel had arrived at Bideford police station to find the place heaving. Nobby's Major Crimes Team was still in the process of setting up the incident room.

The forbidding red-brick building, built on higher ground opposite and above the river, has been closed to the public for years, but local CID and uniform still operate on a day-to-day basis behind its closed doors. The only access road is a steep ramp leading up from New Road, and parking is limited. In addition to MCT, extra officers from other stations in the region had been brought in to form a suitably sized team for a murder investigation.

Everyone was squashed into a station ill-equipped for the scale of the operation now underway, as is all too often the case with murder investigations deemed to require a Major Incident Room away from base.

The office manager's job was not going to be an easy one. Saslow's first thought was that DI Janet Peters, the deputy SIO whom she knew Nobby had selected, had to be competent and experienced or she wouldn't have been appointed to the task. But it quickly became apparent that Janet Peters wasn't Margot Hartley. Saslow was used to working with Hartley and Vogel as deputy SIOs. Their set-up was simple, and had become comfortably familiar. Hemmings held the investigation together at the top. But Hartley held it together at ground level, as an office manager capable of solving seemingly impossible problems of manpower and logistics and making it all look easy. It was as if she never felt the stress and weariness that at some stage or other inevitably overwhelmed all the rest of them during a tough investigation. In addition, she had the enviable knack of bending people to her will without them always noticing it. At Bristol MCIT she was known as 'bloody superwoman', by the mere mortals around her, sometimes in exasperation, but invariably in admiration.

It quickly became apparent to Saslow that DI Janet Peters had probably never even heard of superwoman.

As she and Vogel walked into the station lobby they were immediately confronted by the spectacle of a mildly dishevelled looking woman locked in a loud argument with a tall red-headed man whose temper seemed to be in keeping with that traditionally attributed to people of his hair colour. Both were in plain clothes.

'I need more office space for our team, Detective Sergeant Pearce, and that's that,' she demanded.

'You come in here shouting the odds, and then you expect us to cooperate,' countered the DS forcibly. 'Well, you've got another think coming, I'll tell you that.'

Saslow realized the slightly dishevelled looking woman shouting the odds must be DI Peters, even though they had yet to meet, because she could not be anyone else. And she guessed that the detective sergeant, clearly highly frustrated at the invasion of his territory, was probably the senior permanent CID officer at Bideford.

Vogel walked straight up to the quarrelling pair and introduced himself.

'Can I help?' he asked casually.

DI Peters coloured slightly. Both officers looked embarrassed.

'Just a few teething problems,' said the DI, forcing a smile. 'I'm sure we'll sort them soon.'

'I'm sure you will too,' said Vogel. 'And I'll let you get on with it. DS Saslow and I just need a corner where we can get ourselves up to speed and check through all the data that's been accumulated so far.'

'Of course, I'll see to it, just give me a moment,' said the DI, heading off into the heart of the station.

DS Pearce made as if he were about to follow her. Vogel called him back.

'Just a minute, detective sergeant,' he said, his voice conversational. 'I'd like to know who you thought you were talking to a minute ago?'

The DS didn't seem to know quite what to say.

'Umm, I don't know what you mean, sir,' he stumbled.

'Yes, you do, DS Pearce,' said Vogel, who now sounded

thoroughly steely. 'And if I ever again hear you speaking to a senior officer like that, particularly a senior officer who is a key member of my team, I will have you back in uniform in a thrice. And as a PC. Do we understand each other?'

'Uh, yes, sir, s-sorry sir,' stumbled Pearce.

'Good,' said Vogel, turning his back on the man and addressing Saslow directly. 'Right, let's get stuck in then, shall we?' he said.

'You bet, boss,' responded Saslow, aware that she must sound like a schoolgirl.

Vogel had surprised her yet again, just when she'd worked with him so long and in so many varied and stressful situations that she really thought he could no longer do that. She had yet to hear him ever pull rank on his own behalf. He was the kind of man who didn't need to. And she'd never before heard him pull rank on anyone else's behalf either. It had been a salutary experience.

She was just glad she hadn't been on the receiving end.

Just before noon a young DC, with a mop of very black hair and a thin pale face rather well suited to his worried expression, which somehow looked as if it might be permanent, approached Vogel.

'Ricky Perkins, sir,' he said. 'There's been a development you should know about.'

Vogel glanced up from his laptop.

'Go on,' he said.

'Yes, boss. Forensics have been on. They've checked out the rope Jane Ferguson was found hanged from and it's a line off her husband's boat. Almost certainly, they say. Covered in his prints. Few others, as well, but . . .'

'But no prints from Jane Ferguson, is that what you're about to tell me?' queried Vogel.

'Absolutely right, boss, none at all, apparently.'

Vogel turned to Saslow.

'Which effectively rules out suicide once and for all, and points the finger even more at our Felix. Doesn't sort out the little matter of his cast-iron alibi, though, does it?'

'Ah, but there's something else, boss,' the DC continued, sounding just a tad triumphalist. 'The team doing door-to-door in the area all around the crime scene came across this man who was out walking his dog on Saturday night.'

Perkins looked down at his notebook.

'A John Willis. He saw Felix turning into Estuary Vista Close just after ten thirty p.m.—'

'He did what?' interrupted Vogel, who felt as if an electric shock had just passed through his body. 'Is he sure of that?'

'Apparently so, boss.'

'Did he speak to Felix?'

'No. He said he was on the other side of the road and seemed to be in a hurry, walking fast, looking straight ahead. But he knows Felix quite well by sight, lives just up the hill.'

'It would have been dark, though, and there's no street lighting in Estuary Vista Close.'

'Not in the close itself, but there are lights on the road it turns off. New Road it's called. And it was there that this Willis saw him. On the corner.'

'And is Mr Willis also sure of the time?'

'Yes, boss, says he always takes his dog out for a few minutes at half past ten, just before going to bed. And the team who talked to him said he seemed a reliable sort, too.'

Vogel looked at Saslow.

'Well, that little lot seems to point to our principle person of interest right enough, doesn't it, Dawn?' he began.

Then his mobile rang. Vogel glanced at the screen before answering.

'Yes, Nobby,' he said. 'I think I know why you're calling.'

'You've heard about the latest forensics report and the new witness, I presume?'

For once the detective super clearly had no time for banter or small talk.

'Indeed I have,' said Vogel.

'Right. So what are you planning to do about it?'

'Well, I've not really had time to formulate a plan yet,' admitted Vogel. 'But I definitely think, first off, Saslow and I should now interview Felix Ferguson formally.'

There was a brief pause at the other end of the line.

'You need to do a bit more than that, Vogel,' responded Clarke eventually. 'I want Ferguson arrested on suspicion of the murder of his wife. Straight away.'

'You do?'

Vogel was not entirely surprised, all the evidence pointed that way, and it was pretty much the result he had expected when first on the case. Or it would have been had it not been for Nobby Clarke herself suggesting that there could be some sort of mysterious conspiracy, and putting all kinds of doubts in his mind.

He moved away from DC Perkins and Saslow, turning his back on them and lowering his voice. He didn't want Perkins to overhear the next part of his conversation with Clarke.

'I thought you didn't believe this was a standard domestic, Nobby,' he said. 'I thought that was why you had Saslow and me drafted in, to delve deeper.'

'That's quite right, Vogel, but I do believe in evidence, and it's pretty hard to argue against the weight of evidence we now have.'

'You're under pressure to do this, aren't you, boss?' Vogel whispered into the phone. He didn't even want Saslow to hear him saying that.

'Of course, I'm under bloody pressure, Vogel,' responded Clarke vigorously. 'The brass want this all sorted ASAP. I told you that yesterday. And if I hadn't told you what I did yesterday, this morning's new information – the forensics report and a witness placing a prime suspect at the scene of the crime at the right time – would have led you to arrest Ferguson without any hesitation at all, wouldn't it?'

'I suppose it would, boss, yes,' Vogel admitted reluctantly.

'Yes, and the suspect is the husband of the victim, which we would normally regard as the clincher, would we not?'

'Yes, boss,' agreed Vogel.

'So bloody get on with it then. Arrest the bloody man.'

'Yes, boss,' said Vogel again.

'For God's sake, Vogel, you know I can't stand you calling me "boss". And it's particularly damned annoying because I know perfectly well you always do it when you're pissed off with me.'

'Sorry, boss,' said Vogel.

Vogel and Saslow reached the Ferguson home in Bay View Road just before one p.m. The DCI was confident that Felix Ferguson would still be there. Where else would he be? He had two children, and his home was still a crime scene. And unlike his father he wasn't the sort who would rush back to work regardless.

Vogel was about to make an arrest for an extremely serious crime. The most serious of all. Murder. So he'd brought DC Perkins along, and the three detectives were accompanied by four uniformed officers travelling at considerable speed in two patrol cars, which were rather dramatically pulled to a halt with a screech of brakes and a squeal of tyre rubber outside All Seasons.

Vogel knocked on the door considerably more loudly and aggressively than he would if he were making a routine call.

Mrs Ferguson senior answered the door at once. Vogel suspected she had already been alerted by the commotion of the patrol cars outside.

'Is your son at home, Mrs Ferguson?' he demanded, at the same time pushing past her into the house without waiting to be invited in. This was an arrest. He didn't think Felix Ferguson was the type to try to do a runner, but he knew better than to take any chances.

'He's in the s-sitting room,' stammered Amelia Ferguson. 'W-whatever is going on?'

Vogel didn't bother to answer. He just kept on walking. Saslow and Perkins were right behind him, closely followed by two of the uniforms. The other two remained outside the house on watch.

Vogel paused at the sitting-room door and turned back towards Amelia Ferguson. A thought had just occurred to him. He really didn't want to add to the horrors Felix and Jane's children had experienced over the last thirty-six hours.

'Are the twins with your son?' he asked.

Amelia shook her head.

'No, we sent them to school as usual, we thought that was for the best,' she said.

Vogel was relieved. Although, even in the heat of the moment, it crossed his mind that not many people would think it 'for the best' to send two six-year-olds to school on the day after they had seen their mother hanging dead with a rope around her neck.

He pushed the door open without making any comment. Felix was slumped on the big chair by the window. The TV was on and a football match filled the screen. Felix was drinking already, it seemed. He had a glass in his hand which looked as if it contained whisky.

When he saw Vogel, accompanied by his small entourage, his face took on an expression first of surprise and then of dismay.

He rose to his feet at once, still clutching the glass in his left hand, and took a couple of steps towards the police officers.

'Wh-what's going on?' he asked. 'What do you want now?'

'Felix Ferguson, I am arresting you on suspicion of the murder of your wife, Jane Ferguson,' Vogel announced.

Felix's lower jaw dropped. Other than that he barely moved a muscle.

The two uniformed officers in the room stepped forward and were quickly at Felix's side, one removing the glass and grasping Felix's left hand, the other grasping his right.

Felix let them do so without making any protest. He seemed to have been quite literally struck dumb, remaining in stunned silence as Vogel recited the formal caution.

'You do not have to say anything. But it may harm your defence if you do not mention when questioned something which you later rely on in court. Anything you do say may be given in evidence.'

However, Felix's mother made up for her son's involuntary silence.

'How dare you, how dare you arrest my boy,' she yelled. 'Are you all mad? You must all be mad.'

As the two uniforms began to lead a still unprotesting, but now whimpering, Felix from the room, Amelia lurched towards them.

'Let him go, let my boy go,' she cried hysterically, her voice at screaming pitch.

DC Perkins took a step towards her. Saslow was quicker. She half threw herself in front of Amelia, grabbing the older woman in an arm lock in order to prevent her reaching either her son or the two officers escorting him.

Felix spoke then, for the first time since his arrest.

'Just stop it, Mother,' he hissed at her. 'Stop it. You're only making matters worse. As usual.'

Amelia Ferguson had been struggling, albeit hopelessly, in Saslow's practiced grasp. She stopped at once. Her face fell.

She looked almost as if she had been hit. Then she started to weep.

Vogel gestured to the two uniforms to carry on escorting Felix from the room. In the doorway Felix looked back over his shoulder, and spoke again.

'Just look after my kids, Mum,' he said, as if, in spite of the circumstances, he was issuing an order, rather than making a request.

Amelia nodded, and mumbled something incomprehensible through her tears. She made no further attempt to obstruct proceedings. Vogel didn't like the woman, but he very nearly felt sorry for her. He could see that all the fight had gone from her. It had been bad enough for Amelia Ferguson to witness her son's arrest, but for him to speak to her in the way that he had was clearly the final blow. She looked broken. Vogel was 100 per cent sure she would cause no more trouble.

'I think you can let Mrs Ferguson go now, Saslow,' he said.

With just a small show of reluctance, Saslow did so. For a moment it almost looked as if, without the DS's support, Amelia might collapse. She reached out for a chair behind her, and leaned shakily against it.

'Are you now on your own in the house, Mrs Ferguson?' Vogel asked.

The woman nodded.

'Where's your husband?'

'I don't know,' she said.

And then, with just a touch of what Vogel already considered to be her more normal spirited attitude, added angrily, 'How the hell would I know where Sam is? I think Jane's death has done something to his head. I haven't known where he's been or what he's been up to half the time ever since . . . ever since she died. He's supposed to be on his way home now, but God knows whether he is or not.'

'Well, perhaps you should call him,' suggested Vogel. 'I don't think you should be here alone at the moment.'

He became aware then of some sort of commotion outside. Sam Ferguson burst into the room. His hair was tousled, and his jacket was hanging off one shoulder. He looked dishevelled, as if he had been in a tussle.

'What the hell do you think you're doing, Vogel?' he stormed.

The two uniformed officers who had been on sentry duty outside were hard on his heels.

'Sorry, boss,' said the taller and younger one. 'We tried to hold him back. He gave us the slip. Suddenly took off, like. To be honest, we didn't expect him to be that fleet on his feet . . .'

Vogel held up a hand to stem the flow.

'It's all right, PC Verity,' he said.

Then he turned to face Sam Ferguson.

'I have arrested your son, Mr Ferguson,' Vogel told him, 'on suspicion of the murder of his wife. And if you don't calm down and behave yourself, I shall probably arrest you too.'

'I am calm,' replied Ferguson, with the slightly manic certainty of someone who was anything but. 'I just want to know why you are arresting my son, and why I wasn't told. I should have been told.'

'We are not in the habit of announcing in advance an impending arrest—' Vogel began, only to be interrupted by a clearly still angry Amelia.

'Nobody could tell you anything today, Sam, because nobody knew where the heck you were,' she said edgily. 'What were you doing, Sam?'

Sam stared at his wife, then glanced towards Vogel, and back again.

'I was working, Amelia, like I always am, I told you that, you knew that,' he said pointedly. 'And I hope you told the police that.'

'No, I didn't, Sam, because it's not true. You admitted that on the phone. Things to do, you said. You were gone for six damned hours, the day after . . . after . . . that dreadful thing happened. And I have no idea where you were, do I? I know where you should have been. Here, with your family. You may even have been able to stop this . . . this . . . ridiculous arrest . . .'

Vogel had no time for this. It was turning into a domestic which did not seem to be of any interest to him. Perhaps Sam Ferguson was having an affair. Vogel didn't care. Felix would be taken to the nearest police station with a custody suite and holding cells, which was Barnstaple, eight or nine miles away. Vogel wanted to get there himself as fast as possible in order to begin the interviewing process whilst the young man was still reeling from the shock of his arrest.

'Mrs Ferguson, the arrest of your son is a police matter over which your husband could not possibly have any control,' he interjected. 'However, I am glad that Mr Ferguson has now returned, and hopefully you will be able to give each other some mutual support. We will keep you informed on further developments.'

TWENTY-ONE

Ultimately Vogel and Saslow began the first formal interview with Felix Ferguson just over an hour after his arrest. DC Perkins was charged with the task of liaising with DI Peters in the Major Incident Room at Bideford in case of any further developments.

Felix had volunteered nothing on the journey from Northam, nor whilst he had been processed through the custody suite, not as lengthy a process as usual as his fingerprints had already been taken and DNA extracted, as a matter of routine, for the purposes of elimination if nothing more. But he appeared, to Vogel's relief, to be reasonably sober and perfectly lucid, in spite of having clearly already started drinking before his arrest. Vogel had on more than one occasion been forced to attempt to conduct interviews with subjects under the influence of drink and drugs. It was not normally a successful process.

Felix turned down the opportunity of having a solicitor present, which allowed the interview to proceed more quickly than might otherwise have been the case.

'I don't need a solicitor because I didn't do it,' he said.

Vogel ensured that the video equipment was activated, and recited the names of those present and the time and date, as is standard.

For just a few seconds he studied the man sitting opposite him across the simple table. As always, he asked himself if he really thought this was a human being capable of taking the life of another; not a scientific approach, but something he could never help doing.

In this case his gut instinct told him that Felix Ferguson was probably not a murderer. But there was now significant evidence to the contrary, which couldn't be ignored. Also, everything about Felix, from his appearance through to his behaviour since his wife was killed, suggested that he was a weak man. And Vogel's many years of police experience had taught him that weak people were inclined to be the most dangerous.

'Mr Ferguson, we have arrested you on suspicion of the murder of your wife because, since we last spoke to you, fresh evidence has come to our attention which incriminates you,' said Vogel stiffly. 'Do you understand?'

Felix nodded.

'I understand. But I don't know what this evidence can be, because I'm innocent. I didn't kill my wife. I loved my wife.'

'Well, let me explain.'

Vogel glanced towards the uniformed woman constable standing by the door.

'Could you bring in the evidence bag, please,' he asked.

The PC was gone for less than a minute during which nobody spoke in the small interview room. When she returned she was dragging behind her a large clear plastic evidence bag and its clearly heavy contents.

'Do you recognize the contents of this bag?' asked Vogel.

Felix leaned towards the bag.

'Well, it's a rope, probably a boat line.'

He paused.

'Oh my God, is that the rope which hanged Jane?'

'Yes, it is, Mr Ferguson. And you were also correct when you said that it is a rope which has been used as a line on a boat. Do you recognize it?'

'Recognize it? What do you mean. One boat line is pretty much like another. It looks like it's quite new, hasn't been used a lot. There's no fraying . . .'

He stopped in his tracks.

'I had new lines fitted to the *Stevie-Jo* this season. Are you saying that is my rope?'

'We have reason to believe so, Mr Ferguson. The rope is covered in your fingerprints.'

'Well, that's absurd nonsense,' blustered Felix.

'I'm afraid it's the truth.'

'Well, someone must have taken it off the boat. You can't make them secure, you know. Not on a river mooring.'

'When did you last take your boat out?'

'About a week ago.'

'And did you notice anything missing then?'

'Well no, but if someone had nicked a line, I wouldn't necessarily. There's one at the stern and two aft, port and starboard, and I keep another couple in a locker. There's no key or anything. Anyway, I suppose it could have been taken after that.'

'So, you didn't remove that line from your boat yourself, and take it to your home?'

'No, of course I didn't. Why on earth would I?'

It was apparent that Felix was not thinking clearly, or he wouldn't have needed to ask that question. Vogel did not wish to state the obvious. Nor to lead the interviewee. He made no response.

'Oh, for God's sake,' continued Felix, as grim realisation slowly dawned. 'You think I took the rope home in order to use it to hang my Jane, don't you? Well it's nonsense, I tell you. I still believe she committed suicide. I've always believed that. Look, it makes sense. If she was planning to hang herself, she would certainly know where to find a suitable rope. On my boat. It's obvious, isn't it?'

'I'm afraid not, Mr Ferguson. There are other fingerprints on the rope, which we would expect to have been handled by people other than yourself, people who may have crewed for you presumably, or the chandler you bought it from, and we are currently running the appropriate tests.'

He took a sip from the glass of water before him, hoping to increase the dramatic effect of what he was about to say by making Felix wait.

'There was one set of fingerprints highly significant in their absence. Your wife's, Mr Ferguson. There was not a single fingerprint from Jane. And she most certainly was not wearing gloves when her body was found!'

'Oh, my God,' said Felix again.

'Indeed. Therefore, your wife had never touched that rope. So, could you explain to me, please, how she could have used it to hang herself?'

'I can't. I just know I didn't do anything to her. I wouldn't. I couldn't. I mean – I wouldn't even know how to go about it.'

In different circumstances, and if it wasn't for the weight of evidence, and the lack of any other suspects, Vogel would have been inclined to believe Felix. How many people would know how to set about hanging another human being, in the way that Jane Ferguson had been hanged, and be physically able to do it. Felix was a tall man and looked strong enough. But there was a tad more to it than that. And in this case, it seemed almost certain that the victim had been strangled even before the rope was put around her neck. Something rather easier said than done, unless the victim had been knocked unconscious first of course.

'All right, Mr Ferguson, let's move on. You told us you were at the yacht club on the night your wife was killed, is that not so?'

'Yes, I was. Everyone will vouch for me. Ronnie. Any of the other members. Of course, I was there.'

'All night?'

'Yes. Until nearly three in the morning. But you know this.'

'I'm afraid not, Mr Ferguson. A witness has come forward who can place you near your house, near the scene of the crime, at around the time your wife died. Can you explain that, please?'

'What? No. That's not true. I was at the club all night. Whoever's said that has got it wrong. Made a mistake. That must be it.'

Vogel told Felix about John Willis the dog walker, and how sure he had been, both of seeing Felix and the time that he did so.

Felix didn't respond at first.

'Look, Mr Ferguson, John Willis is a neighbour of yours, he knows you,' persisted Vogel. 'He could even accurately describe what you were wearing. A dinner suit. And I presume you know him, do you not?'

'I know who he is, yes,' muttered Felix with some reluctance.

'So, would you recognize him?'

'Yes, I suppose so . . .'

A thought seemed suddenly to strike Felix.

'But it's dark at ten thirty, pitch black in the close, the houses are set too far back for their lights to shine into the street,' he said, sounding suddenly hopeful. 'How could John Willis have recognized me, or anyone else, for that matter?'

Vogel explained exactly where Felix had been when John Willis said that he had seen him.

'There's street lighting there, as you know,' he pointed out.

'I-it's not very good lighting though,' stumbled Felix, not even sounding as if he was convincing himself.

'Good enough for Mr Willis to be able to see what you were wearing,' the DCI remarked levelly.

'W-well, I just can't explain it, that's all, it d-doesn't make any sense . . .'

'I think it does, Mr Ferguson, and I think you can explain it perfectly well if you choose too,' interjected Vogel. 'Come on. What were you doing returning to your home in the middle of a dinner in your honour? Were you going back to kill your wife? Is that what you were doing?'

'No, no, it wasn't.'

For the first time Ferguson raised his voice, and Vogel could see desperation in his eyes. The DCI continued to apply all the pressure he could muster.

'I think you were,' he persisted. 'And I think you planned it all along. I think you slipped away from the dinner at the yacht club, which gave you an apparently cast-iron alibi, went home, strangled your wife and then did your best to make it look as if she had committed suicide. That's what you did, isn't it?'

'No. It isn't. Really it isn't. I didn't touch Jane. She was alive when I left, when I went back to the club. I swear it.'

Vogel felt the familiar frisson of excitement run down his spine. Was this it? Was this the breakthrough he had been seeking?

'She was alive when you left?' he queried. 'So are you now admitting that you returned to your home on the night of your wife's death whilst she was still alive, at around the time our witness reported?'

Felix nodded. Then he lowered his head into his hands.

'Mr Ferguson, don't you the think it's time you started telling us the truth?'

Felix raised his head and nodded again. Almost imperceptibly.

'OK, so can you first of all tell me what time you left the club in order to return to your home?' Vogel continued.

'Well, y-yes, I suppose so,' Felix responded hesitantly. 'Uh, the speeches, the awards and all the formal stuff, ended about a quarter past ten, I think, and I slipped away just after, when everyone was using the toilets, that sort of thing, or making their way to the bar, when I thought I probably wouldn't be missed. Most people had had a few drinks by then, too . . .'

'I see, and how long were you gone?'

'Oh, I don't know, it's a good ten-minute walk, about thirty-five minutes, I suppose, I'm not sure.'

'So how long were you in your house with Jane?'

'No more than fifteen minutes, I'm certain of it. Maybe a minute or two less. Not nearly long enough to kill someone and string them up over the bannisters, for God's sake. Even if I'd wanted to, which, you have to believe me, Mr Vogel, I didn't. It had never crossed my mind to harm Jane, and never would have done.'

'All right, Mr Ferguson, so why did you return to your home in the middle of this so important dinner?'

'I, uh, wanted to make sure that Jane and the twins were all right. That's all.'

'Did you have some reason to think they wouldn't be all right?'

'No. No. Of course not. I just wanted to check.'

'Couldn't you have done that by phone? And, indeed, if your wife had any sort of problem, wouldn't she have phoned you?'

'Well, yes, I suppose so. But, um, I'm a worrier . . .'

'You don't look like the sort of man who worries unnecessarily,' commented Vogel.

'Maybe not, but appearances can be deceptive, Mr Vogel. I have always worried about Jane. She was . . . could be, fragile. I told you about her dreams.'

'Yes.'

'Well, she'd been going through a bad patch. I hadn't left her alone with the children for weeks. Not in the evening, I mean. She urged me to go to the commodore's dinner, said it was my dinner, and I really shouldn't miss it on her account. That she would be fine. But I knew how tired she was. She was worn out. I just wanted to see with my own eyes that everything was all right.'

'Mr Ferguson, you just said you hadn't left your wife alone

with the children for weeks. Were you worried that she might not look after them properly, or even harm them?'

'No, certainly not.'

Felix answered quickly. Vogel wasn't quite sure whether he was looking directly at him or not. Because of the other man's slightly wonky eye it was sometimes difficult to tell. He thought he saw a flicker of something he could not quite define in Felix's facial expression. Nervousness perhaps? Fear even? Or just distress?

'I still see no reason why you couldn't merely have phoned your wife,' Vogel continued. 'I don't understand why you felt it necessary to rush home.'

'I didn't rush,' replied Felix pedantically. 'You never knew Jane. She would have fibbed. She would have told me she was all right, even if she wasn't. I told you. I needed to see for myself.'

'All right, so you say you were in your house with Jane for about fifteen minutes. What did you do during that time?'

'Do? Well, I asked her how she was. She said she was fine and wanted to know what I was doing there. She said I had nothing to worry about. The children were in bed, sound asleep. But she would stay up until I got home.'

'Why wouldn't she go to bed?'

'Well, she didn't want to have a bad dream without me there to comfort her. Neither of us wanted that.'

'And so, after about fifteen minutes you headed back for the club.'

'Yes.'

'Did you meet anyone on the way, see anyone at all?'

'No. I don't think so. There was nobody about on the hill, I don't think. I crossed the main road and then cut through Bridge Lane to get down to the parade, like I always do. There may have been cars on the main drag, I didn't see anyone on foot though. But then, I didn't see John Willis and his bloody dog on the way up, either.'

'And it seems likely that nobody at the dinner noticed your return, because nobody had been aware of you leaving. Is that what you believed to be the case?'

'I don't know, do I, you'd have to ask them.'

'We are doing so, I can assure you, Mr Ferguson, but so far
we have drawn a complete blank.'

'Well,' said Fergus, sounding a tad desperate, 'if nobody
noticed that I was gone, doesn't that indicate that I wasn't gone
for very long, not nearly long enough to commit murder and
then try to cover it up?'

'The trouble is it seems that very few of your fellow members
were likely to have been sober enough to notice.'

'I was sober,' remarked Felix obliquely.

'Yes, indeed, you were, in spite of the fact that, by your own
admission, you have been drinking heavily lately.'

'I had a speech to make, I always watch my drinking before I
have to make a speech. And I wanted to nip home. So I kept sober.'

'That doesn't really help your case, Mr Ferguson,' remarked
Vogel. 'Neither does the fact that upon your return to the club
you drank so much that by the time you returned home for the
second time, at three o'clock in the morning, you were so drunk
you couldn't walk straight, and were promptly sick over my
crime scene. Now you tell me, would you have behaved like that
if you were still worried about your wife and children? Indeed,
would you have behaved like that if you hadn't known that your
wife was already dead?'

Felix lowered his head into his hands again. Vogel waited
patiently. Eventually Felix straightened up. His face was ashen.

'I can see how it looks,' he said. 'But it wasn't like that.
Honestly it wasn't. Jane had seemed so positive about everything,
so in control of it all, and she insisted that I go back and enjoy
myself. As I had hoped she would, I suppose. I'd never intended
to stay home, if I could possibly avoid it. I'd been enjoying
myself too much. And, to tell the truth, I wanted a proper drink.
I, well, I suppose I have been developing a bit of a drink problem
lately. Jane did point it out once or twice, but I always turned it
around on her, told her that if it wasn't for her and her damned
stupid dreams I wouldn't need to drink. Not very nice, Mr Vogel,
but then drunks aren't very nice, are they? And most of us take
a damned long time and have to sink pretty low before we admit
that we are drunks. You know what, I think this is the first time
I've ever admitted it. But you don't sink much lower than being
arrested for murdering your wife, do you?'

Felix gave a short bitter laugh.

Vogel decided to ignore the confession of habitual drunkenness, for the moment.

Instead he merely said, 'You haven't explained why, if you were so worried about Jane, and her bad dreams, you then stayed out until three a.m., have you, Mr Ferguson?'

'Yes, I have actually,' replied Felix. 'When I get drunk I do the job properly, you see. Sober, I am a responsible and loving father and husband. And yes, I do worry about my family. Drunk, I barely remember I have a wife and children. And that's what happened on Saturday night. I went back to the club, relieved that Jane and the twins seemed fine, found myself some drinking mates, and got stuck in. I was out of my skull, Mr Vogel, and I think your officers would vouch for that. I didn't have any idea how long I'd been drinking for. I didn't have a clue it was three o'clock in the morning, and I wouldn't have given a damn if I had known. That is the gospel truth, Mr Vogel.'

'I see,' responded Vogel. 'So why didn't you tell us before about your little trip home in the middle of the club dinner?'

'Would you, if your wife was found dead in suspicious circumstances? Everybody knows the spouse or the partner is always the first suspect.'

'You lied to a police officer, Mr Ferguson, which is a very serious matter under any circumstances. And you told us you were convinced your wife had taken her own life. If that was the case why would you feel the need to lie?'

'Look, when I got back from the club and those officers told me Jane had been found hanged, of course I thought it was suicide. In fact, I could swear they told me it was suicide. But I was drunk. Very drunk. When you came round, well, it was only six or seven hours later, wasn't it? I was probably still drunk. And Mum had given me that damned stupid sleeping pill. I can't believe she gave it to me considering the condition I was in. And I can't believe I took it either. As soon as you said Jane's death was being treated as suspicious, I thought, they're probably going to think I did it. And if I tell them that I went home, left the dinner and went home, around the time she must have died, they are definitely going to think I did it.'

Vogel had to admit there was some truth in that.

'Didn't it occur to you that lying to the police was a highly dangerous thing to do? That sooner or later you would be found out.'

'I told you, Mr Vogel, I wasn't thinking straight. Then when my head cleared a bit, well, I'd already done it, hadn't I? In any case, I honestly thought the only person who knew that I'd gone home was my poor Jane. And she was dead. So, I had the alibi I knew I needed. I would have been right too, wouldn't I? If it hadn't been for bloody John Willis walking his bloody dog.'

'There is almost always a John Willis,' remarked Vogel mildly. 'That is why every year the police solve between seventy-five and ninety per cent of murders across the country.'

'Look, Mr Vogel,' Ferguson continued almost as if Vogel hadn't spoken. 'You have to believe me, I didn't kill my wife.'

'The thing is, Felix, if you didn't kill Jane, then someone else certainly did, and they did so within a very tight timescale – between just before eleven p.m. when you say you left your house to return to the club, and just before one a.m. when the Barhams returned and found Joanna out in the road. Now how likely is that?'

Felix looked down at the table.

'It doesn't sound likely at all, I know that,' he replied quietly. 'But I promise you I'm telling you the truth now.'

'All right, let's say for the moment that I accept that. When you went home did you see or hear anything out of the ordinary at all? Did you see anyone hanging around outside your home for instance? In your garden even? Or think you did?'

Felix shook his head.

'No, nothing. Certainly not in the garden. The lights at the front of the house go on automatically as you approach. I used the torch on my phone to make my way along the pavement, like I always do, so I was shining it in front of me, and looking down, I suppose. Even if there had been anyone there, I doubt I'd have seen them. I was just concentrating on getting home as quickly as I could, making sure everything was all right, and then getting back to the do.'

Felix sat back in his chair, letting his head fall backwards in a gesture of exasperation.

'I didn't even see John Willis, for goodness sake,' he said again.

'So, there was nothing that gave you any cause for concern, nothing at all that wasn't quite as it should be?'

'No. Nothing . . .'

Ferguson paused abruptly, raising one hand to his mouth, frowning in concentration.

'Well, there was just one thing, our gate at the end of the driveway is electric and operated by a remote control, as you know. You can use a key to open and shut it, but we keep it locked all the time because of the children. Well, when I went back to the house I noticed that the gate wasn't closed properly, it was very slightly ajar. Certainly not locked.'

'And you'd locked it when you'd left to go to the club? Are you sure?'

'Well, yes. Or I certainly thought I had. I pointed the gizmo at it as soon as I'd gone through, like I always do. It's happened before that it's got stuck, usually if there's been something jamming it, a stone or something. But not very often.'

'And you assumed you'd been the last person through the gate?'

'Yes. Of course.'

'Did you ask your wife if she had opened the gate for some reason?'

'No. I mean, she wouldn't have done. Anyway, I didn't think much of it. Not at the time. Just reckoned it was one of those things . . .'

'When you left the second time to return to the club, did you lock the gates again?'

'Of course, I did. And I looked around to see if there was any obvious obstruction. There wasn't. They seemed to close OK.'

'Are you aware that when Anne Barham took Joanna back to your house and found Jane's body, the security gate was open and the front door was ajar?'

'Uh, no, I don't think I was.'

'Also, there was no sign of a break-in. That indicates that it is reasonable to assume that anyone who entered your house had a set of keys, don't you agree?'

'I suppose so, yes.'

'And who has keys to your house, apart from you and your wife?'

'My parents.'

'Nobody else?'

'No.'

'Well, your parents have alibied each other. But, in any case, I don't expect you think either of them killed Jane, do you, Felix?'

'No, I don't. Of course not.'

'You see, then, that there really is nobody else in the frame. I must warn you, Mr Ferguson, I am now on the verge of formally charging you.'

'Do what you like,' said Felix in a resigned sort of way.

TWENTY-TWO

It seemed to Amelia Ferguson that her entire life had fallen apart. The daughter-in-law she'd never liked had died a horrible violent death. Her beloved only son had been arrested for her murder. And the husband who had always been her rock was behaving more like a piece of drifting flotsam.

She stood for a moment in the doorway of her home, watching the little convoy of police cars disappear up Bay View Road. Two or three neighbours had stepped out of their houses to see what was going on. Amelia was the sort of woman who put considerable importance on appearances, and would normally have been horrified to think that her neighbours had seen the police take her son away in a squad car.

Today she did not even notice.

Sam was standing right behind her. She turned to him, looking for, and still half expecting, the comfort and support he had always given her.

She took a step towards him, reaching out to him. He just turned around and walked back into the house. She knew he must be in shock, as she was. But ever since the previous afternoon he had been behaving so strangely.

She followed him slowly indoors, aware that tears were falling down her cheeks, and into the kitchen. Sam was over by the window, with his back to her, and seemed to be gazing out to sea. Then she noticed his shoulders start to heave. He, too, was weeping.

She went to him at once. And to her immense relief he wrapped his arms around her. For a little while they clung to each other in silence.

'Oh Melia, Melia,' he eventually whispered through his tears. 'What is happening to us? I thought we had everything. Suddenly we have nothing. Nothing at all.'

'I know, I know,' she murmured as soothingly as she could manage. 'But we will get through it, won't we? We can get through everything as long as we have each other. And we know Felix is innocent, we know that, don't we?'

'Of course, of course.'

Amelia stood back from him then.

'Come on, Sam,' she said. 'You are always the strong one. You always know what to do. We have to help our boy.'

Sam wiped the tears from his eyes with one trembling hand.

'You're right, of course, you're right,' he said. 'Look, first thing, we must get Felix a solicitor. Trevor Hardwick is the best round here. I'll get on to him straight away.'

'That's better, Sam,' said Amelia. 'You see, you always know what to do, and you always know the right person to do it.'

'If anyone can get Felix home it will be Trevor,' said Sam, sounding just a little more like his old self.

Amelia thought she had read somewhere that people arrested for murder in the UK were remanded in custody as a matter of course, and only got bail in very rare and exceptional circumstances.

Nonetheless she tried to muster an encouraging smile.

Sam left the kitchen and made his way to his home office, telling his wife that he didn't have Trevor Hardwick's number in his phone. Which wasn't actually true. But he desperately needed time alone to think. He was aware that he should also be phoning DCI Vogel. The detective had given him his mobile number. Now that Felix had been arrested, he really should tell Vogel what he had learned from Gerry Barham the previous afternoon.

But he could not quite bring himself to do so.

He sat for a few minutes struggling to compose himself before finally phoning Hardwick.

The solicitor sounded stunned when Sam told him about his son's arrest. As well he might, thought Sam. Hardwick recovered quickly though, asked Sam a number of salient questions, and then said he would make his way at once to Barnstaple police station and offer his services to Felix.

Sam thanked him and ended the call. He supposed Hardwick was bound by some kind of code of confidentiality concerning his clients, but he could only imagine the tsunami of gossip which was about to wash over the North Devon peninsular. He was the mayor of Bideford. He was a highly successful businessman. He thought he was a respected local figure. He hoped he was, anyway. But not for much longer, in any case, he suspected.

Amelia had no idea what was going to hit them. If Felix was brought to trial it would all come out. It would have to. And what would it do to the children? Sam couldn't bear to think.

He would like to share his burden with his wife. She would at least understand his behaviour then, understand why 'her rock', as she called him, was finding it difficult to hold himself together. But Amelia wasn't as strong as she made out, and he wondered if either of them was strong enough to survive this.

He knew he should go back to the kitchen, or find his wife wherever she may have gone in the house, try to reassure her. But how could he, when he feared the worst in every direction?

Almost on cue, the office door opened and in walked Amelia. She had dried her tears, styled her hair and put on fresh make-up. At least she was behaving according to type, thought Sam. She always gave optimum importance to how things appeared.

One of her favourite sayings was 'never let the act drop'.

She asked Sam if he had called Trevor Hardwick, and he was at least able to reassure her that the solicitor was on his way to be at their son's side.

'It's gone half past two,' she said then. 'One of us needs to go and fetch the twins from school.'

Sam knew Joanna and Stevie finished school at three. From the way Amelia had worded her remark it was obvious to him that she was hoping he would offer to pick them up.

He did so willingly. It would get him out of the house, this time for a thoroughly legitimate reason, and give him something to do.

'If anyone comes to the door, don't answer it,' he instructed. 'I'm afraid it's not going to take the press long to get hold of this. It never does.'

He met a couple of teachers outside the school, and a parent whom he knew a little, all of whom expressed only slightly embarrassed regret and condolences over Jane's death. Sam thanked them and made no further comment. They would know that a murder investigation was underway, of course, but the news of Felix's arrest had yet to break. That's when things would turn really grim.

Meanwhile, the twins' form teacher brought Joanna and Stevie to him, holding each of them by the hand. The children ran to their grandfather pretty much as they normally did, but he was aware that they lacked their usual exuberance. He wasn't surprised. And things were going to get so much worse.

'How've they been?' he asked.

'A little quiet,' responded Miss Wakefield. She turned to the twins. 'But you're such brave little soldiers, aren't you?'

The twins nodded. Stevie managed a small smile. Sam did not like to think about how brave these two six-year-olds were going to have to be.

He just wanted to get them home. He probably wouldn't have sent them to school that day. But he hadn't been around to make the decision, had he? And in the event, it was a good thing that they hadn't been in the house when their father was arrested. They were quiet on the journey. Selfishly, Sam was quite glad they didn't want him to talk to them, because, frankly, he no longer knew what to say.

As they pulled into Bay View Road, he was quickly aware that his worst fears had already been realized. A woman photographer was standing by the gate of All Seasons, aiming her camera through the Range Rover windows as he swung his vehicle into the driveway. A young man he vaguely recognized to be a reporter from the *Western Morning News*, known for being particularly quick off the mark, was standing by the porch.

Sam parked the Range Rover in front of the garage, and,

ushering the children before him, headed smartly for the scant protection of the porch, aware of the photographer snapping away all the while.

'Could you confirm that your son has been arrested for the murder of his wife,' called out the reporter, who was doing his best to obstruct Sam's path.

Sam only just resisted the urge to push him out of the way. He just hoped neither of the twins had properly understood what the reporter had said. He sidestepped around the young man then turned to face him, drawing himself up to his full six foot two inches. The photographer was still snapping.

'I have only one thing to say to you,' he announced, hopefully with an authority he most certainly did not feel. 'My grandchildren are six years old. If their picture appears in your paper, any other publication, or anywhere on the internet including social media, I shall not just sue, I shall bring the wrath of God on all your heads.'

Sam wasn't sure quite what he meant by the last remark, but he had the satisfaction of seeing the reporter take a step backwards and the photographer lower her camera. It made him feel very slightly better, although he suspected that feeling would not last for long.

He opened the front door and shooed the twins inside.

Joanna turned to him, wide-eyed, anxious.

'Who are those people, Grandad?' she asked.

'Nobody you need worry about, kitten,' Sam assured her, aware that nothing could be much further than the truth.

'Grandad will make them go away,' he continued. Another lie.

Amelia was standing in the hallway. To be more exact, she was cowering in the hallway.

'Oh Sam, it's started already,' she cried. 'I don't think I can bear it.'

Sam went to her, put his arm around her and kissed the top of her head. He knew she liked that. Although he didn't think it would help much that afternoon.

'There, there,' he murmured ineffectually. 'I'm on the case now. And Trevor Hardwick is with Felix. We should hear from him soon—'

'He's already called, on the house phone,' interrupted Amelia.

'He says Felix has turned down his services, won't see him. This is just all so awful, Sam. I mean, Felix has been arrested for murder, why on earth would he turn down legal help?'

'I have no idea,' said Sam, who actually thought he did have a fair idea of at least some of the reasoning behind his son's behaviour.

TWENTY-THREE

At Barnstaple police station the interview with Felix Ferguson continued without offering up anything more of significant assistance to the investigation.

Felix continued to be unable to explain certain aspects of his behaviour, primarily his visit home during the yacht club dinner, to Vogel's satisfaction. But he stubbornly persisted in proclaiming his innocence.

Vogel asked him again if he could suggest a single alternative suspect. Felix stared glumly at the DCI, his expression suggesting that was a question to which he had no answer. And in any case he had no time to give one.

There was a knock on the interview room door, and DC Perkins' tousled dark head appeared. The young man looked even more worried than usual.

'Sorry, boss,' he began tentatively. 'Could I have a word?'

Vogel's first reaction was one of intense irritation. But he knew that no police officer would ever interrupt the interview of a man under arrest for murder except on a matter of extreme urgency. And he had asked Perkins to keep in touch with DI Peters and monitor any further developments.

The DCI announced formally for the benefit of the video recording that he was pausing the proceedings, gestured for Saslow to stay where she was, and left the room hard on Perkins' heels.

'Sorry, boss,' said Perkins again. 'DI Peters just had a call through from HQ at Exeter, they've had a report they thought we might be interested in—'

'Get on with it, man,' interrupted Vogel impatiently.

'Yes, sir. It's Gerry Barham, as in Gerry and Anne Barham, the couple who nearly drove into little Joanna Ferguson after she'd found her mother's body. Apparently he's gone missing, boss.'

'Gone missing?' queried Vogel. He and Saslow had interviewed the Barhams early the previous morning. And Gerry Barham was an adult as yet not under any sort of suspicion. The DCI was puzzled. He had yet to understand why this had been brought to his attention.

'When did he go missing?' the DCI asked.

'Uh, well, his wife doesn't know for sure.'

Perkins explained how Anne Barham had woken at seven to find her husband no longer in bed, and then gone back to sleep.

'It was about half past eight when she went downstairs and realized he had left the house,' said Perkins.

The DCI checked his watch. It was three twenty-five p.m.

'So Gerry Barham's precise whereabouts have been unknown to his wife for a maximum of between seven and eight-and-a-half daytime hours,' he said. 'How does that qualify for him to be described as missing?'

'I'm sorry, sir. I should have said. He's presumed missing at sea.'

'Good God,' said Vogel. 'Right Perkins. You'd better tell me everything you know.'

Perkins did so. When he had finished Vogel was thoughtful.

'So, a man who is at the most a very occasional amateur sailor took out his boat, generally considered to be inadequate at sea for anything except the fairest of fair-weather sailing, on a day like this.'

Vogel gestured through a window near where they were standing.

Barnstaple, like Bideford, is an estuary town, on a tidal river, but further inland and therefore protected to a certain extent from the extremes of coastal weather. Nonetheless driving rain was hammering into the glass, and it was clear that a gale was blowing. A stubby tree on a patch of grass outside had been bent almost horizontal by the wind. The sky was leaden.

'Why on earth would anyone take any sort of boat out in this weather?' he asked.

'Well it wasn't like this first thing,' said Perkins. 'It was a bright sunny morning, wasn't it, sir? Just like yesterday.'

'For a while, yes,' agreed Vogel. 'But by mid-morning the weather was already beginning to change. In Bideford the wind was blowing right up the estuary. You didn't need a forecast to know what was coming.'

'Mr Barham did tell his wife he didn't plan to be long,' said Perkins.

'Yep. But what was he planning?' asked Vogel, more of himself than anyone else.

He re-entered the interview room, formally ended proceedings, told Felix that the interview would be resumed later, and, once they were alone together, gave Saslow the rundown on what he had just learned from DC Perkins.

'Barham could just have got things wrong,' suggested Saslow who could already tell the way her superior officer's mind was going. 'I mean, as he wasn't much of a sailor, he could just have made a terrible mistake. It might not be significant to our investigation at all . . .'

'Saslow,' said Vogel. 'You don't need to be a sailor to check the bloody weather forecast. A man who is central to a murder investigation has inexplicably taken a small and inadequate boat out to sea in highly questionable weather within a day or so of the event. It seems quite likely, does it not, that he is at the very least in serious trouble at sea? He could well be dead. That would make him the second person living in a small secluded close to have died a violent death within less than two days. And the other was his closest neighbour. When conducting a murder investigation, I do not believe in those kinds of coincidences.

'Come on Saslow. We're going to Instow to see what Gerry Barham's wife has to tell us about all this.'

Anne Barham answered the door before either Saslow or Vogel had rung the bell. She must have heard or seen them arrive outside her house.

Vogel could see that she had been crying. She recognized him and Saslow at once, of course. Her hand went to her mouth and she gave a little gasp.

'Gerry, is it Gerry?' she asked, her voice little more than a whisper.

Clearly she feared that Vogel and Saslow were bringing the news she had no doubt been fearing for some hours now.

'We don't have any further news, Mrs Barham,' said Vogel quickly. 'We just wanted to talk to you again, about the events of yesterday and your husband's disappearance.'

'Uh yes, of course. I don't know what it's got to do with yesterday though. Except, well, I think Gerry was a lot more upset by what happened than I realized.'

Anne Barham led the way into the same sitting room where she had fetched coffee for Vogel and Saslow early the previous morning. This time she offered no such hospitality. The woman was clearly quite distraught. She did not even bid them to sit. The two officers did so anyway, and it was Vogel who suggested that Mrs Barham should join them.

She lowered herself abruptly, and with a bit of a bump, onto a hard chair by the door.

'I just don't know what's happening any more,' she said. 'My Gerry, this isn't like him. He's . . . he's such an orderly man. He used to be a civil servant, you know. Caught the seven a.m. train into central London every morning, and the five p.m. one home. Regular as clockwork. He's always punctual. Even now he's retired he has his routine in everything. Never wavers. I don't think he's surprised me, not really, in thirty-seven years of marriage . . . until now—'

Vogel interrupted her. The woman was in danger of being gripped by verbal diarrhoea. It happened in these situations. Vogel had seen it before.

'Mrs Barham, what I would like you to do is take me through everything that has happened in the period since DC Saslow and I left you yesterday morning until now. Particularly I need to know specifically anything about your husband's behaviour that was odd or out of character.'

'Everything about Gerry's behaviour was odd,' Anne Barham replied straight away. 'He wasn't like my Gerry at all. Not at all.'

She then gave a quite precisely detailed account, perhaps surprisingly so under the circumstances, of Gerry's unlikely absences, the questionable phone calls, and her own growing sense of concern and anxiety.

When she had finished, Anne Barham began to cry. Which was always Vogel's worst nightmare. He didn't know why he couldn't cope with other people's tears, but he never had been able to. He sometimes thought that was the main reason he had always tried to be a good husband. He'd only seen his wife Mary cry a handful of times in their twenty years of marriage. And every time it tore his heart out. So he did his utmost to ensure, as much as was humanly possible, that Mary had no cause to cry.

Saslow, however, was thankfully rather more able to deal with displays of emotion. She got up, walked across the room, crouched down next to Anne, and took one of the woman's hands in hers.

'We know that the coastguards are doing all they can, and the RNLI,' she said. 'There's still a good chance they'll find Mr Barham and bring him safely home.'

Vogel had already begun to think that wasn't very likely, and was pretty sure Saslow didn't really believe what she'd said. But, for the moment, he was glad that she had said it. Anne Barham stopped crying, dabbed ineffectually at her eyes with a paper tissue, and smiled weakly at Saslow.

Vogel then felt able to continue.

'Thank you, Mrs Barham, for giving us such a full account,' he said. 'I have just one or two questions, if you could bear with me. Did you really have absolutely no idea who your husband was talking to on the phone during those calls which you found . . . well, you found them rather mysterious, didn't you?'

'I did. Yes. He dodged my questions every time I asked him about the calls. And then there were those little walks. Nothing little about them, either.'

'Could he have been meeting someone, perhaps?'

'I don't know. But why? Why would he be meeting someone, and not tell me? Gerry and I don't have any secrets from each other, Mr Vogel. I know married people often say that when it's not true at all, but I know it's true of us.' She paused. 'Or at least, I certainly knew it until yesterday,' she added.

'Look, Mrs Barham, I am very sorry to ask you this,' continued Vogel. 'But has there ever been a time during your marriage when you suspected Gerry may have been unfaithful to you, that there might be someone else in his life?'

'No. Never. Not for a moment. He's never been that kind of man, really he hasn't.'

Vogel did not quite subscribe to the theory that every red-blooded male was 'that kind of man' – after all, he was not – but more than twenty years of policing had certainly taught him that most were. However, Anne Barham had answered his highly provocative question with quiet certainty, and totally calmly – indeed much more calmly than Vogel might have expected. This line of questioning not infrequently provoked an emotional outburst from interviewees.

Nonetheless, he persisted a little further.

'I apologize again, Mrs Barham, but unexplained absences and mysterious phone calls are often indicative of some kind of extra-marital liaison,' he said. 'I am sure you realize that. You say, however, that you had never been aware of that sort of behaviour in your husband before yesterday?'

'No. Never. We have always been very close, and since Gerry retired, well, we are hardly ever apart. I mean, don't misunder-stand me. We don't live in each other's pockets. He has his interests, things he does without me. But we're not apart a lot. Once a year he goes up to London for a reunion dinner with old work colleagues. Only the once, you understand. And it would be a pretty understanding mistress who put up with meeting her lover at an annual event, wouldn't it?'

Anne Barham smiled a tight strained little smile. Saslow was no longer holding her hand. Instead Anne Barham was twiddling her fingers, literally, around damp strands of paper tissue.

'Then there's the yacht club, his drinking pals there and in The Boathouse, not that he's a heavy drinker, you understand,' she continued. 'And he's on the parish council and the Bideford regatta committee. He's good at that sort of thing. He plays golf occasionally. And I have my interests too. I'm a collector, Mr Vogel. Rare books and unusual clocks, in particular.'

She gestured towards a bookcase packed with intriguing looking volumes and a glass cabinet containing a selection of specimen clocks.

'I have a little group of friends I go browsing antique fairs with. We occasionally meet for coffee or lunch. That sort of thing. But, quite frankly, Mr Vogel, I don't see how my Gerry would have time for a bit on the side without me knowing, even if he had the inclination.'

The strained smile fleeted across her face once more.

'You mentioned your husband's work,' commented Vogel. 'I think you said earlier that he was a civil servant?'

'That's right, yes. Went into it right after university. Only job he ever had. In the civil service for nearly thirty-five years. Then they offered him an early retirement deal he couldn't refuse. He'd had enough by then, so he took it like a shot. And we came here. Never regretted it for a second.' Anne Barham paused. 'Until now, maybe,' she murmured.

'What branch of the civil service was he in?' enquired Vogel.

Anne Barham frowned.

'Mr Vogel, I really don't see why you're asking all these questions. That's all in the past. I want to know what's happened to my husband today? I am worried sick about him. I want him found.'

Vogel nodded sympathetically.

'Of course,' he said. 'And believe me, every possible effort is being made to find him and bring him home. I am just trying to build a picture of Gerry, so that maybe I can understand what has caused him to behave in this out-of-character way.'

'Well, if you can understand it, I take my hat off to you, Mr Vogel,' replied Anne Barham. 'Because I don't understand any of it. But of course, if you think it will help in any way, I will answer any questions you have. Gerry worked in a number of different departments over the years, he was a—'

Anne Barham was interrupted by the strident ring of Vogel's phone. He'd meant to put it on vibrate, but he would in any case have to check who was calling, as he now not only had Felix under arrest for murder, but also a missing person case upon which there could be news at any moment.

He took his phone from his pocket and studied the screen. The caller was young DC Perkins.

'I'm sorry Mrs Barham, you will have to excuse me, I need to take this call,' said Vogel, stopping Anne Barham in mid-sentence.

He stood up and left the room.

'You were saying, Mrs Barham?' said Saslow, continuing the conversation more out of courtesy than anything else. She thought it likely Vogel might at that very second be receiving significant news. Certainly, he would not have left the room if he hadn't half expected that.

Anne looked as if she was already thinking what Saslow was thinking.

'Uh, what? Um, yes, Gerry worked in various different departments, commuting in and out of central London every day, he'd certainly had enough of it in the end and . . .'

She stopped abruptly. This time of her own accord.

'Look, detective sergeant, I'm sorry, I can't concentrate. Can we wait until Mr Vogel returns? I need to know if he has any news.'

'Yes, of course,' said Saslow.

Anne got up from her chair and walked to the window where she stood looking out. The weather more or less blotted out the view, but Saslow doubted Anne Barham was taking much notice of that. The acting DS didn't even attempt to make any further conversation.

Vogel didn't keep them waiting long. He returned to the room within less than five minutes. Saslow was sitting opposite the door. It was she who saw Vogel's face first. And she knew at once that he had news, all right. And it wasn't good.

As soon as she heard the door open Anne Barham turned around. She too seemed aware just from looking at Vogel of what he was about to tell her. Or the crux of it, anyway.

She didn't speak, just stood stock still, staring at the DCI. Her face was already ashen.

'Mrs Barham, I am afraid I have some very grave news,' said Vogel.

Anne still didn't move a muscle. She continued to stare at the detective.

'Perhaps you would like to sit down, Mrs Barham,' he suggested.

Anne responded with an almost imperceptible shake of her head, still staring at him.

'As you wish,' Vogel continued. 'I am afraid the wreckage of a boat has been found off Hartland Point. We have reason to believe that the boat was your husband's.'

Anne Barham remained silent and quite still. Fleetingly Vogel wondered if she had grasped the import of what he was saying. Then her knees began to buckle, although she seemed to be quite unaware of it.

Saslow was at her side in a thrice. The young DS was small but strong. She wrapped a supportive arm around the other woman and half coaxed, half pushed and pulled her into the nearest armchair.

Anne gave the impression of being in a kind of trance. Vogel wondered if he should give her a moment or two to compose herself before continuing. Suddenly she sat bolt upright. Her eyes blazing.

'Just tell me,' she yelled. 'For heaven's sake, just tell me. Is Gerry dead?'

Vogel kept his voice level and unemotional. Over the years he had found that was the best way. If there ever was a best way.

'Mrs Barham, the body of a man has been found on the rocks at Hartland, near some of the wreckage from the boat, almost certainly washed in on the incoming spring tide. I am afraid we have reason to believe that it is the body of your husband.'

Anne Barham lowered her head into her hands and groaned. It was more than a groan. It was a long low exhalation of breath, an expression of total dismay. It started quietly, low and slow, and grew louder and higher until it developed into an animal howl.

Every death call was different. In Vogel's not inconsiderable experience every human being confronted with the sudden violent death of a loved one deals with it differently. He had, however, never seen a reaction which moved him more than this one.

It was as if Anne Barham's entire world had suddenly ended. As indeed, at that moment, she no doubt believed that it had.

Saslow was still at her side, with a comforting arm around a shoulder. Anne gave no sign that she even knew the DS was there. Certainly, Saslow could clearly now do nothing to give her even an iota of comfort.

Eventually the strange agonized noise, which seemed to come from the very core of Anne Barham's being and fill the room with her anguish, stopped. As suddenly as it had started.

Anne raised her head to look across at Vogel. There were no tears to be seen. Just an expression in her eyes of total devastation.

'Do you know any more? When was he found? Are they sure? Are they sure it's Gerry?'

Vogel answered as simply and factually as he could.

'Enough of the boat remained intact for the lifeboat men who found it to fairly quickly identify the wreckage as being from a boat of the same sort as your husband's, and a little later they found the section of the hull bearing its name. The *Lady Anne*. After you, I suppose?'

Anne Barham closed her eyes briefly. Her face tightened as if she were in pain. Then she nodded in a distracted sort of way.

'Yes. He changed the boat's name as soon as he bought it. I read somewhere that is believed to be unlucky . . .'

She uttered a small mirthless laugh.

'Yes, well, it was a rescue helicopter which first spotted a significant amount of wreckage off Hartland Point about two hours ago,' Vogel continued. 'Hartland lifeboat was quickly at the scene, and its crew later discovered the body of a man wedged in a crevice of the rocks, partially hidden from sight. I was notified, as requested, as soon as it became reasonable to assume that the body was that of your husband.'

'Assume? You mean there is still some doubt?'

'Very little, to be honest,' said Vogel. 'As I am sure you already realize. But, of course, we will need to have the body formally identified.'

Anne Barham gasped.

'I am not sure that I could do that,' she said.

'You don't have to,' said Vogel quickly. 'Another relative, or anyone who was close to your husband, can make the formal identification.'

'My daughter,' said Anne at once. 'Maybe she will do it. She's on her way from London. Or at least I hope she's on her way. I called her earlier. Told her what had happened. That her father

. . . her father was thought to be missing at sea. She couldn't understand it. Well, how could anyone? It just seems so unlikely. All of it. Why on earth, why on God's earth did Gerry take that bloody boat out on a day like this?'

Anne Barham had been speaking quite calmly. The last few sentences once more turned into a wail of anguish. She waved a hand at the sitting-room window. Rain was lashing against the glass, the sky was a leaden dark grey, something somewhere outside was being rattled by the powerful wind, the trees at the bottom of the garden were leaning at a dangerous angle.

'How could anyone survive at sea in a small boat?' questioned Anne in a voice so small it was nearly a whisper.

'Mrs Barham, do you know what time your daughter will get here?' asked Saslow.

It was clear to both officers that the woman should not be left alone.

'No, I don't. I could call her. But what shall I tell her? She'll be driving. Should I tell her on the phone that her father is dead? It might be dangerous, mightn't it, to give her such a shock?'

Saslow looked towards Vogel for guidance.

'Only you can decide that, Mrs Barham,' he said. 'Because of what you have already told her, your daughter is probably already expecting the worst. But perhaps you might like to wait a little while, so that you have time to clear your thoughts, before you decide when and how you will break the tragic news to her.'

Anne Barham nodded.

'All right,' she stammered uncertainly.

'Meanwhile, is there anyone else we can contact who could be with you?'

'I don't want anybody else, and I don't need anyone else,' said Anne, who clearly did need support quite badly.

'Well, we can at least get a family liaison officer over . . .'

'I don't need a family liaison officer,' said Anne stubbornly.

'Look, we'll get one over here, and then you can decide later whether you want him or her to stay with you,' said Vogel. 'It is standard procedure in a case like this.'

'Is it?' asked Anne Barham, her voice suddenly sharp. 'I didn't think the police were required to provide a FLO in a case of accidental death, however tragic?'

Vogel did a double take. Anne Barham had naturally used the police vernacular. Perhaps there was more to this woman than at first seemed. On the other hand, perhaps she was just a fan of crime fiction. Either way, this was not the time to push her on that.

'Well, no, but . . .' he began.

'But you are already treating my husband's death as suspicious, is that it, Mr Vogel?'

'Well, not really, not yet, however at this stage all options remain open, and we will conduct a thorough investigation into the loss of your husband's boat, the events leading up to it, and his subsequent death,' said Vogel. 'It is more than possible, probably likely even, that your husband's death was a tragic accident. But well . . .'

'But, it's the second violent death in this small community in less than two days, and the other person who died is our next-door neighbour,' volunteered Anne.

Vogel shot her a look of guarded admiration. He didn't doubt for one moment that her grief was both overwhelming and totally genuine. But Anne's brain had snapped back into action quickly enough.

'Absolutely,' he said.

'I don't know what to say,' responded Anne, just slightly dithery again. 'My Gerry was a very ordinary man, and he led a very ordinary life. None of this makes any sense. No sense at all.'

An ordinary man, mused Vogel as he and Saslow drove out of Estuary Vista Close a half hour or so later. Was he indeed? And if Gerry was so very ordinary, how the hell had he become involved in the sequence of events which, Vogel now strongly suspected, had probably led to his death, and were beginning to look as if they were anything but ordinary?

TWENTY-FOUR

After leaving the Barham home Saslow and Vogel drove straight to Hartland Point. Gerry Barham's body had been found at the foot of a cliff to one side of a roughly hewn cove, which, the RNLI reported, was inaccessible from the sea due to the rock formation just offshore, and presented problems for approach by helicopter due to the cliff overhang.

There was, however, a steep path, largely taking the form of steps roughly hewn in the rock face, leading down to the cove.

Saslow followed the clifftop track and parked as close as she could to where she believed the path to be, as indicated by the other vehicles already there: two police patrol cars, a CSI van, a Coastguard Cliff Rescue truck, and pathologist Karen Crow's little white Golf. The two detectives made their way to the cliff edge where they could see a uniformed constable standing looking down at the scene below. They introduced themselves and also peered over the cliff. A tent had been erected over what must be the place where the body lay. Vogel already knew that the body had been moved once as, when it was spotted, it had been half covered by the still incoming tide. CSIs were scurrying in and out of the tent.

The rain had stopped, but it was still pretty blowy. Vogel pulled his inadequate coat close to his body and stepped forwards.

'Come on, Saslow,' said Vogel, with a lot more bravado than he felt. 'Let's get down there and have a proper look.'

Vogel was not especially afraid of heights. But he was a city boy through and through. He never felt comfortable with steep paths and uneven ground, the Atlantic Ocean was raging down below, and gusts of wind were hitting him straight in the face. Vogel was way out of his comfort zone.

He noticed a system of ropes and pulleys were in place, and wasn't sure if that made him feel better or worse.

'You'll have to wait a minute, sir,' said the uniform. 'Cliff

Rescue are on site and there's a safety officer who will rope you up and take you down.'

On cue a lithe young woman wearing a hard hat appeared alongside. She quickly supplied Vogel and Saslow with hard hats, and helped them into safety harnesses, each attached to a rope.

'OK,' she said, 'the harnesses and ropes are just in case. You'll be fine. Now follow me.'

She set off briskly. It seemed to Vogel that she launched herself in somewhat foolhardy fashion from the relative safety of the cliff top. Saslow followed at once. Vogel had little choice but to get on with it. The wind continued to whistle disconcertingly around his ears. He moved cautiously down the rough-hewn steps, making sure he had one foot firmly in place before moving the other. Saslow meanwhile was hopping rather more nimbly downwards, without, it seemed, a care in the world.

He was relieved to reach the rocks, boulders, and pebbles below. Although they too presented a challenge to a man who had never been in the least athletic.

Pieces of boat, presumably the ill-fated *Lady Anne*, were laid out on tarpaulins. Crime scene investigators, clad in their protective coverall Tyvek suits, were swarming over everything.

Saslow and Vogel headed for the tent, where they assumed Karen Crow was already at work. There was a cordon around it. A CSI handed them a couple of suits, thankfully just big enough to pull on over their outer clothing. As they fought their way into them, all the more of a struggle because of the strong wind, Karen Crow emerged from the cordoned-off area.

'Twice in as many days or thereabouts, Vogel,' she muttered.

'Always a pleasure,' replied Vogel.

'Not for that poor bastard,' responded the pathologist, cocking a thumb in the direction of the tent.

'He did not have a good death, that's for sure. He's been smashed to pieces, pretty much like his boat. Both arms broken, at least one of his legs, not sure about the other, a fractured skull, and his face is a mass of bloody pulp.'

'Is it what you would expect from the victim of a shipwreck, or could it be something else?' queried Vogel.

'Why would it be anything else?' asked Karen Crow. 'Some nutter takes a small boat out in this weather, what can you expect, for God's sake? I've only been called in to follow routine procedure, surely. And what are you doing here anyway? Is there some reason why this little personal tragedy might be important enough to warrant your attention, Vogel?'

'We think the victim is one Gerry Barham from Instow,' said Vogel.

Karen looked blank.

'From Estuary Vista Close, Instow,' Vogel continued. 'The neighbour who called in the death of Jane Ferguson, having encountered her little daughter right after she found her mother's body.'

'Ah, I see,' said the pathologist, adopting a quizzical expression. 'Well, that explains that then. If this is your Gerry Barham, and no doubt you already have good reason to assume it is, then two people who lived next door to each other have died violently, one after the other. And you don't believe in coincidences, do you, Vogel?'

'No. I don't. Do you?'

'Never have done,' replied Dr Crow bluntly.

'So, will you answer my question now? Could he have been killed by anything other than injuries sustained following some sort of accident at sea?' persisted Vogel.

'Well, considering the state he is in, that might be very hard, indeed, even impossible to ascertain,' said the pathologist. 'His injuries are totally consistent with having been thrown off his boat into the sea and then smashed against rocks by a raging incoming tide. That's what happened by the way. Have you spoken to the coastguards or RNLI yet?'

Vogel shook his head.

'Well, according to the RNLI boys who were here when I arrived, it looks almost certain his little boat was swept out on the tide when the storm was at its peak and the sea got up big time this morning. Then the incoming tides and the prevalent currents washed him and his boat ashore here. You only have to look at the state of the thing.'

Karen Crow waved one arm at the wreckage spread out on the shore.

'You don't have to be a doctor nor have conducted a forensic examination to have a fair idea what that sort of force has done to his body,' she went on. 'Apart from the external injuries which are totally obvious, he is sure to have suffered all manner of internal injuries. Poor bastard didn't stand a chance.'

'The question is, could he have sustained some of those injuries before his boat capsized or broke up?' asked Vogel.

'Well yes, of course he could. And without any help from a third party, too. He could have been thrown all over that boat of his in this weather. Like a rag doll. If, for example, there'd been a big gust of wind and his boat had veered to one side, he could easily have broken something, a leg or an arm, or both. He would then have been left pretty helpless, unable to steer or do anything to even attempt to control the boat. It's all a bit chicken and egg.'

'But what if a third party was involved?' asked Vogel. 'What if someone beat him up then left him on the boat to die? He had a fractured skull, you said. What if someone wacked him with a hammer or something?'

'It doesn't look like a hammer blow to the head, there's no imprint, he could have been hit by some sort of blunt object, something with a big flat edge, an anchor maybe. To be honest, Vogel, I really doubt there's any way of telling, after the damage those rocks over there have done to him. He's a total mess.'

Karen Crow paused, staring out to sea as if she wished the ocean could speak, tell its story. Which was exactly how Vogel felt.

'Look, Vogel, this is your territory not mine,' she continued. 'But if someone stove this man's head in, and left him drifting aboard a small boat which was likely, in a gathering storm of up to fifty-mile-an-hour winds, to be driven by the tide into one of the most treacherous stretches of coastline in the British Isles, then where is this someone, Vogel? That's what I'd want to know if I were you. I mean, is he also dead? Is his body washed up somewhere where it hasn't yet been found, or caught up in something out at sea where it might never be found? In which case, it's not much of a murder scenario, is it, if you die along with your victim? This third party must have been on the boat with our victim, mustn't he? He couldn't have beaten Barham up first then sent his boat off down the river with a dead man at the helm, could he? Bloody thing wouldn't have made it into the estuary, let alone out to sea far enough to be washed back into Hartland.'

'I don't have the faintest idea, Karen, not yet,' Vogel admitted.

'No,' said the pathologist. 'Tell you something, Vogel, I wouldn't like your job. That I wouldn't.'

Vogel had a sudden vision running through his head like one of those old compacted newsreels, of every post-mortem examination he'd ever been to, all jumbled up and joined together to form a cinematic horror story. Only the previous day, it seemed like much longer ago, but it had indeed been only the previous day, he had watched Karen Crow take a circular saw to the head of a rather beautiful young woman, and he had seen her crack open that young woman's ribcage and tear her exposed torso apart.

'You know what, Karen,' he remarked mildly. 'I wouldn't much like your job, either.'

He turned to Saslow.

'Come on, detective sergeant,' he said. 'Let's have a look at our body, shall we?'

He led the way across the last few yards of rock and shingle and stepped inside the tent protecting the dead man from the elements, and from the unwanted attentions of members of the public. Not that there were likely to be many passing by this particular scene.

The body was lying on its back. Karen Crow may have turned it over in the course of her preliminary examination. She hadn't straightened the limbs. The first thing that hit Vogel was the state of the man's face. Only it wasn't a face any more. It was red mush. Red mush with bits of white sticking out, which Vogel assumed were bits of bone. You couldn't even see the eyes. This was bad. Worse than he had expected. Possibly worse than he had ever seen before. His involuntary stomach heave was as bad as he had ever experienced. He turned towards Saslow. He was about to make an excuse. He didn't have time. He just ran for the entrance of the tent and headed, flat out, his feet slithering and slipping on wet shingle, for the shelter of a rocky outcrop forming a shallow cave in the cliff face. He almost dived inside, bent over, and was as sick as he had ever been in the whole of his life.

It was not the first time Vogel had been unable to control his nausea when faced with a dead body. But it was the first time in a very long while.

TWENTY-FIVE

I n Northam, Sam and Amelia Ferguson were trying to keep some sort of normality going, if only for the sake of the children. Amelia took them upstairs and helped them change out of their school uniforms into their tracksuit bottoms and T-shirts, whilst Sam called Trevor Hardwick back. It was a call he had to make, but the solicitor's response was only what he expected.

Hardwick told him that there was a considerable amount of advice he would like to give Felix concerning what he should and should not tell the police officers who interviewed him, and that he could quite probably assist in all sorts of ways. But he could do absolutely nothing at all if a potential client declined his services. And that is what Felix had done. Quite categorically, apparently.

Sam then called the police. He had the mobile number of the senior man at Bideford, a uniformed inspector. He asked where his son was and what was happening to him.

Inspector Braddock told him that Felix had been taken to Barnstaple, which he'd already learned from Hardwick, and that the interview process was ongoing.

'Has he been charged?' Sam asked.

'I'm afraid I can't give you any more information, Sam, really I can't,' said Braddock. 'All I can tell you is that Felix has been arrested on suspicion of Jane's murder.'

'I bloody know that,' snapped Sam.

'I'm sorry, but I can't help you any further,' said Braddock. He sounded awkward and embarrassed.

Sam knew full well that he had put the man in an impossible position and that he should have made his enquiries through the official channels. He didn't care. He was desperate.

'Look, can I see Felix?' he asked. 'Can you arrange that for me?'

'You've got to be joking,' said Braddock. 'Members of the

public can't visit somebody who's been arrested for murder whilst they are in police custody and being interviewed. This case has attracted the attention of the top brass too. Big time. And not just because of who you are, Sam, I'm pretty sure of that. We don't know quite what's going on, to tell the truth.'

'But you do think there's something else going on, then, do you?'

'Nobody tells me anything,' replied Braddock obliquely. 'I'm just the senior wooden top around here. Look, I've got to go.'

And he promptly ended the call without the formality of a farewell.

Sam was thoughtful. Probably without realising it, Inspector Braddock had added weight to what he already knew. But Sam was all too aware that he had only half the picture – if that.

The children came running down the stairs then and into the kitchen, closely followed by Amelia.

She glanced at Sam enquiringly. He'd told her he would call Hardwick and the police while she went upstairs with the twins.

He shook his head slightly and turned his attention to Jo and Stevie.

'Right, you two, off you go to the sitting room and I'll find that film you like and put it on the big screen in there,' he said, trying, with extreme difficulty, to make his voice sound suitably jolly.

When the twins were safely out of earshot he related the unsatisfactory results of his phone calls to Amelia, leaving out Inspector Braddock's expression of puzzlement at the level of 'top brass' interest in the case, but otherwise giving an accurate account. His wife looked as downcast as he felt. But Sam doubted she was anything like as frightened as he was.

He followed the children into the sitting room, looked out the DVD of *The Jungle Book*, currently their favourite film which they seemed happy to watch over and over again even if their concentration rarely lasted until the end of it, and put it on the big TV, just as he had promised. Then he sat down and began to watch the film with them; partly because he knew the twins would like that, and he wanted so much to keep them from being distressed and upset, and partly because, at that moment, he could think of nothing else to do.

Only he wasn't watching the film, of course; just staring unsee-ingly at the screen, whilst the previously unimaginable horror which had suddenly descended upon his family engulfed every iota of his being.

Amelia went to the kitchen to prepare the children's tea. Or that's what she said she was doing. In fact, it didn't take very long to make Jo and Stevie's favourite fish finger sandwiches. They were not normally on Amelia's menu for the twins. She usually tried to provide them with healthier meals, although she did keep a packet in the freezer for special occasions. She supposed this was a special occasion, of the most terrible sort. If fish finger sandwiches would give the twins pleasure, even make them happy, albeit fleetingly, then that is what they were going to get.

She shut the kitchen door behind her. Even the children's laughter, and the noisy cartoon sounds of the film showing on the sitting-room TV, made her nerves jangle. But at least Sam was making a real effort for their grandchildren, and she admired him for it. She knew it couldn't be easy for him to put on a brave face for them, any more than it was for her. He was behaving a little more like the solid capable man she had married, the man who had always been able to solve any problem.

When the children had seen as much of the film as they wanted, Sam brought them in to the kitchen, where they polished off their fish finger sandwiches in a thrice. Not for the first time Amelia marvelled at the resilience of childhood. Although she had little doubt that it would take a miracle to avoid Joanna and Stevie suffering long term damage in the wake of the events of the last two days.

Sam, sitting at the table opposite the twins, listening to their chatter, and even joining in, was somehow managing to continue to play the jovial grandparent. She just couldn't do it. She bustled around the kitchen pretending to be busy, whilst wondering what on earth they were going to do to entertain Joanna and Stevie until their bedtime. She desperately wanted to talk to her husband too. She wondered if one of them should go to the police station, just to be there for Felix, even if they couldn't see him. At the very least Sam should surely call the police again. Or maybe she should. But that was Sam's department. That was what he did. And he was so much better at dealing with officialdom than she was, or he usually was anyway. He always seemed to know someone in authority; if anyone could cut through red tape it was Sam.

With a great effort of will she put a smile on her face and sat down at the table with her grandchildren and her husband. She leaned close to him.

'Don't you think you should call the police again?' she asked softly. 'I can't bear not knowing what is happening.'

He nodded.

'I was just about to,' he said. 'You stay with these two, I'll do it in the living room.'

He wasn't gone long. When he returned he was shaking his head.

'No change,' he said. 'No more news at all. Not that anyone's passing on to me, anyway.'

Amelia lowered her voice to a whisper again.

'They haven't charged him, have they?' she asked, the very thought of it making her heart race.

'I don't think so,' said Sam.

He looked as if he was about to say more when the familiar beep of his phone indicated that he had received an incoming text.

He took the phone from his pocket and began to study the screen, turning away from Amelia as he did so. She couldn't see his face, but she noticed his shoulders tensing – or she thought she did.

'What is it?' she asked anxiously. 'Is it news?'

Sam turned around again.

'No,' he said. 'Uh, not really. But I have to go out for a while. Sorry to leave you on your own with the children, but . . .'

'Where are you going?' Amelia demanded. 'Are you going to the police station? Is it about Felix?'

Sam had already taken his car keys, from one of the row of hooks on the kitchen wall where they kept all their keys, and was halfway through the door. He looked back over his shoulder.

'I'm not sure exactly what it's about but I have to find out,' he said. 'This is something I have to do. And I can't tell you about it yet. I'm sorry. You're just going to have to trust me.'

At a run she followed him into the hall.

'Sam, stop! I want to know what's going on. Where do you

keep disappearing to? This is the third time. What is going on? Please, please tell me . . .?'

Her words fell upon deaf ears. Sam just carried on through the front door and out of the house.

She was about to follow him outside when she remembered the reporters and photographers who were doubtless still waiting there.

She stopped herself just in time. Her breath was coming in short sharp gasps. She could feel her heart beating far too fast, she was sure of it. She was bewildered, frightened and distraught.

In the distance she could hear her grandchildren calling for her. Then little Joanna appeared by her side. The child looked as if she was about to burst into tears. Amelia had to fight to stop herself doing the same. Her grandchildren needed her to comfort them and take care of them. She just hoped she had the strength.

She bent down, reached out for Joanna, and pulled her close.

'There, there, Jo,' she said. 'Everything's going to be all right, sweetheart, Grannie promises, everything is going to be all right.'

But even as she spoke she was starkly aware that this was one promise she would almost certainly never be able to keep.

TWENTY-SIX

Meanwhile at Hartland, Vogel had pulled himself together, cleaned himself up and re-entered the tent which covered and protected the body of the man who must surely be Gerry Barham.

However, he still felt slightly nauseous, and had not looked too closely. He thought, or at least hoped, that he'd seen enough. And certainly Saslow, who'd remained in the tent whilst he had emptied the contents of his stomach amongst the rocks, would have had plenty of time to study the body.

He had no doubt that the DS was well aware of what had happened, but she passed no comment, and certainly knew better than to ask how he was feeling.

Instead she remarked levelly, 'I don't think we can learn too much more here, do you, boss?'

And she thus made it respectable for Vogel to quit the scene as fast as he could.

By the time the two of them had made their way up the precarious path to the clifftop his stomach had more or less settled, although he didn't feel great. But he couldn't dwell on that.

They needed to get back to Barnstaple police station as quickly as possible to continue interviewing Felix Ferguson. Vogel was becoming increasingly certain that, at the very least, the young man knew more than he was letting on. And he was clearly not the only one.

In the relative warmth and quiet of their vehicle the two detectives continued to discuss what may or may not have happened to Gerry Barham, and any possible connection his death might have to the death of Jane Ferguson.

'We need to get on to DI Peters,' said Vogel. 'I want a team diverted to try to find out when Gerry Barham and his boat left their mooring, whether or not he really was alone, and, if not, did anyone have any idea who was with him. Let's re-interview that chap who saw Gerry's boat going towards the estuary this morning. And if there is a single human being in the whole of North Devon who saw anyone, man, woman, boy or beast, acting suspiciously in coastal areas, around the time Gerry is believed to have taken his boat out, I want that person found. I also want Gerry's movements tracked, right through the period from when we interviewed him early yesterday morning until he took his boat out this morning, with or without company, a period of almost exactly twenty-four hours. Let's concentrate on the yacht club, all the houses, pubs, restaurants and shops along Instow front, across the river at Appledore, and Hartland and thereabouts, of course, where we found the body. If a third party was involved in Barham's death, could it have been Felix? That's the big question we need to address when we get to Barnstaple. And we should also get someone to check if Amelia Ferguson can alibi her son, too. We arrested him just before one p.m., so, if he wasn't at home, in theory he could have had time. Maybe. And he is a sailor. But he was sitting with a whisky bottle when we picked him up, and although he wasn't drunk exactly, he looked as if he'd already got stuck in, and certainly not like a man who'd just been battling the elements out at sea. Do you agree, Saslow?'

'I do, boss. He didn't look as if he'd been anywhere. But there is someone, though, a pretty unlikely someone, I realize, whose whereabouts were apparently a bit of a mystery all morning, according to his wife.'

Vogel turned to look at the young detective with whom he had been working now for almost four years, and for whom his respect grew almost as every day passed.

'Of course, Saslow,' he said. 'Sam Ferguson. Amelia was furious because he'd gone off somewhere without telling her and been missing for hours. She also inferred that he'd lied about his whereabouts. Good thinking, Saslow. So let's detour to Northam on the way back and see what Mr Ferguson senior has to say for himself. I agree it's hard to imagine him leaping on and off boats whilst he commits a bizarre murder at sea, but it would appear he created the window of opportunity for himself, and at the very least we need to know exactly what he was up to this morning.'

'Right, boss,' said Saslow. 'It's far from the only theory, though, is it? I was thinking about something else, just an idea, and you're probably going to say it's a daft one, but it would make sense of a lot of things . . .'

She paused, looking as if she wasn't sure she wanted to continue.

'Go on, Saslow,' said Vogel, a tad impatiently.

'Well, we cannot yet be entirely sure the dead man washed up at Hartland is Gerry Barham, can we?' continued the young detective. 'I mean, you sure as heck couldn't recognize him, the state he's in. His own wife couldn't recognize him.'

'Saslow, what are you talking about? If that isn't George Barham lying dead back there in that bloody awful cove, then who the heck is it, and how did he get there?'

'I dunno, boss, but maybe it's somebody Barham got on his boat and then murdered. Maybe Barham himself is off somewhere alive and well. Maybe he staged his own death. His wife said he'd been acting very strangely. Perhaps he was involved in this whole extraordinary sequence of events in ways we haven't thought of yet. Maybe he's done a John Stonehouse. Or the canoe man, you know, that man who pretended to die in a canoe accident and buggered off to Spain or somewhere . . .'

'Saslow, you've been watching too much television.'

'No, I haven't, boss. I work for you. I don't get the time to watch nearly enough television.'

Vogel smiled.

'I've no doubt you're right there,' he admitted. 'All the same, if Barham was murdered by an assailant aboard his boat, we do still have the small problem of how anybody could have safely got off the boat whilst leaving their victim to die in what was presumably meant to look like just a tragic, and very stupid, accident at sea.'

'I know, boss. I don't have the answer to that, either, I'm afraid.'

'Neither do I, Saslow, neither do I. Whoever it was would have had to be a bit of a superman. Or superwoman, I suppose. Now that would be something.'

Saslow smiled.

'Or just a professional, boss,' she offered. 'Someone with top-level military training. SAS perhaps.'

'Perhaps, Saslow, but we don't have anybody of that sort remotely in the frame, do we?'

'No, I don't suppose we do. There is another possibility, though, boss. The obvious, simple one. Assuming it is George Barham lying dead and smashed up out at Hartland Point, which will be proved pretty soon one way or another by DNA and dental records and so on, what about if he really did take his silly little boat out in a moment of madness without checking the weather forecast. And all on his own. Then the weather blew up big time, he got caught in a storm of considerable magnitude, which neither he nor his boat could cope with. The boat was wrecked, and he died. Nobody else was involved at all. The whole thing really is a stupid tragic accident. And the fact that his next-door neighbour died violently, and was almost certainly murdered, the day before, really is just a coincidence. But you don't believe that, boss, do you?'

'No, Saslow,' said Vogel. 'I do not believe that for one moment. Now come on, put your foot down. Ferguson senior first at Northam, and then Ferguson junior back at the nick. I think both of them are holding out on us. And if we put enough pressure on them maybe, just maybe, one of them will break.'

TWENTY-SEVEN

t took Vogel and Saslow just under half an hour to drive from Hartland to Northam. By the time they arrived, there was a small group of reporters and photographers outside the Ferguson home, six or seven of them. There was also a TV news team.

'Good to see the British press corps is still so on the ball,' muttered Vogel unenthusiastically.

The whole assembled throng surged forward as the two officers climbed out of the car and headed for the front door of All Seasons. The door opened before either of them had knocked or rung the bell. At first it seemed to have done so all on its own as neither Vogel nor Saslow could see anyone in the hallway. Then they realized that Amelia Ferguson, who had presumably been peeping out of a window at what was going on outside, was standing pressed against the wall, half hidden behind the open door.

'Come in quickly,' she muttered. 'Please. They're awful those people, awful. They're just vultures.'

Vogel was inclined to agree. On occasions, anyway. But as a policeman of long standing he also believed that a free press was a necessary evil without which a free society could not function as such. And the press did have its uses. Like so many in the police force, he'd fed journalists information over the years and used them in all sorts of ways to assist his enquiries. Sometimes without them quite realising what he was up to.

He and Saslow stepped inside. Mrs Ferguson slammed the door shut behind them, still keeping out of camera shot.

Amelia looked as if she might have been crying. Vogel was mildly surprised. Perhaps the woman did have feelings, after all.

He wished her good evening and told her that he and Saslow would like to speak to her husband.

'He's not here,' replied Mrs Ferguson sharply. She sounded angry and upset. 'He went off again, and again I've no idea where he's gone. Somebody sent him a text. He read it and he just left. Leaving me with the children, not knowing when he'll be back or what's going on . . .' She paused, a thought clearly occurring to her.

'Look, I don't want you to think, I mean, I am sure Sam has a good reason for whatever he's doing. He's probably just protecting me . . . He might have gone to the police station . . . I just don't know . . . I don't want to cause any more trouble . . .'

Vogel thought he understood what she was getting at. This was a difficult woman with a naturally arrogant nature, although there wasn't much sign of that at the moment. But there was little doubt of her loyalty to her husband and to her son, albeit not to her dead daughter-in-law.

'Mrs Ferguson, I don't think you are likely to cause much more trouble than has already befallen your family,' the DCI remarked gently. 'I think you may be afraid of being disloyal to him, but I urge you to give us all the help you can, for your husband's sake, possibly for his safety. There has been a disturbing development. We need to speak to Mr Ferguson as a matter of urgency.'

'But I just told you, I don't know where he is,' said Amelia, looking even more distressed.

'All right, let's go through everything again, shall we?' persisted Vogel. 'Mr Ferguson received a text and then left without any real explanation, is that right?'

'Yes,' Amelia agreed with only a little reluctance. 'That's what happened.'

'How long ago was that?'

'Oh, you only just missed him actually. About ten or fifteen minutes ago.'

'I see, and he didn't tell you who the text was from?'

'No. He told me nothing. He hasn't told me anything for the best part of two days.'

'And am I correct to assume you were unable to see the screen of his phone?'

'That's correct, yes, I couldn't see it, he turned his back on me, then put his phone back in his pocket.'

'All right, now there may be a way of finding out who texted your husband,' said Vogel, who had a bit of a love affair with

modern technology, had been accused of preferring his computer
to people, and was known by his colleagues as 'the geek'.

'Does Mr Ferguson have an iPad which might be linked to
his phone?'

'He has an iPad,' replied Amelia. 'Though he doesn't use it
much nowadays because the phones are so good, and he always
has his with him. But I have no idea whether or not it's linked
to his phone. In fact, I didn't even know that was possible.'

'Do you know where the iPad is, can you show it to us?'

'Yes, it's in the office, in the desk drawer.'

Amelia Ferguson led the way upstairs to a room on the street
side clearly used as an office. Everything in it, the Mac desktop,
the furniture, the books, looked clean, shiny, and in its place.
Vogel was not surprised when Amelia removed the iPad from
the first drawer she opened.

He switched it on. No password. He was straight in. And he
was quickly able to ascertain that the tablet was linked to a
mobile phone.

He opened messages, and there was the text Sam had received
earlier.

> Meet me at the old chapel outside Eastleigh, soon as you
> can. I have something to show you. It's vital that we talk.
> Gerry.

Vogel felt the back of his neck stiffen as he read it and saw who
it was from.

Without comment he passed the iPad to Saslow.

The DS gasped involuntarily as she looked at the screen.

'G-Gerry Barham?' she queried haltingly.

'Must be. The number's plumbed in the phone too, indicating
regular contact. Only this message is timed at 17.43 and we
certainly know it can't be from Gerry, don't we?'

Saslow was about to respond, but Amelia Ferguson got there
first.

'What are you talking about?' she asked. 'What's Gerry
Barham got to do with anything?'

Vogel turned to her, his expression and his voice grave.

'Mrs Ferguson, I have to tell you that Gerry Barham has been found dead following an incident at sea, and we are treating his death as suspicious.'

He reached to take the iPad from Saslow and passed it to Amelia.

'As you can see, the text Mr Ferguson received appears to be from Mr Barham asking your husband to meet him urgently. But we know Gerry Barham cannot have sent it, because he was already dead.'

'I don't understand . . .' said Amelia.

'I'm sure you don't Mrs Ferguson. Do you know this chapel by any chance? Has your husband got any connection with it at all?'

'I know the chapel, yes. Everybody does. Somebody from London bought it years ago to convert into a house, but they couldn't get planning permission. They started to build and were stopped halfway through. It's a bit of an eyesore now. Nothing to do with Sam. I have no idea why he would meet anybody there . . .'

'All right, Mrs Ferguson. Look, I am in little doubt now that your husband is in danger. And to be on the safe side, I'm sending a uniformed team round here. Someone will be with you twenty-four seven until we've sorted this. They'll keep those vultures at bay for you, too. Meanwhile, don't open the door to anyone—'

Amelia interrupted him.

'My God,' she said. 'Whatever is going on?'

'Try not to worry, Mrs Ferguson,' Vogel continued, with a confidence he did not feel. 'Saslow and I are going to find your husband and bring him home to you.'

Saslow was ahead of him. Literally. She was already on her way down the stairs. Vogel followed hard on her heels.

'As soon as we're in the car let's get Peters on the hands-free, we need her to send backup, and make sure we know exactly where this damned chapel is, too,' said Vogel. 'And you know what, Dawn, if we don't get there smartish, I think we'll have another death on our hands.'

TWENTY-EIGHT

The old chapel, about a mile out of Eastleigh up a narrow country lane, had been built in the nineteenth century at the height of Methodism, in common with most rural chapels, almost all now abandoned, throughout Britain.

Many have been successfully converted into residential dwellings. This one was still surrounded by elderly scaffolding and piles of debris bearing witness to the unsuccessful attempt to do just that, which Amelia Ferguson had referred to.

Saslow, who had broken every speed limit on the way, pulled their car to a halt with a shriek of brakes in the layby opposite the dilapidated once-white building. There were already two other vehicles parked there. Sam Ferguson's blue Range Rover, which they recognized at once, and a business-like looking black Land Rover Defender. Saslow and Vogel were out in a flash, running at full pelt across the lane and the overgrown and rubble-strewn patch of rough ground directly in front of the chapel. A door at the far end, which looked as if it had until very recently been boarded up, stood slightly ajar.

Vogel tried to push it further open but failed. He squeezed his way in followed by Saslow.

Once inside he couldn't see anything at first. There were a number of windows, of course, but these were also boarded up, and there was little light.

Vogel could just make out the figure of a man, who seemed to be turning to look at the two officers.

'Mr Ferguson,' Vogel called. 'Is that you?'

At the same time, out of the corner of his eye, he glimpsed a movement. He glanced upwards to where there was a precarious looking balcony, high in the chapel's vaulted ceiling. He could hear something too. A scraping noise. Suddenly he saw a large object begin to appear over the edge, directly above where Sam Ferguson was standing.

'Move Sam, get out the way, move,' Vogel yelled at the top of his voice.

Sam only then seemed to register what was happening. He glanced upwards just as the large object, revealing itself to be a steel beam of the sort used in construction, toppled, or most likely was pushed, off the balcony edge. Simultaneously, and with perhaps unexpected speed and agility, Sam threw himself sideways, landing full length on the uneven chapel floor.

The beam, an RSJ about ten feet long and most likely weighing between three and four hundred pounds, crashed to the ground alongside Sam, sending up a cloud of dust and dirt, and missing him by inches.

'Stay down, Sam,' called Vogel, realising as he spoke that he had no idea if the older man would even be able to get up.

Ferguson stayed down.

Vogel's eyes began to adjust more fully. He peered through the gloom. There must be someone up on the balcony. That RSJ hadn't come crashing down all on its own. The balcony hadn't collapsed, it was still intact, in spite of its precarious appearance. And he didn't think it was any coincidence that Sam Ferguson had been standing directly below the beam when it fell.

There was someone up there all right. Someone who knew how to go about causing fatal damage to another human being. A killer. Someone who had almost certainly already killed twice.

Vogel was listening as well as looking. He thought he heard footsteps. Maybe the sound of someone coming down a staircase, if indeed there was a staircase, but he supposed there would have been once. Or it could have been footsteps on a ladder. And was that the shadow of someone moving towards him and Saslow? Or towards the door? He couldn't quite make it out.

'Saslow, get out of here,' he hissed.

The young DS had not so long ago ended up in grave danger, during a previous investigation which Vogel had headed. She had come close to death and Vogel had felt responsible. He still felt responsible. He wasn't going to risk that happening to her again.

But, of course, Dawn Saslow had a mind of her own. And she was just as stubborn as her senior officer.

'No boss, I'm sticking with you,' she said.

Vogel turned towards her, about to protest. At that moment a dark shape came out of nowhere and at him, cannoning into his body with considerable force. Vogel was knocked sideways onto the ground, the breath forced out of his body. The shape continued to move at speed towards the doorway, its momentum barely slackening, strikingly silhouetted against the incoming light. To Vogel's horror Saslow, whom he knew to be a fast runner, had already taken off after it. And the dark shape was their killer, Vogel had little doubt of that. He tried to shout, to order her to stop, not that there was any guarantee she would take any notice. But he did not have the breath to do so. All he could do was watch, and pray that Saslow did not catch up with that shape.

Then he heard something, something which at that moment he thought was the best sound he had ever heard. The wail of the siren of a police car, clearly approaching at speed up the lane, its siren growing louder by the second. More than one police car, he swiftly realized.

The shape hesitated. Saslow was gaining ground. Vogel found his voice.

'Saslow, stop,' he yelled. 'Our backup is here.'

Somewhat to his surprise she did stop. Maybe she, too, had remembered her last near-death experience.

The shape, now revealed to be a man, surely it had to be a man, wearing dark clothing, turned briefly back, looking towards where Vogel was lying, but the light was behind him and Vogel could not see his face.

In convoy, two patrol cars arrived up the lane from the direction of Instow, and a police four-wheel-drive, of the sort used by armed-response units, appeared from the other, effectively blocking in the three vehicles already parked in the lay-by.

The man turned to the right, then to the left, presumably looking for a path of escape, and back to the right. Then he took off at a run. As he disappeared from Vogel's path of vision he appeared to be making a phone call.

Still breathing with difficulty, Vogel hoisted himself to his feet.

'All right, Saslow, I'll take it from here,' he said. 'You go take care of Sam Ferguson.'

From the lane, again just out of his limited field of vision, he could now hear the sound of a male voice, amplified by a megaphone.

'Stop. Armed police. Stop. And put your hands on your head. Stop.'

Vogel made his way as fast as he could to the doorway of the shed, where he paused before stepping outside, instead peering cautiously around the door.

The darkly clad figure was now standing quite still about twenty yards away, to Vogel's left. The DCI watched with some satisfaction as he obediently put his hands on his head.

Two armed officers moved forward, grabbed his arms, frisked him, and cuffed him, very nearly in one practiced movement.

Vogel approached at once.

'Well done, lads,' he remarked.

The darkly clad figure was wearing a balaclava type hood. Vogel realized he wouldn't have been able to see his head even if there had been proper light in the chapel.

'Get that hood off,' instructed Vogel. 'Let's see who we've got here then, shall we?'

One of the armed officers promptly ripped off the balaclava hood, revealing the lightly tanned face of a man probably in his early forties, with a full head of dark blonde hair and striking blue eyes. He was a tall, rangy looking character, immediately familiar to Vogel. But the DCI couldn't quite place him, at first.

Then he got it.

'I know you,' he said. 'I know who you are. We met at the yacht club yesterday.'

The man did not respond. He stared straight ahead, his facial expression giving nothing away.

Vogel thought for a few seconds. He had a good memory for both faces and names. In fact, Vogel had a good memory for almost everything.

'You're Jimmy Granger, the graphic designer from Instow and new member of the club,' he announced just a little triumphantly. 'Only you're no more a graphic designer than I am, are you?'

'No comment,' said the man.

TWENTY-NINE

Vogel arrested and cautioned Jimmy Granger and asked for him to be delivered to Barnstaple police station.

A shaken looking Sam Ferguson was by then standing in front of the chapel watching the arrest. Saslow was with him, one hand tucked supportively beneath his right elbow.

Sam seemed to be favouring his right leg, and his right hand was bleeding.

Vogel walked across the yard to join them.

'You all right, Mr Ferguson?' he enquired, well aware that the older man clearly wasn't. He was trembling, and his face was ashen.

'Hurt my knee when I fell to the ground, and grazed my hand when I tried to save myself,' Sam replied. 'Other than that, I think I'm OK.'

'Good,' said Vogel.

He wanted some straight talking from Sam Ferguson at last, so he decided to strike whilst the other man was in obvious shock.

'You do realize you were very nearly killed in there, don't you?' he asked.

Ferguson nodded.

'Yes, and I think I would have been if it hadn't been for you two,' he said. 'You saved my life.'

'Perhaps,' said Vogel. 'You can do something for me now. You can start telling me what you know, as you clearly know much more than you have revealed so far, about the murder of your daughter-in-law, and a lot else besides, I reckon. I want the truth, all of it.'

Ferguson nodded again.

'Yes, of course, absolutely everything, I promise you,' he said, with what Vogel was sure was rare subservience. 'Gerry told me I didn't know what I was getting into. And he was certainly right about that. I came here to meet Gerry . . .' Ferguson paused, looking puzzled.

'Where is Gerry? Did he tell you I was here?'

'No, Mr Ferguson, he did not,' said Vogel bluntly. 'I am afraid Mr Barham is dead.'

'G-Gerry, d-dead?' Sam stumbled. 'No. H-how? He wasn't murdered too, w-was he?'

'We think so, yes.'

'And someone . . . someone came after me, too. A complete stranger, I think. I saw his face just then, when he was arrested. I have no idea who . . .'

Ferguson broke off in mid-sentence. There was suddenly real fear in his eyes.

'Mr Vogel, my family. Amelia. The twins. Oh, what have I done?'

His voice grew louder, and there was a note of near hysteria in it.

'Are they in danger too?'

'I think the danger might be over, certainly for the time being, now we've made this arrest,' replied Vogel. 'But in any case, I have arranged for a police presence at your home twenty-four seven. Your family are safe, Mr Ferguson.'

'T-thank you, thank you.'

He'd lowered his voice to a more normal level, but, as he spoke, Sam Ferguson's knees began to buckle. Saslow gripped his elbow more firmly. Vogel stepped forward to take his other arm.

'An ambulance is on its way, we need to get you checked out in hospital,' said the DCI. 'But first, I really want to speak to you before we interview your assailant, and indeed before we talk to your son again. Do you think you might feel up to that? We can sit in our car.'

'Yes, of course, anything I can do, anything,' said Ferguson. 'I can't believe I've been so stupid.'

'Thank you,' said Vogel, who couldn't wait to hear exactly what it was that Sam Ferguson had done which he now regretted so much.

Together with Saslow he helped Sam to the car. Vogel didn't think the other man was badly hurt physically, although his knee looked sore, but he was clearly badly shaken. The DCI remained determined to take full advantage of that.

He sat in the front with Ferguson. Saslow installed herself in the back.

'Right, Mr Ferguson, I want you to begin at the beginning,' instructed Vogel. 'It is becoming clear that you have been afraid of something, or at least that you probably had certain knowledge which was causing you concern, ever since the death of your daughter-in-law. Could you tell me about that, please?'

'Well, we were always suspicious of Jane,' replied Ferguson. 'We didn't like her, Amelia and I, neither of us liked her, I told you that before. But it was more than that. There was something about her. We were suspicious of her past, which seemed . . . so . . . so mysterious. Felix, well, Felix is loyal by nature, always has been, and he loved Jane so much . . . Look, he couldn't have killed Jane, you've got to believe that, Mr Vogel. Perhaps you do believe that now?'

The man had switched to another train of thought. He was obviously desperate to save his son, and Vogel didn't blame him. Vogel had, of course, never been entirely convinced of Felix's guilt. But he wasn't telling Sam Ferguson that yet.

'Clearly we have new strands of enquiry, which I promise you we will investigate thoroughly,' he said. 'Now, please continue with what you were starting to tell me.'

Sam nodded.

'Yes, well, as I was saying, Felix is loyal by nature, and he told us very little, and Jane nothing at all,' he continued. 'When it became apparent there were problems, he just said Jane kept having bad dreams and wasn't sleeping well. He made fairly light of it, but we could tell he was worried, and he's not a worrier. Not normally. Not Felix.

'Then something happened. And I did something I now regret with all my heart. It was about six weeks ago. A weekend. We had the kids on Friday evening as usual. Felix told us he and Jane were going out, to the cinema and for a meal. Something they didn't do very often. In spite of how we felt about Jane we were glad they were doing something normal together. For the sake of the children. About seven o'clock, I think it was, Felix called. He sounded quite stressed. He said Jane had convinced herself she'd left the iron on and the house was going to burn down. Now, she was a worrier. And she could be quite neurotic.

We always thought that. She wanted to go home and check, call off their night out, which Felix had been looking forward to. He asked if I would drive over and check everything was all right and text him back, so he could put her mind at rest.

'So, I did. The iron was still out on the ironing board, but it was switched off, of course. As Felix had always suspected. I was just about to text Felix when I thought I heard a noise upstairs. I went up to check, not really expecting to find anything, opened the door to the master bedroom, flicked the lights on, and saw at once that there was a chair in the middle of the room beneath the smoke alarm, which had been removed, and there were wires hanging down. I walked in, thinking at first that the room was empty, then I turned around and there was Gerry standing behind the door. Trying to hide himself, only not making a very good job of it. I don't know which of us was the most shocked to see each other, to tell the truth.

'He was holding two smoke alarms. I asked him what on earth was going on. He tried to prevaricate, but he clearly had no explanation at all.

'Then, well, I half remembered something I'd read, in a news-paper or maybe online, about surveillance cameras concealed in what appear to be ordinary smoke alarms, so I grabbed the ones Gerry was holding. He barely tried to stop me. Well, I am about six inches taller than him and four stone heavier. Sure enough, one of them was a surveillance camera. I could hardly believe my eyes. Little Gerry Barham was installing a hidden surveillance camera in my son's bedroom.'

Vogel blinked rapidly behind his spectacles. He didn't know quite what he'd expected to hear from Sam Ferguson, but certainly not this.

'So what did you do next?' he asked.

'Well, I told Gerry not to move, then I reached for my phone and started to dial 999,' Ferguson continued. 'Then I stopped. I thought I'd talk to him first. Find out what was going on. I'll be honest, Mr Vogel, it occurred to me very quickly, and I'm really not proud of this, that I might be able to use this situation. And that I might learn the answers to some of the questions Amelia and I had been asking for years.'

'Sam, one of your son's neighbours was putting a secret camera in your son's bedroom,' interjected Vogel, who'd decided formality could be abandoned now that he had just saved the other man's life. 'Didn't you think he might merely be a voyeur?'

'What, little Gerry?' queried Sam. 'No way.'

'So what was he doing then? Why was he spying on your family, in an extremely, uh, intimate manner?'

'He told me that he was in . . . well, a rather special branch of the civil service, that's all he said, and he was suddenly given a big bonus and an early retirement deal generous enough for him to relocate to Instow and live in some luxury for the rest of his life. In return he had to keep an eye on Jane. That's all. He said he never knew why, and he didn't ask. Jane and Felix seemed like an ordinary happily married young couple to him. He cultivated them, and reported back periodically to his employers, and everyone was happy. There never seemed to be any cause for concern. Then Gerry had a drink with Felix, a week or so before I found him in their house, and Felix got drunk and opened his heart a bit, confessed how worried he was about Jane's bad dreams. How she woke up screaming, quite hysterically, and how it was beginning to affect their whole lives. He told Gerry far more than he'd ever told me. Said he felt it was caused by something in her past life that she claimed to have no memory of.

'Well, Gerry reported back. He said that afterwards he wished he hadn't. His controllers suddenly went into overdrive. They said they wanted to know all about these dreams. That it was vital. And they sent him that smoke alarm surveillance outfit. A very sophisticated little number that linked to his phone.'

'Did you ask Gerry how he got in to your son's house? I presume it was all locked up when you got there.'

'Yes. He told me he had a set of keys. He'd sneaked off and got them cut one day when he and his wife were babysitting. Just in case, he said.'

'What did you do next?' Vogel asked.

'Well, I wanted to know about Jane's past more than ever. I told Gerry I wouldn't call the police, in fact I wouldn't tell anyone about our meeting, I would let him carry on with his surveillance unhindered, as long as he shared any relevant material with me. I told him I wanted to see what was going on in my son's life.'

'And Gerry agreed to this?'

'Yes. I suppose he didn't have much choice. I said that if he didn't agree, I'd blow his nasty little operation, whatever it really was, out of the water.'

'Did you see any footage?'

'Yes. Mostly Gerry just called me and told me what he'd seen. But I insisted on seeing at least some of it. It was pretty disturbing stuff. Jane screaming her head off. Felix trying desperately to calm her down and keep her quiet. And then . . . well, there was the time he woke to find Jane shaking little Joanna. We didn't actually see that because it happened in the children's bedroom. But there was film of them in their bedroom afterwards, when, uh . . .'

'When what, Sam?'

'Well, Felix was clearly very frustrated. Furious actually. And he isn't an angry man by nature. He told Jane he would never trust her with his children again. And, uh, well, I am afraid he hit her. Across the face. And his ring caught her cheek, cut it open. There was a lot of blood. It wasn't very pleasant to see.'

'I'm sure it wasn't.'

'No. So, when Jane died, and we learned a murder investigation had been launched, well, I knew right away I should tell you about Gerry and his mysterious surveillance, but I was afraid it would lead you to suspect Felix.'

'Do you still have any of that footage?'

'No. Gerry showed it me, but he wouldn't send me a copy. Not of anything. I had to meet up with him and watch on his phone. It was . . . uh . . . all a bit sordid really, I'm afraid.'

'Yes, it was, wasn't it?'

Vogel knew he was blinking vigorously behind his spectacles again. And his attempts to control it were not succeeding very well.

'You were intruding on your son and daughter-in-law's privacy, spying on them, watching them and allowing someone else, a relative stranger, to watch them in their most intimate moments, in their own bedroom,' commented the DCI. 'Did that not concern you at all?'

'Of course it did. But I so wanted to know the truth about Jane, I really didn't think it through. After the night when Felix hit Jane, I had big second thoughts about the whole thing. I asked Gerry to take his camera down. He said it was too late, I was in it with him, and there were people involved that I wouldn't want to cross.'

'Do you still not know who these people are?'

'Not really, although I'm beginning to guess they are some sort of secret service, or maybe an undercover police unit. And I just knew Gerry was holding back on me about all sorts of things. Jane's death really frightened me. I arranged to meet Gerry yesterday afternoon, on the beach at low tide, and I was much tougher with him. I felt, probably wrongly, that I had nothing to lose. I told him if he didn't come clean with me I would destroy him. God knows how I would have done any such thing. But he seemed to be in as bad a state as I was. Worse if anything.

'It was then that he told me I'd only seen the edited version of the night Felix hit Jane. He showed me the full footage. The camera was one of those activated by movement, of course. The stuff I'd already seen ended with Jane lying down in the bed next to Felix, who already seemed to be sleeping. But there was more. Later, Jane woke Felix up and told him that she really had to talk to him. She'd remembered something terrible from the past, from her childhood. She mentioned a psychiatrist and regression therapy, which had brought it to the front of her mind, but she hadn't been quite able to grasp it. She said she'd remained in a kind of denial until that night when she had frightened Joanna so much, and it had all come flooding back . . .'

Sam stopped abruptly.

'Please go on,' Vogel prompted.

Sam looked as if he was about to continue, then he shook his head.

'No, Mr Vogel,' he said. 'I just can't. You're going to have to ask Felix. I've already intruded unforgivably on the lives of my son and his poor wife, you said so yourself, and with terrible consequences.'

'Look Sam, you've been guilty at least once before of withholding evidence during the course of this investigation. Please don't make the same mistake again.'

'I'm sorry,' said Sam. 'It's just too much, you see. Felix must decide whether to tell you.'

Vogel raised his voice very slightly.

'You are treading very dangerous ground, Sam,' he said. 'You should be aware that I could charge you with perverting the course of justice. And Felix too, if he also decides to hold out on us.'

Sam shrugged.

'You must do whatever you have to, Mr Vogel,' he said.

He spoke quietly, which somehow made him sound all the more obdurate. Vogel considered he was going to get no further with Sam Ferguson on that particular line of questioning. Not for the moment, anyway.

'All right, Sam,' he said. 'Let's move on, for the moment. Are we to presume that the people who employed Gerry to spy on Jane knew whatever it was that she had done, and had her watched all those years because of it?'

'Yes, Mr Vogel,' he said. 'That's what I came to believe, anyway. Although I still don't understand it. Indeed, they may well have been protecting her from afar, until they learned what she had remembered. Which, they wouldn't have done if I hadn't allowed Gerry to plant his damned surveillance camera. Collaborated with him, in fact . . .'

Sam leaned forward slightly in his seat and lowered his face in his hands. He continued to speak, mumbling slightly through his fingers.

'I asked Gerry again yesterday, who and why. He said he had never known why, not really, and I had to trust him, it was better, far better, if I didn't know who.'

Sam looked up.

'He was right about that, wasn't he?' he said. 'They nearly killed me back there.'

'Somebody tried, that's for sure,' agreed Vogel.

Sam might be a big burly man, fit for his years, but he was clearly deeply shaken. His face was ashen, and his hands were still trembling. Vogel thought it was time to get him medical attention, but he had one last question. The most important of all.

'Sam, did Gerry have camera footage of Jane's murder?' asked the DCI.

'No,' said Sam. 'Or at least, that's what he told me. He said the surveillance camera had stopped working. It was the first thing he checked after he and Anne discovered Jane's body. In fact, he said he spent most of the rest of that night fiddling with his phone, checking and double-checking, but the last forage he

FOOTAGE ?

had was from earlier in the evening when Felix had gone up to his bedroom to change into his dinner suit. Gerry didn't know whether something had gone wrong with it, maybe the battery had drained, or if someone had deliberately dismantled it before killing Jane.'

'So that someone would have to have known it was there in the first place, and you don't think Felix had any idea he was being filmed, do you, Sam?'

'I'm sure he didn't,' replied Sam firmly.

'One last thing,' said the DCI. 'I know you didn't harm Gerry, you thought he'd asked you to meet him here, but where were you this morning?'

Sam laughed briefly and without humour.

'I drove to Exeter to try to get a meeting with the chief constable,' he said. 'I thought that if anyone knew what was really going on, it would be him. And I thought he might help me. We used to play rugby together. But he clearly didn't want to see me. I waited for hours before giving up.'

'Why didn't you tell your wife that?'

'Look, it was before Felix was arrested. Amelia still believed Jane had taken her own life, and thought I did too. She would just have worried. When I arrived home and walked in on the arrest, I wasn't going to come out with it in front of all of you. Then later, well, I'd failed, hadn't I? So there didn't seem much point. To tell the truth, I haven't really known what the hell I've been doing since Jane died.'

'All right, Sam, that's enough for now,' said Vogel. 'But you do realize I will have to talk to you again, don't you? Particularly if Felix fails to give us the information we need. Next time, it will be a formal interview at the police station, and if you refuse to offer your full cooperation you will be charged accordingly.'

Sam nodded very slightly. He looked as if he was past caring.

An ambulance had arrived. Two paramedics were standing by it. Vogel escorted Sam over to them, impatient now to get to Barnstaple police station. There were two men detained there who he was, by the minute, becoming more and more eager to interview.

THIRTY

On the way to Barnstaple Vogel spoke to DI Peters back at the incident room to inform her of all that had occurred. He asked her to organize a CSI team to search Granger's flat, which didn't require a search warrant as the man had been formally arrested on suspicion of a capital offence.

'The address should be in the system,' he said. 'On that list of members of the NDYC.'

He also asked Peters to dispatch DC Perkins to Estuary Vista Close to re-interview Anne Barham.

'I wonder what she really knows about her husband's past, Saslow,' Vogel mused. 'A special branch of the civil service, eh? Looks like he might have been some sort of spook. If he was, it's hard to believe his wife didn't have any idea. He must have been darned good at his job.'

'He didn't look like a spook, seemed like a bit of a nerd to me, boss,' said Saslow.

'What would you expect?' asked Vogel. 'James Bond? Think boffin instead of nerd. GCHQ is one of our major secret intelligence services, and it's staffed almost entirely by high-tech whizz kids, mathematicians, linguists, and the like. All top level.'

'OK, but do we really believe the British intelligence service goes around murdering people? That's pretty James Bond, isn't it?'

'They call it lethal force, I understand, Saslow. And I certainly don't believe it's unique to the Russian secret services. I wonder if you remember the death of Gareth Williams, he was a mathematician employed by GCHQ and seconded to MI6?'

'No, boss, I don't think I do,' responded Saslow.

'Ten years ago, probably before you were in the job, you're so damned young, Saslow,' said Vogel. 'I was in the Met, of course. Still a DC. It wasn't our finest hour. Williams' decomposing body was found in a North Face bag, padlocked from the outside, in the bath of his Pimlico flat. Our brass and MI6 collaborated on how the investigation should be handled, and all sorts of restrictions on information were imposed. Nonetheless, there was an inquest, as the law demands, and the coroner described Williams' death as "unnatural and likely to have been criminally meditated", prompting a second investigation. After another twelve months, the then DAC at the Met announced that the most probable scenario was that Williams had died alone in his flat as the result of locking himself in the bag.'

'Wow,' said Saslow. 'That sounds like some cover-up, boss.'

'And all in the interest of national security, Dawn,' Vogel continued. 'It has to be possible that something of that nature was going on here. I'm pretty sure it's what Nobby Clarke was driving at.'

'So you think Jimmy Granger is another spook, do you, boss?'

'I think that the man we have just arrested is almost certainly responsible for two murders and an attempted murder,' said Vogel. 'And I want him brought to justice, whoever the hell he is.'

By the time Vogel and Saslow arrived at Barnstaple police station, Jimmy Granger had been processed in the custody suite. He'd been photographed, and had his DNA and fingerprints taken. He'd supplied his address and other relevant personal details readily enough, but refused to be interviewed until he had a solicitor present. Two phones were found on his person. One was a burner phone with just a handful of numbers plumbed into it, the yacht club and a couple of other Instow numbers including Gerry Barham's, and an unidentified London number. This was the last number Granger had called before his arrest, and the time logged indicated that he had made the call when he'd realized he had little chance of escaping from outside the old chapel. Almost certainly when Vogel had seen him using his phone.

Vogel immediately called the London number, which rang out for more than a minute before cutting itself off. He planned to try it repeatedly, but had little hope of success. He asked Saslow to arrange for the number to be checked out. But neither did he hope for much success with that either.

The second phone had belonged to Gerry Barham, and a text had been sent from it that afternoon, hours after Gerry's disappearance and almost certainly after his death, to Sam Ferguson. The text instructing Sam to go to the old chapel at Eastleigh.

Granger was carrying little else when he was arrested, just some cash, a credit card, and a bunch of several keys. Vogel took a bet with himself that amongst these would be keys to Felix and Jane Ferguson's home, almost certainly also copied by Gerry Barham and forwarded to his mysterious employers.

Granger had the name of what appeared to be a standard High Street solicitor in Exeter. It was way after office hours, and it took time to track the man down. Whilst waiting to begin, Vogel tried two or three times to phone Nobby Clarke in order to report to her directly. She wasn't picking up, which was unusual.

Meanwhile, DC Perkins reported back on his interview with Anne Barham.

'She says Gerry was a civil servant with the Ministry of Defence, working in various departments over the years, usually dealing with finance,' said Perkins. 'Deployment of funds to the military, that sort of thing. I honestly don't think she had any idea he might be anything more than that, boss. He was a mathematician apparently.'

'Ah yes, along with half of GCHQ,' muttered Vogel, who was also aware that recruits to all three British secret intelligence services, MI5, MI6, and GCHQ, were instructed to use the 'civil servant with the MoD' job description in their personal life.

The solicitor finally arrived more than two hours later, to find not a lot was required of him. Jimmy eschewed the opportunity to discuss his case with the man. He had, it appeared, no real reason to do so, as during the formal interview which followed, Jimmy made only one reply.

He answered 'no comment' to every question.

The solicitor merely sat in silence.

Vogel suspected Granger had been deliberately time-wasting. He wondered what behind the scenes skulduggery might already be taking place, possibly instigated by the man's call to London.

Whatever the case, Vogel, who had himself deliberately delayed talking to Felix Ferguson again until after interviewing Granger, now realized that he may as well get on with it.

Saslow activated the video equipment in the small interview room, and made the usual announcement of those present, as a matter of record.

Vogel then took charge.

He began by telling Felix that there had been an attempt on his father's life and that Gerry Barham had been murdered.

Felix turned ashen. He looked shocked and bewildered.

'W-what's happening, Mr Vogel?' he asked haltingly. 'I-I don't understand. Is my father hurt?'

'Not badly,' said Vogel. 'Just bruised and shaken.'

Felix nodded a little absently. He was clearly trying to concentrate.

'And Gerry is dead? Murdered, you say. Does any of this have anything to do with Jane's death?'

'We don't know for certain, but we think so. It would be the most extraordinary set of coincidences if not.'

Vogel then explained about Gerry Barham's surveillance operation, the installation of a hidden surveillance camera in Jane and Felix's bedroom, and Sam Ferguson's complicity in it all.

Felix was incredulous. Of course he'd had no idea he and Jane were being filmed, he insisted. It was unbelievably shocking. He became even more shocked after Vogel asked him if he knew a man called Jimmy Granger. At first he said he didn't think so. Then he said the name might be familiar.

'Wait a minute, he's a new member of the yacht club, I think,' said Felix eventually. 'What's he got to do with it?'

'We think he was sent to Instow by persons as yet unknown, after Gerry Barham reported back on the results of his surveillance on Jane. Probably in order to take whatever action might be deemed necessary.'

For a moment or two Felix stared blankly at Vogel, in silence. He seemed to be having difficulty in taking in everything the DCI was saying. Vogel did not entirely blame him.

'I still don't understand,' he said eventually. 'Why would anything filmed by that damned camera make someone want to kill Jane?'

'I have no idea, Felix,' replied Vogel. 'I was hoping you might.'

Felix shook his head. He did not speak.

'C'mon, Felix,' said Vogel sharply. 'Your wife is dead. You have been arrested on suspicion of her murder. I am trying to get to the truth here. For Jane's sake, please give me some assistance. At least, tell me all you know.'

Felix sat up a little straighter in his chair.

'All right,' he said, a note of resignation in his voice. 'Jane was having terrible dreams, you know that. There was one night, n-not long before she died, when things got particularly bad. I was woken in the night by screaming. I found her in the children's bedroom. She had little Jo in her arms, and she was shaking her. It was terrible. Awful. I snatched Jo away from Jane. And, well, then I lost my temper, I don't often do that. I was in shock, I think. I, uh, I hit out. I struck my wife in the face . . .'

Felix paused.

'But presumably you know that?' he queried. 'You'll have seen it all by now, I assume. I mean, we were being filmed. In our own bedroom. Jesus!'

'No,' replied Vogel, adding disingenuously, 'your father doesn't actually have the footage, but we do expect to recover it in the near future from other sources.'

'He's seen it, though? Damn him. Must have done. And presumably told you all about it?'

'He told us that he had seen film of you hitting your wife, and how your ring cut her face,' said Vogel. 'You lied to us about that, didn't you?'

'Yes,' Felix admitted. 'But wouldn't you? It was the only time I ever hit Jane, and I was ashamed. In spite of the circumstances, I regretted it as soon as I struck her. And I knew it would look bad for me, after I realized I was your prime suspect.'

'What about your wife's other bruises?'

'I told you before. She fell in the garden playing with the twins. That was absolutely true.'

Vogel thought it almost certainly was. But he intended to pile all the pressure he could on the other man.

'Is it, Felix?' he asked.

'Yes, yes, I promise you, Mr Vogel,' said Felix.

'All right. Let's say I accept that, for the moment, and we move on. What happened next that night?'

'Uh, nothing much. We both went to bed and to sleep. At least I slept. I don't know about Jane.'

'She woke you up, didn't she? In the middle of the night?'

Felix sighed.

'Yes. OK. She woke me up. So you know about that?'

'Yes. The camera was activated by movement.'

'Then if you know what happened, why are you asking me about it now?' asked Felix wearily.

'I don't know what happened,' replied Vogel honestly. 'Your father indicated that Jane shared with you something of considerable enormity. That she remembered something terrible about her past which she revealed to you that night. And almost certainly it was what she remembered that started the chain of events leading ultimately to her death. But your father wouldn't tell me what it was. He said he had intruded enough on you and Jane. I need you to tell me, Felix, exactly what Jane remembered.'

'You said you had sources who were going to give you the film from that night, so why do you need me to tell you anything?' countered Felix stubbornly.

'Because I don't know how long that might take,' replied Vogel, which in itself was true enough. 'And I don't want any further delay in completing this investigation. I should remind you that you are already guilty of withholding evidence. As is your father. And I should warn you, as I already have him, that I am on the verge of charging you both with perverting the course of justice.'

Felix smiled without humour.

'Not much of a threat as I'm banged up already accused of murdering Jane,' he said.

'But you have not been charged,' murmured Vogel.

Felix looked thoughtful, as if he could maybe see a glimmer of at least a certain degree of hope.

'All right,' he said. 'Look, one of the reasons I didn't tell you this before, is that I didn't really believe what Jane said she'd remembered. I mean. I couldn't. I couldn't believe it. If I'd let myself accept what Jane told me as the truth, it would have been the end really, the end of our life together, it would have had to be . . .'

Felix stopped, lowering his head into his hands.

'Please go on,' said Vogel. It was half an instruction, half encouragement.

Felix looked up. There were tears in his eyes.

'J-Jane said that when she came round after I'd found her shaking Joanna, long-buried memories started to return,' he began haltingly. 'Q-quite terrifying memories, which she believed were what lay behind her nightmares, causing her to wake up screaming hysterically. She said she thought her regression therapy may have taken her back to the cause of her bad dreams. But she truly had never known exactly what they were about until that night. Then she just blurted it out.

"'I killed my own sister, I stabbed her to death, that is what my dreams are about," she said.'

Felix paused to wipe away the tears which were now running down his cheeks.

Vogel remained silent, with difficulty. He certainly had not expected this. He knew he was blinking at speed behind his spectacles. He was aware of Saslow sitting very still beside him. Both of them were waiting anxiously for Felix to continue, desperate that nothing should stop him from doing so.

'Jane looked absolutely stricken, and I was just completely stunned,' Felix began again, after just a few seconds.

"'When you found me holding Joanna, shaking Joanna, it all came back to me," she said.

'She'd remembered back to when she was a little girl, to one night when her mother came into the bedroom she shared with her sister, and a kind of horror story unfolded. She suddenly became aware that her sister was dead beside her. And, that she was holding a knife. A knife dripping blood.

"'I was screaming, and my mother was screaming – at least I think the woman was my mother, she must have been, but it wasn't clear," Jane told me. "Everything else was crystal clear. I had this knife with a big long blade in my hand. And there was blood everywhere."

'Well, I just couldn't believe my ears. I didn't handle it well. I didn't handle it at all. I just jumped out of bed shouting that it couldn't be, she must be mistaken, the damned trick cyclist had messed with her brain. It was all just another dream.

'Jane wouldn't have it. She said she was quite sure of what had happened. That she was suddenly very certain about her early childhood. She'd been one of twins, like our children. And the sister who died, the sister she had killed, had been her twin. That seemed to make it even worse, somehow, if anything could be worse.

'I still insisted that I didn't believe her. That it couldn't be real. It was all just inside her head.

'But the truth was I didn't know what the hell to believe. I did know that if I admitted to myself that I had any doubts at all, I would have to leave Jane, I would have to destroy our family because I wouldn't be able to trust Jane with our children. I just ran out of the room, leaving Jane with tears running down her face. And afterwards I went into a kind of denial. I was worried sick, of course, but I just kept on telling myself it had only been a dream, it must have been only a dream. Jane had never killed anyone, whatever she thought she remembered. The only way I could carry on was to convince myself of that. And tell no one. I wouldn't even talk about it to Jane.

'Then later, of course, I believed it was the reason that Jane had killed herself. Which we all thought she had. At first, anyway. I felt so guilty that I hadn't helped her.'

Felix stopped quite abruptly. Vogel decided it was time to intervene.

'Yet, after Jane's death, you withheld this information from the police, even though you must have known how significant it could be,' said Vogel sternly. 'Why did you do that?'

'For my children,' replied Felix. 'I feared it all becoming public knowledge. As it probably would have done at an inquest, let alone a trial. How could I let my children grow up thinking their mother was a killer?'

Vogel was a father. He couldn't help feeling considerable sympathy for Felix Ferguson. He decided to put the other man out of his misery. In as much as anything could under such tragic circumstances.

'All right, Felix,' said the DCI. 'You should know that Jimmy Granger has been arrested on suspicion of the murder of both Jane and Gerry Barham, and of attempting to murder your father. And in view of this development, I am going to arrange for you to be released from custody.'

Felix sat back in his chair and closed his eyes, just for a few seconds. Vogel could see the relief washing over him.

'I still don't understand, though, Mr Vogel,' he remarked. 'Suicide would make an awful sort of sense. But murder? Why would Jane's dream, true or not, make anyone want to kill her? Now. All these years later.'

'I don't know,' said Vogel honestly. 'But I intend to find out . . .'

Quite abruptly, Felix sat bolt upright.

'I've just realized something,' he said. 'If my father hadn't made that wicked pact with Gerry Barham, Jane would still be alive. Nobody would have known that she had remembered the cause of her dreams. Nobody would have known anything.'

'Well, we can't be sure of that, Felix,' said Vogel.

'Oh, yes we can,' said Felix, the horror of it showing in his eyes. 'If he had reported Barham to the police, none of this would have happened. I don't see that there is any doubt about that.'

At three in the morning, after another two unsuccessful attempts at interviewing Jimmy Granger, an exhausted Vogel and Saslow prepared to return to the Seagate.

On the way Vogel called DI Peters, who was also still at work, to check on developments at the incident room.

She quickly told him that the second interview of Sid Merton, the witness who claimed to have seen Gerry sailing towards the estuary on the morning of his death, had produced highly significant results.

'When pushed he admitted that the person at the helm of the *Lady Anne* had been wearing a woolly hat pulled down over his ears and sunglasses, that the boat had been right in the middle of the river, and that he couldn't be absolutely sure it was Gerry, but had just assumed it was because it was Gerry's boat.

'He also said that, upon reflection, there had been something a little unusual. He'd noticed that the *Lady Anne* was towing one of the rubber dinghies the NDYC members use as tenders to get out to their boats on their river moorings. Apparently, they usually leave them on the moorings.'

'Do we know if those dinghies have outboards?' asked Vogel.

'Only small ones, boss, about two hp, but yes they do,' replied DI Peters.

'Do we know if one of those dinghies could get someone ashore from way out in the estuary? Particularly in the weather we had yesterday.'

'I've already had it checked out, boss. Apparently the answer is yes. It could do the job. And don't forget the weather didn't kick up until three or four hours after Barham set off.'

'Well, well,' said Vogel. 'That might solve one mystery, mightn't it?'

He then asked Peters if there was any news from CSI at Granger's flat.

She replied that she wasn't sure if they'd even got there yet. HQ at Exeter had diverted the team she'd allocated to a major road traffic accident on the Devon link road, involving more than one fatal casualty.

'They said that as Granger was in custody he couldn't hide any evidence there might be at his home, so there was no urgency,' Peters reported.

Vogel cursed silently. He remained unable to contact Nobby Clarke. Peters' CSI news added to his unease. He feared he might no longer be entirely in charge of his own investigation.

'What about Granger's keys?' he asked.

Peters replied that CSI had the keys, which they would be checking out as part of their further investigations.

When they finally got to any of the crime scenes, thought Vogel.

Peters also told him that all attempts to trace the London number stored on Granger's burner phone had failed. As Vogel had more or less expected.

'It's unlisted,' she said.

Vogel had blue-toothed his phone through the car's speakers so Saslow could hear the conversation. She'd been unimpressed.

'How the heck can a number like that be unlisted?' she asked Vogel irritably, after he'd ended the call. 'I didn't think there was any such thing. It's an 0207 number isn't it?'

'Was,' said Vogel. 'I'd take a bet it no longer even rings out. I'll try it again later just to make sure. With the people we are dealing with anything is possible. They play by different rules to the rest of us.'

'And since when did teams on a murder enquiry get diverted to an RTA?' Saslow continued.

'I'm not sure I know the answer to that, but I do know I'm not happy about it,' said Vogel.

'Surely, we've got Granger bang to rights, anyway, though, haven't we, boss?' continued Saslow.

'I do hope so, Dawn,' said Vogel. 'And I think we now know how he staged Gerry Barham's death too. I reckon it was Granger that Sid Merton saw at the helm of the *Lady Anne*, and Gerry Barham was already dead and hidden from view. Then, when he was far enough away from shore, Granger rigged up the rudder so that the boat would carry on going out to sea until it ran out of petrol, whilst he decamped into the dinghy to get himself home. Once the storm got up, the helpless *Lady Anne* was swept in on the next tide and smashed to pieces – as the RNLI reported, and just as Granger had planned. The North Devon coast must be one of the most unforgiving in the country, too. We've seen that for ourselves, Saslow.'

'Yes, boss,' agreed Saslow. 'Simple, when you say it quickly, boss.'

'In as much as anything is simple about this case, Dawn,' said Vogel.

Yet again he tried to call Nobby Clarke.

'She's still not picking up,' he muttered, after being diverted once more to voicemail. 'And I don't like it, not at all.'

THIRTY-ONE

Vogel was woken by a phone call from DC Perkins just before six a.m.

'Boss, I've got something to tell you and you're not going to be happy,' he began. 'The custody sergeant at Barnstaple's just rung me. He's a mate. Seems Jimmy Granger's been released from custody. Insufficient evidence to detain him.'

'What?'

Vogel sat bolt upright in bed, instantly wide awake.

'What d'you mean released? When? On who's authority?'

'About half an hour ago apparently. Orders from MCT HQ at Exeter.'

Vogel felt his heart sink.

'The big chief herself, boss,' Perkins replied. 'Detective Superintendent Nobby Clarke.'

Vogel ended the call almost straight away. Immediately, and for the umpteenth time, he tried to call Nobby.

For the umpteenth time he got her message service. This time he didn't bother to leave another message.

She would know what he was calling about, for sure. As she would have known all damned night that he was desperate to speak to her. And now he knew why she wasn't picking up. Vogel leaned back in his bed and closed his eyes. His mind was in turmoil. For once in his life he really didn't know what to do next.

It looked like Nobby Clarke, too, had allowed herself to become embroiled in some sort of high-level conspiracy.

Apart from his wife, and perhaps Saslow, Nobby was the only person in the world whom Vogel trusted absolutely. He considered her to be a copper with heart and integrity, and had always admired her independent spirit, her passion for justice, and her near compulsion to always question authority.

Secretly, she was the copper he aspired to be. Or she had been until now.

If he couldn't trust Nobby he wasn't sure there was any point in continuing to be a policeman.

Nonetheless, he determined to carry on going through the motions. He called DI Peters. She was in the incident room, and answered straight away. Vogel suspected she had been there all night. That sort of work ethic was something which she did have in common with Margot Hartley.

'I was just going to call you, boss,' she said. 'CSI finally got to Granger's flat. They're still at it, but their first impression is that it's been cleaned up and cleared out. There are some clothes, presumably his, there, but virtually nothing else. No paperwork of any kind, not even an electricity bill, no laptop. Nothing personal at all.'

Vogel was not surprised. Granger himself could not have cleared out his flat as he'd been in jail until half an hour earlier. But it seemed there had been people to do the job for him, and the delay in the arrival of a CSI team had given them the time.

'I see,' he commented non-committally. 'Any news on that RTA the CSIs were diverted to, by the way?'

If Peters followed his train of thought, her voice gave no indication of it.

'Yep, seems some wires got crossed and the first report was

way off,' she replied evenly. 'No fatalities at all, and nobody seriously injured either.'

Once again Vogel wasn't surprised. He told Peters then that Granger had been released, trying not to let his anger show.

Peters muttered something he didn't quite hear. She sounded vaguely uncomfortable. He had the feeling she might already have known, and also knew that the man had been released without the knowledge of her SIO.

'I still want us to keep an eye on him,' he said. 'Let's find out where he's going. He obviously hasn't gone back to his Instow flat, if he ever really lived there. He's probably in his car, heading out of the area. That Defender we have on file. Get a call out to Traffic. Devon and Cornwall, and Avon and Somerset. We should be able to pick him up on the North Devon link road or the M5 with a bit of luck.'

Less than ten minutes later his phone rang again. It was his senior officer at the Avon and Somerset, Detective Superintendent Reg Hemmings, head of MCIT.

'Vogel, we need you back,' he said. 'You're to wind up your part of the Ferguson investigation pronto and get on the way to Bristol. You and Saslow . . .'

'For God's sake, boss, what is going on?' asked Vogel. 'A man whom I am quite sure has killed two people and tried to kill a third has been released from custody. I'm the SIO on the case and I wasn't even officially told, let alone consulted. The whole thing stinks, boss.'

'That's not the information I've been given, Vogel,' countered Hemmings. 'Seems it's all been a storm in a teacup, a suicide and an accident at sea. My instructions are that we should get out, and leave the local boys and girls to clean it up.'

'It wasn't a storm in a teacup for Gerry Barham, that's for sure,' said Vogel, who was mildly surprised to find that his policeman's black humour remained intact. 'And Jane Ferguson did not commit suicide. Karen Crow made that pretty clear.'

'Not entirely clear, apparently, Vogel. In any case, I've been told that the Crown Prosecution Service would not be confident of a prosecution. Your mate Nobby didn't reckon there was enough evidence to charge this Jimmy Granger. You must realize that.'

'It's a cover-up, boss,' said Vogel.

'Oh, get down off your high horse, man,' responded Hemmings. 'And get your arse back to Bristol. You did all you could.'

Vogel could think of little more to say. And barely had the will to say anything. He was despondent.

He made one more attempt to call Nobby Clarke. This time she picked up. And she spoke first, before he had the chance to.

'I wouldn't have let this happen without a damned good reason, Vogel,' she began, sounding as feisty and confident as ever. 'You should know that.'

'I don't know any such thing because you have told me zilch,' countered Vogel. 'I have been trying to speak to you since yesterday evening, as you are well aware. You appointed me SIO of a murder investigation. You asked for me, you brought me here. Now you have ordered the release of a man who I'm darned sure has killed twice and attempted to kill a third time. And you didn't even have the decency to tell me yourself. I had to learn it from a DC. What on earth is going on, boss?'

'Look Vogel, there's always been doubt in this case. A woman, known to be neurotic, hanged, and a man who was barely an amateur sailor took a boat out in a storm. Suicide and an accident at sea. Those are the obvious conclusions. We were making too much of it. Then there was an incident on premises which are clearly a health and safety nightmare.'

'For fuck's sake, boss, don't give me that shite,' Vogel stormed.

The DCI rarely swore, and was known for his calmness in a crisis. He had never felt less calm. A cold fury was consuming his entire being.

'I cannot believe this is you talking. Have you been fucking got at or something?' he continued.

'Remember who you are speaking to,' responded Nobby quickly.

Vogel was having none of it.

'Don't even think about pulling rank with me,' he said. 'And, since you brought the subject up, I don't think I know who I'm speaking to anymore.'

'Oh, Vogel, I just told you, this operation has been scaled down for a very good reason—'

'It hasn't been scaled down, it's been as near as damn closed down,' interrupted Vogel. 'And, if there is a good reason, then tell me what it is. Just tell me, boss.'

'I can't do that, Vogel. I'm sorry. You are just going to have to trust me on this.'

'Trust you, Detective Superintendent Clarke?' queried Vogel, with cold formality. 'I will never trust you again as long as I live. And I never ever want to work with you again. In fact, right now, I don't even want to stay in the same police force as you.'

Vogel and Saslow had arranged to meet for an early breakfast. He greeted her with the news that they had both been recalled to Bristol.

Saslow didn't think she had ever seen her boss look so severe.

He then told her about the release of Jimmy Granger and the closing down of the MCT incident room in Bideford, and the conclusions which had been officially drawn concerning the deaths of Jane Ferguson and Gerry Granger, and the attack on Sam Ferguson.

'Christ,' Saslow blurted out. 'Surely Nobby hasn't gone along with that.'

'The detective superintendent has been the one issuing the orders,' said Vogel grimly.

'What?'

Saslow was shocked to the core.

'She wouldn't. I mean, why? She must have a good reason. Surely?'

Vogel laughed humourlessly.

'So she says, however, she hasn't chosen to share that reason with me.'

'But you two are so close, you speak the same language—'

'We were, and we did,' interrupted Vogel. 'It's over now. And so is this job. Get your stuff together. I'd like to make a last visit to the Bideford MIR, then it's back to Bristol for us.'

Saslow could hardly believe her ears. This wasn't her governor. He sounded totally defeated.

'Boss, if there's anything you'd like to do, you know, under the radar, well I'm up for it, really I am,' she said.

Vogel smiled sadly.

'Thank you for that, Saslow,' he replied. 'But I am afraid there is nothing either of us can do. Not this time, not with this one. The plug has been pulled.'

The MCT team were already packing up at Bideford police station when Saslow and Vogel arrived.

DI Peters looked flustered. Saslow wasn't surprised. No sooner had she got to grips with the behind the scenes management of a major murder enquiry, than the whole investigation had been pushed to one side.

There seemed to be cardboard boxes everywhere. Laptops, printers, and stacks of paper were being packed away, or fed through a shredder.

'I wasn't expecting to see you, boss,' she said. 'The guvnor told me you were on your way back to Bristol.'

'I am,' said Vogel. 'This is a farewell visit. And to say thank you.'

'For what?' asked Peters. 'We'd barely got started. We certainly hadn't anything like finished.'

It was obvious to Saslow that the DI shared Vogel's frustration.

'As you know, boss, I've been ordered to leave everything to local CID and shut our operation down as quickly as possible, and unfortunately that includes the tracking of Jimmy Granger's car,' Peters continued. 'Traffic reported an early spotting of the Defender heading north on the M5 by Taunton, but, I'm sorry, boss, I've had to call off the hounds. Oh, and whilst two of the keys Granger was carrying when you arrested him were to his flat, CSI never did get around to checking if any of the others belonged to the Ferguson home. They were his personal property, of course, and had to be handed back to him as soon as we knew he was going to be released.'

Vogel looked as if this was only the news that he had expected.

He had been almost entirely silent on the short drive from Appledore to Bideford. And he remained largely uncommunicative throughout the much longer journey from Bideford to Bristol.

His phone rang several times. Each time he glanced at the screen but did not pick up. Saslow would have cheerfully bet a month's salary that the calls, or at least most of them, were from Nobby Clarke.

She had never seen her senior officer look broken before. In fact she had always considered him to be indomitable. And she was absolutely sure that it was Nobby Clarke's apparent betrayal of her own team which had left him that way.

She wished he would talk to her, but knew better than to ask any questions. In any case, the DCI had already made it clear that he knew few answers.

As they approached Bristol, Vogel asked Saslow to drop him at his home on the outskirts of the city. That in itself was highly unusual. It was still only mid-afternoon. There was little doubt in Saslow's mind that, under normal circumstances, Vogel would have wanted to return to work at MCT for the rest of the day, and expected her to do the same. But these were not normal circumstances.

Like Vogel, Saslow found herself upset and more than a tad angry, as she continued to drive into the city centre, heading on autopilot for Kenneth Steele House. Suddenly she swung the car off the main drag and headed in a totally different direction.

'The damned brass have turned their backs on us, right enough,' she muttered to herself. 'They can do without me until the morning, too.'

As usual, Vogel gave his wife Mary a full account of events. Or as full an account as possible. He invariably found her listening ear, and her occasional quiet comments, helpful in the extreme. On this occasion she could not help at all.

Mary knew how much he respected, and indeed liked, Nobby Clarke, and she looked as shell-shocked as he felt when he related his earlier conversation with the detective superintendent.

Vogel could not sort out his head at all. He took the family dog for a walk in the park to get some fresh air. He listened as his daughter, who suffered from cerebral palsy but was an excellent swimmer, regaled him excitedly with a blow-by-blow account of her latest competition triumph the previous day.

He sat down for an unhurried dinner with his wife and daughter, something he all too often missed, and always enjoyed. But he could not begin to relax.

After dinner he helped Mary clear up, and later, once Rosamund had gone to bed, the two of them sat down to watch a movie

which Mary said was reputed to be one of the best of the year.
Vogel could not concentrate on it at all.

Just before ten p.m. the doorbell rang. Vogel looked at Mary.
Mary looked at Vogel.

'I'll go,' he said, rising to his feet.

Unexpected visitors at that sort of time slightly disconcert most
people. For a police officer, dealing as a matter of course with
society's underbelly, such calls are particularly disconcerting.

Vogel walked softly along the hallway and peered through the
spyhole in the front door. The security light in the porch had already
switched itself on and the visitor's face was clearly illuminated.

It was Nobby Clarke. For a second Vogel thought about not
even opening the door to her. He couldn't quite do that. He
opened it, and stood in silence looking at her.

'I was going home, then I found myself driving here to you,'
she said. 'You wouldn't pick up. So, it's the mountain and
Mohammed and all that . . .'

Her voice tailed off.

'You'd better come in, then,' said Vogel flatly.

He led the way into the sitting room. Mary was already on her
feet. She greeted Nobby warmly. Slightly to Vogel's annoyance.

Then she offered to make tea.

'I'm sure you two need to talk,' she said.

'We certainly do,' said Nobby. 'Thank you, Mary.'

Vogel was unimpressed. He knew the detective super wouldn't
have driven all the way from Exeter for nothing. But he could
not imagine anything she might tell him which would even begin
to lessen his disappointment in her.

'Right, Vogel, you are clearly going to carry on throwing your
toys out of the pram unless I give you an explanation, so that's
what you're going to get,' Clarke announced. 'But you have to
swear that you will never breathe a word of what I am about
to tell you to a living soul, not Saslow, and not even Mary.'

Vogel glowered at her, and shrugged. He said nothing.

'You're still behaving like a child, Vogel, nonetheless I am
going to put my trust in you, and I hope you don't make me live
to regret it,' she continued.

Vogel found her tone extremely irritating, and didn't feel that
Nobby Clarke was in any position to discuss trust. He did,

however, want to hear whatever it was that she had finally decided to tell him. So he still said nothing.

'Do you love your country, Vogel?' she asked.

'What sort of damned fool question is that?' he growled, all the more irritated now. 'Something your low life spook friends would come up with, I should think.'

'Do you, Vogel?' Nobby persisted.

'Yes, of course I love my country,' he snapped. 'It's the clowns who run it I can't stand.'

'You have a point there,' responded Nobby. 'But of course, we are fortunate to have people at the very top who, whether you like them or not, have for centuries given this country a stability envied throughout the world.'

'Didn't know you were a royalist,' said Vogel.

'I'm not. I'm a pragmatist. As I believe you are. And I believe that if something isn't broken you shouldn't mend it.'

Vogel was intrigued in spite of himself. He said no more, instead waiting for Nobby to continue.

'All right,' she said. 'This is the story. Jane Ferguson did not kill her twin sister as she feared. But there was some truth in her dreams. She did have a twin sister. And the little girl was murdered. But by her mother. Not by Jane—'

Vogel interrupted sharply. He could not help himself.

'So, just to make things really perfect, you're telling me Jane Ferguson was an innocent woman who had harmed nobody,' he snapped. 'And we're letting her murderer walk away scot free. Now, ain't that just great!'

'Vogel, please. Will you just keep quiet until I've finished?'

Vogel grunted.

'The twins' mother, not the woman who brought Jane Ferguson up, had developed serious mental health issues, not helped by a reliance on drugs and alcohol,' Nobby Clarke continued. 'One night she quite literally took leave of her senses and attacked Jane's twin with a knife, killing her. Woken by the children's screams, their father came in to the room, just as the mother was beginning to turn her attentions on Jane. He grabbed the woman, pulling her off, and pushed her out of the way. Forcefully. He was a strong man. A military man. He killed her, without, it is alleged, meaning to do so. Nonetheless he killed her.'

Nobby took a deep breath.

'This man, the father, was one of those at the very top,' she continued obliquely. 'The woman was his mistress – who, although disturbed was apparently very beautiful – with whom he occasionally spent the night. Not unusual in those circles, and perfectly acceptable as long as appearances were maintained. It was believed that if a scandal broke around him, of this magnitude, it could rock the very bedrock of this country. Certain security agencies were charged with covering the matter up. It all went on record as a domestic tragedy. A deranged mother, under the influence of drugs and alcohol, killed her children and then herself.'

Nobby stared at Vogel, as if trying to gauge his reaction. He tried not to react again. Not yet.

'You notice I said children, Vogel?'

He nodded.

'Yes. It was decided that the cleanest way to clear the matter up was to kill off the entire family. Only the father would not hear of any actual harm being done to his surviving daughter. So Jane was put up for adoption, to someone trusted to keep the whole thing under wraps. She was only six. And she was so shocked by what happened, that she seemed to wipe the whole episode out of her mind. Which suited everybody—'

'Why would anyone agree to adopt a child and help cover something like that up, to keep such a terrible, dangerous secret?' interrupted Vogel. 'It doesn't make sense to me.'

'In certain areas of society, where the wider repercussions of a scandal breaking could be so very grave, this sort of thing is far from unheard of,' replied Nobby. 'Camilla's husband, Colonel Parker Bowles was complicit for years in covering up her affair with the Prince of Wales—'

'As far as I remember the prince has never been suspected of killing anyone,' Vogel interrupted again.

'Oh, all right, Vogel,' responded Nobby briskly. 'Just listen, will you! Taking into account her age, and the immensity of the shock she had suffered, it was hoped that Jane would never remember her previous life, in particular the night her mother and her sister died. Indeed, the mental health professionals who dealt with her at the time thought it unlikely that she ever would. But the security services kept an eye on her, just in case. After her adopted mother died and she married, Gerry Barham was entrusted with the job. On a need to know basis. He never knew the full story, or he might have been more aware of the danger in reporting back about Jane's dreams. He was a semi-retired spook, of course, of the deskbound boffin type. MI6 seconded to GCHQ, most of the time.'

Vogel realized he was once again beginning to blink rapidly. He so wished he didn't do that.

'Danger is an understatement,' he said. 'The bastards killed Jane Ferguson, and Gerry Barham, and we are letting them get away with it.'

'I'm going to say it again, Vogel. Jane Ferguson committed suicide. Gerry Barham's death was a stupid accident. And what looked like an attack on Sam Ferguson was also an accident—'

'Don't be ridiculous,' interrupted Vogel. 'For a start, Jimmy Granger, or whatever his real name is, had Barham's phone on him when we arrested him, and undoubtedly sent a text to Sam Ferguson enticing him to the old chapel near Eastleigh. Where we nabbed him red-handed.'

'Granger found the phone at the yacht club and was intending to return it to Gerry Barham. The text was sent before he found it. He was at the chapel because of his interest in ecclesiastical architecture.'

'Boss, you are talking errant nonsense, and you know it.'

'Perhaps, but this is the official version of what happened, and I honestly believe that if we had persisted in opening that other can of worms this whole country could descend into anarchy. I was only told what lay behind it all because the powers that be reckoned it was the only way they could get me to call you off and stop the investigation. It worked too. Look around you, Vogel. There is a big republican movement in the country nowadays, and, thanks to Brexit and no Brexit, what passes for our government is in crisis. Confidence in our so-called democracy is probably at the lowest ebb in modern times.'

'Who are "the powers that be" in this, boss? Who got you to call off our investigation?'

'I really can't tell you that, Vogel. It was somebody I would never have expected to be involved. I was summoned to London late last night.'

Vogel was thoughtful.

'What are you thinking, Vogel? I do hope you are going to go along with this. You know how much it goes against my grain. But we have no choice.'

'I was thinking, what members of our extended royal family would have been at the right age to be sowing their wild oats thirty-odd years ago, when Jane Ferguson was conceived.'

'Let's get this straight, Vogel. I did not say the father was anything to do with our royal family. I have not and cannot specify who he is. Not even to you. Neither did I give any indication of his age when Jane was conceived.'

'No, you didn't give any indication of his age, did you, boss? And that opens up all manner of interesting possibilities, too.'

Nobby Clarke sighed, a tad theatrically.

'Vogel, I need to know, are you on side or not?'

'What will you do if the answer is no, have me bumped off too?'

'Don't be ridiculous, Vogel. You're a police officer doing his job, and I am the senior officer who put you on the case—'

'Except neither of us are doing our job, are we?' interrupted Vogel.

'Let me finish,' continued Clarke. 'You are also the one copper I respect more than any other, and that's why I want and need you to understand the decisions I have taken. Nobody needs to be "bumped off", as you put it. Everything is being arranged. There really is no case for Jimmy Granger or anybody else to answer. That's how it has to be.'

Vogel felt quite desolate.

'I'm on side, boss,' he announced suddenly. 'Like you said, I don't have any choice.'

EPILOGUE

Sam Ferguson told his wife everything. He had no choice, either. She would not leave him, of course. But neither would she ever forgive him. His only son also made it clear that he would never forgive his father. And that he was going to leave.

Right after his release from police custody Felix Ferguson told his parents that he intended to take his children away and build a new life for them somewhere many miles from North Devon and their terrible memories. Felix said his mother would always be welcome, wherever he went. But he never again wanted to see the father without whose complicity in the surveillance operation at his home, he believed his wife would still be alive.

Felix was the one person who might have been expected to pursue every possible avenue of protest when Jane's death was suddenly dismissed as suicide – particularly given all that he knew about events surrounding it, including the surveillance operation at his home and the arrest of Jimmy Granger. But he did not do so.

Felix no longer cared about anything except his children's future. And, for their sake, he wanted the past buried almost as much as those who had summarily called a halt to Vogel's investigation.

In addition, Felix was quite sure that in not making a fuss, and therefore protecting his children from unknown further consequences, he was doing what Jane, the most devoted of mothers, would have wanted.

Anne Barham immediately made plans to sell her house in Estuary Vista Close and look for a flat in suburban London close to her daughter, son-in-law, and grandson. She did not wish to remain in Instow for a moment longer than she had to.

Her dream retirement with the husband she had loved for most of her adult life had ended in a way she could never have imagined. A truly horrific way. Anne grieved for Gerry dreadfully, in spite of feeling betrayed by him. She'd really never had any idea that he'd worked for MI6, and it still seemed barely possible to her that her quiet unassuming husband had been some sort of spy.

Jimmy Granger ceased to exist almost immediately after his release from custody. The blonde-haired, blue-eyed man, who had been known by that name, parked his Land Rover Defender outside a motorway service station motel on the M4, not far from Heathrow, picked up a brown leather bag that had been left for him at reception, and checked into his pre-booked room.

A few hours later he left the motel and set off for the airport by taxi. He now appeared to be completely bald, and his eyes, without the tinted contact lenses he'd previously been wearing, were a murky grey rather than strident blue. The picture in the passport which had been in the brown leather bag – along with a new credit card, a considerable sum of cash, some clothes, and a few other necessities – matched his new appearance exactly.

Immediately after Nobby Clarke's revelatory visit, David Vogel sat down and wrote a letter of resignation to his superior officer, Detective Superintendent Reg Hemmings.

Only when he had finished did he consider his wife and his daughter, and her special needs. Vogel had joined the police force when he was eighteen. He had never had another job. He had no professional skill other than being a policeman. He had no other source of income.

Perhaps even more importantly, he knew no other way of life.

He sat looking at the letter, which he had folded neatly and placed inside a plain white envelope, for several minutes.

Then he ripped it up.

The following morning he reported for duty at Kenneth Steele House. It was what he did. There was nothing else. It was what David Vogel would always do.

Lightning Source UK Ltd.
Milton Keynes UK
UKHW011834151020
371668UK00002B/34